THE THROWER'S APPRENTICE

R.L. AIKEN

ISBN

978-0-6485683-1-5

For my sisters,

Jen and Cath
with love

ACKNOWLEDGMENTS

There are a bunch of people who read this book for me before it was a real live book. Their comments were invariably favourable and their support invaluable, and I thank each and every one. My thanks also to my writers group for their advice and help. They are a fantastic bunch who know what it is to sit alone with only an imagination and a keyboard for company; to be staring out the window wondering, appearing to be not doing very much at all, while actually working really hard. And I could not do this without Annie Seaton, a fantastic writer and a great friend, who does such lovely covers for me and all the technical stuff that my Luddite brain just can't get the hang of. My thanks to my family for loving me and being the first to buy my book; and to my daughters and my wonderful husband, I love you all. Thank you all for coming on this ride with me...

xxx

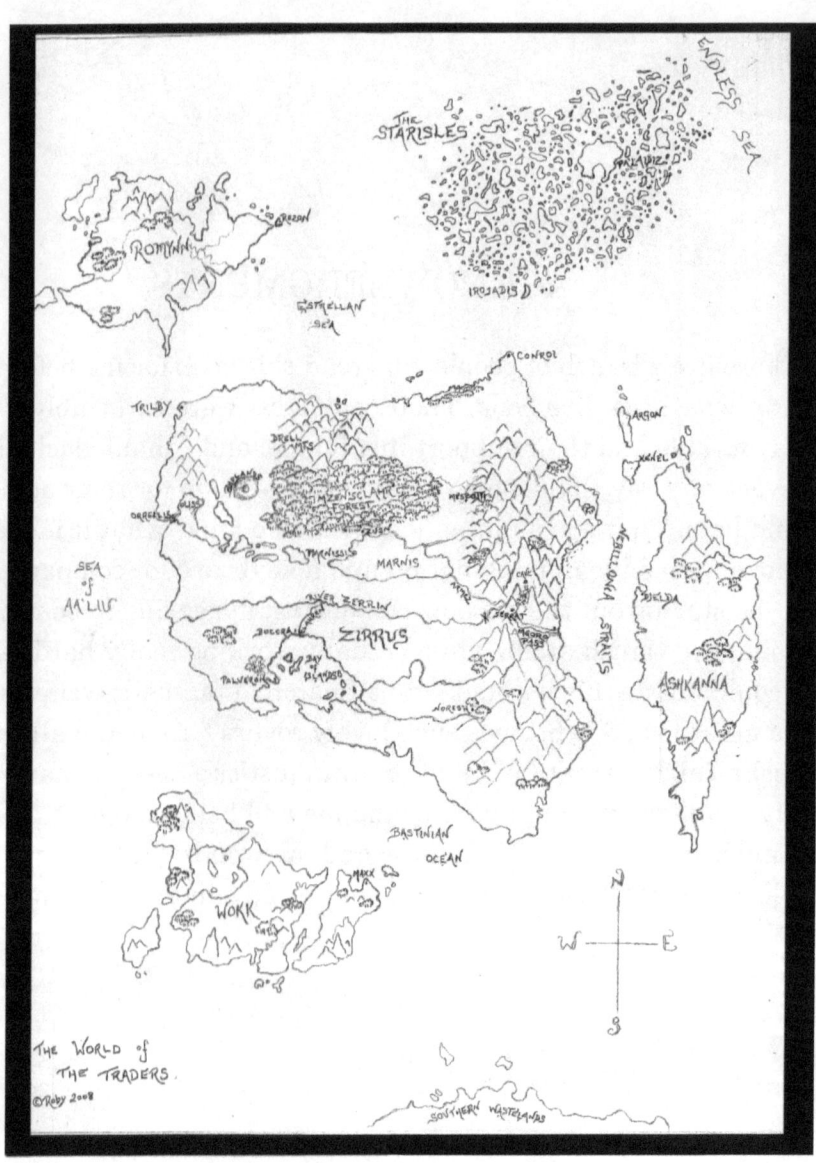

THE WORLD of
THE TRADERS.
©Roby 2008

PROLOGUE

At Great Court on Zirrus, Queen Virrisian was in her private rooms, pushing away the remains of her lunch. She'd had a tedious morning putting petty courtiers in their place, and she planned on ignoring everyone for the rest of the afternoon. Almost everyone.

Across the over-laden table, her master-at-arms, Sir Azeron of Maxx, buttered another roll and looked out the window. Snow swept past the thick glass, and the city of Palveron below was hidden behind the blizzard. Only the closest towers of the castle could be seen through the gaps of swirling snow, the wind tearing at them as if bent on their destruction, as if the gods were joining forces against them. Azeron shoved his chair back from the table and put his feet on the lacy tablecloth.

"Orm was quaking in his tiny boots," he said, tearing off a piece of the roll and shoving it in his mouth. "It was all I could do not to laugh outright, the cringing fool."

Orm of the treasury was the only one of King Tenelon's court who still remained in the castle. Previously a mere underling, he had been given the running of the treasury by

Queen Virrisian soon after she'd come to power; she had found his gift for numbers was outweighed only by his pathetic sense of survival, a trait she'd happily exploited. He was as worm-like as his name suggested, a small, balding man with soft white hands and a face like a bat, and he kept the treasury filled with young lads calculating long tables of figures and cataloguing jewels. His soft hands had wrung together as he'd stood before the queen that morning, begging her to allow him to lower taxes. As he and everyone else had known, despite him bringing a dozen of his pasty-faced boys and as many brave courtiers as he could persuade to come, he had been refused. He had, as Azeron had said, quivered in his tiny boots and slunk off with his retinue.

"Orm should keep his mind on his figures," said the queen, with a dismissive shake of her hand.

"It is his figures that bother him," said Azeron. "If you take from the people before they have time to make more, there will be no more to take." He shrugged and devoured the rest of the roll. "They say people are getting poorer."

"And while they grow poorer, they also grow weaker," Virrisian said. "And while they grow weaker, my soldiers grow stronger." She twirled a glass between her fingers, the wine dark as blood in the crystal. "As I desire it."

"Your soldiers are your biggest expense," said Azeron. "Garrisons on every coast and scattered inland, not to mention the quarters here, filled with men and women willing to do your bidding." He raised one black eyebrow at her. "I suppose you have a purpose for them?"

"Of course," she replied. "When have you ever known me to do something without reason?" She sipped at the wine. "Once the small problem of the rebels is taken care of, I'll take over the running of Nebillonia Straits and the islands there, Argon, Xenel and the others. Then perhaps a few of the Wokk islands." She sipped again at the wine. "If I control the Straits and Meoro Pass, my reach goes further than our mere shores." She spoke casually, as if she were purchasing a country property. "Then I shall take Wokk itself."

"A fine plan," said Azeron, his voice as mild as hers. "But don't you think the other Lands might take offence. The Wokkii for example." He raised a brow. "There *are* those in my homeland who will do as you bid, as ever, but there are others who may resist the idea."

"Probably," she answered. "Yet I have a… let us say, a solution to that."

"May I ask what that solution is?" he said.

"No," she answered, her lips curling into a smile. "But I promise you, we shall not have to worry overmuch about the other Lands. They will come around to my way of thinking." She drained her glass. "Eventually." She put the glass down and looked at him across the table. "I suppose you have plans of your own."

"The rebels you mean?" he asked, and shrugged. "I have my spies. Those who have been heading the raids at Conroi have been caught, we are following several people in the Lakes' country, and as for those between here and the Clahren," he shrugged again, "it's only a matter of time. We took the two women in Boccra who made the weapons before the Wintering. They're no doubt having a merry time at the garrison there." He yawned and stretched his arms. "I shall order their deaths after first thaw. Something nice and public. As a warning. But we have half the Wintering yet to wait before more can be done." He looked back out at the snow blasting against the windows and changed the subject abruptly. "What of the old queen? Will she be allowed out of seclusion this year?" He laughed. "*Seclusion.* That always amuses me."

The queen was not amused. "She'll stay where I can watch her," she said. "I don't trust her and I never have."

"This I know, yet I found no reason for it when I questioned the old woman, E'Nith. Neither have your spies ever found

anything of use, even those from Wokk who have the most...
persuasive methods. There is no need to worry about her."

"Yes, Azeron, so you think, but no one saw that babe born,
only its corpse, and I'll not have *her* out in the World again
causing trouble, babe or no."

"Yes, yes," said Azeron, taking his boots off the table. "I
have heard all this before, and I know you have your reasons,
even though you haven't seen fit to divulge them to me, but
we've been watching that old nurse roam the castle for years
without finding out a thing. She does not speak well," he smiled
humourlessly and bobbed his head to her, "no thanks required."
The smile disappeared as quickly as it had come. "And nothing
goes in but food, occasionally some paper. She is searched
before entering the Glade Room. The only message you ever
allow out is to that old knight, Vulcan, on the eve of the
Wintering, and you read those yourself. Face it, my dear queen,
Tenelon's 'prophecy' was mere madness. There *is* no child."

"You were not *there*, Azeron," she answered, eyes
narrowing. "You did not see him, nor hear his words."

"Yes, but I *have* heard them repeated many times since,"
he replied. "He spoke of light and darkness and birds, birds of
metal and birds who save people. He spoke of a child who
would be saved by sisters and brothers it did not have, and an
old one who knows the way in. 'In' *where*?" He leant forward
and spoke quietly. "It was madness, that's all. You have
nothing to fear, my queen. Tenelon's words were *not* prophecy,
but Green Fever eating his brain. The Land is yours, as it has
been these fifteen Winterings."

She looked at him for a while and then nodded. "You're
right, Azeron," she said. "Even when the trader wench came
there was nothing, though they were in the city half the year."

"No Trader was near the city when the old king died," he
prodded. "First snow was already here when the babe was
born, dead or no, even though you'd been searching for it since
the old king died. As I said, I know you have your reasons for

4

that, but every ship in the harbour was searched and your Wokkii scoured the countryside, two were almost lost to the blizzards, but your suspicions came to nothing."

"I know," she answered. "But I could not be sure that the child was born when she said it was. How do we know the babe buried with Tenelon is hers? Irinesta had many friends once." She was silent a while longer, looking out at the snatches of tower through the blizzard. She smiled a small, tight smile. "But yes, you're right, the Land *is* mine and I do not fear an old woman the World has forgotten. And we needn't let E'Nith roam any longer. She shall be kept with her mistress in the tower of the Glade. Tell the guard at the door." She filled her glass again. "Don't stop watching the Traders, though, when the year begins," she added, the smile widening. She sipped at the crimson wine. "I have plans for them, too."

"Yes, my queen," Azeron murmured. He wondered what she meant, but he said nothing. He had found it more profitable to bide his time. He raised his glass to her. "As you wish."

* * *

In the Glade Room, the old queen, Irinesta, also sat staring at the blizzard. Her pen hung poised above a near-blank page, eyes fixed on nothing until E'Nith put a cup of tezz beside her and brought her from her reverie. The old woman smiled at her when she looked up, and patted her hand.

"You tink of her?" she said. She spoke awkwardly, as she had since someone had cut off the tip of her tongue the Wintering after Tenelon died, but Irinesta never had trouble understanding her.

Irinesta nodded. "Yes. It's always worse in the Wintering," she said. "It brings that other Wintering to mind." She smiled wryly. "As you well know."

"Zoon," said E'Nith, patting her hand again.

Irinesta smiled. "Yes, E'Nith," she said. "Soon. But a few more Winterings yet."

5

She put down her pen and looked about the room as she drank her tezz. A bright fire burned in the grate, another in the small stove where E'Nith prepared their meals. The carpets were looking scruffy, the curtains and coverlets a little threadbare, but the room was warm despite its size, and still beautiful. Her eyes lingered on a collection of stones on a shelf beside her bed, but the mural dominated as always, and she looked a long time at the painted, smiling faces in the trees surrounding the empty glade before turning back to her desk. The blizzard still raged against the panes, the World lost behind the swirling white, just as she was lost to the World. Irinesta sighed and picked up her pen.

* * *

Others also watched the blizzard. Those Sir Azeron of Maxx thought happily ensconced in the garrison on the Clahren River were not happy. Nor were they at the garrison. They watched the blizzards and grieved. And they waited.

Fezzik had barely spoken in the days that followed the deaths of Pim and his little Zeffy. His throat had been raw from grief and the great howling cry that had filled the streets of Boccra when the guard rode away leaving two small girls dead in their wake.

Little Pim, the child of Pelazarus, his dearest friend, had breathed her last as the prison carriage carried her mother and Verlie away; her final whooping gasp followed by a soft sigh and then nothing more. Zeffy, his beloved youngest daughter, lay broken in his arms as he howled in the street, her head a bloody mess, her face beautifully perfect, hands curled beneath her chin, eyes closed as if in sleep. The other children, some injured, all shocked beyond tears, had watched silently until the villagers, roused from their own appalled disbelief, had rushed forward.

The Faunist had bound their wounds, set Florry's broken arm, and helped him prepare the children for burial. Her tears fell on the little bodies as she dressed them and wrapped a soft

6

scarf around Zeffy's blood-filled curls and the place where the back of her head used to be. Fezzik tied a pretty bonnet over the wadding. The Faunist stood beside him as the grave was dug at the end of the garden, and she and the villagers had watched with him, faces grim, as the hastily built and decorated box was brought and the two girls were laid side by side in it and lowered into the earth. Afterwards, she gave the children hot drinks laced with herbs and soon they slept, their faces still pained even in slumber. The babe of Pelazarus and Pemba, a frail tiny girl born after her family had been evicted from their farm during the last Wintering, was taken home with her. She had offered Fezzik the same respite as the children before she'd left, yet he would not take it; his mind was already turning to his wife and Pemba.

Fezzik had sat on the veranda all through that long, awful day, not hearing the murmurs of condolence spoken by the many people who visited nor the pained replies of his parents, not touching the cups of tezz put beside him by his mother, not seeing the bright day about him or feeling the cool wind blowing from the south. He sat staring north, tears rolling unheeded down his cheeks at times, his shoulders heaving with silent sobs at others. When the children woke during the afternoon he roused himself to try and comfort them, but the rawness of his throat kept the words back and all he could do was to take them in his big arms and hold them as they sobbed against his chest. His mother fed them soup, and though, at her insistence, he had tried some, the hot liquid caught in his throat and he could eat nothing. The Faunist had brought them another draught that evening, and though the children uncomplainingly took the brew, Fezzik again refused. He had sat outside late into the night, his eyes moving between the little mound of fresh-turned earth at the end of the garden and the river glinting in the moonlight.

He made himself wait until just before first snow. He had plenty of volunteers, all ready on the night he chose, sliding out of the trees, from the fields and across the river to a bend above the garrison. The night was cold, first snow just days away, the moon shrunk to a thin sliver, the starlight sparkling only on the weapons in their belts and in their fists. The few boats had ferried them silently downstream where they clambered one by one into the tunnel at the base of the bluff; the tunnel above the waterline that had been found by Fezzik, Fozar and Pelazarus so many years before. They had a few tiny covered lamps to light the way, and people filled the tunnel and the little cave where the three had camped as lads. Fezzik, his huge shoulders barely squeezing through the tunnel, had wiped away tears as he'd found the stubs of candles still on the rocky shelves in the cave where they'd left them. He had shed many tears lately, but he was growing used to the leaden weight of grief curled below his heart, the throbbing pain that flared into a blow if he poked at it too long.

In the small hours after midnight they crawled higher through the tunnel and out into the night, creeping up through the boulders surrounding the hole, the rock pile crowning the bluff barely touched, the hole leading beneath unfound after these many years. Down through the rocks they crept, weapons drawn, bowstrings notched with arrows fletched by Verlie and Pemba, the triangles at the tips also made by the two women in the forge at Boccra. It seemed only fitting.

The sleeping guard within the garrison never stood even a slight chance, for Fezzik had another asset besides surprise and he used it well.

Late one night, ten days after Verlie and Pemba had been taken and the two girls buried, a woman had come to Fezzik's house. He had been staring sleeplessly into the fire, for sleep had become an enemy, coming seldom and with tortured dreams when it did, and he had started at the sudden knock. The children, all still pale and inclined to weep at the slightest thing, were asleep, not denied that refuge as Fezzik was, and he had taken up a sword before opening the door. The woman stood there, a short woman with square shoulders and a chin to match. She had come inside and closed the door behind her, ignoring the sword in his hand, and she had begun to babble. Her name was Bithani, and it had taken him a while to understand her, but when he did he almost killed her right there in the kitchen.

She was of the guard. She had looked back when her companions had staunchly ignored the devastation left behind. None had spoken of it at the garrison afterwards, she said. She had come to try and help, to make amends in some small way. She'd had a sister who'd been trampled by horses when she was young, she said, her plain face crumpling. She pulled at her square shoulders, made them squarer, and looked him in the eye. She had not joined the queen's guard for this, she said, yet she was not permitted to leave it. She could atone only one way. She gave Fezzik a map of the garrison. Details of where Verlie and Pemba were held were clearly marked and she answered his questions about patrols and numbers without shifting her eyes from his. She also marked the room occupied by the head of the guard without question when Fezzik asked for it. She supplied details of supply wagons, where the guard patrolled, who their spies were. He had met with her twice more in the days leading up to their raid. He had found her useful and she assured him she was eager to continue to be so. When they attacked the sleeping garrison, they were armed with knowledge as well as weapons.

Those awake and patrolling the wall were swiftly dealt with, their cries arousing a few of the guard sleeping inside. As Fezzik's people rushed to meet them, a band went through the corridors, straight to the dank, tiny rooms where Verlie and Pemba were kept isolated from each other as well as the World. Others were also freed from the prisons, and Pemba and Verlie were taken through the garrison, across the courtyard and out through the gates. A covered wagon waited down the slope, and they were bundled into it as the others fought the guard above.

Fezzik, after a while, had come striding through the battle; he had found who he'd sought and his sword was stained with her blood. He'd felt little as he ran the blade into her unwomanly chest, her cries had gone unheard in his ears; that it had been too easy for her was his only thought. She lay now in a widening puddle of blood on the floor of her room.

He had called to them and they'd come, elated and bloody, to crowd about the wagon, smiling at the two white-faced women, yet they had not lingered. They set fire to what buildings they could within the garrison and melted back into the night to hide their weapons and wash the blood from their clothes; to bide their time until another day, when they could again strike a blow against the queen and her guard.

Fezzik had driven Pemba and Verlie back to Boccra where they'd wept beside the grave, then they'd gathered the other children from the house, hushing their cries of joy as they were reunited with their mothers. They collected the baby from the Faunist, and in the quiet of the sunrise hours they left the village to live the lives of fugitives, hidden in barns and lofts and cellars, making plans and weapons.

The Wintering was being spent in the relative safety of an isolated farm, planning what they could do when spring came. Fezzik also thought quietly about what he would do to the landingholder, Qwintum, when next they met. He had been unable to find him at the garrison, and was determined that this would be the last Wintering the man would see.

Of the dozen or so soldiers spared from the massacre at the garrison on the Clahren, none could say from whence it had come or how the wall had been breached. One, a squarish woman with a plain face, had shrugged when asked if she knew who had attacked the garrison; shaken her head when asked if she had seen the person responsible for killing the head of the guard. She did not know, the soldier named Bithani said unblinkingly, she could tell them nothing. This did not seem strange; none of the others knew anything either.

There was no time to fill the garrison with fresh young guard before first snow, and word of what had happened there would not reach Great Court until after the Wintering.

* * *

CHAPTER ONE

Two Moons after first snow, Shaeli was pacing the sitting room of Flin's house in Palveron. Ebony paced the sofa, watching intently as her mistress stalked up and down. Every so often Shaeli would stop and stare out through a gap in the shuttered windows; Ebony would stop expectantly too, and then she would continue her march up and down the sofa as Shaeli resumed her pacing.

The Wintering was passing slowly in Flin's house. They practised skylights if the weather permitted, but they had been permitted seldom and the sluggish hours of the day passed far too slowly. Sometimes they practised throwing skylights along the upstairs hallways, creating bugs or caterpillars, making flowers blossom on the ceiling, conjuring dragonflies and butterflies which they sent gliding down the hall. Shaeli learned much about embroidering detail into her skylights, but there was only so much that could be done in a hallway, and the tiny skylights expended little strength. The nights dragged too, as if accompanying the days in a slow dance; she went to bed long before she was tired to lie reading or staring out the windows at the snow slapping against the panes. Flin's house held many wonders, but she had inspected them all in the first long days of the blizzards which kept them from practising, and she missed the warmth and the companionship of Cave more with every passing day. Flin, Qiren and Illen had been more than kind, and Shaeli had grown very close to them all. She was warm, well-fed, cared for, and she was learning much, but still...

Shaeli sighed, stopped pacing, and plonked herself down beside the jevvi, ruffling her thick winter coat. Ebony ran to a bowl on the table beside the sofa and came back with a fat, round nut which she offered to Shaeli.

"Do you want me to crack it, or hide it?" she asked. Ebony put the nut behind her back. "Alright, then, but no peeking."

Ebony shook her head, placed the nut in Shaeli's hand, and put her hands over her eyes. The fingers cracked apart and one big dark eye looked out.

"No cheating, Eb, or I won't play," Shaeli said sternly, and Ebony covered her eyes again, curled up into a ball, and wrapped her thick tail about her.

"That's better," said Shaeli. "But just to be sure," she added, taking a light rug from the back of the sofa and dropping it over the ball of fluffy jevvi, "that should help." She laughed at the small indignant chitter from beneath the rug. "Well, I'm sorry, but you shouldn't peek."

She looked about the room, and then began to wander about, opening draws and lifting the lids of numerous ornamental jars, moving books and swishing curtains. Finally she selected a spot, placed the nut there, but continued her roaming, bumping furniture and eyeing the lump under the rug on the sofa.

"You're not peeking, are you?"

A muffled chatter of denial.

"Good."

She continued to move about the room, displacing objects and making noise. Ebony was very tricky. Finally she went back to the sofa and lifted the rug. Ebony smoothed her fur, ruffled her tail and looked at Shaeli accusingly.

"It's no use looking at me like that. You peek if you can and you know it."

Ebony pretended not to understand and looked expectantly about the room.

"Go on, then. See how quick you are."

The jevvi bounded off the sofa, her pointy nose high in the air, whiskers stiffly out. She roamed the room just as Shaeli had, sniffing at the drawers and jars and bookcases, and in moments she was nosing a chair in the corner. Shaeli smiled.

Ebony leapt onto the chair, nuzzled at the cushions, selected one, and dragged it to the floor. She worked the buttons with her tiny fingers, felt about, and then her head disappeared inside the cushion cover. She emerged victorious with the nut and bounded back to Shaeli, who dutifully cracked it for her. This was the prize in the game; the finder had the nut cracked for them by the hider – if they found it. Shaeli was generally the nut cracker. Ebony chewed the nut slowly, then took another from the bowl and looked at Shaeli.

"Alright," she said. "If I must."

She covered her eyes. Ebony chattered.

"I'll have you know I never cheat," Shaeli replied loftily through her wrists.

She listened as Ebony scampered about the room, trying the same distraction techniques as Shaeli had, yet much more quickly. Soon the jevvi was back, pulling at Shaeli's skirt until she took her hands away from her eyes.

"Back so soon?" she asked.

Ebony nodded, and smiled her unusual smile.

Shaeli began to wander about. She felt cushions, swished curtains, and looked in the wood-box beside the roaring fireplace. She felt along the bookshelves and looked into vases; she knelt on the floor, put her face on the carpet, and peered beneath the furniture. She stood on a chair and ran her hand along the curtain rail. That's where she was when Flin entered the room. Her back was to him as she stretched her arm up.

"Shaeli," he said. "Come down."

"Alright," she answered. "I'm just looking for..." She stopped. "*Aha*, found it," she cried, turning and jumping from the chair.

Flin stood in the doorway. Beside him was a lady, an elegant lady in soft velvet robes with a fur stole in her hands and an amused look upon her face. She was tall, her figure still impressive despite her obvious years, her face powder-pink, the painted mouth curved at the corners, her hair a cloud of white curls piled atop her head.

"I'm very happy for you, my dear," the lady said, her voice mirroring the amused curve of her lips. "What is it?"

"Ah, a nut," Shaeli said, holding it out.

"Very nice," said the lady. "But a strange place to keep nuts, I must say."

Shaeli pointed to the jevvi. "Ebony hid it. Now she has to crack it for me. It's the rule."

She threw the nut to the jevvi, who caught it and cracked it with her strong molars, delicately peeling away the shell and placing the bits in the bowl. She ran across the floor, held out the nut to Shaeli, scampered up her arm and peered at the woman from her shoulder.

"It's her favourite game," Shaeli said with a shrug. Ebony rose and fell with her shoulders.

The woman smiled. "I'll wager you seldom win so easily. Jevvies have an incredible sense of smell."

"I know," Shaeli replied seriously. "And they also cheat."

They looked at each other, and then began to laugh.

"I can see a great deal of your mother in you, my dear," said the lady, and Shaeli looked at Flin.

"Shaeli," he said. "May I introduce you to the Lady Arinola. Lady Arinola, this is Shaeli."

"Oh, I've heard my mother speak of you," Shaeli smiled. She put Ebony on the sofa, and moved towards the woman. Arinola put out her hand, but Shaeli by-passed that and hugged her instead, adding a warm kiss to the soft cheek. "Mam would send you that, I'm sure," she said, as she stepped back. "She was sorry to have missed you. We spent much of the year in Palveron."

"So I believe, Shaeli. Thank you for that greeting, I was very sad at missing Purple Leaf." She looked at Flin. "Sir Vulcan told me they were here, and that Shaeli had stayed as your apprentice." She looked back at Shaeli. "A gift for skylights, I hear?" Shaeli nodded and Arinola continued. "Good for you. You must be very talented for Flin to have taken you. He has not the patience for apprenticeship." Flin cleared his throat and looked at the ceiling, and Arinola laughed. "You'll be missing your family, though, and the Wintering at Cave?"

Shaeli nodded again. "Yes. I feel at home here now. Flin has been so kind, and he and Qiren and Illen are like family, but, yes, I do miss everyone." She looked about the room. "I never realised how much there was do at Cave, and I'm..." She stopped and looked at her feet, embarrassed.

"She's bored, my lady," laughed Flin. "I'm afraid the blizzards this Wintering have kept us housebound. We have barely had enough good weather to practise our skylights in the garden, let alone find some entertainment for our young guest."

"You can't help the weather, Flin," smiled Shaeli.

"May I ask how you made it down here?" Flin inquired.

"Some of my men cleared a path," Arinola replied. "And I wore my snow-shoes. I thought the break in the snow would hold a while longer." She twinkled at Shaeli. "I was bored, too. So I said to Vulcan, 'let's go and see the young people', and here we are."

"Why didn't you come by sleigh, Arinola?" Flin asked.

"It's not far, Flin," she said. "And I didn't want the horses to get chilled."

Shaeli smiled, but her mind was gaping. The Lady Arinola must be as old as Wyshka, and she *knew* that Sir Vulcan was an old man, for she'd met him several times throughout the year. Flin had told her the streets were treacherously icy, and only the hardy – or the foolhardy – traversed them on foot between blizzards.

"Where is Sir Vulcan?" asked Flin.

"He saw my men to the kitchen," Arinola replied. "They were rather cold after the walk with the baggage."

"The baggage?" Shaeli asked.

16

"Yes, my dear. If we are caught by a blizzard we shall have to stay until it passes. One always takes baggage when visiting during the Wintering. Ah, here he is. All safely settled?"

Sir Vulcan entered the room, and nodded at the question. He was silver-haired and straight-backed, his shoulders unbent by his years. "Yes, Arinola, but we'll not be leaving any time soon," he said. "Those lads are exhausted." He shook Flin's hand and kissed Shaeli's cheek between sentences. "You've worn them out."

"Oh, piffle," Arinola replied, tossing her immaculate white hair. "'Tis only across a road or two and down a lane." She handed Flin her stole, the glitter of rings on several fingers of the white hands. "And we shall stay as long as the Wintering says we may."

"Well, I don't know about you, Arinola, but I could do with a brandy," said Sir Vulcan, rubbing his hands together. He looked hopefully at Flin.

"Vulcan, we just had lunch before our walk. Don't you think it's a little early?"

"Arinola, that 'walk' aged me. I feel I've missed the afternoon and reached evening, age-wise. And it will warm us."

"Very well," she replied, seating herself on the sofa beside Ebony, reaching out a soft hand to stroke the thick brown fur. "I shall join you."

Sir Vulcan looked at Flin again.

"What about a hot, mulled wine with the brandy in it?" Flin asked. The visitors agreed and he busied himself by the fireplace.

Shaeli nibbled on the nut Ebony had shelled for her as Flin set a clean poker in the fire. As it heated, he mixed red wine, cloves, brandy and other liquids and flavourings into a tall metal jug. He tasted the brew as he mixed, and when he was satisfied, he took the poker from the flames and plunged it into the jug. The room filled with the aroma instantly, and it smelled so delicious that Shaeli found herself nodding when

17

Flin offered her a mug. She'd never tasted it before, though she'd enjoyed its aroma several times, and she sipped tentatively at the hot brew. She found the flavour sweet and rich, and felt the wine's effects immediately as it melted its way down her throat and settled like a warm cushion in her stomach.

Arinola was speaking to Flin. "I'm planning on throwing a small Winter ball, Flin, and was wondering if you would consider a little performance during the evening."

"I think that may be arranged," Flin said. "We have no previous engagements, and I'm sure Qiren would agree." He grinned. "I don't need to ask Shaeli."

"That's true," Shaeli smiled. "I'd love it." She turned to Arinola. "You live close by, my lady?"

"Arinola, my dear, please. Yes, my house is directly above Flin's, but a street away. I regularly see little bursts of colour from my balcony."

"But what if there's a blizzard, Arinola? How do the people get there?"

"They come when they can, my dear. Some arrive days before, just to be sure."

"And they all stay in your house?"

Arinola nodded. "Oh, yes, it's great fun. You'll enjoy it."

"Arinola's house is rather grand," said Vulcan. "I have taken advantage of her hospitality and ensconced myself in one of her suites since my retirement from court. She could sleep a small village beneath her roof."

"Will we stay with you, too?" asked Shaeli.

"Of course. You must all come well before the evening. It wouldn't do to be without our skylights, and I'm particularly interested in seeing you perform. Your parents must be very proud."

Shaeli nodded. "I'm sure Mam would rather I was at Cave, but she knows I have to practise, and I'm very lucky Flin found

18

me." She smiled at Flin. "Yet we have done very little since the Wintering set in, and we're getting itchy fingers, aren't we?"

Flin laughed. "We are, and we have a performance to prepare for now. We shall have to hope for a break in the blizzards."

"You have half a Moon yet, Flin, and I've never known you to need much practise," smiled Vulcan.

"Why weren't you out when we arrived?" asked Arinola. "The snow was quite light, almost pleasant."

"It's the wind that stops us," explained Flin. "It's coming from the south-east, and gusting. You probably felt little of it down on the street, but if we tried throwing in this wind, the beams would fly back in our faces."

"Oh, I see. The same as on a boat or a Trader, you have to toss water down-wind or you get wet," Arinola said.

"That's right," Flin nodded. "But skylights are only affected by very strong winds, of which we've had plenty this Wintering."

"We have to wait for the wind to swing back south, so we're more protected by the headland and Great Court," said Shaeli.

"Well, we shall hope for that, then," said Arinola brightly. "I'm sure the gods will give you ample time." The shutters rattled against the windows, and their heads turned. "Perhaps tomorrow, then," said Arinola, as if the gods had heard her.

Sir Vulcan went to the windows, and peered out the thin gap that Shaeli had been looking through. "Another blizzard," he said, as he turned back. "It may be we shall have to take advantage of your hospitality, Flin, unless it's a short one."

"I think you should. You are both welcome, as always. I'll tell Yorrow there will be two more for dinner. Help yourselves to more wine," he said, as he left the room.

Vulcan re-filled his mug and Arinola's. Shaeli still sipped on her first one.

"Where is Qiren?" asked Arinola.

"He and Illen are in the library. They found some old drawings of elves in a folder and they've been making a proper book of them." Shaeli laughed. "Flin didn't even know they were there, because the library came with the house."

"How wonderful, I must look at them later," Arinola replied. "But who is Illen?"

"Qiren's wife. You haven't met her?"

"No, but I will be pleased to. Elfin women are always so beautiful."

"Oh, she's not elfin," said Shaeli. "She's my aunt Eenis' sister." She explained briefly about Illen and Eenis and how they'd been separated, and Arinola's face grew sombre.

"The poor things," she sighed. "I remember that terrible half-elf. What was his name, Vulcan?"

"Periqol. A cruel one he was. Killed scores of people and destroyed three or four villages."

"Where did he come from?" Shaeli asked.

"No one knows," said Vulcan. "It was rumoured his father was one of the People. A Warlock, some said, who took an elfin maid for wife. But they were only rumours, nothing could ever be found about his life before he started his rampage of rape and pillage."

"Our good King Tenelon dealt with him swiftly, though," said Arinola.

"That he did," said Vulcan. "He sent our best to bring him to justice, in company with the elves."

"My grandfather, too," said Shaeli. "Purple Leaf was trading nearby, in Noresh, and he rode with the rescue party. That's how Eenis met my uncle Jeth."

"Your grandfather was a fine man, Shaeli. I met Povann many times when your parents were courting," said Arinola.

"It's odd to think of them as courting," mused Shaeli.

"They were a lovely couple. Your father was such a handsome young trader. Mareesha knew, the first Wintering after they'd met, that she would not be separated from him again. She insisted the whole time she would not be at Great Court for the next Wintering, and told Irinesta she'd have to look for another Faunist. Irinesta was heartbroken when she left, but she was so happy for your mother she could never begrudge it. Oh, I wish she could see you *and* your mother."

"Irinesta? The old queen?" asked Shaeli. "I'm sure Mam misses her, too. She used to talk about her a lot, when I was little." She sipped at her wine, warmed to the toes by its fruity heat. "We saw her once, a few years ago, up on the balcony, and I often saw Mam staring up at the old queen's tower whenever we were near Great Court this year. She always asks my aunt Asheen for news."

"'Tis all we can do. Ask for news and see her on the balcony occasionally. I was with her the night Tenelon died, you know, as was Vulcan. I'll never forget the look on her face when he kissed her farewell and breathed his last." She wiped a tear from her eye. "We all wish she would come out of seclusion."

"Not all, Arinola," said Sir Vulcan. "Only those of us who remember her. There are many now who do not."

"I know. All these new young faces above black and scarlet uniforms. Everything has changed." Arinola sighed. "You had your letter from Irinesta before the Wintering, Vulcan, didn't you?"

Vulcan nodded. "Yes, but it was hardly a letter, merely a note on the anniversary of Tenelon's death, saying she is in good health and E'Nith cares for her, as always."

"Perhaps I can see E'Nith in the corridors somewhere, and let her know that Mareesha's daughter will be throwing skylights from my house. She should see them from the tower of the Glade."

"That's a strong wish," Vulcan replied. "E'Nith speaks to no one, you know that, and she is always accompanied by guard. She gathers a few things and returns to the tower. Most think she is deaf, and she'll not stop to listen. She moves like a ghost through the castle."

21

"Yes, *most* think she is deaf, but I have known E'Nith for a long time. She thinks of no one but Irinesta, and if a message *can* reach her, E'Nith is the only way," Arinola said. "There is no harm in wishing it. I am going to Great Court in a few days, weather permitting, and if the gods are kind, E'Nith will cross my path."

"Perhaps so," smiled Vulcan. Again he crossed to the window and peered out. "It seems this is no small blizzard and we shall have to stay the night."

"That is just as well," said Flin, re-entering the room. "Yorrow would be unhappy if I changed the number for dinner again."

"Well, we must keep Yorrow happy," said Vulcan.

"It is one of the reasons Vulcan does not mind being stranded here," said Arinola. "He knows you have the best cook in the city, Flin."

"Say that when Yorrow is around, Arinola, and you will have a friend for life," chuckled Flin.

"I will be sure to," she smiled. "You know I'd steal him off you if I could. Shaeli was telling us Qiren has brought his wife with him this time."

"Yes," Flin replied. "Illen is a lovely woman, and pleased to be back in the World after so long. Shall we go and join them in the library?"

Flin re-warmed the jug of wine and took it and extra mugs with them, and they went down the hall to the library where Illen and Qiren pored over the old drawings. Introductions were made, mugs filled and refilled – Shaeli was already feeling light-headed with the wine's effects – and the drawings on the desk were admired.

The drawings were mainly of elves, a few showed dragons or drell, and one or two were maps with faded, old-fashioned script on them. Qiren had found them high up on a dusty shelf one day when he was bored and searching for something to read. Flin had chosen some to have framed, and the rest were to be bound; Qiren and Illen were preparing which order they were going to be bound in.

Shaeli had looked through the collection many times, admiring the beautiful work. There were a few unfinished sketches – headless torsos, faces floating on the page, disembodied dragon wings – and Qiren had decided they were all very old, and should be preserved.

Shaeli's favourite was a small coloured sketch framed in the centre of the page. It showed the Lady Shahlita with Wipp standing beside a great tree, looking off into the distance. Shahlita was pointing at distant mountains – the range where the dragons once lived, Qiren said – and it was by the bangles on her arms that Shaeli had recognised her. Qiren had been amazed Shaeli had recognised an elfin lady long since dead, and she had told him she had studied many things elfin with the Warlocks at Cave – it was not a lie, after all – and she named several other elves from the pages in the folder and spoke a few words in formal elf, impressing him all the more.

Every time she saw the drawing it made her think of the bangle Nol had given her, now safely back at Cave with Almarnoch. She had decided to place the tapestry bag holding the wand and Nol's box in Almarnoch's hands for safekeeping. When she had first stayed with Flin, during the year, she had brought the bag with her, stashing it under her bed or in the cupboard, but before Purple Leaf had left for the Wintering she had given it to her father to deliver to the High Warlock, knowing there was no safer place for the wand than with her old friend at Cave. She had worried for a while that he would look in the box and see the bangle, but in the end she thought it mattered little; she would tell him of Williver's request to find Shahlita's bangles, for she thought it time the Warlock knew. She planned to tell him next Wintering, and somehow she felt that Williver would agree. If she saw him in her dreams before then, she would ask him about it, but his visits were becoming fewer and farther between and Shaeli missed him.

Lady Arinola and Sir Vulcan were delighted with the collection, and Shaeli searched the pile for the one of Shahlita to show them, but she could not find it. Flin noticed her searching and smiled. He left the room unnoticed, and returned moments later.

"Is this what you're looking for, Shaeli?" he asked. In his hands he held the sketch, beautifully framed. He set it on a chair and stood back as Shaeli admired it.

"Oh, Flin, it looks lovely," she cried.

"I hoped you'd think so," he said. "Because it's yours."

"Mine?"

"Yes, Shaeli," said Flin. "Your mother told me that your birth-day fell during the Wintering, and I thought this a fitting gift."

"Mine?" said Shaeli again, gazing at the framed picture. "To have in my room?"

"Yes, while you're here," said Flin. "But you may take it with you whenever you leave us, though I hope that won't be for a long time yet."

Shaeli launched herself at him and hugged the thin man until he begged for air.

"I'll have to give you presents more often, Shaeli," he said, brushing blonde hair out of his eyes when she released him. "It brings great rewards."

Shaeli blushed. "Thank you, Flin," she murmured. "I love it."

"I'm glad," he said. "Now, more wine anyone?"

Shaeli shook her head; her throat felt tight and she did not speak. Illen noticed the tears in her eyes and came over to give her a hug.

"We've all become very fond of you, you know," she murmured, her eyes warm with feeling.

"Thank you, Illen," Shaeli whispered. "You're all so kind, it's just…"

"I know. You miss them." Illen smiled. "But you have the ball to look forward to now, and the rest of the Wintering will pass quickly after that. When first thaw comes we shall leave for the Starisles where we'll see them again. I look forward to it almost as much as you."

She gave Shaeli another quick hug and drew her over to the others, and Shaeli did her best to find some gaiety inside herself. Sure enough, it was there, and she found herself enjoying the afternoon and evening immensely.

Arinola and Vulcan were witty, entertaining people, keeping them amused with a huge array of tales. Qiren and Flin had known them for many Winterings, and the two matched the visitors tale for tale. They told wicked stories about certain courtiers during dinner, and then moved on to the best scandals in the city. Arinola hinted that one of the scandals belonged to her own family, but she would not be drawn to divulge any details, saying only that she had had a very wicked grandfather.

Shaeli laughed so hard her cheeks began to ache, and when it was time for bed she was almost sorry the day was over. As she slipped beneath the blankets, she hoped the blizzard would hold for a day or two so the visitors would have to stay longer and the Wintering would pass more quickly. She watched the flames in the fireplace dancing as her lids began to droop, and she decided Illen was right. There was a lot to look forward to.

* * *

Arinola and Vulcan were snowed in for that day, and the next, but the morning after that they woke to an almost clear sky. A thin layer of sunshine shone weakly on the city, and soon after breakfast the visitors left, the men who had brought them shovelling a path back through the snow. Shaeli waved until they were out of sight, and then went to find Flin, who still sat at the breakfast table.

"Are you ready?" she asked him.

"Almost," he replied, through a mouthful of toast. "I'll just finish my tezz. Put your coat on and I'll meet you on the terrace."

"Alright," she said. "I'll tell Qiren. I think he's in the library. Come on, Eb," she said, scooping the jevvi off the floor. "We're going outside."

Soon after, the three of them stood on the terrace, looking down on a garden waist-deep in snow.

The long terrace was on the bay side of the house, and a wide set of stairs led down to the garden. Stone walls on two sides sheltered the terrace from much of the winds, and what snow there was had been swept clear, but the garden was deep in thick mounds of snow, the trunks of the trees marooned in tall drifts. The low fence on the cliff side was completely covered, the space where they threw skylights was a bank of white sloping down to where the ground ended abruptly at the cliff's edge. The tide thundered against the base of the cliff and the waters of the bay were metal-grey.

Flin looked down the steps. The last four were covered in snow. Ebony was on the fifth step, tentatively poking at the pile of white. She scampered to one side, climbed the railing, and launched herself off into the lowest branches of a tree. Flin watched her leap from branch to branch, little arms and legs outflung, gliding easily between branches, then he looked back down at the snow.

"I can get the men to clear it," he said. "But it may take a while."

"We may see another blizzard soon, Flin," said Qiren. "And in the meantime we cannot practise."

"It looks pretty slippery out there, too, near the edge," said Shaeli, nervously. She stood in the corner beside the wall at the end of the terrace. She could not see the water throwing itself against the rocks at the base of the cliff, but she could hear its roar. She felt a bit dizzy and her knuckles were white as she let go of the railing. "We could throw out off the veranda, between the trees and the wall," she said. "Or reach around the wall."

"There isn't room to work together," said Flin. "It's never blown in like this before. It usually takes only a short while to clear a path. The winds are *usually* from the south, that's why I bought this house." He was growing petulant and glared at the house as if it had turned the winds on purpose. "And we can't throw straight up, because the eaves hang so far over and the trees are in the way."

"What about over the other side?" said Qiren.

"No, the stables are over there."

Qiren nodded. He knew horses were skittish around skylights.

"What about over the end wall?" asked Shaeli. She pointed to the end of the terrace where she'd been standing. "Couldn't we put something over there to stand on and throw out over the top. It's not that high."

Flin's face brightened immediately. "No, Shaeli, it's not that high, is it? The sideboard from the hall ought to do. I'll see to it immediately."

He had several of his men carry the broad side-table out, and he followed with a chair for stepping up to it. They pushed the table against the wall, covered its polished surface with a rug to protect it from their boots, and climbed on top.

The wall reached Shaeli chest-high when she stood on the table; Flin and Qiren had no trouble reaching over. The wind had dropped, and the patchy sky held as they threw skylights out over the edge. Flin asked Shaeli to throw with the vistrella, and he wove a sequence of skylights around the silver-and-purple shapes she threw with the black gem. Qiren highlighted them both, trying out a few ideas, and by lunch, when the next blizzard arrived, they had worked out a rough program for the performance at Arinola's.

Flin was so pleased with the new throwing space that he had his men begin constructing a more permanent platform.

Over the next few days, when the weather permitted, the sideboard was moved back and forth until the platform was completed. When it was done, it had a set of stairs at one end and Flin was delighted that they had no need to worry about clearing a path down to the garden ledge. Several of Flin's staff also congratulated Shaeli on her idea; it was much easier, they said, to spend a few days building a platform than the whole Wintering shovelling.

Shaeli was the most pleased of all; she had not liked throwing from the cliff with its jagged edge and the long drop below, but from the platform, with the wall in front of her and the terrace behind, it was not quite so frightening – as long as she did not look down. Her eyes had been drawn there, once or twice, and been held against her will. The wall beneath the terrace went straight down into the rock, and there was only a slim ledge between the wall and the brink of the cliff, drifts of snow clinging precariously to the thin perch. Once, as her eyes had been riveted to the scene, a clump of snow had slipped away and fallen onto the rocks at the base of the cliff, tumbling slowly down as if flying, until suddenly its icy body smashed against the black rocks. She had turned and sat down on the platform with a thump, her eyes closed and her stomach trying to curl up into a ball and crawl away. After that she learned not to look straight down, and she kept her eyes on the islands in the bay, or the skylights they threw into the air.

* * *

CHAPTER TWO

The days before Arinola's ball passed quickly, and one afternoon there was a lull in the storm clouds. On Flin's advice, Shaeli had packed several days before so they would be ready when the weather allowed, and they bundled into a sleigh for the trip to Arinola's. Ebony burrowed into Shaeli's jacket as they drove in towards the centre of the headland and turned up towards Great Court, but they passed only one lane before turning back to the left, heading again towards the cliff. Arinola's house was the last on the high side of the street, an enormous edifice taking up the space of two, surrounded by tall trees and an imposing wall, yet the wrought iron gates were wide open, and small balloons flew from them.

"She must have had a Warlock come and give them Lift," said Shaeli, looking nostalgically at the little balloons as they passed through the gates.

"Arinola has a Warlock on staff," said Flin. "Her gardens are elaborate and require a lot of attention. Her roses are famous in Palveron."

"You don't have a Warlock for your garden, Flin, do you?"

"No, my trees are the variety which does not require Warlock protection. Another reason I purchased my excellent house." The house had come back into favour with the new throwing platform; the unhappy width of its eaves forgotten.

The bells on the sleigh jingled as they drove through the grounds beneath trees laden with blossoms of snow. As Flin had said, the gardens were vast and elaborate even under the white blanket, and Shaeli wondered how they would look during the year.

Arinola stood at the top of the stairs as they drew up in front of the house, the enormous door behind her wide open. She was muffled against the cold by a large overcoat with a fur

29

lined hood, and was calling greetings before they'd alighted from the sleigh. Her house dwarfed her, white columns holding up the roof above the doorway, grinning gargoyles perched on each corner, gleeful despite the snow on their heads. The house rose three storeys above the ground, peaked attic roofs towering above them, more leering gargoyles crouched on each one.

Inside was a huge entry hall with a white marble floor, with white figurines of fairies many times their actual size gracing recessed alcoves. On each side of the entry hall, two white-carpeted staircases curved upwards to the first floor, the void above reaching all the way to the roof, the twin staircases mirrored on the floors above. Doors and hallways opened from a dozen places off the entry hall. Shaeli thought she would get lost in so huge a house, and she tried not to ogle as she stood inside the doorway.

Arinola bustled in behind them, and they discarded their coats, which were taken by two discreet young maids. Sir Vulcan wandered out from one of the doorways, a steaming mug in his hands.

"Ah, Flin," he said. "Just the man I was hoping for. I can't get these toddies right. Come and help."

"Vulcan," scolded Arinola. "They may want to settle into their rooms first. We have not even said a proper hello." She kissed everyone's cheeks, and patted Ebony, who sat on Shaeli's shoulder, huge black eyes peering above. "Dear little thing, she looks like she wants to explore." Ebony fixed her eye on Arinola and chattered, her tail shivering. "I think she understood me," Arinola laughed.

"Oh, she knows what 'explore' means," smiled Shaeli.

"I don't mind helping Vulcan with the wine before we put our bags away," said Flin. "Anyone else?"

The others shook their heads.

"Excellent," smiled Vulcan, leading them into the room he had just exited. Their things were left looking forlorn in the entry hall; a small pile of baggage in a white void of space.

The room they entered was a library, three times the size of Flin's, the shelves reaching to the ceiling. Two thin staircases spiralled up to a walkway which ran around the walls above their heads, and there were little ladders on wheels here and there, more on the walkway above. Almost every bit of the walls were filled with shelves, and every shelf was filled with books. Shaeli had never seen so many books in her life, let alone all in one place, and she stared about her until she realised she was ogling again and tried to contain herself.

The fireplace, longer than three normal fireplaces joined together, roared with a huge load of wood, elegant lamps shone in every corner – she suspected with Warlock-fire, they had that sort of glow – and there were thickly padded arm-chairs and couches clustered throughout as well as several tables and desks.

Vulcan ushered Flin over to a corner where a sideboard held dozens of bottles, and while the others seated themselves amid one of the clusters of couches, the two concocted a warming brew. Soon Vulcan was offering them a mug from a tray, and as they sipped on the drinks, they heard bells from outside.

"That will be more guests," said Arinola. "I'll go and greet them." She left the room and Vulcan chuckled.

"She knew as soon as that blizzard stopped that we'd see some guests. She's had the servants running around putting the finishing touches to the rooms."

Arinola was soon leading the other party into the library, and before introductions were over, another group had arrived – neighbours from down the street who walked in on snow-shoes. Arinola saw them from the windows filing across the garden, but before Vulcan and Flin had mixed another batch of mulled wine, another two sleighs had pulled into the driveway

31

and more people had walked in on foot. By nightfall, when the next blizzard hit, there were twenty people already under Arinola's roof.

The snow fell through the night and the next day, but another break in the weather the morning after that saw twenty more arrive. When the next blizzard struck and the streets became impassable once more, Arinola's house was filled with guests ready to be entertained. The dull days of the Wintering had given others besides Shaeli a near-terminal case of boredom.

Shaeli's room was in the north-eastern wing on the top floor, Illen and Qiren on one side, Flin's around the corner, and it had taken Shaeli several escorted trips before she managed to find her room on her own. Her windows looked over the bay on one side and a conservatory on the other, and from a tiny jutting balcony she could see Great Court looming above.

Shaeli and Illen talked about the strangeness of living in such a huge house, eating with vast amounts of people, encountering strangers on every landing. Neither had ever experienced such a thing before and felt lost in such a grand place with so many servants. The dining rooms were eternally full, someone was always mixing drinks in the library, and they had enormous trouble remembering everyone's names. Conversations were swift, tangled beasts, filled with things of which they had no knowledge – but they agreed it was a thrilling time nonetheless.

The following morning, the day of the ball, arrived with leaden skies and snow-filled gusts crashing against the windows. Though the Wintering shuddered furiously about the house the mood inside was light and airy, the atmosphere permeated with spring.

During the afternoon, Shaeli wandered the halls with Ebony as a strange quiet filled the house. Everyone was resting in anticipation of the ball, but she was nervous, as was becoming her custom before a performance, and she had not been able to rest. She *had* tried. She'd lay on her bed – a high, four-poster, lace-hung structure – but had begun pacing the room and peering out the windows at the snow. Below was the glass roof of the conservatory where the guests would watch the skylights, but she could not see the tiny balcony above where they would throw their lights. The balcony was high up under the eaves somewhere, and she hadn't accompanied Flin and Qiren when they inspected it the day before. She imagined it was tiny and open to the elements, a gargoyle leering down at the long drop to the ground.

She left the room and walked down to the library, but for once it was empty of toddy drinkers. She looked at a few books but could not concentrate on the words, so she wandered away and found herself following Ebony down the hallway that led to the conservatory. The first time she had seen it she had been amazed, for inside the glass-walled room, it seemed as if the Wintering had never been.

The room was vast, its walls and ceiling almost entirely made of glass, and it was filled with green plants and bright flowers – in pots, in walled beds, and hanging from the paned ceiling. Stacked outside were shutters to cover the structure from the worst storms, but the thick glass in the walls of the room were layered three deep, and seldom did hail or wind crack more than the outer layer. The structure was also protected by the house Warlock, but Arinola said the plants needed little of his magic to grow; the glass was the magic.

Inside, the plant life thrived, and Shaeli wandered about marvelling again at the novelty of such a room. Tables and chairs were nestled in leafy nooks; a waterfall, minute and perfect, ran from a rock wall in one corner; tiny, exotic blossoms nestled in mossy cracks. A fountain with fat, smiling cherubs pouring water from jugs sat in the middle of the room, lilac water-lilies gracing its surface. Blossoms hung from climbing vines as if spring had called them from their beds, but the glass ceiling above looked up to a snow-washed afternoon.

She squinted up at the blizzard. She still could not see the balcony where they were to stand tonight, but she could imagine the winds that howled around it. She was glad she hadn't gone with the others to look at it; she didn't want to think about it, being outside, up there, and if the wind was too strong they would have to abandon the performance anyway. Flin had decided that if that happened they could throw a few skylights up into the stairwell above the entry way, and she almost hoped for that.

She wandered over to the other side of the indoor garden, looking inland. She could see lights already in some of the windows of the southern wing and it was barely mid-afternoon. She sighed and walked back to the smiling cherubs in the fountain, wishing she could rest like the others.

She sat at the edge of the fountain, dabbling her fingers in the water until Ebony, who had left her to roam the garden, bounded over. She held a nut in her small hand.

"Where did you get that?" Shaeli asked her, and jumped as a voice spoke behind her.

"I hope you don't mind," the voice said. "I gave it to her."

Shaeli turned and saw a man coming towards her. He was older than her, she thought, but not by many Winterings, his features even and handsome, and she suspected he had something of the people from across the sea in his lineage. His brown eyes and dark skin had the cast of the Irikai, and those eyes were warm and smiling as he approached. Shaeli found herself smiling back.

"It will only cause you grief," she said. "She will want to hide it for you to find."

The man grinned. "Is it that hard?"

Shaeli grinned back. "You don't want to know." Ebony chittered. "Come on, Eb, you'd win in here and you know it. Besides, there's only one nut."

"Well, not exactly," said the stranger, rattling his pocket. "I brought supplies."

34

Ebony spoke again and Shaeli stroked her, looking up at the man. "You'll have to crack it for her if you can't find it," she said. "And I have to warn you, the chances of finding it are extraordinarily slim."

"That good, eh?"

Shaeli nodded. Ebony looked eagerly at the man.

"I like taking chances," he said.

"Well, if you're sure," Shaeli said. "But remember I warned you, you can't win." She looked seriously at the man. "You have to shut your eyes."

"Perhaps I'd better introduce myself first, then," he said, holding out his hand. "Pizar, of Maxx."

She shook the proffered hand. "Shaeli, of Purple Leaf Trader," she said automatically, then she thought again. "Apprentice to Flin, master of skylights."

"I thought so," he smiled. "I was told he had a new and very pretty apprentice. I look forward to the skylights this evening."

"I *was* looking forward to them," Shaeli smiled, fighting the blush that wanted to rise on her cheeks after his compliment. "Until this afternoon."

Ebony tugged at Shaeli's sleeve. Shaeli looked at her, and then at Pizar.

"You asked for it," she said. "Cover your eyes."

He obediently covered them with his hands and Shaeli looked at the jevvi. "Don't make it too hard," she said, and then covered her own.

Ebony bounded off as soon as their eyes were hidden, and they continued their conversation from behind their hands as Ebony rustled about amongst the leaves.

"You must have arrived with the last batch of visitors," said Shaeli. "I met most of the people who arrived the other day."

"Yes, I think we were almost the last," he replied, and Shaeli noticed how deep his voice was when she could not see him. "We came down from Great Court almost at the last moment. Our captain is an old friend of Lady Arinola's, and he said she always likes a few soldiers at her balls, even if they do wear black and scarlet."

"You're with the queen's guard, then?"

"Yes, only one of many."

"Where is Maxx? I've heard of it, but I'm not sure which Land it's in."

"It's in Wokk," he said. "The north-eastern tip on the east island. Not a big place, but almost a city, right on the coast."

Shaeli had been right about him being a descendant of the Irikai: Wokk natives were fair and blue-eyed.

"I love the sea, don't you?" she asked. "The smell of salt in the air is so clean and crisp. It's the one thing I miss at Cave."

"I've always been fascinated by the Traders. To travel to all the Lands and to Winter in the fabled Cave with all the other travellers."

"It is wonderful," she admitted, and then her voice changed. "This is my first Wintering away."

"Oh," he said, gently. "I didn't know." He was quiet for a few moments. "How strange all this must be to you."

Just then, Ebony came back and tugged at Shaeli's sleeve. Shaeli took her hands from her eyes.

"She's hidden your nut," she said, touching his arm.

He lowered his hands, and blinked. "The chase begins," he grinned, and offered Shaeli his hand.

She took it, and rose, but let go of it as soon as she'd gained her feet; his hand felt unduly warm and damp beneath her fingers. They continued their conversation as they searched for the nut.

"It must be vast, to hold all the Traders' ships, your Cave," said Pizar.

"Oh, yes," replied Shaeli, feeling about beneath some ornamental grass. "It's huge, but beautiful, with the fire-pits and all the candles and lamps. An amazing sight." She began to realise just how magnificent as she spoke of it, and she felt the now-familiar twinge of homesickness.

"It's difficult to reach, isn't it?"

"Well, yes, unless you fly. It's a long way from Serrat, the closest town, and the Valley of Stones is practically impassable."

"Is there no way over the mountains?" he asked, his hand in the foliage of a hanging basket.

"No *easy* way, but sometimes we have strangers find their way down to the Long Lea." He looked at her, puzzled, and she explained. "It's an enormous meadow that runs below Cave where we grow food during the year."

"But I thought all traders travelled the Lands during the year." He moved on to the next basket.

"Most do, but the old ones, traders who have retired, and the Warlocks are always there, and always young people having their Cave year." Again that look, and an explanation. "Somewhere around our fifteenth Winter we stay at Cave for the year, while our families go into the World to trade. We learn new skills, and help with the crops for the Wintering. Shall we have a look near the waterfall?"

"Alright," Pizar nodded. "We have something similar on Wokk," he said, as they walked over to the little waterfall, "but we live with the elders within the town, so we may still see our families. It must have been difficult for you."

"Yes, but this is harder. When I had my Cave year I had many friends, and my grandmother, and the Warlocks. Here is... well... it's a little different."

Pizar nodded again, but she could not see his face, for it was hidden in foliage as he searched beneath some tall pots of soft green fern.

They did not find that nut, nor any of the others hidden throughout the indoor garden during the afternoon, yet the time passed quickly, much to Shaeli's delight, and when they parted to dress for the ball, she felt she had found a friend in Pizar.

* * *

She introduced her friends to Pizar after dinner. He was wearing his uniform, so starched that it almost crackled, and when he asked Shaeli to dance, his white gloves were cold and stiff under her hand, yet his manner was far from stiff as he whirled her expertly about on the dance floor, making her laugh with amusing stories about people she didn't know. He, in turn, introduced her to his friends from the guard, and his captain, Arinola's old friend, Sir Collett.

Sir Collett was a stocky, barrel-chested man with a moustache like a thick brush and shoulders like a horse. His voice when he greeted Shaeli was a gruff bark, yet the words he spoke were gracious and kind. He remembered her mother and talked of "happy days, long gone", before going off to ask Arinola to dance.

"What a nice man," said Shaeli.

"You wouldn't think so when he's yelling at you at sunrise after all-night duty," Pizar grinned. "It's not a happy sight. It's, 'in my day' this, and 'when I was a young guard' that, and so on, and tells anyone who will listen he will retire in two years. He's the last of the old king's guard, and most think him an awful bore."

"Oh dear," giggled Shaeli. "And he seems so gallant for such a big man."

Pizar also introduced her to Skeltom, Arinola's Warlock, who was also from Maxx. She had seen him stalking the halls before this, but had not met him officially. Here were the features of a Wokkii native which one would expect: the white-blonde hair, the ice-blue eyes, the pale skin. Skeltom was tall and thin with a beaky nose. His eyebrows were white, and his skin was so pale it was pink. His large head was balanced precariously on his long neck – or so it seemed, for it wobbled about when he spoke as if in danger of falling, and Shaeli found herself strangely paused to catch it the entire time they talked with him. Besides the odd, head-wobbling habit, Skeltom also stood with his hands clasped together as if in prayer, his long, bony fingers folded over, except for the forefingers, which he kept upright like a little tent, and they tapped together as he spoke. Shaeli, reminded of a praying mantis by the tall Warlock, tried not to giggle as she thought that the head wobbling and the finger tapping were somehow connected. Pizar told her that Skeltom was a very powerful Warlock, absolutely amazing with plants, and that Arinola was lucky to have him. Shaeli wanted to ask had his head always wobbled like that, but she didn't want to be rude.

After dancing and an elaborate supper, Flin disappeared to check the weather, and when he returned, he whispered to Arinola and she asked the guests to move into the conservatory. Shaeli's heart took a swift dive into her stomach and she sought out Illen for the comforting words she knew would be forthcoming. Illen did not disappoint her. By the time she had climbed the stairs behind Flin and Qiren, her heart had returned to its appointed position, though it still bumped quite badly against her ribs.

One of Arinola's servants stood at the entrance to the last stairwell, a door beyond Flin's bedroom. He stood patiently with a pile of fur-lined cloaks over his arm, and as they donned them Flin pulled something from his pocket. Shaeli was tucking her hair into the furry hood of her cloak when he approached.

"I know you won't part with that amulet Shaeli, but I had this made for you, so there'll be no more mixing up your stones during a performance." He put the object in her hands. "I hope you like it."

Shaeli looked at him, and then at her hands. In them was a broad belt, made from thick purple velvet, with small, deep pockets sewn onto it. It had no buckle, but two long ties, and Shaeli saw its use immediately. She tied it around her waist, with the pockets at the front and the ties at the back, tried one of the pockets, and found it small, but easy to put her fingers in, and deep enough to hold even her longest stone. She hugged Flin.

"*What* a good idea, Flin," she said. "Thank you, I love it." She pulled out the vistrella and tucked it into one pocket, placed the finger of smoky quartz in another, and the green triangle of verdena and the blue stone in two others. "I won't get mixed up now."

Flin beamed as he flung his cloak about his shoulders. "Good. Now, let's go and dazzle the guests with our brilliance," he said.

He went through the door, Qiren followed, and Shaeli straggled behind them. Illen did not move, and Shaeli looked back at her.

"Aren't you coming?" she asked, and Illen shook her head.

"No. I'll watch with the others," she said, smiling. "Don't worry, Shaeli, you'll be fine."

She turned away and Shaeli continued up the narrow staircase to another doorway, this opening into a large room with a peaked ceiling, the sides sloping so steeply they almost touched the floor on either side. It was chilly in the cavernous attic, strange shapes shrouded in dust cloths loomed in the shadows, and across the floor lay a set of double glass doors, the panes small and thick. Through them Shaeli could see the balcony from where they would throw their skylights, and the soft white blur of the snow still falling outside.

Beside the doors was a small brazier with three mugs of tezz steaming on its lip. The brazier was filled with fire-rocks and lit with Warlock fire. It did not smoke or burn, yet a steady warmth came from it. Flin chuckled.

"Arinola thinks of everything," he said, and handed them each a cup.

Shaeli sipped nervously at the tezz, and when Flin moved to the doors she took a deep breath, put down her cup, and followed him. She almost laughed when she stepped outside. She had worried about the terrace needlessly. It was high, yes. The snow still fell, but barely, and the wind had dropped. The terrace was small, yet a grilled railing bordered it on every side, and reached high above her head. The grillwork of the wrought iron was intricately braided, and Shaeli felt perfectly safe in the pretty enclosure.

At the front of the cage there was a broad opening, from Shaeli's chest height to well above Qiren's head, and along the bottom of the opening was a wide shelf. Flin leant on it and looked down at the conservatory. *That* made Shaeli's head swim.

"They should be organised by now," Flin said. He looked at Shaeli, who stepped up to the opening beside him. "Ready?" he asked, and she nodded.

She turned to Qiren on her other side. "Ready?" she grinned, and he nodded back, lips twitching.

They turned forward and Flin's many-faceted gem erupted with an enormous golden orb which lit the windows and the glass roof below with yellow fire. Qiren was right behind him with a sequence of huge red flowers which flew from his wand on invisible threads, exploding within Flin's ball. Shaeli punctured their centres with silver and purple from her vistrella with one hand and green leaves with her verdena from the other.

And so it went, through a sequence of gold orbs punctuated by spinning red wheels and whizzing green fireflies, to a soft rain of purple and silver, then bluebird-shaped lights which flew in circles downwards before fading to soft sparks on the roof of the conservatory while tiny rainbows arced above. More they threw, skylights dancing from their fingers; a flood of butterflies, leaping dolphins, fat spiders falling on shining strings, on and on, and almost before Shaeli had time to enjoy it, it was over, and Flin was throwing the last golden orb into the sky, completing their sequence. She had barely noticed the cold which had turned her cheeks pink and the end of her nose red; her fingers had not felt the bite of the Wintering as she threw, but suddenly she was very cold. She shivered, pulled the cloak about her, and transferred her stones once more to the safety of her amulet beneath the thick fur.

The moon broke through a gap in the clouds and the scene was transformed into a world edged with silver. The Bay of Islands glittered with a thousand diamonds, the trees in Arinola's garden proudly wore their thick white coats, and the castle crowning the skyline shimmered with light, its outline starkly black against the sky. Shaeli sighed as the moon hid its face again and the Land became shrouded in shadows once more, and she turned and went inside, followed by the others. They warmed their hands again over Skeltom's brazier before descending the stairs where the servant was waiting to collect their cloaks. Shaeli put her new gem belt in her room as she passed and checked on Ebony, who was curled asleep before the banked fire.

They went down the stairs and the entire party was in the entrance hall to greet them. As they reached the last flight, applause erupted and they descended amid cheers.

Shaeli blushed as she reached the bottom, embarrassed, but proud, and she thanked people for their praise, but stayed close to Flin as they were surrounded. At last each guest had congratulated them on their performance and drifted off to dance or eat again, but Shaeli began to drift into a daze. She could feel the drain of magic and it was not long before she and Illen went upstairs. As she snuggled beneath the mound of quilts, she realised that the Wintering was going by at last, and she hoped the rest of it would pass quickly. Despite the excitement and the amazing experience, she still longed to see her family.

* * *

Across the Land, in the vast Cave below Mount Zerrinius, all but one of Shaeli's family thought of her often. Mareesha and Jarris found her in their thoughts a dozen times a day, Shanna and Neesha talked of her almost as often, lamenting the fact they would not see her perform in the Starisles in the spring; it was time for their Cave year, and although they were excited, they mourned the fact that they would miss their sister's performance. Jeth and Eenis talked of Shaeli too. Eenis was eager to be reunited with Illen after the Wintering, and Jeth loved hearing his wife talk so eagerly, so openly of her feelings that he encouraged every conversation. Her brother and cousin thought of Shaeli less often; their days were full helping with the new Arrow Trader being built in one of the rear caverns, and most evenings Tarkoda dragged Andos to wherever the prettiest girls had gathered. Tarkoda was well liked, but few of the girls took his flirting manner seriously; Andos was at his least nimble in front of them, for they left him tongue-tied and shy. Wyshka and Olver had Shaeli in their thoughts every day; the Warlocks too, spoke fondly of her, but the strength of her gift weighed on Almarnoch's mind. He wished he had spoken to her before Purple Leaf left before the year, yet he had to console himself with the fact that the gods had taken her education out of his hands. They would do as they would.

Only Dari never thought of his cousin. He was happy enough in himself, practising his art and striving to be the best Warlock he could. He spent long hours going over incantations until he had them down perfectly, and while he grew more knowledgeable, the time spent alone isolated him from the other traders, made him distant from their daily lives. He did not know he was looked upon as rather odd, and he would not have cared if he had; he hoped only that Almarnoch would soon find him worthy of going to the Warlock Island. The High Warlock continually said how quickly he was learning, how he was learning much faster than Garrit had, faster even than Llevvis. Perhaps in a few more Winterings... Then he would go to Palveron, and when he was a fully-fledged Warlock with a staff of his own he would seek out Garrit and they would have a fine time together.

* * *

CHAPTER THREE

While the rest of Wintering did not pass as quickly as Shaeli had hoped, eventually, as is always the case, the time did go by. She spent it practising, growing ever more controlled in her throwing, and once when the weather permitted, she visited her aunt Asheen's. They stayed at Lady Arinola's again too, but with much fewer guests and a great deal more fun.

Pizar and two of his friends from the guard called on them and were snowed in for a day, and they kept them amused with tales of the terrible Sir Collett and his rigorous training. Pizar continued to show interest in the Fleet, and asked Shaeli many questions about her family and the traders.

Each morning as the end of the Wintering grew nearer, Shaeli thrust back her curtains in the hope that the blizzards had ended, and one morning she was greeted with the usual banks of snow on the ground, but overhead the clouds had large rents in their thick hides and the sun shone weakly through the gaps. She whooped, dressed as quickly as possible, and rushed down the stairs, but by the time she got there, the wide rents in the clouds had shrunk to thin slits, and the sun battled to be seen, yet it was the beginning of first thaw – she could feel it. Eight days later, Flin knocked on her door before breakfast.

"Best gather your things today, Shaeli," he said. "Tomorrow we begin the journey to the Starisles."

Shaeli laughed. "I've been packed for three days, Flin. I'm ready whenever you are."

Flin chuckled and left her in a dither of excitement, though sleety rain slapped against the windows. Thin sleet continued throughout the day while Flin's servants rushed around the house and preparations were made for their departure. The pile of baggage grew higher and higher in the entry hall, and

45

every time Shaeli passed it her stomach did a little dance, as it had when she'd found out how they were getting to the Starisles.

"Well, we're not going by carriage," Flin had smiled when she'd asked him about it. "We do not have time to wait for the snow to melt, Shaeli, or for your Fleet to arrive. We go by sea."

"By sea?"

"Yes. We'll board the first ship to leave Palveron, and we'll reach the Starisles in six or seven days."

"I've never been on a ship," she said. "What *fun*."

Flin laughed. "And you from a Trader. *I* do not look forward to the trip," he said. "I'm not a good sailor, which was no easy thing for one growing up on the Starisles."

They were going to leave in the sunrise hours, and after dinner Flin advised her to have a good night's sleep before the journey.

"I don't think I'll be able to sleep," she answered. "My last night in Palveron, and tomorrow the journey to Pa'laidiz. By *ship*." She took Ebony from her perch on the back of her chair and twirled about the room with her, but the jevvi voiced her displeasure loudly and Shaeli took pity on her and stopped twirling.

She took Flin's advice and went up to bed, hoping to bring the morning more quickly, yet she slept badly, waking fitfully, her head filled with jumbled dreams and half-formed thoughts. When she was woken by a maid in the grey, sunrise hours, she felt groggy and stupid. She wished for one of Sahli'en's potions as she stumbled through breakfast, and she was yawning as they waited for the carriage. Illen emerged from the kitchens and passed her a small cup.

"Yorrow thought you might need this," she said. "I've had one, and they make a great deal of difference. I felt so dull this morning."

"I know the feeling," said Shaeli, downing the brew. It was not nearly as palatable as Sahli'en's or her mother's may have been, but the effects were excellent. By the time the carriage drew up, her eyes had grown bright and her brain more focussed, and she smiled and thanked Flin's cook when he joined the party. Yorrow merely nodded, but his face did not crack.

They drove through the dim streets of Palveron, the thoroughfares cleared of snow by the Warlocks after the last blizzards had swept through, but still lined with muddy slush. The docks were between the great headland and the long sweep of bay where her aunt and uncle lived, the ships packed together in the sheltered harbour so closely their masts looked like a forest of leafless trees, and when they drove along the wide boardwalk between the docks and the warehouses, their baggage was already being carried to a ship moored at one of the larger wharves. It was a large, sturdy-looking ship, three tall masts rising from the deck and a dozen sailors swarming in the rigging, their voices loud and raucous, like a flock of seagulls in the still morning air.

Shaeli stepped down from the carriage just as the sun stepped over the horizon. Small ice floes dotted the bay and the water turned silver around them.

As they gathered their belongings, another carriage pulled up, and Shaeli was touched to see that it was Iyri and Asheen, come to bid them farewell, and they held a hurried, hugging conversation before she walked up the gangplank behind the others. Flin greeted the ship's captain with familiarity, clapping him firmly on the shoulder and introducing them all, and then they headed out into the bay.

The ship, its buxom colourful figurehead riding the cutwater, sailed easily through the ice-studded harbour. Her aunt and cousin became small figures on a toy wharf far behind, and then they disappeared into the blur of ships and shoreline. Palveron's buildings spread out, and then grew smaller under the castle on the headland, the first rays of the sun brushing the towers gold. They sailed past the islands, Flin happily rambling on with a fountain of interesting facts and stories about them as the sun rose.

They passed close by the Island of Dead Kings where towering statues and elaborate mausoleums sat silently amid wide-branched trees and frosted bushes. Another clump of huge trees stood silent sentinel on the peak of the island, and white birds wheeled and cried dolefully overhead. Except for the mournful cries of the birds, an air of quiet hung over the island and Shaeli thought it looked a lonely, eerie place.

They sailed past the Faunist and Warlock Islands at a greater distance, admiring the green gardens of the Faunist's and marvelling at an unnaturally blue mist which hung about the trees of the Warlock's, and then the three islands also grew small in their wake.

Other islands passed, the wind grew stronger, and Shaeli felt it in her stomach when they hit the open waters of the Bastinian Ocean. She stood on deck, her hair whipping about her in strings, her face dusted with salt-spray, revelling in the feel of it as Ebony clung tightly to her shoulder. It was almost as good as being on a Trader, only lower and much bumpier.

The others retreated quickly below for the air was freezing, yet Shaeli stayed on deck, her face into the wind until her skin was numb with it and Ebony was shivering and complaining in her arms, then finally she went below. Ebony gave Shaeli a black look and went and curled into a tight ball in her basket, one hand over her head.

By midday, Illen and Flin had also taken to their beds. Qiren held on until mid-afternoon, and then he too retired. Several other passengers had boarded with them; a merchant and his wife who went to their beds about the same time as Illen and Flin, and an insipid looking gentleman who'd boarded in a cloud of scent with a kerchief over his nose and disappeared immediately into his cabin. Shaeli couldn't understand their queasiness; she found nothing untoward in the ship's movement, it made her feel alive.

She saw Yorrow during the afternoon, and chatted to him for a while, yet he was very short on conversation, answering her chatter in a series of monosyllabic grunts, and she soon ran out of things to say to him. Ebony ignored her and stayed in her basket sleeping, and Shaeli found herself alone, wandering the decks, alternately watching the sailors climb about and yell at each other, or the shores of Zirrus slip past. The vast Land was a green and white mass to the north, and as Shaeli watched it from the railing late in the afternoon, the captain stopped to speak with her.

Captain Mahi was a tall man, his skin bronzed, his eyes a clear blue, the lines cut deeply around them from years of squinting into the sun. He was an old friend of Flin's – they had grown up on neighbouring islands – and he shook his head and laughed at his friend's lack of sea legs. He told her they would travel around Zirrus' southern tip, and up through Nebillonia Straits to the Starisles, and then he asked her to join him and his crew for dinner. He smiled as he told her the invitation included her party and the other passengers on board, yet she was the only one who had managed the movement of the ship. When she told him she had lived all her life on a Trader, he laughed loudly and patted her shoulder.

"I've always wanted to fly a Trader myself," he said. "It looks like a grand way to move about in the World."

Shaeli smiled back. "It is," she said. "The grandest. You should try it sometime."

"I'm sure *The Painted Lady* would object though," he said, patting the railing just as he had patted Shaeli's shoulder, yet with more feeling. "She is a jealous mistress, yet the Fleet has always intrigued me."

Captain Mahi spoke to her more on the subject at dinner that evening and those that followed. He was full of questions about the Traders and how they worked, and Shaeli was happy to answer them. As they sailed round the bottom of Zirrus and up through the Straits, they began to scan the sky for the

Traders who Shaeli knew would already be flying into the World. When they finally saw one – Little Cloud, heading south – Shaeli whooped and waved, but they were too far away to see her and Captain Mahi shared her disappointment.

As they sailed up the Straits and approached Meoro Village, she saw more Traders in the skies, naming each one for the Captain, and speculating on where they might be heading. Night Wing was the only one which flew close enough for them to clearly see the rainbow undersides of the Zoi's wings shimmering in morning sunlight, but they did not see Shaeli waving from the deck of the ship. When Meoro Village came into sight she hardly believed it when she saw that not only was a Trader moored there, but that it was Red Arrow.

Her face as she told Mahi of her friendship with the family made him smile broadly, for he had already told his men to dock. He said they always stopped at Meoro Village to see if there were any passengers and to collect fresh water, and she may as well use the time to visit her friend. Shaeli almost hugged him in gratitude. She flew downstairs to tell a pale Flin of the stopover, yet he merely groaned and flapped a hand at her.

"Go," he said. "Enjoy."

She was at the gangplank before it touched the wharf, and she flew across it as the grinning sailors were still tying its ropes. They had become fond of the young trader for her soft manner and strong stomach.

Shaeli ran up the street to the Landing, bolted up the stairs, and still had breath to call Kirrit's name as she leapt onto the deck. It was surprisingly empty, and she hurried across to the stairs, and though it was dark below, she kept going, calling Kirrit's name as she went.

At the bottom, only one hall led back through the Trader – unlike Purple Leaf's two – and she was halfway down it, bedrooms full of bunk beds and store-rooms on either side, when Kirrit came through the door at the other end, drying her

50

hands on a towel. Her eyes grew huge and her smile wide as she ran down the hall and threw her arms around Shaeli.

"It *is* you," she cried. "We were just talking about you, and I thought I was dreaming when I heard your voice. *Mam,*" she called over her shoulder. "It *is* Shaeli." Her voice dropped. "The gods I missed you this Wintering," she said.

"I missed you, too. I missed everyone," Shaeli answered, hugging her again. "How is Mam and Da, and the twins, and the boys and, oh, everybody?"

"Fine when we left Cave three days ago," Kirrit grinned. "The girls were that nervous about Cave year, but Tajindi was putting up a brave front for them."

Delphi came down the hall and hugged her. "Goodness, girl, where did you come from?" she said.

"Yes, Shaeli," prompted Kirrit. "Where *did* you come from?"

"Hello, Delphi," smiled Shaeli. "We were sailing past – we're on our way to the Starisles, Flin and Illen and Qiren and me, on a ship, *The Painted Lady* – and I saw you. I told the captain how Kirrit is my best friend in the whole World, and he was bringing the ship in for water anyway so..." She shrugged. "Here I am."

"Well, that *was* nice of him to let you come up," Delphi smiled. "How long can you stay?"

"Oh," said Shaeli, stumped. "I never thought to ask." She looked guilty. "Probably not long."

"But I've so much to *tell* you," said Kirrit. "You can't just rush off."

"I *wish* you could come with me," said Shaeli. "It's hard not having any of the Fleet around."

"Well, then, why don't you ask this captain of yours if Kirrit can fit on his ship?" said Delphi. "She could do with a dose of you, Shaeli. She's been that grumpy all Wintering."

"*Mother,*" said Kirrit, hands planted on hips. "I have *not,* and Shaeli can't ask that." She looked at Shaeli. "Can you?"

Shaeli grinned. "I don't see why not," she said. "There's a spare bunk in my cabin, and I'm sure Flin wouldn't mind." She looked at Delphi. "Do you mean it? I can take her?"

Delphi nodded. "If it's alright with this captain. After we trade on Ashkanna we were going to fly up to the Starisles anyway. Kirrit insisted we had to see your skylights. Go on, go ask."

Kirrit grinned and Shaeli grabbed her hand, and they raced back up the stairs, intending on going down to the ship, but when they reached the deck, they found Captain Mahi standing on the Landing, admiring the balloon. He unhesitatingly gave his permission to Kirrit.

"It'll be nice to have someone for the lass to talk to besides my rough lot," he smiled. "And I'm sure Kirrit will have as fine a pair of sea-legs as Shaeli."

This time, Shaeli did hug him, and the girls flew back down the stairs to pack Kirrit's things. Delphi gave Mahi a tour of the Trader while they waited, and was showing him the Zoi in the shade beneath the Trader when they came down with Kirrit's bag.

"'Tis a pity my husband and the rest aren't here," she was saying. "But they're all at the markets. They'll be sorry they missed you and our Shaeli. The boys will be green when I tell them where Kirrit's gone."

"Tell them you had to force me, Mam," Kirrit grinned. "I'd *so* much rather stay here."

"I'll not be telling lies to my family, miss," Delphi grinned back. "Your Da will have a hard enough time believing it was all *my* idea without making it more absurd."

"It was a wonderful idea, Delphi," Shaeli said, hugging her. "Thank you."

"You're welcome. Just mind she doesn't get up to too much mischief." Delphi looked at Mahi with narrowed eyes. "I trust your men are a *dependable* lot." She stressed the word as if it had many meanings.

The Captain nodded. "You may have faith she will be well cared for while she is on my ship, madam," he said.

Kirrit's face had grown pink during this exchange. "Mam, *please*," she said, rolling her eyes. "I'm not a little girl anymore."

"I know, Kirrit," said Delphi, sweetly, kissing her daughter's cheek. "That's exactly what I'm worried about."

They said their good-byes – Kirrit through pursed lips – and Shaeli told Delphi to give a hug to each of her family from her, with an extra kiss for Baroz. Then Kirrit was tugging her arm and they were following Captain Mahi back down to the ship.

Shaeli proudly introduced Kirrit to all the sailors, and then crept down to tell Flin. Again he flapped a hand at her from his bed in the darkened cabin.

"Capital idea," he mumbled as he flapped. "Have fun." And he turned his pale face again to the wall.

* * *

The next morning Illen surprised Shaeli by joining them for breakfast. Yorrow had been brewing thin broths for the sea-sick trio – much to the disgust of the ship's cook – and Illen declared she had woken with a mind for something other than soup.

Illen was delighted with Kirrit's presence, declared Delphi a very smart woman, and she joined them after breakfast as they sat on deck talking about Cave. She was anxious for news of Eenis, and smiled when Kirrit told her of the amazement of the entire Fleet at Eenis finding her long-lost sister. Kirrit asked after Qiren, and Illen tried to hide her smile as she told them how badly he had taken to the sea.

"He lies moaning and saying he is dying," she said. "I keep telling him that no one ever died from sea-sickness, but he refuses to believe it."

Ebony suddenly dropped down from a rope above their heads, chittering happily as they jumped in fright. She had forgiven Shaeli for the initial freezing introduction to sailing, and had soon learnt to enjoy the ship. The sailors marvelled at the way the jevvi flew through the rigging, leaping from one slim rope to the next, arms and legs held wide as she glided between the sails. She had greeted Kirrit noisily the day before, jumping up on her shoulder and smelling her red hair, and now she grinned her funny grin at them. Shaeli was pretending to scold the jevvi when a sudden rumbling stopped her.

A mass of low cloud was rolling across the horizon ahead, its depths filled with the blackness of rain. It came low through the mountains on their left, boiling across the water and obscuring the straits in moments. A fork of lightning shattered the black mass, followed by another low rumble. Shaeli looked at Kirrit.

"Five leagues?"

Kirrit nodded. "About that." She scanned the skies. "I hope none of the Fleet are close by."

"It's a bad one," agreed Shaeli. "Hail in it, I'd say."

Kirrit nodded again.

"I'll ask Mahi if he wants us to secure anything," Shaeli said, and she got up and went to where the captain stood on the bridge.

Illen had watched the exchange quietly. "Will it be a bad storm, Kirrit?" she asked. "It looks a fair way off, perhaps it will miss us."

Kirrit shook her head. "No chance," she replied. "The wind is behind it, and all storms travel south at this time of year. Back to the Southern Wastelands beyond Wokk."

The air cooled and a breeze sprang up, ruffling Shaeli's hair as she came back across the deck.

"They're alright up here, he said, but we can go downstairs and check, and help the cook. Come on, Ebony," she said, scooping up the jevvi. "We'd best go below."

While they were storing things, the movement of the ship grew progressively more erratic and the rumble of thunder increased until it surrounded the ship in shuddering waves. Illen had warned Qiren and Flin of the coming storm, and she sat with the girls in a tiny sitting-room, her eyes glued to the ceiling. Kirrit wandered about, lurching every now and then as the ship rolled. She grinned over at Shaeli.

"Bit rougher than a Trader, eh, Shaeli?" she said.

"A bit," Shaeli nodded back.

"Want to go and see?"

"On deck?"

Kirrit nodded. "The storm's pretty close," she said, and, as if to prove the point, the grey light in the room flickered brightly, and their faces turned white. The flash of lightning was coupled immediately by a clap of thunder. The ship shuddered.

"Let's go," said Shaeli.

"Perhaps you shouldn't," said Illen. "It may be dangerous."

"We'll be alright," said Kirrit. "We know how to keep out of the way. Come on, Shaeli."

"We won't be long," said Shaeli. "Keep an eye on Eb for me." She kissed Illen's cheek and followed Kirrit up the stairs.

They both had to push the door open at the top, and then the wind caught it and almost wrenched it from their hands. They shuffled outside, giggling, and slammed the door behind them, but the sight of the storm surrounding the ship sobered them instantly. Lightning turned the World white and black and white again. Wind whipped the breath from their throats.

There was an overhang outside the door, and they each grabbed one of the posts holding up the shelter above the doorway to steady themselves as they looked ahead.

All around them were roiling masses of cloud, black hearted, and the blacker sea boiling against the sides of the ship, but the rain had not yet begun to fall. The wind buffeted them and a wave slapped the side of the ship, washing foaming water across the deck. The sky was shattered by another jagged bolt, and snatches of shouted words came from above where the Captain was on the bridge, three men helping him hold the wheel. The air around them took on an odd green hue, and Shaeli yelled one word to Kirrit over the screaming of the wind, waves and thunder.

"*Hail.*"

Kirrit nodded and replied, but the words were lost to the wind and another wave cracking against the side of the ship. The bow of the ship ploughed steadily through the black waves, and then suddenly it was gone. Hail fell as if tossed from a bucket, and at once the deck was covered in white, but beneath the overhang they were safe from the ice pelting down.

Kirrit pointed to the right across the boiling sea, her mouth moved and although Shaeli did not hear the word, she knew what Kirrit had said, and she nodded. *Ashkanna,* she had said.

She looked out the other side of the ship, to the left, and saw in the flashes of lightning the coast of Zirrus looming much closer than she'd expected. The mountain range rose blacker against the black sky, the tops lost in dense cloud, the jagged tumble of rocks that lined the sea beaten in fury by the waves. The mountains reached right to the coast here and the rugged and dangerous shoreline was uninhabited. The huge rocks looked like giant's teeth waiting to eat the ship whole.

The hail eased and the green light of its passing began to leave the sky, yet it was replaced by chundering rain that began gusting in beneath the overhang. Kirrit pointed to the door with her head, and Shaeli nodded. Together they wrenched it open and Shaeli held it while Kirrit slipped inside.

As she turned to go in, she glimpsed a light across the churning waves. She only saw it for an instant, but the distant flicker was unmistakable. She frowned, squinting through the rain, and she saw it again. Her frown deepened, for it was not from far-off Ashkanna that the light had come, but from the closer coastline of Zirrus; from a place where no one lived.

* * *

By nightfall the storm had passed, and though the seas remained rough, stars began to break through the clouds overhead. Illen declared that despite the tumbling she felt well enough for dinner, and they dined as usual with the captain and those of the crew not on duty. The storm was discussed, and Mahi told them they were headed over to Ashkanna now the winds had shifted.

Illen had admitted to a great deal of nervousness, and Kirrit said she had been a little bothered, but only when they were on deck. Mahi was surprised at their venturing out, but looked perplexed when Shaeli asked him about the light she'd seen on the Zirrus coastline.

"It must have been a trick of the storm," he said. "Some reflection from the lightning."

Shaeli conceded that could have been the case, but secretly doubted it. It had not looked like a reflection.

After Illen went to bed, Kirrit and Shaeli chatted for a while, and then they tucked themselves into bed in their cabin with a steaming mug of tezz to continue their gossiping.

Shaeli learned that Almarnoch had been disconcerted when she did not return to Cave, and Kirrit had seen him deep in conversation with her parents many times. Shaeli guessed the reason, and told Kirrit everything that Flin and Qiren had told her about the strength of her gift, how very few people could levitate with the vistrella, and their amazement at her channelling the Warlock's power. Kirrit looked at her, eyebrows raised.

"They can't move things with your stone?"

"No," said Shaeli, then she grinned. "Though Flin keeps trying."

"And you think Almarnoch knew, and didn't tell you?"

Shaeli nodded. "I'm sure he knew – how could he not? And he *would* have told me, I know, and that's why he was upset when I didn't come home for the Wintering. He's probably worried about me, that's all. Like Williver." She told Kirrit about her dream as she lay in the sun at the Autumn's Eve Hunt. She repeated Williver's words and her promise to be careful, and then she looked at her friend. "Oh, and don't say anything to the others about Williver, I haven't mentioned him, or my dreams."

"Have you seen him since?"

"Not since Autumn's Eve, no, but I'm sure he'll show up sometime."

Kirrit nodded. "Rhubic told me you'd gone to the Hunt. He said it was a sight, and great fun until the man with the bird full of maggots."

Shaeli shuddered, remembering, and Kirrit changed the subject. "Did I tell you that Dari has gone to the Bay of Islands?"

"No. Good for him. I didn't think he'd be ready for another few years," Shaeli smiled.

"Neither did he apparently, but Almarnoch seemed to think he was."

"Did his lights last all year?"

"Almost, and when they did the Lift spell he just glowed. Eenis cried when he flew off with Taffka and Renn on Golden Eagle, but he was so excited, anyone could tell. Oh, and you should have seen Tarkoda flirting with Bonn all Wintering. He kept asking her to go and spot glow-worms with him," Kirrit rolled her eyes. "My brothers followed them mercilessly."

Shaeli shook her head. "Aren't they a little old for that?"

Kirrit nodded. "Yes, but they were bored and forgot they're grown men."

"Poor Koda. I'm amazed she'd want to be seen with him, seeing as she thinks I'm such a freak."

"You wouldn't care what Bonn and Shylo thought, would you, Shaeli?" said Kirrit, her lips pursed as if she'd just sucked a lemon.

"No," Shaeli said, hoping she sounded convincing. She changed the subject again. "Who else is courting?"

Kirrit's face darkened. "Jezzyn. And Rennan. I'm sorry, Shaeli."

Shaeli studied her feelings, and then smiled. "It's alright, Kirrit. It doesn't matter, really. Rennan and I were never very serious. That reminds me, how's Bic?"

Kirrit blushed. "Fine, but we're not serious either. He still misses his family, but he's much better than he has been since Yellow Star was lost. I saw him watching Ooli a lot, all Wintering, but I don't think anything came of it. Besides, I want to look at all the boys in the World before I settle on one."

"*All* of them, Kirrit? You'll be looking a long time."

Kirrit laughed. "That's the idea, and the Starisles seems a good place to start. How long will it take to get there, do you know?"

"Well, we're past halfway, but I know we have to drop one of the passengers somewhere on Ashkanna, and the others at Xenel Island, so probably another few days."

"A bit slower than flying?"

Shaeli nodded. "A bit."

"Why aren't there more passengers? There's obviously room."

"Mahi said people are always nervous about sea travel until the ice melts. He'll have a lot more on the return journey."

"Are we going straight to Pa'laidiz after Xenel Island?"

"I think so. We have to start practising with the other throwers, and learn the music. Flin says it takes quite a few to perform the skylights."

"How many people are there that throw skylights?"

"There are barely a few hundred people in the World who throw, and many have only limited power. There are elves, of course, but few who are willing to leave elven lands to perform, like Qiren. Flin's not sure who we'll be performing with, it changes each year. I'm nervous already, just thinking about it."

"Don't be. From what you've told me you're stronger than all of them. You just listen to Flin. He sounds like he knows what's going on."

Shaeli nodded. "He does. He's very sure of himself and full of information – when he's not on a ship, that is," she giggled. "Fancy growing up on the Starisles and getting sea-sick."

"Like being a trader and afraid of heights," Kirrit said. She yawned loudly, and missed the look on Shaeli's face. She finished her tezz and snuggled down. "I think I need to go to sleep," she said.

"Me, too," said Shaeli, mirroring Kirrit's yawn. She turned out the lamp, and looked up at the round window. It was very like her window on Purple Leaf, and she could almost imagine she was there with the stars and clouds drifting past. "Bright and peaceful dreams, Kirrit," she said.

"You, too," Kirrit murmured from beneath the mound of blankets.

* * *

The next morning they moored in a bay on the north coast of Ashkanna, and the man with the perfumed handkerchief disembarked. Later they docked at Xenel Island and the merchant and his wife wobbled their way across the gangplank. As they sailed past Argon Island that afternoon they talked of Ishaan, and Shaeli was tempted to tell Kirrit about Ishaan's entering the Zoi cave, but she stopped herself; Almarnoch had asked her to tell no one. Her feelings were all mixed up when she thought about Ishaan; she had liked him so much, and he had betrayed her so badly by going into the cave when he knew it was forbidden, *and* he had looked at her wand secretly, when no one was home. She had tried a hundred times to find a reason for his behaviour, but in the end she could not excuse him, and thinking of him reignited the ember of her anger. She was pleased when Argon Island shrank in their wake and she could relegate him to her memory again.

The next night, Shaeli gave the crew a small show, throwing her skylights off the stern, lighting the sky with her quartz and azulis, her amber and eroscia, creating flying fish, dolphins and spinning octopi, then tossing small balls out into the sea where they bobbed among the waves before disappearing. Captain Mahi and his men applauded loudly; even Yorrow had come on deck to watch Shaeli's skylights.

They sailed across the open sea and began tracing a path between the first of the Starisles. Here, spring was already beginning to blossom; warm winds blew down from the north, and the gardens on the islands were showing bright splashes of colour. At last, Pa'laidiz came into view, and soon they were sailing into the harbour, and the pastel town with its backdrop of mountains opened out before them.

Pa'laidiz harbour was a wide arc, almost bowl shaped, two promontories hugging the harbour and giving it protection from the sea and winds. The city was concentrated around the busy harbour and town square, the houses spreading out on the harbour's arms and up into the low hills behind. Above them the mountains rose steeply, their sides tangled with rainforest.

Flin and Qiren had been rescued from their beds, and they sat with the baggage as the ship moored at one of the wharves. Both had pale faces and grey patches below their eyes, and both looked longingly at the city. Flin said goodbye to the captain much less enthusiastically than he had greeted him, and Mahi laughed.

"Goodbye, my friend," he said. "Always a pleasure."

"Very funny," mumbled Flin, covering his mouth with his thin fingers.

Shaeli hugged Captain Mahi as they left his ship, and he smiled and kissed her cheek.

"May the gods go with you, Shaeli," he said. "I hope we meet again."

"So do I," she smiled. "Thank you so much. It's been a wonderful journey."

Flin, leaning on Yorrow's arm, groaned loudly as she said this, and Shaeli laughed and thanked Mahi again before following the others down the gangplank. Flin sank down onto a trunk as soon as they reached the end of the wharf while Yorrow went to find a carriage.

Kirrit stood in a dither of impatience, her eyes darting in every direction. Ebony too, watched the surroundings from the vantage point of Shaeli's shoulder. Behind them, the bay was awash with all manner of craft. To the left, on the far side of the wharves, lay the big square that held the Landing, and while no Traders were moored there yet, there was still plenty to see. Shops displayed samples of wares brought from the Four Lands, and many people wandered about examining the produce and haggling with the storekeepers. The trees lining the streets beyond were just beginning to blossom, and the city rose above in layers of blue and pink and lavender. Down here, men yelled at each other; ladies bought fish fresh from the boats; children ogled the comings and goings; merchants negotiated prices, but the city rose serenely above, untouched by the flurry at its feet.

The girls watched, fascinated, until Yorrow arrived with a carriage and an extra cart for the bags and trunks, and before long they were driving along the waterfront and through the square with its empty Landing.

Yorrow sat with the driver and directed him along the road that ran beside the harbour's western edge. The road rose and left the water behind, and as they drove further, the road dropped and curved back towards the harbour, and then a tree-lined laneway opened out on the left. They followed it between wide-lawned houses, until, halfway along, a pair of wrought iron gates closed off the lane.

The gates opened noiselessly as they approached. Two men, one on either side, nodded as they drove through, and closed the gates behind the baggage cart. Now there were no houses on either side, only wide lawns and tall trees, with glimpses of water between the trees on the left. At the end of the lane the trees opened out, and Flin's house stood before them.

It was pale blue with white trim, two storeyed, many-gabled, with verandas running around both levels. The windows sparkled in the sun and the front door stood open, flanked by smiling servants waiting to direct the baggage. Best of all, they had come around the bay in such a way that the house looked back across the water to the city, and it was very close; Shaeli guessed half the distance of the trip by road. She could see the waterfront below the stately township, and Mahi's ship, moored at the eastern end of the harbour – that must have been how Flin's staff knew they were coming – *and* she could see the square and the Landing. How wonderful.

She grinned at Kirrit as they helped a wobbly Flin and Qiren down from the carriage and inside the house. Ebony bounded ahead, much to the amusement of Flin's staff, and sniffed the air. It was as light and airy inside as it looked from outside, its rooms large, most with window-seats in broad bay windows.

Flin gave mumbled instructions to the servant at the door, then he wobbled his way upstairs. Illen asked for their room, and she escorted an embarrassed-looking Qiren up. The girls were shown to their room, Shaeli carrying Ebony behind a maid and a man with their bags, up the stairs and down a hall. At the end of the hall, a door opened into an enormous room.

Two beds with carved heads and feet were on the left, a small table and low chairs beside a fire-place on the right. There was a small fire in the grate, though there was barely need for it with the sun streaming in, but it gave the room a welcoming air. Two doors led off either side; one into a dressing room, and the man took their bags in through the panelled door. On the other side, the door led to a bathroom, a white room with a window of glass patterned with leaves and flowers. At the far end, double doors led out to the veranda. The maid wanted to unpack for them, but the girls assured her they could do it themselves and the servants left.

The girls looked at each other, exploded into delighted laughter, and explored the room again, one pace behind the inquisitive jevvi. They looked at the dressing room, the bathroom, tested the chairs beside the fire-place, and walked out onto the veranda to admire the view. They leant against the railing while Ebony clambered up the elaborate grillwork and ran along the length of the rail, sniffing the air some more, testing every new scent with a quiver of her whiskers.

"I think we'll have trouble with that dressing room," said Shaeli, soberly.

"Why's that?" frowned Kirrit.

"We'll never fill it," Shaeli laughed. "It's bigger than my bedroom on Purple Leaf."

Kirrit grinned. "Did you see the size of that bath? You could swim in it."

"I know," giggled Shaeli. "Flin's partial to fancy bathrooms. And the view. Do you realise we can see a Trader as it arrives?"

They gazed across at the city, arguing happily about who would be the first to come, and then they went back inside and Kirrit threw herself down on one of the beds.

"This'll do me," she grinned, as Shaeli tested the other bed. "It's like lying on a cloud."

When they had unpacked their belongings, they found that Shaeli was right, the dressing room still looked rather empty, and they made a pact to try and fill it with some new outfits before they left the Starisles. They found Ebony and wandered through the house, getting their bearings, knocking on doors upstairs until they found the others, and then looking through the sitting-rooms, studies, dining rooms and library downstairs.

They found Yorrow rearranging the kitchen and he gave them something to eat, and then they wandered outside to explore the grounds. Shaeli put Ebony's long fine chain on so she could explore but not disappear, and the jevvi scampered about, her nose and ears turning a dozen directions.

There were statues and fountains in the garden, a small topiary, and back near the gates a little gardener's house with boxes humming with bees nearby. Ebony sniffed the air longingly – she loved honey – but Shaeli did not let her get too close. They wandered down to the edge of the bay and found a boathouse, and inside two boats sitting upside-down on blocks. A thin wharf stretched out over the water beside it, and they walked along its length. The wharf was one of scores that poked into the harbour, and the girls sat at the end and dangled their legs over the water. It was clear and clean, patterned a dozen shades of blue, and there were several different kinds of fish swimming lazily around the pylons.

Shaeli anticipated swimming here when the weather warmed, or taking one of the boats for a row, and she knew it would not be long now until she saw her parents. She had Kirrit with her, Flin would soon recover and they would practise for the skylights, and they had Pa'laidiz waiting to be explored. She looked back at the pretty blue house, and smiled. She felt happier than she had for a long time.

* * *

CHAPTER FOUR

Flin and Qiren both recovered quickly from the sea journey, and a few days later they accompanied Illen and the girls into the town centre. They had found that they would not be needed for skylight practise yet and their time was their own for the next nine or ten days.

Qiren had been to Pa'laidiz many times, but it was Flin who was in his element. He was born on an island close by, and sailed regularly to the city as a boy with his friends; short trips did not bother him – he had not even known he was prone to sea-sickness until he was ten. People stopped to greet him as he showed them everything there was to see; the shops, the restaurants, the parks; the most elaborate houses and the impressive edifice of the Starcluster, who governed the Starisles. He told them of a performance he had given there as a young man, when an unfortunate flock of birds had flown into a skylight just as it had exploded. The birds had fallen to the ground, unhurt, but dazed and almost blinded by the light. Flin made them laugh as he described well-dressed ladies and gentlemen gathering the flock of groggy, stupid birds together in an enclosed garden to recover, dignitaries from several Lands among them.

They also drove into the countryside around the town; rolling hills dotted with nut and fruit farms, small villages producing unsurpassed wood carvings, and one day they travelled high up the mountain in the centre of the island to feast on food and the view. Across the water, scores of islands lay in the patterned sea like mossy pebbles, the water dappled from sand and coral reefs, hundreds of birds wheeling in the sky. Flin pointed out kelp beds on one island, shellfish and mollusc farms on another; the peak of the island where he had grown up, Shilipnos in the west; Altorri, the Starisles' second

66

biggest island, to the south; and the Endless Sea at the edge of the World, far beyond the tiny islands scattered to the east.

The days passed by, and though she was enjoying herself, Shaeli began to grow impatient for her family to arrive. Blue Dolphin had flown in and gone again with a delivery of salt for Zirrus, Dragon Wing had also been and gone, but neither had news of Purple Leaf.

A few days after they'd picnicked on the mountain, she and Kirrit went into the town to hunt for the new clothes they had promised themselves. Flin had surprised Shaeli on their first shopping expedition by asking her how much of her money she wanted. She had looked so confused he had laughed, and explained that he was paying her weekly, with additional funds for each performance, as was customary in an apprenticeship. He had just assumed that because she had not asked for any coin, she hadn't needed any. Today she had enough to buy herself and Kirrit each a new dress – something lovely for the festival.

They had a fun morning, choosing materials and styles for the gowns in Flin's tailors where they were fussed over as if they were royalty, and they bought presents for their families and a lovely set of silver pens for Flin in appreciation of his generosity. Shaeli also bought the twins a silver bracelet each to give them at the end of the year, and then they had lunch at a little cafe overlooking the harbour. They had just walked outside when Kirrit grabbed Shaeli's arm.

"Look, Shaeli," she cried. "Purple Leaf!"

The Trader was flying across the harbour, and without a word they both began to run, down the hill, through the streets, across the square to the Landing where the Trader was just mooring, Kirrit, as always, easily ahead.

She waited impatiently for Shaeli at the bottom of the Landing, and they hurried up the stairs just as a startled Andos was tying up at the top. He was the beneficiary of the first of the hugs and kisses, and soon Shaeli was surrounded by her parents, Eenis, Jeth, and Tarkoda, and she was so happy she laughed and cried at the same time.

Eenis asked after Illen, and Shaeli pointed to Flin's blue house down the western arm of the harbour, and told her they would have been seen. She was right, for it was not long before Qiren, Flin and Illen arrived.

That night they all dined at Flin's blue house, and Shaeli spent the entire evening in bliss. She learnt more of the passing of the Wintering at Cave, and Purple Leaf's journey through Zirrus, and she told of meeting Kirrit in Meoro Village, and the journey on *The Painted Lady*.

After dinner Flin told them how well Shaeli had done, and Mareesha was interested to learn of the performance at Lady Arinola's and she asked many questions about Arinola and Sir Vulcan and Sir Collett. Jarris told Shaeli that Almarnoch had sent his love, and his sincere apologies for not telling her more about her gift, grinning when he said that Almarnoch admitted he had been disconcerted by Shaeli's power, and disgusted with himself for not seeing it for what it was.

"Almarnoch prides himself in knowing many things, and foreseeing their effects," Jarris chuckled. "But I think you almost frightened him, Shaeli." His face sobered. "Yet he adds his cautions to the others. He bids you be wary, and take great care who you trust."

The next day brought thunderheads, and the greenish hue of hail filled the sky during the afternoon. Jeth and Jarris eyed the storm warily, yet when the hail finally came it barely penetrated Almarnoch's magic, and the balloon suffered no damage. That night they gathered in the big room on Purple Leaf to eat.

Shaeli went over everything in the Trader, each room and every object in it was touched and sighed over, even the store-rooms, much to Koda's amusement, and she also went below to visit the Zoi with her brother, Kirrit and Andos.

That night she slept with her family on Purple Leaf for the first time in many Moons, and she woke feeling more refreshed than she'd felt since before the Wintering.

* * *

A few days later, Shaeli went with Flin and Qiren to meet the others who would perform the skylights at the Summer Festival. There were six of them, all known to Flin and Qiren, and Shaeli felt lost amid the talk of music and skylights for the festival.

The event was being choreographed by a woman called Moneq, who had written the music and would conduct the orchestra, and they met at her large house in the hills above the town.

Moneq was tall and dark, her thick, wiry hair streaked with grey, her slanted green eyes overhung with thick brows. Her strong arms poked out of the wide sleeves of her gown as she gesticulated wildly to the group of throwers, sketching her vision in the air at one moment and demonstrating a theme on the piano the next. The throwers agreed generally with her vision, and began apportioning tasks and lights amongst themselves.

Shaeli sat quietly as parts were cast and tasks assigned, and then she slipped out to use one of the bathrooms. When she returned, an argument was taking place between Moneq and one of the throwers, Horler, a tall, reedy man with a crooked nose.

"Give me one good reason why *not*, Moneq," he was shouting, as Shaeli entered the room.

"Because the music builds too *quickly*, Horler," Moneq replied. "It is sharp and pointed, not soft. There is no *place* for gliding birds." She demonstrated by pounding the keys.

Shaeli thought it did not sound very bird-like either.

"But it's a transition, moving from one strain to the next, and we *need* a change of pace that reflects that, something that moves the lights to the next phase," Horler said. "Birds are movement, *and* they will tie in with the opening."

"Birds are too *soft*, Horler," Moneq replied emphatically. "The music is much too precise. They are wonderful in the opening, I agree, but here, they will not work."

They stood, glaring at each other, and Shaeli opened her mouth and spoke quickly, before she lost her nerve. "What about birds that turn into arrows?" she said.

Moneq and Horler spun to look at her. Every other eye in the room turned to her also.

"What did you say?" demanded Moneq.

"Arrows," said Shaeli, slightly intimidated by the looks, but pushing on nonetheless. "They're sharper, more to the point, it will still tie in with the opening sequence, and they could move the lights to the next piece."

Moneq looked at her a moment, and then her face curved into a smile. "Birds that turn into arrows," she said. "Yes, I believe that would work, my dear. Excellent idea. And you shall do them." She looked at Flin. "Your clever little apprentice is capable of this, yes?"

Flin nodded and Moneq turned back to the discussion. Everyone stopped looking at Shaeli, but she caught Flin's eye and he winked at her.

As the afternoon passed each thrower became familiar with their tasks and the music, and when they finally left for the day, Shaeli was exhausted. As she drove home with Flin and Qiren her mind was a whirl of music and instructions.

Each day for the next seven days they went to Moneq's house to practise in the huge expanse of garden behind the house, so Shaeli saw little of her family during the day, but they were given a few days off after the intense practising, and Shaeli swam in the clear waters' of the Starisles, enjoyed the warmth of the spring sunshine and time spent with her family, but the days moved swiftly towards summer after rehearsals began again. They alternated between practising at Moneq's and at a secluded, private bay on the other side of Pa'laidiz, away from curious eyes. Half of the spectacle of the summer skylights was the mystery of the music and what form the lights might take, and great steps were taken to ensure the practises were done in secret. The skylights were always choreographed especially for the music; and always the music was written especially for the night. The throwers and musicians were all sworn to secrecy.

Shaeli liked the piece written by Moneq. It was a strong, exciting piece, yet she did not find it as moving as the haunting melody played during her first skylights so many Winters before. She learnt her part as precisely as always and drew the admiration of the older throwers with her aim and control. Shaeli delighted in the fact she still had a connection with her lights even after they'd flown from her fingers, and she could turn a sliver of light into a blazing ball of colour no matter how high it rose into the air, or throw beams that would blossom into every imaginable shape; she had learnt how to direct her magic, to give it shape and texture, to change it as it flew.

It seemed the eve of the festival had arrived much more quickly than it should have, and Shaeli began to suffer from her usual bout of nerves. She woke on the morning of the festival with a lump in her stomach, and she had trouble eating Yorrow's marvellous breakfast.

Kirrit had seldom seen this nervous, distracted Shaeli; broody and uncommunicative, yes, but she did not know whether to be amused or sympathetic with this pre-performance friend, so she aimed for somewhere between the two. She prattled on about nothing as they drove into town to meet Tarkoda and Andos, and her own brothers, for Red Arrow had arrived a few days before.

For most of the day the crowd of young traders succeeded in keeping Shaeli's mind off the performance as they enjoyed the sights of the festival. Several times they turned her away from contemplating the huge pontoon being set up in the harbour where the orchestra and the throwers would perform, and whenever Tarkoda saw a tight, pinched look on her face, he'd throw his arm about her shoulders and show her some new delight of the festival, or tempt her with one of the many delicacies available. As the day passed she lost some of her nerves, and she appreciated the efforts of the others to calm her. She saw her parents late in the afternoon before she and Kirrit left for Flin's, but she barely heard Kirrit prattling as they dressed for the evening. Their new gowns had been delivered, yet the beautiful dress did little to draw Shaeli's mind away from the coming skylights.

She did manage to calm down a little by talking to herself very sternly – until Kirrit and Illen left in the carriage. They were watching the spectacle from the decks of Purple Leaf with the rest of the traders, and after the carriage drove off, Shaeli began a fresh round of trembles, no matter how sternly she spoke to herself.

She walked with Flin and Qiren down to the wharf on legs she could not quite feel, and as they waited for the boat that would take them out to the pontoon, she shivered beneath her long cloak, and ran her fingers over the bumps of her gems in the pockets of the wide sash tied around her waist, checking and rechecking to assure herself of their presence. She took deep breaths of the tangy air as the dusk turned its thoughts to evening.

The trip across to the pontoon was mercilessly quick, and then Qiren was helping her up the ladder to Flin, who somehow already stood above her, and she was dragged atop the deck.

The pontoon was a massive structure, only rocking slightly on the swell of the bay, its broad surface easily accommodating the orchestra and the throwers. Shaeli was faced with a vast flock of musicians tuning their instruments and a gaggle of fluttering magicians.

Moneq strode amongst all, a spectacle of waving arms and hair which had a life of its own. The black mane flew around her like a fountain as she strode amongst the orchestra and the throwers, arranging that, calming this, organising that over there, all the while telling everyone they would be *fab*ulous, *won*derful, fan*taaas*tic, darling.

Shaeli stood beside Flin, remembering her cues, remembering the music, remembering to breathe, but above all that was the excitement. It was a life unto itself, filling her with a breathless anticipation, a sense of wonder, and, strangely, it was the excitement which helped to calm her. She was *here*, at Pa'laidiz, about to perform in the biggest skylights in Four Lands, and almost her whole family was watching. She wished the twins could have been here, and she closed her eyes to send them her love.

Moneq's voice boomed suddenly in front of her, and as she opened her eyes, she was grabbed and embraced tightly by the tall woman. "Do not worry, my dear, the gods are already with us," Moneq said. "Look at this fabulous sky. You will be *won*derful, I know it. Your timing is impeccable."

Shaeli barely had time to thank her before Moneq moved on, but she was grateful for her words just the same. Now the time was so near, she felt ready – nervous and excited and awestruck – but ready. She began to think it would be alright. When the music began, there was no time to think.

She was a part of the opening sequence of slow-rolling wheels, and she reacted as always, her aim sure, her timing, as Moneq had said, impeccable. Giant flowers blossomed in the air, dragonflies flitting among them. A waterfall appeared, surrounded by blue shadows and framed with dark trees, and silver fish leapt from the waters and turned into white birds racing across the sky.

Shaeli was vaguely aware of the roar of the crowd across the water, but the knowledge barely registered, so intent was she upon Moneq's cues and the music. The magicians drew two

73

ships in the sky, tall-masted ships that rode on tumbling waters and fired brightly coloured balls at each other until one sank beneath the skylight water. She led the way into the final theme with an arc of silver birds that turned into arrows shooting far across the waters of the bay, and her hands became a blur as the orchestra wound up into the final crescendo. The sky was a maze of colour, the stars invisible behind the curtain of skylights. The final chord leapt into the air with a burst of light from every magician. As the last strains echoed across the water, each thrower narrowed their beam to a thin, bright stream directed into the stars, and with a sharp wave of Moneq's baton, the beams extinguished as one.

There was silence over Pa'laidiz for one long, drawn-out moment, and then the crowds lining the shores erupted, and those on the pontoon were washed with the sounds of delight. It was over. They had been a success, and after the musicians had packed their instruments; after the throwers had slapped backs and kissed cheeks in congratulating each other, still the roar of the crowd washed over them.

Shaeli's head buzzed as she removed the gems from the belt and put them back in her amulet. She smiled her thanks as her cheeks were kissed again and again, and she practically floated down to the boat. The trip to shore was filled with grins and congratulations, but it was their arrival which brought the tears.

Standing on the wharf were her family, and all those from Red Arrow and Blue Dolphin, but there also, their smiles wide, were half a dozen of the children from her Cave year. Rennan, Rhubic, Jezzyn, Bic, Ooli and Crylla stood with a grinning Kirrit, applauding and whistling as the boat drew up. She was surprised to see Crylla, knowing her father, Lunn, thought Shaeli a traitor, thought she had aided Ishaan in broaching the sanctity of the Zoi cave. Crylla had sided with Bonn and Shylo after Shaeli had saved Taffka too, and something of this showed in her eyes, yet Shaeli pretended she didn't see it, and greeted her as warmly as she did the others. She was hoisted up to the dock and surrounded; she was hugged and kissed and hugged again, her mother was crying; her father, too. Scattered sentences filtered through.

"Never been prouder in my life," said Jarris.

"Aren't you surprised, Shaeli?" said Ooli. "Jezzyn had her Da land on the other side of the island, so you wouldn't know we were here."

Jezzyn's parents stood grinning with Delphi.

"Darling, it was wonderful," said Mareesha, hugging her tightly.

"Absolutely," smiled Eenis, beside her, Illen nodding behind them.

"We all stowed away on White Star with Bic and Jezz," boomed Rhubic. "Great skylights, Shaeli."

Rennan, kissing her flushed cheek. "Wouldn't have missed it for all the wine in Romynn," he said, smiling.

"Oh, Shaeli, it was gorgeous," Jezzyn smiled. "Kirrit didn't give us away?"

Shaeli shook her head and looked at Kirrit, who grinned back.

"No way, Jezz," Kirrit said, looking particularly pleased with herself. "The look on Shaeli's face was well worth keeping the secret."

"And you know how hard that is for our Kirrit," smiled Baroz, kissing Shaeli's cheek. "You were a marvel, Shaeli, just as I always said you were."

"Thank you, Baroz," she smiled. "But I had a little help."

Her eyes met Flin's through the crowd, and they smiled at each other as the others milled around. Then she was swept away by her friends into the wave of the festival, and Shaeli spent the rest of the night riding the wave from one part of Pa'laidiz to the other, buoyed up by her friends and her soaring spirits.

She finally crept into the blue-and-white house in the dark hours before sunrise. Kirrit still partied with the others in town, yet the exertion of the skylights had wearied Shaeli long before the others had even begun to think of their beds, and she had found a small carriage to take her back to Flin's despite their many protests. She could have slept the night on Purple Leaf, but she had nothing but her grand gown to put on tomorrow, and the huge bath in her room at Flin's had been calling to her. She wondered vaguely if she was getting a little spoilt.

When she tiptoed inside the house, she was surprised to find Flin waiting for her, a small glass of port in his hand and Ebony curled up on his knee.

"Why, Flin," she said. "What are you still doing up? Hello Eb," she added as the jevvi woke and bounded over to her. She leant down and tickled her ears, and Ebony went over to the stairs and leapt up onto the banister. She yawned loudly, and Shaeli laughed. "We'll go up soon. I'll just say good night to Flin."

"I wanted to make sure you arrived home safely," Flin said, rising and stretching his arms. He walked across the room and put his hand on her shoulder. "Did you have a good time?"

"Yes, *won*derful, as Moneq says," she grinned. "And I want to thank you, Flin. If it wasn't for you, I would never have been here."

"I cannot take all the credit," he smiled.

"But if you hadn't seen that skylight in Palveron, I wouldn't *be* here."

"Oh, I think you would. Illen would have introduced us eventually."

"Well, maybe," she conceded. "But it's still you I have to thank. Horler told me you have never taken apprentice before, and I'm so grateful that you took me."

"Yes, yes, well," Flin blustered. "It was... different this time, and... and it has done us both a lot of good." His face grew serious. He moved a step closer, and looked at Shaeli intently. "Indeed, it is I who have much to thank *you* for."

"Me? Why?" Shaeli was suddenly acutely aware of how quiet the house was.

"Because you have brought much into my life that I had not even known I missed," he said, and he reached out a hand and stroked her cheek with one thin finger. "I have known much laughter lately, Shaeli, and I have only you to thank for it. You have become very, very dear to me. It was only tonight when I saw you amongst your friends that I realised just *how* much you mean to me." He leant forward and kissed her, not on the cheek or forehead, as he usually did, but on the lips; a warm, lingering kiss. Then he stepped back, the mood shifted, and he was his normal, amiable self again. "Shall I walk you to your door?" he asked.

Shaeli nodded. She felt she had almost imagined the incident, yet she still felt the warmth of Flin's lips on her own. After he had left her at her door with a soft goodnight; after she'd undressed and sunk into the warmth of a fragrant bath; after she'd climbed into bed and tuned out the light, she wondered, what did it mean?

* * *

CHAPTER FIVE

The rest of the time on the Starisles passed swiftly, though the summer was more than half over when they left.

Shaeli spent a lot of time with her friends and family, exploring Pa'laidiz and the surrounding islands, and she practised with Flin almost every day, who gave no sign of what had passed between them on the night of the festival. Shaeli did not refer to it either, and tried to deal with their relationship as she always had, yet every now and then she caught Flin's eye and the memory would leap unspoken between them. She loved Flin, yet she knew it was only the love of a friend, and while she tried hard to be as easy and casual around him as always, she was also careful not to be alone with him, hoping that by ignoring the kiss, he would somehow understand. It seemed that he did, for the incident was never repeated.

The other Traders, except for Red Arrow, left to continue trading, and their plans were made. Horler had invited them to perform in Marnissi, and Flin was delighted when Jarris offered to fly them there, and then back to Palveron. Purple Leaf could trade on the way, and though it would be crowded, it would be an easier journey than by ship and road.

One afternoon a few days before they were to leave, they were lazing under the trees beside the water at Flin's. They'd had a long, slow lunch, and swum a great deal, and while the boys still had the energy to row out onto the harbour, Shaeli and Kirrit were laying in the shade on a blanket. Shaeli only realised she was almost asleep when Kirrit's toe dug into her calf. The sound of the world swam back into her ears. She opened one eye and looked at Kirrit.

Kirrit cocked her head towards where their parents sat with Flin, Illen and Eenis some distance away. Jeth and Qiren were down on the wharf fishing, and Shaeli listened as Flin talked. His voice was faint, but it came wafting across the grass with the breeze.

"It would make it much easier for her I'm sure, Delphi," he was saying. "I feel it imperative Shaeli keep up her practise again next Wintering, and yet I also know she was incredibly lonely during the last."

"And you think Kirrit would make a difference?" asked Delphi.

"I'm sure of it," replied Flin. "We did our best to keep her amused, but Kirrit could only benefit her, don't you agree, Illen?"

"Yes, I do," Illen said. "The difference in her when we picked up Kirrit at Meoro Village was amazing. If Shaeli agrees to return to Palveron, I think Kirrit would make it much more like home. Qiren and I will spend one more Wintering there also before we must return to elven lands, but without Kirrit... well, I think Shaeli will not continue her practise with Flin, but return to Cave with Purple Leaf."

"And you think this is not a good thing, Flin?" asked Mareesha. "To break her training for the Wintering?"

"No, Mareesha. I think that she is so close to becoming a master of skylights that to halt her training now would only set her back. She would have to retrain to reach the point she has already reached. You know there is no halt for the training of Faunists, Wintering or no."

"Nor for Warlocks," said Eenis. "We'll see little of Dari until he is finished on the Warlock Isle."

Mareesha nodded. "Well, we can only see what she says. Jarris and I were almost prepared for it."

"I'll have a talk with her then," said Flin, standing up and looking towards the girls. Kirrit and Shaeli pretended they were very interested in the sky as Flin looked at them. Flin looked back at Delphi and Baroz. "And may I tell her that Kirrit is welcome also?"

Delphi and Baroz looked at each other, and Baroz shrugged. "She's a woman grown," he said. "You best ask her."

"Delphi?" asked Flin.

"As Baroz says," she frowned. "But you can tell her she has my blessing."

Flin nodded. Even he knew that without Delphi's blessing, grown woman or not, Kirrit stood no chance of Wintering in Palveron.

Shaeli and Kirrit had listened to this exchange with their eyes on each other's faces, each pair of eyes growing huger. Shaeli had not contemplated staying in Palveron for the Wintering; she had not thought of much past the festival and seeing her family. Kirrit had thought Shaeli might not come back to Cave, but she had never contemplated being able to stay in the city with her. By the time Flin reached them, the news glowed on their faces, and he saw it plainly.

"Oh," he said. "I see you could hear us. I'm sorry I haven't discussed this with you, Shaeli, but I didn't want to worry you before the festival."

"That's alright, Flin," she said. "But, if I *do* stay in Palveron, it's true? I can have Kirrit?"

"If she wants to," Flin smiled.

Kirrit screamed, and threw herself on a laughing Shaeli. Shaeli looked up at Flin.

"I think that's a yes," she said.

* * *

It was crowded on Purple Leaf as they flew to Marnissi; people were bumping into each other at every turn and there were beds on floors in every corner, but they had a fine time, with both Flin and Qiren declaring it far surpassed travelling by sea. Despite a slight queasiness initially, both were in fine spirits.

The only person who was obviously uncomfortable was Yorrow, lost without a kitchen to dominate. He hung around the Trader looking forlorn until Eenis asked his advice on preserving a large supply of berries she'd picked up, and then the two became great friends. Eenis had recently taken more interest in cooking, and they would talk endlessly over cups of tezz on ways to cure pork or the best thing to do with leftover pudding.

Purple Leaf traded along the way, yet the trading was not as robust as it had once been. Many times they passed empty fields and heard tales of farmers too bereft of coin to buy the seeds needed to sow new crops, or those who'd had to sell off much of their stock to pay their taxes. Of the fields they passed ripe with produce or newly harvested, there were stories of raiders – rebels they called them – stealing whole carts on the way to market, or robbing the fields themselves. Tales were told too, of the burning of barns, of cattle stolen by rebels, their targets those who supported the queen or her ever-increasing guard. Others said, though more quietly, that more barns were burnt by the guard themselves, and that the rebels seldom targeted any supplies not destined for the soldiers' many outposts or the queen's coffers. Retaliation by the guard was only ever whispered about in corners, with many furtive glances over hunched shoulders, but widely known just the same. The queen's soldiers were becoming ever more forceful in their demands on Zirrus, taking over lands, bullying townsfolk, helping themselves to anything they said they needed. Vocal objectors and their families had been disappearing in the night; bodies were found beaten and bloody by roadsides. Most towns and villages had tales like this, of guard and rebels; all had a family or two who were dependent on goodwill for their survival, who had lost homes to taxes or to "the queen's need being greater", which meant the guard could take your land if they needed it for a new garrison or to supply their needs.

Several times the throwers gave a small show, and the faces of the people would grow brighter, at least for a while, yet as they flew across the Land and saw more of the poverty and despair, they knew that a few skylights would do little to help their increasingly hard lives.

They were to perform the same routine in Marnissi as they had at Arinola's during the Wintering, and so they re-familiarised themselves with the piece in the impromptu shows they gave as they flew south. Beyond that, there was a performance again at the Autumn's Eve Hunt, and Flin had already begun choreographing. It would incorporate elements of both their most recent performances and Shaeli was not too worried about learning it. The skylights on Pa'laidiz had bolstered her confidence enormously, and she was infinitely more sure of herself – when it came to skylights, at least. She'd had little opportunity to practise the stronger form of her magic, yet it was clear the throwing of skylights had intensified the accuracy of this, too. The magic which flew from her fingers was a strong, clear source of power, and she had such control that she no longer worried about her magic overstepping the boundaries as it had the time she'd wounded Ishaan at Cave. Flin helped her refine her strength, yet soon there would be little he could teach her, for though his skill at skylights was surpassed by no one, Shaeli's strength with the deeper magic was clearly far stronger than his. He often said it was only a matter of time before Shaeli was the best thrower in Four Lands, and he was constantly frustrated with his inability to make a twig even tremble with her vistrella, let alone lift anything.

Late one night they flew into Zuen and moored at the Landing outside the town. As usual, all was quiet in the pious village on the shores of Lake Marnis as the sun had set long ago, and only the light on the landing had shone through the darkness. When they woke next morning, they walked into the village to stretch their legs, and the streets were bustling, but they drew shakes from many heads that they had not risen with the sun, already above the peaks of the mountains to the east. Before they left Zuen, they walked along the edge of

M'Zen'sclahr Forest, to see if the fairy cluster they had seen the year they had flown Princess Crissita to Romynn was still there. It was, but the cluster was empty, the tree to which it had been attached had lost a large limb to lightning, and part of the cluster lay shattered on the ground. The rest was abandoned, its tiny rooms empty, the air around it bereft of flittering lights, and they turned away, disappointed. No one noticed the fairy in purple-and-grey watching them from one of the empty rooms; a single fairy watching the forest's edge, like a tiny sentry at an isolated outpost. As they walked back to the Trader, the purple-grey fairy left the abandoned cluster and flew into the dark interior of M'Zen'sclahr.

* * *

Later that morning they moored at the Landing in Marnissi.

Marnissi Landing was an impressive structure, large enough to moor six Traders, very gaudily painted, with a gabled roof over the centre to protect buyers from the weather. Another Trader, Sea Mist, was moored there and greeted Purple Leaf on their arrival. They were to fly out next morning, but on hearing that Shaeli was to perform they promised to return.

The days passed quickly and Sea Mist returned early on the morning of the show, followed by Four Winds and Green Arrow – Kirrit's cousins – who had heard from Red Arrow of the performance and had also come to watch.

The show was put on by the shores of Lake Marnis, and the sight of the skylights reflected in the lake's surface was an astounding sight. This time, Shaeli also had the luxury of watching, for after their piece, Horler performed, and then he asked Flin to join him, and the two did an unrehearsed piece, creating duelling skylights which chased each other across the sky before exploding into miraculous shapes; huni deer, trees, ships, even a Trader, complete with Zoi, which brought mighty

83

cheers from the members of the Fleet. The night was a great success, and the next day Purple Leaf flew south.

When they crossed over the River Zerrin, they could see in the distance the Clahren, the tributary which led to the Bay of Islands, and they flew down and followed it until they could see the bay ahead. By late afternoon they came to a familiar village, Boccra, near the sandstone house which Flin had rented before the Wintering, and they moored there for the night.

Next morning, Flin mumbled something about "unfinished business" before disappearing into the village. He came back some time later, suggesting they go down to the bay before they left.

As they walked down to the water they passed by the walled sandstone house, and he said they should have a look inside. The others dubiously followed him through the gates and Flin turned to look at them as they gathered inside the walls.

"Welcome," he said, pulling a few keys on a fine chain from his pocket. "Welcome to my new house. My door is open to you all." He unlocked the door and threw it open, arm outstretched as he spoke. He laughed as the others took in the information and moved forward to congratulate him. "I couldn't resist," he said. "I heard the owner had need of coin, and it's such a fine house. We shall be able to spend much time here before the Wintering. Our little home away from home." He beamed at them all, but it was Shaeli's smile of approval he was waiting to see.

* * *

After the late start, they flew across the edge of the bay, the green of the land beside it beginning to look a little weary as it was baked by the summer sun. Just after midday, Shaeli was standing on deck with Eenis and Illen, and, seeing familiar landscape, gave a cry of delight. She recognised the inn where they usually lunched on their way to the sandstone house, and she and Eenis persuaded Jarris and Jeth to moor at the tiny Landing so they could visit.

As they flew in to land, Shaeli could see the inn keeper, Borsal, and his wife, Dorkit, standing in the doorway. They both wore identical frowns of puzzlement until they recognised the faces on the Trader, and then they began to smile and wave.

The Landing adjacent to the inn was a very primitive affair, the stairs rickety and thin, but the landing posts were still firmly pointing at the sky. Shaeli was seized by a momentary claw of fear as she stepped from the Trader onto the wobbly Landing, but then Tarkoda was beside her, taking her hand and squeezing it, and she smiled her thanks and they descended together. Dorkit and Borsal met them at the bottom, marvelling at the Zoi and apologising for the state of the Landing.

"Terrible old thing," said Dorkit. "I keep tellin' Da he ought to have it fixed. Hello, nice to meet you," she smiled, as Shaeli introduced those they had not met.

"Fix it? What for, Mother?" scoffed Borsal. "So she at Court can send one of them landingholders to spy on us?" He looked at Jarris. "We rarely see Traders here, anyway. Most of my stock comes straight from the city. Well, usually, that is, but we've had a bit of trouble with raiders on the roads, even though we already give half our food away to those hereabouts who are struggling. But lately that don't seem enough, and a few wagons have disappeared. Not as I blame 'em much, the way things are."

Jarris nodded. "Nor I," he said. "We return this way in half a Moon or so. Perhaps we can make a delivery for you?"

Borsal beamed, and clapped him on the back. "Let me buy you an ale, sir, and I'll tell you what I need, and where you can pick up what I've already ordered."

"But… but what about the Landing?" cried Dorkit, giving her husband a startled look. "It's in a terrible state, and I'm sure it's too much trouble for these nice folk."

Tarkoda answered. "As long as the landing posts hold firm, it doesn't matter if the Landing itself is gone. And it's no trouble at all. It's what we do."

"Them posts were put in the ground by my grandfather's grandfather, and haven't moved a hair since. And besides," Borsal winked at Jarris, "perhaps I can put a nail or two in the Landing that won't show up to *her* inspectors."

And so while Jarris and Eenis discussed Borsal's delivery, the others were given beverages by Dorkit, who bustled about as usual, serving them and the couple of locals sitting at the long bar, yet to Shaeli it did not seem the easy bustle Dorkit had always possessed. There was a skittishness about her; a nervousness of darting looks and tight lips about the fixed smile, looks that darted from her husband's back to the stairs which led to the rooms above, but her chatter was normal, her gaze calm and friendly when their eyes met, and so Shaeli thought little about it. She chatted with Tarkoda, Kirrit, and Andos as they drank, looking around her.

She saw one of the men at the bar staring at her, a tall man with thinning ginger hair and very little chin, and she gave him a small smile. He smiled back, but Shaeli didn't like the look of it at all. It was a sly smile, full of crooked, yellow teeth and a hint of cunning. A smile that seemed to gloat over terrible things that had not yet come to pass. Shaeli shuddered and looked away.

They left soon after, Borsal and Dorkit waving them off from the front of the inn, and though Shaeli was sure she'd heard Dorkit say they had no guests, she saw the curtains in one of the upstairs windows shift just a little.

* * *

It was dark when they reached Palveron, yet so bright was the city that they had no trouble seeing the enormous square holding the Landing. The city unfolded beneath them, its streets ablaze with Warlock light, the people walking about or dining at one of the many inns and restaurants. Music wafted up here and there, voices were raised gaily, shouts of mirth and ribald laughter hung in the air above the vibrant city. Here, there was little sign of the poverty that abounded in the countryside.

Golden Eagle was moored in its customary place at the spacious Landing, and they were greeted by Rafi, Renn and Taffka when they arrived. Rhubic also came up from the nests; he had been brought to Palveron by Rennan's Trader, Kingfisher, after they'd left the Starisles following Shaeli's performance, for the Head Trader still had need of his help, and it was accepted that Rhubic of Red Sun was now also Rhubic of Golden Eagle.

All the travellers were loathe to end the journey so abruptly, and they decided to stay another night on Purple Leaf, especially after Eenis and Yorrow confessed they had made a feast to commemorate the journey.

It was a wonderful feast, too, the entire company relaxed and happy, and it was long after the midnight hours when they finally reached their beds. Next morning, it was time for them to part, and while Shaeli and Kirrit would spend most of their time on Purple Leaf while it remained in Palveron, Flin, Yorrow, Illen and Qiren loaded their bags into one of Flin's carriages and moved back up the hillside to Flin's house.

As the days passed, Purple Leaf took on a load to trade, and the supplies requested by Borsal. Mareesha finally caught up with Lady Arinola, and the two spent an extraordinary amount of time ensconced in intimate conversation, Sir Vulcan of Conroi or Mareesha's sister, Asheen, occasionally joining them. Kirrit, Andos, Shaeli, and Tarkoda spent as much time together as possible, exploring the city and visiting Asheen and Zander, and Iyri and Meart, who had married on the last day of spring and lived with Zander and Asheen in the white house on the bay.

Purple Leaf stayed in the city ten days before leaving, and when they did fly away, it was with the promise to return for the Autumn's Eve Hunt.

Kirrit was impressed with Shaeli's room at Flin's, and thrilled with her own, which adjoined Shaeli's, and it took her very little time to settle in. Ebony immediately began to roam, finding her food and water bowls in their customary position, fruit where it always was, and it was clear she was very comfortable back at Flin's.

Shaeli took a few days to adjust, for while she also felt comfortable at Flin's, she still felt vaguely *un*comfortable about the thing which had bothered her all along; the thing she had almost gone home for: to see the twins. She knew they would be broken-hearted at her not returning for the Wintering, but she consoled herself with the fact that her parents would bring them to the Starisles in the spring.

Almarnoch, too, she missed terribly, yet her parents had told her he was content now that she knew the extent of her gift, and content also – at least for now – to let Flin and Qiren guide her. Her father had told her that Almarnoch still worried over her, yet even the old Warlock could not say from whence the worry came.

The days passed quickly with rehearsals, shopping, visiting, and soon Purple Leaf was back, and a few days later Red Arrow also arrived.

Over the days before the Hunt, several more Traders arrived; Sea Mist, Rainbow, Running Bird, Little Dove, all flew into Palveron, mooring at various Landings throughout the city. Lastly on the very morning of the Hunt, Silver Hawk arrived, the Trader, which, many Winterings before, had brought the injured herald, Gremon, to Djelda to deliver the news of Virrisian's ascension to queen. Kaplan, his wife Narla, and sister, Teila, like the others, had come especially to see

Shaeli's skylights, and again she was warmed by the support shown by the Fleet.

It was an enormous party that arrived at the Royal Parklands for the Autumn's Eve Hunt, seven packed-full carriages spilled their party out onto the grass, yet as soon as their area was set out with blankets and umbrellas, they disappeared by small groups into the tide of the Hunt crowd.

This year the crowds seemed less, yet still there were thousands of people there. Shaeli had a lovely time showing the others the sights, the stalls and the small hunts. Tarkoda won first place in the slingshot competition, Kirrit found a prize in the flower-bed hunt, and the rest of the day passed with no surprises, no visits from Williver, and no disruptions to the Hunt itself. Shaeli was persuaded to go and watch the judging of the Hunt, and, while there was no repeat of the strange fugue state that had affected her so oddly the year before, she found herself searching the crowd for the faces which had stood out so clearly to her then. She found several she recognised, both the queen's people and the others, and her eyes were drawn again and again to the watchful figure of Sir Azeron, master-at-arms, who sat beside the queen, goblet in hand, eyes incessantly scanning the crowd. Of the big dark-bearded man she had seen the year before there was no sign, and though she had not really expected to see him, the memory of his unspoken cry made her shiver every time she thought of it. While the judging was taking place there were many wary looks on the faces of the crowd, but the judges found their winner and he took pride of place beside the queen with no added excitement whatsoever.

Later, Shaeli, Flin, and Qiren performed their skylights to an enthralled audience, and Shaeli was swept away as usual with the music and her part. The nerves which customarily attacked her before each show were present until the moment the music began, and then the performance took over and the skylights were all she knew.

When they finally reached Flin's house, long after the midnight hours had put themselves to bed, Shaeli was exhausted and fell into bed too, waking the next day with the sun already high in the sky and the sound of Kirrit's voice drifting up from the garden.

The next Moons came and went more quickly than Shaeli could believe. Autumn, always short, seemed to pass even more quickly. Purple Leaf traded up and down Zirrus' west coast, and a couple of times Shaeli and Kirrit accompanied them on short journeys. Ebony loved being on the Trader again, exploring every nook, from the rigging surrounding the balloon to the Zoi quarters, even when the giant birds were there. Tarkoda found her several times chattering to the Zoi, the birds cooing and looking intently down at the tiny creature as if they could understand each other.

When Purple Leaf flew away, Shaeli shed tears, yet they were few, and she consoled herself with the fact that the Wintering would pass and she would see her whole family on the Starisles in the spring, her sisters included. And Kirrit, who had farewelled Red Arrow a few days earlier, was with her, and she would not let Shaeli mope too long. She organised shopping and visits, and kept Shaeli occupied with a constant stream of questions and gossip. Before the Wintering took hold, they also made several trips to the sandstone house on the bay. It was on the last of these trips that she saw Pizar again.

She had not seen the young guardsman since the Wintering, and though she'd looked for him and asked after him, all she could find out was that he had left Great Court for one of the queen's outposts.

It had been a dry summer, the autumn much the same, and the countryside was looking as ragged and patched as an old quilt. The chill Wintering winds were beginning to blow from the south, and the Land was parched beneath the thin sunshine as they drove around the bay.

They stopped for lunch as usual at The Fish and Field, the inn of Borsal and Dorkit, and they also delivered a crate to Borsal, an order which had not been filled before Purple Leaf left the city. Jarris had asked Flin to drop it off because he didn't trust it to normal delivery routes.

Borsal had overseen the unloading of the crate — not large but quite heavy — jovially voicing his gratitude again and again. Dorkit hovered in the doorway watching, and then fed them an enormous lunch while serving her other customers and seeing to one of the many grandchildren who seemed to be always under her feet.

The inn seemed unusually busy that day, the company merry and talkative, and they were later than usual leaving. Yorrow had stayed in the carriage as he always did, and Shaeli saw him have a hurried conversation with Flin and Qiren as she said goodbye to Dorkit and her family. She saw Flin's brows contract and Qiren peer up the road ahead, yet they said nothing as she boarded the carriage. She leant out to wave at those gathered before the inn, Dorkit and Borsal smiling, surrounded by small children, and then the inn was gone, lost in their dust.

A short while after they'd left the inn, they heard hoofbeats and voices ahead, and the driver pulled their carriage to a halt. Shaeli saw Flin's hand go to the pocket in which he kept his throwing gem, and Qiren's hand go to his wand before they alighted. Illen had also noticed, her eyes reflecting Shaeli's alarm, yet they left the carriage without hesitation, Kirrit close behind with Ebony in the curl of her arm.

Before them, barring the way, was a large group of men, yet Shaeli's alarm fled as she recognised them as the queen's guard. The emotion was instantly replaced with surprise; Pizar was at their head.

Pizar was speaking to one of his men, and, strangely, Shaeli recognised this man also. Though he was in the black-and-scarlet of the queen's guard and looked quite different, she saw that it was the ginger-haired man who had smiled at her so sickeningly at the inn the day they had visited on Purple Leaf. The man took half the company and rode past them, following the road back towards the Fish and Field, and the look he gave her as he passed made her shudder all over again. The others in the company stayed where they were as Pizar dismounted and walked towards where Flin and Qiren stood on the dusty road.

Shaeli had initially feared rebels – though they had little with them worth stealing, and she did not doubt Qiren and Flin could deal with anything – but this was something entirely different; a lovely surprise. She rushed forward, all smiles, ready to greet Pizar, but the words stopped in her throat as she saw the looks on the three faces and heard their words.

Flin was speaking as she neared. "It's ridiculous, Pizar, and you know it. Your information is wrong," he said emphatically. "These people are simple country folk, not masterminds of subterfuge, and we were delivering taps for the ale kegs, not contraband."

"Did you see these taps, Flin?" Pizar asked.

"Well, no," Flin admitted. "But Borsal and his wife are honest folk."

"Perhaps, but they are well known to sympathise with the rebels. We believe they shelter traitors from justice and supply them with weapons. *And* they speak open treason about the queen."

"If you arrested everyone who spoke against the queen, the jails would soon overflow," said Flin.

Pizar's face was grim, yet he ignored the comment. "My men have been following the crate you just delivered to that inn since it left the forge; a forge which makes moulds for spear tips and arrow heads, not keg taps. It was delivered to *your* house, Flin."

Shaeli spoke up. "But Flin was just doing my father a favour," she said, and, as Pizar looked at her, she added, "Hello, Pizar."

He nodded. "Hello Shaeli. What do you mean? Was this your father's idea?"

"Well, no," said Shaeli. "It's just that he was unable to make the last delivery, and he knew we pass by this way and asked Flin to drop it off it for him. Purple Leaf made several deliveries to Borsal, because Borsal was worried about rebels."

"And why would Borsal be worried about the rebels if he was plotting *with* them?" asked Flin. "He said he'd lost several wagons already."

"Borsal has *never* lost a wagon," said Pizar, flatly. "Not so much as one keg." Flin blanched at this, and Pizar carried on. "He's worried about the guard searching his wagons, about us finding something." He looked at Shaeli. "And as to your father's previous deliveries, they were searched soon after the Trader departed, and luckily, we found nothing. It would go badly for the traders if they were thought to be aiding the rebellion."

"My father would *never* be disloyal to Great Court, Pizar," Shaeli retorted, her temper flaring instantly. "No trader would."

Kirrit was at her shoulder, and Shaeli felt the same smouldering anger from her.

"Perhaps not knowingly, Shaeli," said Pizar, his face softening slightly, his voice softening with it. "But they do not always *know* what it is they carry. They may be deceived also." He looked at them all. "As you have all been deceived. These people are not the innocents you believe, and they will see justice when they are caught." He smiled a tight smile. "But that is not your concern. I believe you were merely doing a favour, and were unwittingly involved, as was Purple Leaf. You may go on with your journey. You go to your house on the bay, Flin?"

Flin nodded. "Yes, Pizar. A few days away before the Wintering. But how did you know about it?"

"Oh, one hears things," Pizar answered casually, then he turned to Shaeli. "I hope you're not still angry with me. I meant nothing against traders. You know I have the utmost respect for the Fleet."

"Yes, Pizar. I know. But you must realise they'd never do anything like that."

"That's just as well." He looked past her and smiled – a real smile this time. "I'd say by the look on her face that this is another of your traders?"

"Oh, yes, this is Kirrit of Red Arrow. Kirrit, Pizar."

Kirrit nodded, but not at all politely.

"Perhaps we shall see each other this Wintering. I shall soon be returning to duty at Court," Pizar said. He straightened his shoulders and his smile. "It is time I left. I suggest you tell your Fleet to be very careful about what they carry next year. There will be regular searches for contraband, on ships, boats, carts, carriages, *and* Traders, after this Wintering. Queen Virrisian wants the rebels caught."

He nodded and walked back to his men, swung himself into the saddle, and rode past them, following the rest of his men – those led by the ginger-haired man – back down the road towards the inn.

* * *

CHAPTER SIX

Three days later, they began the trip back to Palveron. They reached the Fish and Field at midday, a crisp and lovely late-autumn day. What awaited them robbed the loveliness from it.

The courtyard was empty, the stable a blackened mess on the ground. The tiny Landing, too, had been burnt and only the landing posts remained. The inn itself was an empty shell, bereft of life, its windows broken, the front door hanging from one hinge.

They alighted from the carriage to silence. Utter silence. Qiren called out, but no one answered.

Illen looked about, fear shining brightly in her eyes. Something about the cold silence, the dusty ground, the smell of harsh smoke, gave rise to an unspeakable terror within her and she struggled to keep her countenance, but it was too much. She ran to Qiren and buried her face in his shoulder.

"We must leave, Qiren," she cried. "There is evil here."

Qiren comforted her. "'Tis past evil, Illen. Not *long* past, but gone, just the same." He looked at Flin. "The damage has been done."

Flin nodded. "We should take a look inside," he said.

Illen clutched at the elf's arm. "No, Qiren," she cried. "Don't go in there. Don't leave me."

Shaeli spoke. "You stay here with Illen and Kirrit, Qiren," she said. "I'll go with Flin." She patted Illen's arm. "We won't be long."

Flin nodded. "We'll be fine," he assured them.

Qiren's grip tightened about Illen's shoulders, Kirrit moved to put an arm about her too, and together they led her back towards the carriage where Yorrow and the driver stood talking in low tones beside the horses.

95

Shaeli looked at Flin. He took her hand and gave it a squeeze, and though he smiled, she noticed he held his throwing stone in the other hand. Her own fingers moved to rest on her amulet.

"Just a quick look," he said. "To make sure there's no one here."

"But what happened, Flin?" she asked. "Was it rebels, or...?" She let the sentence fade.

"Pizar's men?"

She nodded.

"I'd guess so," Flin replied grimly, as they entered. "But from the looks of it, they didn't give them an easy time of it."

The room was littered with rubble; broken chairs and tables; shattered glass. Arrows stuck from walls. A small axe lay buried to its hilt in a window-frame. A sword lay in two pieces on the floor beside a large dark patch that stained the wood. Other dark patches lay on the floorboards, testament to the battle waged here. Shaeli wanted to look away, but her eyes were drawn to the dark stains again and again.

Flin led her on, through the kitchens – here too, there were signs of a struggle – and out the back door. Dorkit's small garden lay amazingly unruffled, the green herbs nodding in the sun, the surrounding hedges screening the sight of the burnt stable and empty courtyard. They lingered only a moment, but as they turned to leave they heard a slight noise; a creaking scratch of a sound.

Flin motioned for Shaeli to stay still, and he crept forward, his stone held out before him. The noise had come from a lean-to at the corner of the building. Flin took the door handle and wrenched it open. There was a scurrying noise from inside and he reached in and pulled someone out into the sunlight.

It was Dorkit, but a Dorkit neither had ever seen before. A shivering, jabbering, flailing Dorkit. A Dorkit with hair tangled, with hands scratching, with face snarling. Gibberish fell from her mouth, spittle flew from her tongue. Her words made no sense.

"Took 'im from us," she screeched. "Them above did fight. Watched 'im fight ten, but couldn't help. All in the box. Buried fast. Nothing to find. But them knew it was there. Them searched." She rolled her head. "Held the child, 'til we'd say." She sobbed dryly and looked at them, eyes wild. "You. *You* led 'em. Now them's taken all, and we're left, and 'im … 'im's *gone*. It's *you*. All you." She flew at Flin, arms outstretched, fingers clawing for his eyes.

Flin held her away, her fingers scrabbling uselessly in the air. "Dorkit," he said, his voice striving to calm her. "Dorkit 'tis us, your friends. We mean you no harm. Where is everyone? Where is Borsal?"

"'Im's *gone*," she cried. "Gone. *Gone*." And suddenly she collapsed into a weeping heap at their feet.

Flin and Shaeli looked at each other, aghast. What had happened here?

The answer soon came. As they stooped to bring Dorkit to her feet, two of her daughters came hurrying around the side of the building.

One, half her face swollen and coloured with an enormous bruise, took Dorkit in her arms, cradling her like a babe. Dorkit looked up at her and wept more loudly. The other daughter told the tale as her mother moaned at their feet.

Virrisian's guard, led by the ginger-haired man, had ridden in and demanded Borsal give them the crate Flin had delivered. Borsal did so, but the man, upon opening a crate filled with keg taps, had become incensed, accusing Borsal of swapping crates, and he had ordered his men to search the premises. Borsal had refused to allow them upstairs, and a fight had begun. The details after this became sketchy, but it seems there had been members of the rebellion hiding upstairs, and they had joined the fight.

Dorkit, her daughters, and their children had fled to the kitchens, and only heard the sounds of the battle. But then the ginger-haired man had burst into the kitchen and pulled one of the children, a young girl of eleven Winters, out into the fray, her mother screaming and dragging at his back.

Borsal and his men had laid down their arms instantly, begging for the child to be released yet still denying knowledge of the alleged crate of weapons. The man – three of his guard dead around him – had not believed them, and he had put a knife to the child's throat. Her mother, hysterical, had dragged at the arm that held the knife, and in the scuffle Borsal had rushed them.

Just then, another group of the guard had ridden up and burst into the tavern. By the time they entered the room, Borsal lay dead with a knife in his heart and the ginger-haired man still held the child. Her mother lay sobbing, three of her teeth on the floor beside her.

This new man – *Pizar*, Shaeli thought to herself – had shown contempt for the actions of the other, and had ordered the child released. Yet, still he had ordered the tavern searched, and still he had arrested all the men and taken them away. *And* he had not objected when his men had fired the barn. He'd said it would deter others, Dorkit's daughter told them. Then they had left, taking the prisoners and their dead with them, leaving Borsal lying in a pool of blood.

Dorkit had helped her daughters dig his grave, laid him in it and said a prayer to the gods. Then she had collapsed, and she had not made much sense since.

Flin and Shaeli did not know what to say when she was finished. Their most sincere condolences sounded hollow, even to their own ears. The women waved away their words and all offers of a lift. Their homes were not far, they said, and they would have to learn to keep a better eye on their mother until she regained her senses. No one mentioned that this may never happen, yet it was in all their thoughts.

Shaeli and Flin walked with them back across the courtyard, and bid them farewell. They stood watching as the three women, shoulders bowed with sorrow, arms about each other, disappeared over the brow of a hill.

* * *

The Wintering was half over before they saw Pizar again.

The blizzards had been fierce, they'd practised only sporadically and had been housebound for much of the time. They had visited Arinola and been snowed in for five days, yet they had had a wonderful time in the grand house, and she had begged them to give a performance for her again. It was there that they saw Pizar.

He came, as he had the previous Wintering, with the last wave of guests. Shaeli and Kirrit were sitting in a corner of the library, a mulled wine in their hands, legs drawn up beneath them, giggling, when they saw him. Their laughter died away as he entered and was greeted by Arinola. A stiff greeting, for her, because Flin had told her what had transpired at the Fish and Field.

They had discussed the incident many times over the past Moons, and though they agreed that Pizar was not at fault for the death of Borsal, he *had* arrested every man at the inn and ordered the firing of the barn. And he must have known the character of the man he'd sent before him.

He gave the girls a thin smile now across the crowded room, but he made no move to greet them, instead going to greet Skeltom, Arinola's Warlock.

Sir Collett, who had again brought Pizar and several other young guardsmen, was given a much warmer greeting by Arinola, and then he went straight over to Sir Vulcan and Flin, who were mixing mulled wine. The next guests brought Shaeli to her feet.

Garrit, Almarnoch's former apprentice, who she had not seen since he had left Cave, stood in the doorway, and beside him, eyes scanning the crowd, was Dari.

Shaeli leapt out of her chair and ran across the room. Kirrit, seeing Dari also, was a pace behind her. Dari saw her only a moment before she leapt on him, and he stumbled a little before giving her a firm hug and a kiss. Kirrit was next, and she asked the obvious question.

"Dari, what are you *doing* here? I thought no one left the Warlock Isle before they'd finished training."

He grinned. "Only those who excel at protection spells," he said. "I've been Wintering in the Warlock House at Great Court, training with Garrit and some others. There's twelve of us from the Island, doing advanced tree protection." His pride was worn plainly on his face.

"That's wonderful, Dari," said Shaeli. "But how is it you're here? Does Garrit know Sir Collett?"

"Who? Oh, no. We came down with some of the guard, but Garrit is a friend of the house Warlock, and that's how we knew of the ball. Garrit missed it last Winter."

"Not this time," said Garrit, turning to greet Arinola. "I'd not miss one of the Lady Arinola's balls two Winterings in a row. And I hear we are having skylights," he smiled. "Hello Kirrit, Shaeli. You two have grown a great deal since I saw you last."

"Hello Garrit," said Shaeli. "It *has* been a long time, and it's such a surprise to see you here. You, *and* Dari." She took Dari's arm. "Let me introduce you to Lady Arinola. Arinola, this is my cousin, Dari, who is almost a full Warlock, and studying with Garrit for the Wintering."

Dari held out his hand. "I'm very happy to meet you, Lady Arinola," he said. "Thank you for your hospitality."

Arinola took the hand and kissed his cheek for good measure. "Happy you could be here, my boy," she smiled. "Traders are always welcome in my house. We should have a fine time, and I trust the ball will give you a welcome respite from your studies. There are many pretty young ladies here, and their heads are always turned by skylights *and* Warlocks."

Dari blushed slightly. "I fear I will be busy watching the skylights also," he said, artfully shifting the subject. "I have not seen Shaeli's little lights for several Winters, and I'm looking forward to it."

Shaeli squeezed his arm and smiled at him, remembering how withdrawn they had been from each other as children. She hoped that she and Dari could now be friends.

She saw Illen and called her over. Illen and Dari had not yet met, as he had been at Cave when Illen had been reunited with Eenis, and he was given a hug from his smiling aunt who was delighted to meet him. Of course, she had heard much from Eenis about Dari and was eager to befriend him.

They gave Dari a mulled wine, and then took him to find his bedroom. Shaeli felt almost at home in the enormous house now, and they found Dari's room easily, a few corridors along from their own. Afterwards they gave him a tour of the house, and he was ridiculously excited about the conservatory, exploring every aisle and exclaiming over many of the plants and flowers. When they joined the other guests he made straight for Skeltom and Garrit to discuss the amazing glass room. Shaeli and Kirrit stood smiling as Dari gushed his excitement, asking Skeltom endless questions about sustaining hybrids and the protection of tree orchids. Shaeli and Kirrit were captivated by Dari's enthusiasm and Skeltom's head-wobbling, finger-tapping answers.

Across the room she saw Pizar talking to Flin, and the tight look of Flin's mouth as he regarded the other man. Pizar appeared to be talking earnestly, and after a while Flin's mouth relaxed and he smiled. He noticed Shaeli looking at them and motioned her over. With a little trepidation she excused herself, and walked across the room. Kirrit watched her go, and then turned back to the others as Garrit spoke to her.

Pizar greeted her politely, and she returned the greeting without smiling. He did not make either of them suffer with unnecessary conversation, but broached the subject of the Fish and Field straight away. Although he spoke evenly, Shaeli noticed his hands trembled slightly.

"I know you're upset with me, Shaeli, and I understand completely. It must have been a great shock to you all when you returned to the inn. As I have just been explaining to Flin, the death of Borsal was a most unnecessary and unwarranted act. The man who perpetrated the incident has been dealt with firmly, and I regret that any of you were upset." He licked his lips. "The last thing I wanted to do was harm our friendship, but my orders clearly stated that anyone suspected of rebellion against the queen was to be taken for questioning. I had no choice but to comply. And they *were* harbouring rebels, as we suspected all along. Those who were innocent have already returned to their homes."

"But what about the barn, Pizar, was it necessary to burn it?" Shaeli asked. "And poor Dorkit. What about her?"

Flin watched them silently.

"The barn was a deterrent," Pizar said. "In practise I should have burnt the inn, too, but I ordered my men to leave it as it was, so the poor widow should still have her business, if not her husband. I had no idea she had lost her wits until Flin told me just now, but I hope to the gods she finds them again." Shaeli was mollified a little, and Pizar could see it. He pressed the point. "I *am* sorry for the woman, Shaeli, truly I am, and that any of you were involved, but I must do my duty. My orders are what they are. The rebels are tearing the Land apart. 'Tis barely safe to use the roads. The Land is in an unfortunate state, and it is my duty to try and protect people."

Shaeli nodded, but Flin spoke the words she was thinking.

"The *rebels* are not responsible for the state of the Land, Pizar, and unless you are blind, you must realise that," he said.

Pizar stiffened. "That may be so, Flin, but there is nothing I can do about that. Affairs of Court are far above the head of one of the queen's guard." The stiffness left his shoulders a little as he took a deep breath. "I merely do my duty, and in this case, I'm sorry it involved you all, and I hope it will not affect our friendship."

"You're right, of course, about doing one's duty," said Flin, amiably. "Although sometimes duty and right are not always the same thing. But, as for myself, I think you were not to blame for the *entire* sorry business, and harbour no ill feeling towards you on that score. Yet I shall miss Borsal and the ale at his fine inn."

"I agree," said Shaeli.

As they drank a toast to Borsal, Shaeli noticed Pizar's hands still trembled slightly.

* * *

Two nights later was the evening of the ball. Shaeli and Kirrit spent the afternoon alternating between pretending to rest and talking about the guests and the coming evening.

A blizzard had raged around the house all morning but had eased during the afternoon. By the time they began to dress, the wind had died and light snow fell in large soft flakes. The ground was lumped with white, the trees wearing crisp new gowns, and the soft snow continued through the food and the dancing. It was still falling when they entered the conservatory where Shaeli left Kirrit with Sir Vulcan to watch the skylights, and then she joined Flin and Qiren at the door. They were just about to leave when Arinola stopped them, announcing the Warlocks had something to show them all first.

Skeltom, Garrit and Dari stepped forward. Skeltom and Garrit each held a long staff, and the three bowed to the company. Skeltom spoke.

"We would like to give the guests a taste of the spring to come, so we may honour the Wintering for bringing it to us," he said, his head, as always, wobbling just a little. He bowed again and moved to a huge orchid which hung from a giant tree fern.

Garrit moved to one in a tree nearby and Dari to a large spray hanging beside the little waterfall. Each of the orchids had many long stems hanging from the rich green leaves, but only a tight bud showed where the flowers would begin.

The Warlocks began to chant in low voices, and soon the air started to vibrate and the staffs to glimmer with magic. As the tone of the chant rose, each of the sprays on the three plants began to blossom, slowly pushing out buds which separated and opened, dropping down as gently as the snowflakes outside and blossoming into richly coloured flowers. The heady scent of orchid perfume filled the air, and by the time the chant reached its crescendo, each plant was flourishing with waxy, dappled flowers. The guests were applauding before the glimmer of magic had faded.

Shaeli clapped loudly as the Warlocks bowed again, and smiled her congratulations when she caught Dari's eye. His plant had a few buds still unfurled at its tips, but he had done beautifully and Shaeli was happy for him. She waved as she left the room with Flin and Qiren, and he waved back, his face glowing with pride.

She went up through the house chattering, forgetting to be nervous until they ascended the last set of stairs to the attic with the iron-lace balcony. Again there was a cup of tezz waiting for them on a brazier glowing with Warlock-flame, and fur-lined, hooded cloaks warming beside it. They left the tezz until later, put on the cloaks and walked out through the doors, the cold biting at their faces and fingers as they positioned themselves before the opening. Shaeli stuck out her tongue and a few snowflakes fell onto it and she tasted the sweetness of the Wintering.

When they were ready, Flin opened with a cast of glittering birds which flew across the roof of the conservatory and into the trees around the garden. Shaeli followed with a series of huge balls that flew invisibly into the sky and then exploded into a cloud of silver and blue butterflies. Qiren and Flin then drew a giant huni-deer in the sky, and Shaeli gave it silver horns. On they went, skylight after skylight filling the night, colour reflecting in the hundreds of panes below, until it was over.

Shaeli studied the sky for a moment before she went back inside to warm numb fingers over bright flames and drink tezz. Thick cloud hung heavily over the city, eager to drop its burden of blizzard, no star was to be seen, and the air bit cruelly at her cheeks, but it had been a wonderful night, and she sighed and sent a thought to her family at Cave. If they had been here it would have been perfect.

When they descended the stairs, the guests – Arinola, Vulcan and Kirrit at their head – erupted into enthusiastic applause. They stopped at the lowest landing where Flin and Qiren bowed and Shaeli did a low curtsey, and they went down to be embraced and congratulated.

* * *

Dari and Garrit stood at the edge of the crowd, outside the door to the library. Garrit had just filled their glasses again with strong mulled wine and Dari's face was flushed with it and the many glasses he had drunk during the evening.

"She seems to enjoy the attention," said Garrit, watching Shaeli.

"Always has," said Dari. "Has to show off and out-do everyone. Always has," he repeated, slurring his words slightly. "Whole family thinks they're better than most, even those twins." He looked at Shaeli over the rim of his cup. "Ha. *Twins.* I wonder if she knows one of them is a bastard, left behind in the sunrise hours by a beggar." He swallowed. "Always been too proud, always thought they were better than *my* family, though we live on the same Trader." He gulped at his glass again. "Lived. *I'll* not be a trader again. If you hadn't needed me here, I would've stayed at Great Court. At least there we use *real* magic."

"But I do need you, Dari," Garrit smiled. "We won't fail again, and we've waited a long time."

"I still don't know how she found it before, that time I took it at Cave. *Or* why you want it if you've decided not to sell it."

"It matters not how she found it then," Garrit said through his fixed smile. "Perhaps she saw you leave the Trader as you saw the bastard twin arrive, from the window of the privy. What matters is, if it *is* here in Palveron, we shall try again, if not, you shall find it when you return to Cave."

"And then what?" asked Dari, draining his glass. "What good is it?"

Garrit's smile grew greedy. "If it is what I think it is, it will mean I... *we* hold great power. Power enough to give us whatever we desire."

"Surely Almarnoch would know if it is powerful," said Dari. "You know he was the first to see it. He said it was elven, old and bereft of magic."

"*Hush*. Someone may hear."

"They are all too busy with the throwers," Dari said, yet he lowered his voice. "And it would be written about, surely?"

"It is *not* written about. Only spoken of in hushed tones on the Island of Warlocks, and then by few. It was only by chance I found out about it. Elven magic is of little concern to us," he said. "Yet if the High Warlock suspects what it is, and I'm sure he does, for he is no fool, then he'll not let it go easily. We must hope it is here in Palveron."

"Well, it's time you told me," said Dari, his voice petulant. "I'm not a child any more, Garrit, and if you want me to get it for you, I want to know why."

"Alright, Dari, *hush*," said Garrit, looking over his shoulder at the library door. "Not here. Come into the conservatory, it will be more private. But first we better go and congratulate your cousin on her fine performance. It would seem odd otherwise."

"Alright," said Dari. "But then I want to know."

They walked over to Shaeli, both smiling, both kissing her cheek and congratulating her. Then, when her attention was taken by one of the guard – one who had accompanied them from Great Court and was obviously on friendly terms with her – they slipped away to the conservatory.

* * *

Pizar, who had come to congratulate Shaeli after them, had emerged from the inside the library, where he had listened with interest to the cryptic conversation between the two Warlocks. As he spoke to Shaeli, he watched them go down the hall to the conservatory. He watched them over Shaeli's shoulder as he smiled and talked of the skylights, then he excused himself, and followed Garrit and Dari down the hall to the plant-filled glass room.

* * *

When the guests began to leave with the next break in the weather, Shaeli was sorry to see Dari go. He had been a link to Purple Leaf, and she was glad they were friends. She had kissed him and Garrit, and told them a dozen times to be sure to visit. She had hugged Pizar too, and waved as they drove away with Sir Collett and the others to go back up to Great Court.

* * *

In the carriage, Dari looked at Garrit.

"Not much point visiting. It's not there," he said softly.

Garrit nodded and shrugged.

No one could know of what they spoke, but Garrit noticed one of the guard looking at them – the one who was friends with Shaeli. But it did not matter. At worst, the soldier would think Dari a very poor cousin.

* * *

Pizar regarded the two Warlocks briefly before looking back out the window of the carriage. He had something very interesting to discuss with his cousin Azeron, master-at-arms to the queen, when he returned to the castle.

* * *

At Arinola's, Shaeli and Kirrit were packing their things. Ebony scampered about, getting in the way and making them laugh. They were in fine spirits after the holiday at Arinola's and the success of the ball, and when Flin came to see if they'd finished, he found them giggling amid half-filled bags.

"Hurry up, you two, we'll be leaving soon," he said, but he smiled. "I expect you downstairs promptly, or at least before morning," he said as he left the room.

"We won't be long, Flin," Shaeli called after him. "We're more organised than we look."

Kirrit looked at Shaeli with one eyebrow arched. "Are we?" she asked. "More organised than we look?"

"Well, no, but it sounded good."

"We'd best hurry then," Kirrit said, and she started shoving things into bags. "Dari's grown up alright. He was such a *stuffy* child."

"I know," nodded Shaeli. "Solemn and a bit grumpy. He changed as soon as he discovered he could make Warlock magic. I'm glad it made him happy." She closed one bag and moved onto another. "Garrit and he were always good friends, and though *I* was never that fond of Garrit, I'm happy he's looking after Dari. He did ask me one funny thing, though."

"Who, Garrit?" Kirrit's words were muffled as she looked under the bed for forgotten items.

"No. Dari. He asked me if I still had my wand, and if it's here in Palveron. He joked I should use it for skylights."

"Your what?" said Kirrit, coming back out from under the bed, one slipper in her hand. "Oh, your *wand*." She found the other slipper, stuffed them both into an over-stuffed bag and tried to close it. The clasps didn't touch. "I'd almost forgotten about that wand. When did you find it again?" She sat on the bag, forced the clasps together, and snapped them shut. "*There*," she said, triumphant.

"The year the twins were born. Most don't remember it, and I gave it to Almarnoch to look after. Funny," Shaeli said, as she closed the last bag. "Funny, Dari should ask about it. You know he tried to steal it once?"

"Did he? Why?" asked Kirrit, piling bags beside the door.

"I'm not sure," said Shaeli, scooping Ebony up off the bed.

"He always *was* a bit of a sneak," Kirrit said. "Ready?"

* * *

CHAPTER SEVEN

Despite the weather being bad, Flin, Qiren and Shaeli managed to find time to complete Shaeli's training. They threw small skylights up and down halls and up near ceilings, and when they could they threw light after light out over the wall from the platform built the Wintering before, Kirrit usually joining them despite the cold. She never failed to be delighted in Shaeli's ability, and whooped her appreciation until her throat was hoarse.

Shaeli found these final lessons fine-tuned her magic, giving her greater awareness of each throw and enhancing the subtleties of shape and colour. She understood why Flin had wanted her to continue training without a break, for the more she practised, the more ingrained her technique became in her subconscious. She could tell exactly how much pressure need be applied, how much to veil, when to trigger the exact shape she required for the maximum effect. Soon there was little more they could teach her, all else would be learned from experience, and only time would give her that.

One evening, as the Wintering was losing its bluster, they sat comfortably sipping sweet port after dinner. They had talked of their homes; Illen as a child with Eenis; Flin of the Starisles; Kirrit and Shaeli of Cave; Qiren told of the elven lands where he'd grown up at the southern end of the mountain range that ran down Zirrus' coast, high up behind Noresh in a wide valley. It had been very cold there, bitter in the mornings, he said, but they were warm and had good company.

"It will be good to see them all again, though I'm sure they will hardly have missed us," Qiren smiled.

"I hope they have missed us a little," said Illen. "*I* have missed the peace of elven lands a great deal in the bustle of the

World. It is so beautiful there. Yet now I shall miss the World too, and those in it."

"You should come and Winter at Cave after the year, before you go back to the elven lands," said Shaeli. "I know Eenis would love it, and so would I. Think of the show we could give the Fleet, Qiren." She thought for a moment. "Flin, you should come too. I want you to meet everyone. Almarnoch and Llevvis and Wyshka."

"*What* a good idea," said Kirrit. "Cave is wonderful. You *should* come. All three of you." They laughed and Kirrit shook her red curls and frowned. "I'm serious. There's no reason why you couldn't, after the Starisles, is there?"

"Well, no," said Flin.

"But what about the Autumn's Eve Hunt?" asked Shaeli. "Aren't we doing that?"

"I thought not," replied Flin. "We've done it two years in a row and I'm inclined to give Horler or one of the others a chance. He'd jump at it, I'm sure." Shaeli's face fell and Flin laughed. "I thought you'd be happy to have the rest of the year off after the Starisles, Shaeli. You've been working solidly and deserve a rest." He yawned and stretched. "We all do. *I* look forward to a quiet year."

"There's no reason you couldn't think about coming to Cave then, is there?" asked Kirrit.

"No, Kirrit," laughed Flin. "There's no reason why we couldn't *think* about it."

"Good then. That's settled," said Kirrit, as if Flin had just agreed to go. "What about you Qiren? Illen?"

"Well, I'd love it," said Illen. "And as Shaeli says, Eenis would too." She looked at Qiren. "But it depends on whether there is anything pressing we must go home for."

Qiren smiled. "Not especially. You know we must go and see... friends before we return to our home, but I *suppose* we could think about it, too."

"What a wonderful plan," said Kirrit.

"Imagine the look on Eenis' face if we tell her you're coming to Cave. She'd smile for a Moon," grinned Shaeli.

"It *would* be nice to surprise her," said Illen. "I hadn't considered it before, but it sounds lovely."

By Winters' end they had almost decided on it, and as the blizzards drew to a close they began to gather their things for the trip to the Starisles. They would again go on Captain Mahi's ship, *The Painted Lady*, and Shaeli and Kirrit tried not to let Flin and Qiren see how excited they were about the trip, knowing what bad sailors the two were.

Finally the blizzards swept back across the Bastinian Ocean, throwing their last fury down on Wokk as they went, then creeping reluctantly back to the frozen wastelands to the south. Six mornings later they stood shivering on the dock in the thin sunlight as the baggage was taken aboard.

Flin, despite the ordeal ahead, was in fine spirits as they waited, and Shaeli realised it was because he was excited to be going home, back to the Starisles. As they sailed past the islands a short while later, he turned his face into the wind, a broad smile on his face, and Shaeli smiled with him as they scudded across the water.

* * *

From her tower in Great Court, Queen Virrisian watched the ship dwindle into the sunrise. Azeron had told her about the thrower's new apprentice, information that had been passed to him by his cousin, one of the guard. She'd merely nodded and told him to have his spies watch them. Now, as the ship shrank into the bay, she toyed with the keys on the fine chain at her waist. When the ship had gone, she took one of the keys, unlocked a small box and placed it on the table beside the window. She took the contents out, and began to chant in a soft voice, her face hovering over the half-stone in her hand. The patterns in the stone began to writhe. Queen Virrisian smiled at the voice which answered her song.

* * *

By mid-afternoon Flin was in his bed, the smile gone, the infectious sense of anticipation with it, and that was the last they saw of him until they reached Pa'laidiz.

Qiren fared little better, staunchly lasting until dinner, yet when the meal was laid before him he went a delicate shade of green and hastily exited the room.

Illen managed better still, as she had the year before, but the sea-sickness struck her sporadically during the trip, and they never knew when she would be up.

Shaeli and Kirrit were left to themselves again, yet they did not mind; they had expected it would be so. Most of the crew was familiar to them from last year, and Mahi was as generous as ever, giving them much of his time, and showing again his undiminished interest in the Fleet. Ebony also took delight in being aboard *The Painted Lady* again, climbing the rigging with the hand of an experienced sailor, gliding from rope to rope, something the crew took as much pleasure from as the jevvi.

It seemed, too, that the Fleet knew they would be travelling by ship, for unlike the last year, when they saw Traders only in the distance, every Trader they saw changed direction to fly within earshot, and so Mahi actually met some of the Fleet as they flew by.

They had a marvellous trip, and when at last Pa'laidiz was in sight, they were almost sorry it was over. Yet the excitement of the town and the familiarity of Flin's house saw them enjoying the time before Purple Leaf arrived, and arrive it did. Amid squeals of delight and a plethora of tears, Shaeli was reunited with her sisters.

Shanna and Neesha — both a head taller, both with figures fuller, their green eyes and smothering hugs unchanged — had grown into lovely girls. Neesha was still a smidgin taller, but they both had marvellous dark hair in different shades of deep brown, and cheekbones beginning to push through baby-fat cheeks. Both talked at once, running over each other and finishing each other's sentences, asking questions and telling of their year at Cave. Shaeli barely had time to hug her parents before being swept away to hear of their year.

Flin, who had been the first to see Purple Leaf as it flew across the harbour mid-morning, invited the girls to come and stay at the blue house, and the twins leapt at the chance. Mareesha smilingly agreed – she did not have the heart to keep them from their sister – and Shaeli had a few quiet moments when they went to pack their bags.

Illen and Eenis had been ensconced in quiet conversation since they'd boarded, and Eenis came and took Mareesha's arm, a smile on her thin face.

"Mareesha, wonderful news," she said. "Illen and Qiren have met Dari during the Wintering, *and* they are thinking of Wintering at Cave before returning to their home."

"That *is* wonderful, Eenis," smiled Mareesha. "What an excellent idea."

"Why, thank you very much," said Shaeli, smiling. "I thought so too, when I thought of it. I don't know why we haven't before. Thought of it, I mean. It's so simple. And Flin will probably come too, so he can meet everyone."

They walked over to join the others, who were talking about the same thing.

"And you'll return to Palveron first, Flin?" Jarris was saying.

"Probably, but it matters not. I could leave from here if I wished. My people in Palveron have instructions if I do not return before the Wintering, and I left Yorrow there to boss them about. I left word we would not be performing at the Autumn's Eve Hunt, so apart from the Summer Festival, I have no plans." He smiled. "I must admit, when it was first mentioned, I did not take the idea of Wintering at your Cave seriously, but the more I thought of it, the more interesting the idea became. And I admit, I am eager now to meet everyone who I have only heard about, and to see the Cave of the Traders."

"So am I," said Shaeli. "I can't believe it's been two Winters since I was there. I miss Wyshka and Almarnoch and Llevvis and the all the old ones. When I was little, I never wanted to go to Cave, I just wanted to keep flying and trading, but now I long for it. Long peaceful days and warm nights around the fire-pits. Oh, it will be such fun."

"There's almost a whole year to get through first, my girl," smiled Jarris. "Spring has only just touched the Lands, and we've a lot of trading ahead of us."

"Were you stopped by the guard on Zirrus, Da?" asked Shaeli.

"No. Why should we be?" Jarris looked puzzled. His face grew grim as Shaeli told him of the inn of Borsal, and how Pizar had told her there would be random searches of Traders throughout the year. "That's ridiculous," he said. "No matter how we might disagree with the queen, it would not be right to *knowingly* aid the rebels."

"That's just what I told Pizar," said Shaeli. "Traders are not disloyal to Great Court."

"There may come a time when traders may need to make a choice, Jarris," said Flin.

"What do you mean?" Jarris asked, turning to look closely at the thin man.

"You know how this unrest grows," said Flin, "and how the queen grips ever tighter on the purse-strings of Zirrus. This flows outward, to all Lands. I hear Romynn is sending a delegation of ambassadors to Great Court to try and reason with Queen Virrisian, yet I fear they'll get little satisfaction. It may be that the Romynnii will take umbrage."

"Romynn would never challenge Zirrus, Flin," said Jeth. "It is not strong enough."

"Not alone, no. But the Ashkannii are no happier with the situation. Queen Elenes is as diplomatic as always, but Sir

Vulcan informs me she is keeping a careful eye on things. And the Starisles, too, are most displeased with the plight of Zirrus' people."

"Even where I come from, it has been noticed," said Qiren. "And *that* was two Winterings ago. The gods only know what they think of it now."

"So, Jarris, there may come a time when you have to decide: Great Court, or the People."

"I hope not, Flin," Jarris answered. "I hope I never have to choose."

* * *

Fezzik, laying in the bushes on the banks of the Clahren, had made his choice long before, and the needs of the People had far outweighed the needs of Great Court. He, Verlie, Pemba and the children had Wintered with a few others at an isolated farmhouse, and even before first thaw, his band of rebels had restarted their battle against the queen's guard. Two isolated outposts had been attacked, and although both had been successful, the second had seen him lose three good men, and six others had been injured. Two of them – one a big woman whose family had all been killed when soldiers had fired their farm without warning in the sunrise hours just before first snow; the other an old man whose sons had been held in the garrison for inciting others – were with Verlie, Pemba and the children in a narrow valley to the south, still recovering from their wounds. The sons of the old man had been freed, and were now lying in the scrubby bushes beside Fezzik.

They were many leagues above Boccra, more than halfway to the River Zerrin, and if their information was correct, there would be wagons returning to the nearby garrison with taxes and supplies sometime during the afternoon. He had no reason to doubt it would be so; the soldier, Bithani, who had provided him with the information about the garrison above Boccra, had given him many more useful pieces of knowledge already this year. She had also been, slowly, carefully, seeking others in the guard who thought as she did, and though she'd only trusted two enough to reveal her relationship with the rebels, those two had proved very reliable.

There were men scattered along both sides of the road and women with bows in the trees. All had scarves or bits of material wound about their faces, as did those who waited with the boats tied to the base of the steep bank, and sweat had soaked into Fezzik's. He passed a hand across his eyes and blinked at the brow of the hill to the south. A rider appeared, then another, then a score more. He whistled softly and wiped the sweat again from his eyes, his body tensing, sensing the tension from the bodies lying around him. It mattered not how many times he did this, it was always the same; the tension, the dread that welled up within him, the fear, but always the tight knot of anger surging forth to fuel him; Pelazarus seemed to stand at his shoulder in such moments. The faces of Brinn, Pim and his Zeffy appeared when he closed his eyes and sent a silent prayer to the god Ettorr for strength, and when he opened his eyes again three wagons had followed the soldiers over the hill, another clump of soldiers were just topping the brow behind them. He whistled again, and then he waited, growing more tense, more wary until the first soldiers reached him. He let them pass, the first wagon, the second passed too, and as the wheels of the third went by, he whistled again, three short sharp bursts, and with a cry he leapt to his feet and drew his sword.

The women in the trees had already downed half a dozen soldiers by the time his feet hit the road, and the clangs of metal meeting metal had begun. Fezzik's attention was taken dealing with the rearguard for a while, and as he fought one particularly hairy, ugly soldier, a loud boom sounded behind him, and there was a flash of white light. The ugly soldier grinned then, and Fezzik only had time to wonder at it before the man rushed him. He had just thrust his sword between the ribs of the soldier when a second boom erupted and there was another flash of light, followed by screaming. As he turned, one of the trees holding the women with bows was falling, split in two. One half thudded onto the road carrying the screaming women; the other half went rolling down the bank into the river. His people, those that could, stopped to look at the smoking tree fall, others kept fighting, but Fezzik's eyes were already searching the wagons.

The Warlock stood on the second wagon, atop the boxes and crates, his staff held out before him. His long white plait and pale skin gave away his Wokkii origins, and his intentions were just as clear. Before Fezzik could move, the Warlock loosed another bolt of light, and two of the rebels bore the brunt of it, both bursting into flames, screaming as they were engulfed. The bushes behind them started burning too and as Fezzik leapt forward, he saw that arrows aimed at the Warlock turned away from him in mid-flight, arcing impossibly around his body. Fezzik groaned and then whistled one sharply piercing note. They would have to retreat. The soldiers had dropped before them, many lay wounded or dead in the dust, but they could not fight this.

The Warlock turned his way when he whistled. Their eyes met and Fezzik dived instinctively, rolling sideways as he hit the dirt. The bolt hit the ground beside him and he kept rolling. Some of the rebels were running, others fought the soldiers still, but two of his people were felled as they ran towards the trees where the archers were trying to scramble down. The women in the shattered tree were emerging, those that could; two were still screaming, trapped beneath the branches as the Warlock aimed his staff at another tree. He lazily fired a bolt and then turned back to Fezzik, who was up and running again. The Warlock raised his staff, his face impassive, and there was a flash of rose-pink and his staff flew from his hands and broke in two as it hit the road.

Fezzik skidded to a halt, eyes scanning the dust and the smoke. From the trees on the other side of the road came a woman sitting astride an enormous horse, the biggest horse that Fezzik had ever seen. She wore a grey robe, her hair hidden beneath the hood, but her dark eyes stood out clearly from the shadow that fell over her face. She held a slim twisted staff out before her, a huge pink stone resting at its tip, and she pointed the staff at the Warlock on the wagon.

"Since when do Warlocks use their power against the People?" she said, the words spoken not loudly, yet with a commanding resonance. "You dishonour your calling and do not deserve the staff of your office."

"You have no part in this," the Warlock shouted, his face no longer impassive but outrage-red. "You cannot take it upon yourself to break my staff."

The woman shrugged calmly. "You may take it up with those on the Warlock Island if you wish. If you give me your name I would be happy to mention it for you when I next return there." Her horse, as if unbidden, moved two steps forward. The Warlock on the wagon did not speak. "No?" she said, tilting her head and giving it a shake. "Then for now I suggest you take your rabble and leave. You may have the first wagon but leave the rest. The people have more need of it than the queen. And you may tell her I said so, when next you see *her.*"

The Warlock was momentarily taken aback, but then he snorted and leapt down from the wagon. "Load the dead and wounded and follow me," he said, and he picked up his broken staff, mounted the nearest horse, and rode north without looking back.

The fighting had died away with the appearance of the woman, soldiers and rebels standing sword to sword, watching the brief exchange and the retreating Warlock. The soldiers loaded their dead and wounded onto the first wagon, and drove after him, eyes on the unmoving woman on the huge horse. The rebels watched them go, then began to tend to their own wounded.

Fezzik walked over to the horse. His head did not reach its shoulder, and he looked up. The woman was fine-boned, striking, and he would not have been able to say whether she was thirty or fifty. She had Irikai blood in her too, he could see that now in the earthy colour of her skin, and she was obviously one of the few female Warlocks in the World.

"I thank you. We would have all been dead if not for you," he said, looking to where the others were pulling a woman's body out from the branches of the fallen tree.

She gave him the same shrug she had given the Warlock, as if it was not to be avoided, like getting wet in the rain. "His actions were a betrayal of all that Warlocks stand for," she said. "Only in times of war can a Warlock use their power against others." She smiled wryly. "And I have heard no rumour of war."

"Yet this is a new low, even for the queen," Fezzik said. "She may start a war yet, my lady."

"You have no reason to call me lady," she said. "I am only Bekerra. And you are right. The queen will be displeased when she hears of this. I will make myself unpopular. Again." There was that fatalistic shrug and then she studied him for a moment. "Where do you go, after this...?" She cocked her head.

"Fezzik," he said.

"Where do you go after this, Fezzik?"

"South, Bekerra, to where my family hide from the guard. The queen seeks us," he said simply, copying her calm shrug.

She nodded, then looked away. "I will ride with you," she said, her eyes on where the wounded were being tended. "It may be that I shall have to avoid Palveron for some time." She sighed. "The world has mysterious ways sometimes," she said.

When the wagons had gone, the wounded and dead lowered down to the boats to float away to safety, Fezzik rode south.

With him were the two sons of the wounded old man, and
Bekerra, the female Warlock and her enormous horse.

* * *

CHAPTER EIGHT

The next Moons passed with Shaeli practising for the festival and spending time with her family. Captain Mahi's ship arrived again, and before he left Shaeli gave him the long-awaited tour of the Trader and Jarris took him on a flight above Pa'laidiz and the surrounding islands, to his great enjoyment.

In between Purple Leaf's trading trips around the islands, Shanna and Neesha spent a lot of time at Flin's house on the harbour; from their first visit, they were enchanted by the house and the view. Purple Leaf would trade on the Starisles until after the festival, and then they had planned to trade down Zirrus' coast and go across to Ashkanna for the remainder of the year, yet in light of the news they would be taking extra people to Cave, they were undecided as to what to do. There was room on the Trader for them all, though they would be very crowded, even more so than the previous year now that the twins were back on board. Blue Dolphin, who spent most of its time taking salt backward and forwards from the Starisles to Zirrus, had some room and would take people if needed, but that would not be until the end of the year. After throwing the dilemma to and fro, they finally decided they would wait until after the festival and then decide.

Shaeli saw this dilemma only on the periphery of her consciousness. Her focus was on the task ahead: the skylights. This year the piece was much more intricate, the composer and choreographer much less encouraging and much more demanding than the flamboyant Moneq. A very short, very dark-haired man, Crisiv had created a piece of music spectacular in its theme, but exhausting to its players. Shaeli had been given the task of creating dozens of flowers in blossoming trees with very strict timing, as well as many other tasks throughout the piece. She was so worried, despite Flin and Qiren giving her endless support, that she began to dream of trees with skylights as blossoms.

As the day of the festival neared she began to wake early in the mornings, and so that she would not disturb Kirrit, she would go out onto the veranda and watch the sun come up over the ocean. Ebony would usually join her and they would sit munching fruit while Shaeli watched the sun cast brilliant colour into the sky.

One morning, ten days before the festival, she woke earlier than usual. She was groggy, disconnected. She rubbed at her eyes, for she could not see very well. She half-dressed in a daze, pulling a thin shirt on over her nightgown. Ebony woke, and watched.

Shaeli ignored the creature, as she ignored the figure sleeping in the other bed, she merely admired the red hair that was spread on the pillow as she walked out on to the balcony. Her head pounded. There was something she had to do. What was it? Oh, yes. Take the boat out. Out onto the sea.

She took no notice of the little jevvi following her as she went down the stairs to the garden, nor of the black thunderheads filling the sky to the west. She walked across the dew-wet grass with billowing black-hearted clouds behind her. She walked with bare feet and a muddled mind.

Something pounded behind her eyes, and she knew if she just got in the boat and went out to sea that the pounding would go away. There would be quiet. No dreams. No yelling. No pain.

She walked down the wharf as thunder rumbled at her back, yet she did not hear it. She thought she heard someone calling her, Williver, maybe, but it was too far away and she was too tired.

She saw the boat, foggy and indistinct within the mist wrapped around her sight, and she stepped down into it and untied the ropes. She did not notice the jevvi jump in behind her, nor did she feel the tug on her sleeve or see the eyes which were black pools of puzzlement.

The oars were in the rowlocks, and she put them in the water and pulled at them for a while, but the effort tired her, and she let them drop. She did not notice when first one, then the other, fell into the water. She lay in the bottom of the boat, her head on her hands, and when the rain began, she did not feel it. It was merely the pounding in her head.

* * *

She was dreaming.

She was almost five and the black wind was coming for her.

She was in bed, in her room on Purple Leaf. She felt tiny. Something had woken her. She listened. She listened and the black wind roared in her ears.

She blinked and the growl of a jenka sounded somewhere. Other sounds, echoes of past voices, whispered in her ears.

Then Williver was there, and she was big again, and Williver was yelling, but she couldn't make out what he was saying. All she could hear was the roaring in her ears. The black wind pulled at her, but Williver held her tightly, pulling her away from the wind...

Then she lay at the edge of the dreamworld. She was wet and cold and she was jumping and spinning and rolling around. Wind screamed at her. Fat drops of water pounded her skin. It was dark and the air cracked around her. Something was pulling at her hair.

Then, later, she didn't know how long, she was hot, and the light beyond her eyelids was white. Her head still pounded and the world still moved, and though she thought she was already dreaming, she longed to sleep. It was so hot.

Then she grew cold and wet again and the white light was gone and the pounding made her shiver. There was rain pricking her skin and she was swirling around and her head was throbbing. She heard Williver again, speaking in a strange tongue. She thought she heard Ishaan too, far away, but his words didn't make sense either. She tried to call out to them, but she could barely speak.

"I'm here," she whispered through cracked lips. "I'm over here."

Later still, she felt bumps. Little thumps and bumps, and then a large thud. Some kind of awareness shone through the fog in her mind, and she heard a child's voice.

"Bring her in," it said. "The black wind seeks her." There was a murmur and the sigh of soft winds. Then the child's voice came again. "This will be the one who seeks the way in."

Then there was nothing. Nothing but the call of the black wind.

* * *

At first they did not miss her, and when they did, they did not worry.

A powerful storm had swept through in the sunrise hours and the world was bright and clean behind it. They thought she and Ebony had gone for a walk. Then Kirrit found Shaeli's amulet under her pillow, and they began to wonder. When Flin noticed the small boat was missing, they began to worry. They sent word to Purple Leaf, to see if she was there. Jarris came back, for she wasn't, and they worried more.

Qiren showed Flin a footprint at the bottom of the stairs. Just one, showing a small bare foot. Beside it, the print of a jevvi. Both were sheltered from the rain by an overhang. There were no other footprints. Which meant she must have left *before* the storm.

When they found a scrap of material stuck on a nail on the wharf where the boat had been tied, they began to search the harbour and waters surrounding Pa'laidiz. By mid-morning they were frantic.

Scores of boats searched the sea around the islands. Neighbouring islands were searched too, and when nothing was found, nothing but a single oar floating in the bay, the search went wider. During the afternoon, the sky darkened, and another storm swept across the islands. By the time the sun went down, they had found nothing, not on any island anywhere near Pa'laidiz. As darkness fell, the search was abandoned. Rain still drummed the roofs. The searchers left with the promise they would resume at first light.

Flin watched them go, and knew what they would say amongst themselves. He had heard them muttering about the fierce storm that had torn through in the sunrise hours; a black storm, they called it up here, because of the way it drained light from the World. The wind which had accompanied it was a swirling, mighty beast, known to sweep everything, even small animals, away with it. Hopes of finding her now were slim. He did not know how he would answer Mareesha's questions, but when she asked, he did his best. He tried to speak calmly and give her hope. She had drifted further than they'd thought, he said. She was probably on some tiny uninhabited island, and they would find her tomorrow. Yes, certainly, they would find her tomorrow. And all the while his mind was racing, searching for the answer. *Where was she?*

Why she had taken the boat was a question asked so many times it had no meaning anymore. There was no doubt that she *had* taken the boat, but as to why – why she had not taken her amulet, or shoes; why, when she *must* have seen the impending storm, did she go at all? – to these questions there *were* no answers. And to Flin it mattered little. Only one thing mattered: finding her.

As the long night wore on, he offered his sleepless guests sustenance, yet he took none himself. He watched the drawn faces around him, heard their murmurs and endless questions. He willed the sun to come up so they could go and find her.

By nightfall the next day, Mareesha was inconsolable and Flin had no words left to comfort her. Kirrit and the twins had kept vigil on the water's edge throughout the long second day. They left it only when the first star shone. Eenis brought them in, dried their eyes, and gave them hot tezz. She would not give up hope, she said, for miracles happen every day, if you look for them.

Jarris heard her say it and gave her a crooked, wobbling smile, then he left the room, his hand over his eyes.

* * *

Flin was up on the morning of the third day long before the sun. He went outside and stared at the horizon until the silver of the early rays were reflected off the clouds to the east. He knew the people of Pa'laidiz would search one more day before they gave up, and he closed his eyes and prayed to the gods that today they would find her.

The search had been widened, encompassing all the islands almost to the edge of the World. That she could have been swept out to the Endless Sea was almost impossible; so many reefs and islands lay between Pa'laidiz and the last tiny islands to the east. That the small boat had even been swept out of Pa'laidiz harbour was unlikely. Flin knew it was much more likely her boat had been swamped and sunk in the black storm the morning she'd left. He knew what the townsfolk would say: Shaeli and her little jevvi lay with their boat at the bottom of the harbour. Yet he could not give up. Not yet.

He heard a noise behind him, and he turned and saw Tarkoda coming across the grass.

Koda, like his father, Jeth, and Andos, had been out with the boats for two days and had paced the house through the interminable night hours, his face grey. They tried to smile at each other, but it didn't work, and so they stood silently together, staring at the place where the sun would rise. When at last the edge of the sun leapt over the rim of the ocean, the clouds began to dissipate, burning off even as the rays touched them.

It would be another perfect day.

Flin watched a flock of birds take off between the eastern islands. Watched them whirl and reel in the sky. Saw one had

127

stayed on the ocean's surface. Saw it was not a bird, but a boat, growing bigger as he watched it. Slowly, for there was little wind, it approached the harbour and turned in. Flin watched it cut a silver V down the harbour. He saw two people, one in the rear, one in the bow; the one in the bow a hunched, huddled figure.

Strangely, the small boat headed straight for them, and almost before he had begun to hope, Flin recognised the huddled figure and ran down to the wharf. Tarkoda was a pace behind him, for he too had recognised the figure in the boat.

She could not even manage to throw them a rope as her companion brought the boat in to the wharf. The man with her, his eyes dark, his hair tied at the nape, threw a rope across to them. Flin caught it and tied it, and then Koda had her out of the boat. She was dressed in boy's trousers, cuffs ragged, and an old shirt, far too big. Ebony was with her, and Tarkoda was hugging her, and Flin was beside him, his arm about her, his eyes scanning her sunburnt face.

They scarcely had time to thank the man who had delivered her to them before he was away again, sailing back into the sun. They did not mind. Shaeli was returned.

* * *

For the first few days they did not worry that she was vague and distracted. She was so tearfully happy to be back with them all, and they thankful that she was, that they did not at first comment on her lack of energy, putting it down to her ordeal, yet she regained none of her past vigour. She was confused, easily agitated, and found even the simplest task difficult. When they *did* discuss it, it was hard to put a name to it. Jarris saw a lack of curiosity; Eenis a lack of animation. Mareesha found her listless, and gave her tonics and soups. Everyone could see she was tired. She slept from sunset to mid-morning, and was often found napping throughout the day, sometimes falling asleep while someone was talking to her.

Flin spent every moment he could with her. She was so obviously unable to take part in the skylights, that he, Qiren, and the other throwers were furiously rehearsing a changed version of their performance. He agonised every time he had to leave the house and raced back to it at the first opportunity.

Kirrit and the twins tried distracting her with stories and little treats, but she would just smile wanly at them. She rarely spoke.

Tarkoda and Andos took her for drives in Flin's smallest carriage, brought her gifts and flowers. She would thank them and then go and lie down, turning her face to the wall.

She "forgot" to wear her amulet; her hands lay idle in her lap. She stared endlessly at nothing, her eyes dark and unfocussed.

Ebony went everywhere she did, her anxious eyes rarely leaving her mistress' face, and Shaeli would stroke the creature absently, but pay little attention to her.

Many times they wished Ebony could talk, for though they gently asked Shaeli what had happened, she could not tell them. Her eyes would fill with tears and terror, and she would hug herself, her lip trembling, so they stopped asking and could merely hope she would return to herself.

* * *

When the day of the Summer Festival came, ten days after her ordeal began, Shaeli did not want to go. Mareesha made the others go into town, for she could not see the point in them all missing the day, and she and Flin stayed with Shaeli at the blue house. Shaeli did not want to go into Pa'laidiz to watch the skylights that evening either, so they all stayed at Flin's with her.

After Flin and Qiren left, they went onto the upper balcony, and everyone thought Shaeli would become excited by the skylights. She sat quietly with a rug about her knees, though it was not cold, and as the first strains of music drifted across the water, faint but audible, they looked at her expectantly, but she just sat staring across the harbour as the skylights began, her face expressionless. Mareesha and Jarris looked at each other, anguish in their eyes.

Shanna and Neesha sat on either side of Shaeli, pointing out each new skylight as it blossomed, encouraging her to watch, yet they could see that she struggled to smile. When the skylights ended, they heard the applause from the town, and Shaeli stood and said she wanted to go to bed.

"Flin will be disappointed if you don't wait for him, Shaeli," Mareesha said gently.

Shaeli nodded and turned to sit again, but footsteps on the stairs stopped her.

"Surely they're not back already," said Illen, looking at the stairs.

Yet it was not Flin and Qiren. It was an elf, tall and fair, his eyes blue as summer skies; an elf unknown to them all. All except Shaeli. The rug she was holding dropped to the floor. Her eyes grew huge, and she took a step forward.

"Am I dreaming?" she said.

"No, little one," said the elf, a half-smile on his face. "I am here."

She stared at him. Then she gasped. Her face grew pale. Fear darkened her eyes. They went from the elf to her mother.

"Mam," she said, her voice a mere tremble. "The girls…" Then her voice rose, high and shrill. "Oh, the gods, the black wind *knows*." A hand went to her mouth and she turned back to the elf at the head of the stairs. "Williver, you…" she began.

And then for the second time in her life, Shaeli fainted.

* * *

When she woke, she did not open her eyes. She knew there were others in the room, for she heard them whispering. She lay still. Remembering.

It had been a dream. A strange one; like a Williver dream almost, but unlike it at all. Someone, or something, had been in her head. Something black. Shaeli had hated the feel of it. It was like a wind, sweeping her mind away...

The black wind blew her mind before it, back into the past, and she was laying in her bed on Purple Leaf, and it was dark. She heard voices through the wall. Mam's and Da's and someone else's, a woman's. She didn't know whose, but the black wind did. She felt it grasp at the voice.

"You *must* take her," the stranger's voice was saying. "Her life depends on it. *Please.*"

"But to deceive the Court? The whole realm?" That was Da. "Surely there is another way?"

"There *is* no other way. I cannot protect her. You *can*. No one can know Tenelon's heir lives until she is old enough to take the throne. Virrisian will have no recourse once my child is of age. It *will* rule." The voice began to sound more desperate. "Please. Give me your word you will protect her." The voice broke, and the next words were said around sobs. "She is all I have to remember my husband. She *must* be held safe."

Mam spoke. "Jarris, *please.* You know how vital this is. We have no choice."

"No, Mareesha, you're right. We have no choice. I see that now. Please," Da said, "please get up. We will do as you ask, and we will return the child to you when she is grown. I give you my solemn promise."

There was more weeping, and words that Shaeli could not make out. Then she heard her father's voice again.

"Worry not, my lady," he said. "I swear she will be loved as our own."

Then the black thing swept her mind away...

And she was standing beside a creek, pulling the wand from the mud. She saw her hands, small hands, holding her wand, still encrusted with mud from the bank where she'd found it. She could see bits of the braiding and one of the gems embedded to its surface. She could even hear the jenka growling in the bushes above...

Again her mind was swept before the black wind. Scenes slipped by like pages turning in a book. Almarnoch with the wand in his hands, the twins behind him in their basket on Purple Leaf; Ellirra in her little wagon, the box on her lap, the dragon-scale bangle glittering in the candle light, and an echo of her voice, *It sounds a nice place, Iden. Trilby.* Then came the twins in the barrel in the creek in Orrellis, meeting Blenny and Spotjaw, the images going faster and faster; the little tree blossoming into fire beside the meeting hall on the Long Lea; the rock hovering above Taffka's head; her first performance at the Autumn's Eve Hunt. The black wind blew harder, it began to make her head ache, and the pain grew so quickly that she cried out from it. It throbbed and spun in her head, bursting against her temples, searing the backs of her eyes.

The black wind told her she could make the pain stop. Make it go away. All she had to do was find a boat and take it onto the sea. And jump into the cold, dark water.

Shaeli saw the sense in that. She saw the cool water close over her head; the dark water taking the searing, throbbing pain away, and she knew that was what she had to do. At the edge of the dream she felt a space, a black void of nothing that promised peace.

But then Williver was there. And though the black wind tore at his hair and she could not hear his voice, she saw his hand held out to her and she reached out to him. He grasped at her fingers, pulled her into his arms and held her tight as the black wind raged around them, seeking to drag them both away. Shaeli sensed the huge void somewhere behind them, and she knew if it were not for Williver's arms around her that she would be sucked into that void and never return.

Williver drew them away from the edge slowly, she did not know how. The pain lessened in her mind, and then they were free. Somehow Williver brought her back to herself. Just before she woke she felt the black wind roar in anger.

Yet when she did wake, she was not entirely *there*. Some part of herself had been caught in the limbo at the edge of the void and she had remembered nothing of the dream. Nothing but the need to find a boat.

Now, as she lay with her eyes closed, she remembered snatches of that voyage, too. The storm raging around her, Ebony on her shoulder, clinging to her hair to keep from being taken by the wind. The hot sun beating her mercilessly as she drifted. Rain slashing her face again. Williver's voice. Ishaan's too she'd thought; a far-off echo. Darkness and bumps and landing on an island. The memory of the island was hazy and incomplete, but there had been... *someone* who had looked after her. A man had brought her back to Pa'laidiz, and she must have been able to tell them where she'd come from, though she didn't remember it. She remembered the man's eyes had been dark and filled with concern. She remembered too that the other one had been a child...

As these memories returned, Shaeli began to focus on one thing. How this had happened, or why, was unimportant; one tiny piece of it was all that mattered.

Snatches of a conversation heard when she was almost five, in the middle of the night, had meant nothing. Yet now, the implications of the words she had heard so long ago – words which lay buried in the recesses of her mind – these words now made sense. And she knew also that now they were in danger. Now the black wind knew, too. She opened her eyes.

* * *

133

CHAPTER NINE

Her mother was sitting beside her. Tarkoda, her father and Williver stood talking in the doorway. She was in her room. Hers and Kirrit's. They must have carried her in. The others were still out on the balcony; Kirrit with her arms about the twins, the three of them clustered at the window peering in at her.

"Shaeli," Mareesha said, as she opened her eyes.

"I'm here, Mam," she said, sitting up. "I'm fine now," she squeezed her mother's hand. "I'm back. Properly this time."

Yet Mareesha was not convinced. She thought Shaeli looked strangely at her, and the words she had spoken before she'd fainted echoed in Mareesha's mind, but then Shaeli's eyes moved past her to the elf who had caused her faint. Shaeli leapt off the bed and into Williver's waiting arms.

"Williver," she said, her voice muffled against his chest. "At last I can see you. Truly, here in the World."

"Yes, little one," he smiled. "Yet I would not have asked for it to be under these circumstances."

She shook her head. "Me either," she said, and then she hugged him anew. "Thank you, Williver. You saved me. I don't know what would have happened if you hadn't come."

"I heard you cry out, and for a while I did not think either of us would be able to escape. I *had* to come and see if you were alright. I could not find you in the dream world."

"I couldn't remember any of it. I could hardly remember *myself*. Not until I saw you. That's what made me faint. The remembering." She squeezed him again, tears filling her eyes. "But I'm so happy to see you."

The others watched this exchange, puzzled. Only Illen and Kirrit had any idea who the tall elf was. There had been little time for explanations as they'd lifted Shaeli from the floor and

134

taken her into the room. All they knew was that the elf was a friend of Shaeli's, and that Shaeli was herself again.

They heard voices and Flin and Qiren came up the steps. Qiren took one look at the elf beside Shaeli and he rushed through the door and embraced him. Now it was Shaeli's turn to be puzzled.

"You *know* each other?" she asked.

Qiren looked almost sheepish, but it was Williver who spoke.

"Yes, Shaeli. Qiren and I are cousins."

"*Cousins?*" She frowned. "But why didn't you tell me?"

"We thought it best Qiren should train you without you knowing I sent him."

"*You* sent him? To train me?" Shaeli spoke slowly as if she was having trouble comprehending his words.

"Yes. I was unsure how strongly the gift lay in you," said Williver gently, "though I suspected its depths, and I knew of no one else who I could trust to guide you. Qiren, in turn, trusts Flin. Qiren was to have come to see me before he returned to his own lands, to tell me of your progress."

"Illen, did you know of this?" Shaeli asked.

Illen nodded. "Yes, I knew," she said.

"And you, Flin?" Shaeli said, turning to him. "You knew too?"

"A little of it," Flin admitted. "Qiren convinced me to take you as apprentice. I knew he had been sent by one of his own people; someone who wanted your gift trained properly, but that's all." He looked abashed. "I must admit I was not at all enthusiastic about the idea. Qiren had to bribe me with promised performances." He smiled at her. "But we had not met then."

Shaeli did not return the smile. She lifted her chin. Her hands trembled. "So you've been lying to me, the three of you, all along?" she said. She looked at them each in turn, yet she ignored their startled protests and rounded on Williver. "Lying to me because *you* asked them to. Why would you do that? I *trusted* you, all of you." Her lip trembled but she would not cry. She had done enough crying lately. "I thought you were my friends," she cried.

Illen moved forward. "Of course we are your friends," she began, but Shaeli shook off her hand.

"I *trusted* you," she said again, her voice still high with accusation. "And all along you were keeping secrets from me."

"It wasn't like that," Williver said, taking her by the shoulders and looking into her eyes. Shaeli saw there was no guile there, only deep caring, as always, but the frown remained. "I asked Qiren to work with Flin because I thought you should be trained properly, that's all," Williver continued. "And they did not mention it because I asked them not to. I did not want you to begin apprenticeship with questions or expectations. I wanted you to learn with joy, with the natural progression of magic. I sought only to protect you. None of us would harm you, you *know* that."

Shaeli looked at him, and sighed. He was right. "Yes, I know," she said. "But that *still* doesn't explain why you didn't tell me you knew Qiren," she said. "I even asked you, that time you visited me at the Autumn's Eve Hunt, and you *lied* to me."

"Not exactly lied, Shaeli. I was merely evasive," Williver answered. "And I knew then that you were in safe hands and you would be trained properly. There was no need for you to wonder or put yourself under pressure. You had only to learn freely, and you did."

Shaeli believed him. She had always trusted Williver, and he had almost lost himself trying to save her from the black wind. Her anger ebbed away.

"We did not want you to worry," said Qiren gently. "And I would not have wanted it any other way. From our first meeting I knew Williver was right, the gift lay strongly in you. It was a joy to teach you."

"And to be with you," Illen added. "You know how much we all care for you."

"And I might not have liked the idea in the beginning," said Flin. "But, Shaeli, you know it wasn't long before I *wanted* to."

"I know," she said, smiling a little then. "It was when I showed you the vistrella."

"No, Shaeli," he said, relishing the spark that had returned to her eyes. "It was even before that."

"Alright then," she said. "But no more secrets. I don't like not knowing what's going on."

"Then I fear you may not like what else I have to tell you," Williver said, glancing at Qiren.

Shaeli followed the glance and looked at them. "What else is there?" she asked, suspicion colouring her eyes dark grey.

"There is much more to tell you, my friend." Williver looked at the faces circling this exchange. They had listened to the conversation in silence, and although Kirrit was the least confused, there was surprise and puzzlement on every face. "There are a lot of explanations to be had, all around, I think."

"I agree," said Jarris. "I want to know what's going on, and I'm sure the rest of you feel the same."

They all nodded; Eenis and Jeth, Tarkoda, Andos, Neesha, Kirrit and Shanna. Mareesha's face was pale, but she nodded with the rest.

"Then I suggest we go and make ourselves comfortable," said Flin. "This sounds like it could take a while."

* * *

Shaeli felt a growing sense of urgency as the night wore on. She felt as if she had woken from a very long sleep, as if she had been living in a world separate from this one, and her senses tingled.

They all gathered in Flin's sitting room; all except Jeth and Eenis, who left to go back to Purple Leaf and the Zoi, but the others would stay under Flin's roof again.

137

Proper introductions were made, even Illen had not met Williver in person, and Shaeli kept looking at the tall elf beside her, unable to believe this was not another dream.

Mareesha and Jarris sat opposite Shaeli and Williver as they spoke, Illen and Qiren nearby. Tarkoda, Andos, Kirrit and the twins sat slightly outside the circle, and Flin stood by the empty fireplace, his eyes rarely leaving Shaeli's face.

Shaeli, Ebony on her knee, had explained about Williver and their shared dreams, much as she had explained to Kirrit at the beginning of their Cave year. Koda and Andos had looked abashed when she'd said it was their teasing which had initially made her not speak of it, but relieved when she said Almarnoch had later forbidden her to do so. Everyone was amazed, but it was Shaeli who asked the question she had never asked before.

"How do we, Williver? I haven't asked before, though I've wondered a hundred times. How *can* we meet in dreams?"

"It is an uncommon ability, to travel in dreams," he said, with no trace of self-importance. "It's a talent given by the gods, much like the gift of magic in other forms, though much rarer. The gift is given in varying degrees, mostly as the ability to travel within one's *own* dreams, but sometimes, as it is with me, there is the ability to connect with the dreams, and minds, of others. I first met you in a dream when you were just a babe, your thoughts still without form. I don't know why we were drawn together, but you seemed to enjoy our visits, and so I continued them, though infrequently."

"Is that because it's tiring, Williver? Like throwing skylights?"

"Partly," he said, slowly. "But mostly because in our lands, as it is in yours, this is a gift that is not encouraged."

"Why not?" Shaeli asked.

"Because in the wrong hands, it is a dangerous gift," he said soberly. "The ability to see into the mind of another also brings with it the ability to *guide* that mind. To guide it. Or strip it bare."

Shaeli's face paled. "That's what happened to me," she gasped. "Something bad was in my mind. Something black."

Williver nodded. "I felt the blackness too. I know of no other who has this ability in elven lands, and there has been no one with the gift in your World for many years. Yet it is strong, the gift of this other."

"But what did it want with Shaeli?" asked Jarris. "Why should this person want to see into her mind?"

"I did not see what it sought," said Williver. "I found Shaeli only after she'd cried out, and there was only a blackness, as she said, like a wind." He looked at Jarris solemnly. "It was telling her to take a boat far out onto the water and jump into the sea."

Mareesha gasped. Shanna gave a small cry and then covered her mouth.

"But I didn't remember that part," Shaeli said, her eyes far away. "About jumping into the sea. I only remembered about taking the boat."

Her mother broke her reverie. "It is fortunate Williver heard you and was able to bring you back, Shaeli. Just as you brought me back."

"Brought *you* back, Mam?" Shaeli asked, frowning. "From where?"

"From the blackness. From the wind." Mareesha spoke quietly, but everyone could hear the tremble in her voice. "The time you kicked me, Shaeli, I was affected in just the same way that you describe, yet it was pain that brought *me* back." She smiled sadly and met Shaeli's eye. "Do you remember?"

"Of course, Mam." Shaeli looked her mother straight in the eye. "It was just after the twins were born."

Understanding passed between them, and suddenly Mareesha knew what the strange look on Shaeli's face had been. Some of the sense of urgency that had been growing in

Shaeli as the night passed dissipated. Her mother knew, and that was alright. The burden was no longer hers alone.

"We are not the only ones who have felt the touch of the black wind, either," Mareesha said. "I believe others have had their minds invaded, with much more terrible results." And she briefly told of the fisherman on Zirrus' west coast, and of Gremon, both driven to madness after seeing the black ship that flew so high in the sky.

Williver had heard it rumoured of in the elven world too, and while no one could see a connection between the incidents, they concluded that all these things must be linked. It was a frightening conclusion.

"But do you remember *anything* of what it sought, Shaeli?" asked Flin. "Can you remember what you saw *before* Williver came?"

"Well, lots of things, like pieces of my memory flicking past." She looked at them, all turned to her, waiting for some clue. She tried to steer them as far away from the twins as she could. "I remember seeing my wand," she said, grasping at that, unable to say anything else until she'd had time to speak to her parents privately. "I was small, and I'd just found it near Lake Marnis."

"I feared it was so," Williver said.

Shaeli was completely taken by surprise. "*What?*" she said.

"The *wand* again," said Kirrit quietly, but no one looked at her; they were all staring at Williver.

Williver was looking at Qiren.

"'Tis as we thought, then," said Qiren.

Williver nodded.

"What do you mean, Williver, 'you feared it was so'?" said Shaeli. "Why should anyone be interested in a broken old wand? It has no power, Almarnoch said so."

"It has no power, *now*, little one. It does not mean its power cannot be regained. And many are those who would like to possess it." He took her hand in his, and looked earnestly at her. "The wand held by your High Warlock was once the most powerful wand ever to be seen in the World."

"The most..." Shaeli started, amazement unbalancing her tongue. She tried another tack. "Are you *sure*, Williver?" she asked, but she knew by his face that he was. She looked at Qiren. "And you knew of this, too? You and Illen? Why did you never ask me about it?"

"We knew the wand was safely held at your Cave. It was decided it was best left there, lost as far as the World was concerned, until the right time came," Qiren said.

"Who decided?" asked Jarris.

"And what's 'the right time'?" added Shaeli.

"There are few who know of this, Jarris," said Williver. "We decided. And the time is almost upon us."

"*What* time? And *why* was it the most powerful? Whose was it? And what did it do?" Shaeli was shaken by this strange news, so unexpected, so... well, so ridiculous. Questions streamed from her, her mouth moving as each question formed itself in her head. Yet she was surprised into silence by the answer.

"Can you not guess, little one?" said Williver, softly. "The task I gave you to find Shahlita's bangles was so they would be reunited. Reunited with the wand of Shahlita. The wand of Dragon Light." The murmurs of puzzlement were silenced as he continued. "Little is known of it in your World. A hundred Winterings have passed since the last dragon was seen, and there are none of your kind who remember them. All that is known in your Lands is that the dragons were banished by the sorcery of a Warlock, the reasons of which are subject to hearsay and rumour. A fear of the dragons was created amongst your People, and so when they left, there was only relief, and few questions were asked about their passing. In our Lands, it was a very different story.

"From time immemorial the lives of elves and dragons have been intertwined," Williver continued. "Though dragons

"Long did he bide his time. Many Winters after he had come, he acted. In the midnight hours, just before first snow, when the dragons were all gathered in their cave, he struck. He stole Shahlita's wand, a horse, and disappeared into the mountains.

"Shahlita woke to find her wand gone, Kriv missing, and they began to search for him. Three days later, she was woken in the sunrise hours by the echo of a dragon's cry; a haunted scream of pain that had invaded her dreams. She took three other wielders, and followed Kriv into the mountains.

"It must have been a mighty battle, but little is known of it. Neither the three wielders, nor Shahlita ever returned, nor were their bodies ever found." Williver shook his head and then went on. "Yet she must have defeated Kriv, for he was never seen again either, but he had done great mischief before they stopped him. The bodies of dragons lay scattered in and around the cave. Two crazed dragons wreaked havoc in Four Lands until they, too, disappeared a few Winterings later. It was these two rogues who helped create fear among your people." Williver drew a deep breath. "Of the others, there was no sign. No bodies, nothing in their lair to show where they'd gone. The dragons had vanished, Kriv, and four of our most powerful elves gone with them."

There was silence as the tale was digested. Williver seemed spent by the telling, and passed a hand across his brow.

"Williver," Shaeli said. "Are you sure that my wand is Shahlita's? Really sure?"

"Yes," he said. "I suspected it when you first found it, but now I'm sure. We think that whatever magic was used on the dragons, perhaps the magic can be reversed. Perhaps the dragons could be returned to the World."

"That would be wonderful, Williver," persisted Shaeli. "But how can you know? How can you be so sure my wand is the same one?"

"Because it has been confirmed, Shaeli. It has been confirmed by those who made it *and* the bangles. By the Ammerr."

The word leapt around the room in varying notes of surprise. Andos even laughed. The people of the sea were fantasy, legend.

"The *Ammerr*," breathed Shaeli, her eyes huge. "How, Williver? And why? *When* did they?"

"Why? Because he... they did not believe me, and then they began to worry, and needed it confirmed. As to when and how, it doesn't matter, suffice to say that it *is* Shahlita's wand."

"And now someone else knows of its existence," said Qiren. "It has always been feared that it would fall into the wrong hands, but as so little is known of it in your Lands, we thought it safest where it was, in the hands of the traders. That is now no longer the case. It must be retrieved, and sent to elven Lands for safekeeping."

"I'm not sure I agree, Qiren," said Williver. "I think it is exactly where it was intended to be. But you're right. Someone knows about it." He turned to Jarris. "You must go to the Cave of the Traders, Jarris. To protect yourselves, as well as the wand."

Jarris stared at him for a long time, and then he nodded. "We can leave at first light," he said.

* * *

They packed during the sunrise hours, and in the grey pre-dawn light they drove to the Landing. Jeth and the Zoi were quickly roused and as preparations for lift were being made, Williver drew Shaeli to one side. She smiled sadly at him.

"We're not going to Cave with the others, Williver, are we?"

He shook his head. "No. There is something we must do. I knew you would understand."

"And we can't go there on the Trader?"

"No," he said again. "It would bring them more danger."

"Who will we take with us?"

"Flin, if he will come. Your brother. It is best to keep it a small party."

"Not Qiren?"

"No. I think it best he stay with the Trader." He looked grimly at her. "They may have need of him."

"Oh, Williver, you don't think...?"

"It is best to take no risks, little one. And with luck, we shall not be far behind them."

"May I see if Kirrit will come?"

"If you wish, but we travel light, and quickly."

Shaeli nodded, and was silent for a moment, then she looked at him with an expression he could not read. "There's something else Williver. Something you don't know. Something I need to tell you." And then she began to cry.

* * *

Qiren saw Shaeli talking with Williver on the Landing and the tears on her face, and wrongly guessed it was because her family were to fly to Cave without her. He knew where they were going, and why. He turned and looked down to where Tarkoda and Jeth were just finishing harnessing the birds. A movement in the shadows caught his eye, and he peered across the square, yet he could see nothing. Still, the hairs on his neck had risen and he felt vaguely uncomfortable. Flin stood with Jarris on the fore-deck, and Qiren called to him.

Flin came down the short flight of stairs, and crossed the deck. "What is it?" he asked.

"I'm not sure," Qiren replied. "Maybe nothing. But I think we should leave."

"Jarris says we are ready." Flin squinted at the horizon. It was white with unspilled light, the sun moments away. "The others are below?"

Qiren nodded. He looked over at the Landing. "Williver," he called. "It's time we left."

The elf nodded, and he and Shaeli began to walk across to the Trader. Jeth bounded up the stairs and began to untie the rope beside the landing gate. Jarris stood beside the rope on the fore-deck. Tarkoda was down releasing the rear anchor. They could hear the flutter as the Zoi stretched their wings. Williver stepped onto the Trader's deck. As Shaeli went to follow him across to the Trader, a voice spoke out from below.

"Halt. In the name of the Queen Virrisian, I order you to stop."

Shaeli looked down and could see several of the queen's guard in the square. The colours of Zirrus looked so out of place here on the Starisles that she stopped, surprised. Then she saw the Trader lurch, and knew Koda had let go the last anchor. Her father had slipped the rope he held, and was slowly coiling it, his eyes on the square as it began to fill with grim-faced men and women in scarlet and black until they stood shoulder to shoulder, row upon row.

Shaeli was suddenly very afraid. She was still standing on the Landing with Jeth, who held the only rope that now attached them to the Landing, and that little gap between her and the Trader that she had always been so afraid of began to widen. But Tarkoda was still down the stairs. She could not jump to safety and leave him there alone.

"Hold on to it," she said to Jeth, and she turned to the stairs.

"No, Shaeli," she heard Jeth say, and Williver echoing the same words from the deck.

As she reached the top of the stairs, Tarkoda reached the bottom, but he was grabbed by two of the guard. One spoke again.

"You will not attempt to leave," he shouted. "You will re-tie your ropes and unharness your birds. You are detained in the name of the queen."

"Why?" Jarris yelled from above. "What have we done?"

"You are charged with treason and aiding the rebels. You are to be escorted to Great Court to stand before Queen Virrisian."

Shaeli had no idea what she was going to do until her fingers were drawing a stone from her amulet. She heard thuds from behind, yet she did not turn. She had felt Flin beside her often enough to know it was he. Williver stood behind her right shoulder; she felt him also.

It was the quartz she had drawn, and she held it in trembling fingers. Beside her, Flin had drawn his stone, and Williver held something in his hand also. She felt an instant of surprise when she realised it was a wand.

"Release him," Shaeli said, and, though she did not feel it, there was command in her voice.

"Hold him," yelled the head of the guard.

"I said," commanded Shaeli again. "*Release* him." And she threw two bolts of light from her stone. Bolts from Williver and Flin flew at the guard in the rear.

Shaeli's lights streaked at the two holding Tarkoda, stopping a hands-width from their faces, the red and blue of Shaeli's anger and fear shimmering in their depths. The men recoiled for a moment, but it was all Tarkoda needed. He leapt from their grasp and bounded up the stairs, grabbing Shaeli's arm as he passed and dragging her towards the Trader. She let the two balls explode at the base of the stairs, and the guard was temporarily dazed. It was well that it was so.

Though Jeth still strained at the rope, the gap between Landing and Trader had widened and Shaeli hesitated, but Tarkoda yelled at her to jump, his hand still tightly around her arm, and she did, closing her eyes. She felt the deck come up to meet her and the thuds as Flin, Williver, and Jeth followed them, and then Jeth shut the landing gate and they rose into the air.

Shaeli began to rise, but Koda held her where she was as arrows began to fly through the air above their heads. The balloon puckered with a dozen shafts, yet they made little impression on the material protected by Almarnoch's spells, and most bounced harmlessly away. Within moments the

Trader was over the harbour and the arrows could not reach them. They stood and watched Pa'laidiz and the queen's guard dwindle behind them.

"Well," said Williver, tucking his wand back into his vest. "So it begins."

"But why should Virrisian's guard want us?" Jarris called. "We have not aided the rebels."

"'Tis not about the rebels, Jarris," said Qiren. "It is about the wand. And Shaeli."

"Shaeli? But..." Jarris stopped, looking at Shaeli's pale face. "Then, it is the queen who wants the wand," he said. "The *queen* we are up against." He passed a hand across his brow. "I had not thought..."

"It makes sense though, doesn't it?" said Qiren gently. "Whoever it is with the power to strip minds is in league with the queen."

Mareesha had come up, unseen, behind them. "Then we must be careful," she said.

They turned to look at her. She was touching the small scar on her brow, and her eyes were looking ahead, to where Zirrus lay far across the sea. She did not know she was repeating words spoken by the once-queen Irinesta many Winterings before.

"We must be very careful," Mareesha said.

* * *

CHAPTER TEN

They skipped across the Starisles, stopping at only the smallest islands where they knew there would be no chance of encountering any guard. That there had been such a large contingent on Pa'laidiz was unusual, and they were horrified by the thought that they had been sent specifically for Purple Leaf. They shuddered to think what would have happened if they had delayed lift.

Shaeli and Williver spoke to Flin, Tarkoda and Kirrit as they flew, and when the coast of Zirrus loomed ahead, she knew it was time to tell her parents she would not be going with them. She'd had a private talk with them soon after they'd left Pa'laidiz, had her suspicions confirmed and assured them of her silence. While she could not help looking at her sisters in an entirely new light, at least her fears were shared. Now, she found her father on the fore-deck and stood behind him, wondering what to say.

"Best just be out with it, Mouse," he said without turning.

Shaeli almost cried. He had not called her Mouse in a very long time. "We... we have something to do before we go to Cave, Da," she began.

"I thought something was up," he said, looking over his shoulder. "I suppose it's important?"

"Yes, Da."

"And we're to go to Cave without you?"

"Yes, Da."

Jarris sighed. "Best go tell your Mam, then."

"And, Da..."

"And?"

"Koda's coming with me. And Kirrit."

"Oh, well," he said. "At least you'll have your brother, I'm glad of that, but I don't know what I'll tell Delphi when I see her."

Shaeli smiled at the thought of Kirrit's staunch mother. "With any luck we'll be there before them," she said, and she turned to go and find her mother.

* * *

They avoided the large port city of Conroi on Zirrus' northern tip, landing instead at a small town to the west. They landed at midnight, and though the flight from the Starisles had been a long one, Jarris and Jeth had the Zoi harnessed before sunrise. That they would be pursued was understood, and the Trader would travel into the foothills, to a town on a high bluff where they could rest the Zoi in safety.

Shanna and Neesha seemed bewildered by what was happening and Shaeli hugged them extra hard, studying their faces as they watched the preparations for lift, wondering. Her parents had not told her which one was not her sister, and she did not really want to know; both were equally important to her.

When they were ready, they made their goodbyes quickly; all had unsaid words on their lips, but there was too much to say and no time in which to say it. Tarkoda had helped harness the Zoi, and he took extra care to touch each bird before he released the landing ropes, and then he stood back as the birds spread their wings. The lead female watched him as he walked away, a sword at his waist, his slingshot tucked into his belt beside it.

Shaeli held herself firmly until the Trader had dwindled into the sky, and then she let her face crumple. Tarkoda and Kirrit both had similar expressions.

"Come on, then," said Shaeli, shouldering her pack. Ebony scrambled up her skirts and perched on top of the pack. "No use standing here watering the grass." She sniffed, wiped at her eyes, and looked at Williver. He carried a light pack and a quiver of arrows on his back. In one hand was a long, slim bow and a thin blade was strapped to his waist. "So what do we do now?" she said.

"Travel west as far as we can before we hit the Drell Mountains," Williver said, and shrugged. "I am not familiar with the Land past that."

"I am," said Tarkoda, his hand resting on the slingshot given to him by the drell, Blenny, for his birth-day, many Winterings before.

"I also know it well," said Flin, who carried no weapon other than his throwing stone. "Yet if we can, we should try and find someone to take us by sea. It would be faster and easier, unless we buy horses, yet the Drell Mountains would halt us still."

Shaeli knew how much Flin hated to travel by sea, and she gave him a grateful smile.

"That's true," said Williver. "Shall we go to the docks?"

They gathered their bundles and walked through the streets where people stared at them; it was not often they saw an elf in the World, or even a jevvi.

"I seem to be attracting attention we can ill-afford," said Williver, pulling up the hood of his cloak.

"You, *and* Ebony," said Kirrit.

"The sooner we leave this town, the better," agreed Flin.

"You think they'll be looking for us?" asked Shaeli.

Williver and Flin nodded in unison. Kirrit began to look about nervously.

"'Tis certain they are looking for Purple Leaf," said Williver. "It will not be hard to trace its journey."

"Da should be able to stay well ahead of them," said Tarkoda. "But they'll know we got off here." He smiled at Williver. "And as you say, elves are not common in these parts."

They reached the bay and stood watching the small boats tied to the wharves, trying to find one likely to take them west.

"Oh, the gods," Kirrit said. "*Look.*"

A ship was just rounding the point. Its mast flew the queen's standard, and on its deck stood dozens of her soldiers.

They turned as one, heading back into the streets, hurrying through the little town, unmindful now of the curious stares. When they reached the outskirts, they began to run. They could all see the beginning of the forest to the west, and they did not stop running until the trees closed behind them. Shaeli and Flin slumped against a tree on one side of the wide path, breathing heavily. Kirrit and Tarkoda had sweat on their brows, but breathed more evenly. Williver showed no sign of exertion. He stood just inside the wall of trees, looking back to the town.

"Gather your strength," he said, without turning. "I fear they will not be far behind us."

Flin and Shaeli looked at each other. Flin raised a brow at her and she giggled. There was a touch of hysteria in the sound. They were not used to exercise such as this; their lives did not involve distance running.

Ebony had clung to the pack as Shaeli ran, and she looked disgruntled with the bouncing she had received. Shaeli held her close, then put her on her shoulder.

"It might be more comfortable there, Eb," she soothed.

"They come," said Williver. "Move. Into the trees. Quickly. They will think we have followed the path."

He took Shaeli's hand and led her into the trees, the others close behind. When the trees grew thinner and closer together, he released her hand, and led the way between the tangle of trunks. Branches pulled at their clothes and packs as they followed Williver blindly, not knowing in which direction he led them. Suddenly he stopped.

"Be quiet," he said. "They enter the forest."

They listened, trying to hear what Williver did, and after a while a distant clatter wafted to them on the breeze, and then it was gone. Williver listened a moment longer, and then he turned and led them on. Soon the trees grew thinner, the branches growing more and more crooked, twisting and leaning back the way they had come. The soil beneath their feet became soft and pale, grasses grew in thick clumps, and then they emerged on the coast. They squinted against the sun. It was not yet high in the sky; little time had passed since Purple Leaf had gone.

A long beach stretched out before them, the sand between them and the sea broad and white. To the right, far down the beach, was the town they had left, its buildings outlined above the bay.

"Rest for a moment," said Williver. "Then we must go on. It will not take them long to realise we are not ahead of them. Our advantage lies in them not knowing which direction we have gone."

"What are you thinking?" asked Flin.

"Keep to the trees, close by the beach. It gives good cover, yet we can see. We will make for the town down there," he pointed down the long expanse of beach. "With luck, we shall find a boat or horses before they find us."

They looked down the beach, and none of them could see anything but sand and scrubby trees, yet they knew the town was there. Elven eyes saw better than those of the People.

They adjusted their bundles and followed Williver back into the trees where the firmer ground made for easier walking. They talked little as the morning wore on and concentrated only on putting one foot before the other. Ebony ran along beside them, either in the brown-green grasses or leaping between tree branches, her tiny arms flung out. The sun, dappled by the trees, crawled up their backs and their clothes became damp with sweat. Before the sun was overhead, Williver stopped them again, and through the trees they heard the sound of Virrisian's guard, this time even the echo of their voices. They crept on as the noise receded, and twice more as the afternoon wore on they stopped as Williver listened, yet he was the only one to hear anything. As they waited, they ate a few of the provisions Eenis had packed for them that morning, resting their legs and easing the packs from their aching shoulders. Each time they picked the packs up again, they seemed heavier. The only thing that grew lighter was the water bottles that each of them carried.

At dusk they began to see the town Williver had spoken of, yet the sun began to set behind it and it had grown no closer.

"'Tis clear we shall not reach the town tonight unless we walk with the moon." Williver looked at them. "Yet I think you need rest more. We'll have to sleep among the trees. I hear a small stream ahead where we can fill our flasks."

They followed him through the trees, their feet tripping over themselves, until, as Williver had said, a small stream crossed their path, and they shrugged off their packs and pulled out some more of Eenis' packages. Shaeli was so tired she could barely think, and had to keep reminding herself to chew. The others were not much better. Only Williver did not seem tired.

They did not dare light a fire, and, though the summer night was warm, they pulled their cloaks from their packs, and wrapped themselves in them. Shaeli and Kirrit lay together beneath the overhang of a small tree and were soon asleep, Ebony curled between them. Tarkoda, though he tried, could not stay awake either. Flin and Williver sat talking quietly as the moon rose, and then Flin curled himself up not far from the girls.

Williver sat listening to the night. Small animals crackled through the leaves, an owl hooted in the distance. Once he thought he heard a voice, yet it was far away, and he could not tell from which direction it came. Soon after, he, too, slept.

* * *

When Shaeli woke, she could not imagine where she was. There was a lump beneath her head and something was sticking in her thigh. She sat up, dazed, and then she

155

remembered and looked around. Thin light filtered through the trees, dappling the ground and the lumps made by the others, who were still huddled in their cloaks asleep. At least that's what she thought, until she realised there were only three bundles on the ground. Williver was not there, nor Ebony.

She rose to her feet and could not help groaning aloud as her muscles did. Her legs and back were plaited with dull aches, her shoulders and neck stiff, the beginnings of a headache curled at the base of her skull. She looked around and took a few paces forward, then breathed a sigh as Williver emerged from the trees. Ebony leapt from branch to branch above his head, and in one huge leap, she glided through the air, arms and legs splayed wide, and landed at Shaeli's feet.

"Good morning, little one," Williver said, his lips curving at the sight of her.

"Hello," she said, still hardly used to the fact she was seeing him in person. She tickled the jevvi's ears as Ebony ran up her skirts and nuzzled her cheek. "Where were you?"

"We went upstream to fill our flasks with water. 'Tis brackish here."

She nodded. "Is there any sign of... them?"

He shook his head. "No. They must still search behind us. Yet that does not mean some have not gone ahead. We must be cautious."

"I feel almost as if I were in one of our dreams," Shaeli said. "Everything is so strange."

Williver smiled. "I wish it *were* a dream." He took her hand. "We'll be alright, you know. Try not to worry. Come, now. It is time we woke the others."

Shaeli sighed again, and went to wake Kirrit. A Moon ago she had been practising for the skylights on Pa'laidiz, sleeping in the beautiful room at Flin's, her family all close. And now...

She pulled the leaves from her hair as they ate and drank the fresh water in their flasks, then they shouldered their burdens gingerly, trying to find the least painful position before they headed upstream.

Williver had found a place where the stream was narrow, a few rocks making natural stepping stones, and they refilled their flasks as they crossed and then followed the stream back down to the beach. The clear water became cloudy as the stream grew shallower before running from the trees, cutting a curly path through the white sand. The sun was just over the horizon, yet already they could feel its heat. To the west, the town ahead was patterned with the new sun and the last of the night's shadows.

They moved back into the trees, and began to walk once more. At mid-morning they came out on top of a low rise where the trees were almost bushes, so battered were they by the sea winds, and they could see in every direction. The town ahead was close enough now to make out the houses, and like the town far behind, this one was also built around a wide bay flanked on the western side by a long low headland. To the left, the scrubby forest drizzled into wide plains which disappeared in the southern haze.

As they descended the hill, the trees thinned. The canopy grew sparser, and they began to see the end of the small coastal forest that had sheltered them so well. When the trees grew too thin to provide much cover, they stopped.

The town was now clearly visible, and though it looked like just a sleepy fishing village, they were nervous about approaching it in the middle of the day. They could imagine the stares of the townsfolk and the words whispered behind fingers.

"Perhaps we should wait for darkness," said Tarkoda. "We are less likely to be noticed then."

"True," said Flin. "But people are wary of those who travel by night. Just before dusk is better. Travellers looking for a bed." He looked at Williver. "And perhaps they will not notice an elf wrapped in a cloak as easily."

Williver nodded. "You're right, we cannot know the guard do not lie in wait for us. We should wait until sunset, and trust to luck."

They went back to where the trees where thicker and settled in to wait for nightfall. They drowsed, spent with two days of travelling, as the sun dropped in front of them. The trees around them came alive with tiny birds, brown and dappled as the tree trunks, leaping and twittering through the curling branches. The little birds scolded them as they left the cover of the trees, the peeping calls following them as they approached the village.

Scrubby grass covered the ground between the trees and the first of the houses, and they felt vulnerable as they crossed it, accustomed to the safety of the coastal forest. Voices called here and there as they approached, but they saw no one. They had donned their capes before leaving the trees, and they pulled up their hoods as the buildings closed around them, hoping Williver would not be noticed. Shaeli had Ebony tucked beneath her cloak. The streets were almost empty and the few people they did see paid them little attention as they made their way to the waterfront, looking for an inn in which to spend the night.

Only one thin arm of wharf stretched into the bay, a few larger boats moored along it. Other boats were pulled up on the sand, and here, too, there were few people. Through the gloom, Shaeli could see an empty Landing further round the bay, and she looked at Tarkoda.

"No luck there," he said.

"Do you know where we are?" she asked him.

He nodded. "Yes, I recognise the Landing, but I'm sure we haven't landed here for a long time."

"That looks like an inn further down the street," said Flin. "Why don't I go and try and find some rooms? You can wait here until I know it's safe."

"Good idea," said Williver.

Flin went down and disappeared through a doorway. A picture of a rooster with a pipe in its mouth and wearing a fine waistcoat swung above the entrance. He was soon back.

"We have two rooms, with a door between. Dinner is to be served within the hour." He looked at Williver. "There is an entrance hall before the stairs, with a door into the tavern opening off it. Four of Virrisian's guard are sitting inside."

"We can't go in there," cried Shaeli. "They'll see us."

"I think not," said Flin, a tiny smile playing about his lips. "It seems the owner of the Fancy Fowl is no admirer of the queen, nor her guard. The four have sat in his tavern since their arrival this morning. It seems they were disgruntled at being out all night searching for fugitives, and they have drunk themselves into a stupor and are snoring at his best table. He mentioned he would happily give comfort to any fugitives, should they turn up at his door." Flin let the smile turn into a grin. "He knows not what he says."

"Does he know who they seek?" asked Williver.

"No. He imagines five desperate criminals, not five friends travelling to Romynn."

"Romynn?" Kirrit asked.

"Well, I thought it best to not reveal our true destination," said Flin. "And I implied we did not wish to eat with the queen's drunken guard, so our dinner is to be served in our rooms, and the owner is to make enquiries about a boat to take us along the coast." He looked very pleased with himself, and they agreed with him as he led the way down the street.

As he had said, the hall before the stairs was quite short, and though Shaeli tried not to look, she could not help herself. Through the doorway to the tavern she had a glimpse of the four soldiers, three with their faces planted on the table, one leaning back in his chair, snoring loudly. She had a sudden desire to giggle very loudly.

At the bar sat several men, and behind the bar stood the tavern owner. He was looking at the soldiers contemptuously, but he saw them and waved as they passed the doorway.

"A good evening to you," he called. "Your dinner will not be long."

Flin stopped to thank him, and then he followed them up the stairs. "This way," he said at the top, and turned to the left.

Two doors stood open down the hall, and he led them into one that held four beds and a large table and chairs. A doorway between the two rooms was also open, and in the second smaller room there were two beds. Both rooms looked down over the street.

They closed the doors to the hall and took off their packs. Shaeli and Kirrit dropped theirs on the beds in the smaller room, and found a basin and a jug filled with water where they could wash some of the grime from their hands and faces, but Shaeli was not surprised when Flin told them he had arranged for baths for them all after dinner.

When their meal came, Williver slipped into the other room, taking Ebony with him. The jevvi had taken an instant liking to the elf and happily rode Williver's shoulder into the room.

The owner and his wife set out trays of stew and bread on the table, keeping up a constant chatter as they did so, most of it about the unworthiness of the queen's guard.

"Well, they can only be as good as their mistress," said the owner of the Fancy Fowl. "And we know what *she's* like."

"Now, now," said his wife, looking rather nervous. "It doesn't do to speak ill of the queen." She looked at Flin and bobbed. "There's a pie under that cloth for later, and let me know when you want me to start the boiler for your baths."

"Thank you, dear lady," smiled Flin. "And do not fear speaking ill of the queen near us. We care little for politics and think only of the pleasant journey ahead." He looked at the owner. "Any word yet on a boat?"

160

"Ah, yes. Chessy downstairs says he'll take you, past the Drell Mountains at least."

"Splendid," said Flin. "Tell him I'll be down to speak with him after I've had dinner. Put his ale on my account until I come and I shall settle it all with you then. We wish to leave early."

"Very good," he smiled. "Chessy'll not argue with that. I shall see you directly."

"Enjoy your dinner," said his wife, bobbing again, and the two left the room, shutting the door behind them.

Williver came back in, and very little was said until the trays were empty, and then Flin left to go down to speak to the owner of the boat. Soon after, the wife of the tavern owner was again tapping on the door, and they all had the luxury of taking turns in the bath at the end of the hall. Williver ducked up and down the hall while someone watched the top of the stairs, so he would not be seen, and then Flin, his thin brown hair slicked across his head, told them of the arrangements he'd made with the owner of the boat. It was not a large vessel, he said, but it would suffice. They were to be at the wharf well before sunrise, to catch the tide.

"Will you be alright, Flin?" asked Shaeli.

"I shall endeavour to be," he answered firmly.

"What of the guard?" asked Tarkoda.

"Two still snore downstairs. Two have found beds in another tavern." Flin smiled. "Our good landlord told them there was none available here."

"Excellent," said Williver. "Then we had best go to *our* beds. You have arranged for us to be woken, of course?" he smiled.

"Of course," said Flin. "And we'll have fresh provisions ready to go too."

"As I thought," replied Williver. "You are a very efficient man, Flin."

"My thanks," said Flin. "Now let's all go to bed."

* * *

They were woken before the roosters began crowing and
ate a hurried breakfast before thanking their hosts and
heading for the docks. Of the queen's guard, there was no sign.

Chessy, a short, wiry man, waited for them, yet he did not
lead them down the wharf but along the thin beach. He stopped
beside a boat that had its nose resting on the sand and a long
rope tied around a rock. It had only a small cabin in front and a
wide, open rear, a single mast standing high above the deck.
Chessy grinned at their dubious silence. Several of his teeth
were missing.

"She doesn't look much, I know, but she's fast, and sound."
He looked at Flin from under his brows. "Ye said ye wanted to
get there as soon as ye could," he said.

"So I did," Flin said. "She looks a fine vessel. How long will
it take, do you think, to sail us past the Drell Mountains?"

"Ten, maybe, twelve days, I reckon. 'Pends on the wind.
How long we stop. Not much room to sleep on her, or stretch
your legs," replied Chessy. He peered at the water. "Best we
catch that tide. If one of you will help me push her out, the
others can get on board."

"I'll help," said Tarkoda, and when the others were
standing on the small deck, he passed Flin up his pack and
cloak and helped Chessy push the boat off the sand. He felt the
current at his knees, and they turned the boat towards the
mouth of the bay.

"On with ye, lad," said Chessy, and Koda hauled himself
aboard, then turned round to pull Chessy up.

"Thank ye," Chessy said, when he stood dripping on the
deck. "Now best you go forward with the others while I ease her
over the waves."

Tarkoda nodded and joined the others in the little cabin. It
was rather cramped, but comfortable enough, with padded
benches on which to sit and a small table on one side.

162

On deck, Chessy pulled up the sails. They filled with a soft breeze, and when they passed from the bay into the open water the breeze grew stronger and the sea changed from a dark blanket to a perfect mirror as the sun rose. The boat was as fleet as Chessy had said and the land to their left passed quickly.

Shaeli sat in a patch of sun in a corner of the deck, her eyes closed, feeling better than she had since she was on Purple Leaf. She let Ebony roam, knowing she would be safe, and Chessy grinned at the jevvi, admiring the way she scrambled fearlessly about his rigging. Shaeli looked from Ebony to Flin, to see how he was coping. He smiled at her raised eyebrows.

"Fine so far," he said. "Smooth as a Trader."

By afternoon, though, it was a different story. They flew above the sea's surface like a stone skipped from a child's hand, the wind at their backs. The sea grew choppy, whitecaps and foam leaping about them, and Flin grew pale. Before long he was hanging over the railing.

Chessy laughed and threw in a line to drift behind them, hoping to catch dinner, he said. This made Flin retch all the more. When he staggered inside, they made room for him to lie down on the longest bench, where he mumbled something that sounded like an apology and closed his eyes.

The others watched the sun stretch before them while the shadow of the boat grew longer behind, and just before nightfall, Chessy said he knew a good place to stop, and would Koda go forward and anchor them. He had caught a few nice fish, he said, and was looking forward to dinner. Flin groaned.

* * *

They slept on their cloaks on the bank near the boat. Chessy had pulled in close to the side of a small promontory, its steep side making a natural wharf, a small grassy area above the tide line giving them a comfortable night. They had a small fire, and Chessy slept curled in a bedroll beside them.

163

Williver had managed to avoid Chessy the day before, but as they were heading out to sea just after first light, he stood looking forward over the roof of the cabin. A gust of wind blew his hood back, and Chessy saw him clearly. His eyebrows rose, he lowered his head, and when he raised it, he looked Williver in the eye.

"'Tis pleased I am to have one of your kind on my humble boat, sir," he said. "Pleased indeed. The little jevvi was a treat, but this is a most welcome surprise." He smiled broadly, and treated Williver with great respect for the remainder of their journey.

Days passed with the land sliding by, and on the afternoon of the sixth day the Drell Mountains began to loom ahead. Chessy stopped well before they reached them, and said he hoped to be past them by this time tomorrow. Before darkness fell he cast many superstitious glances at them, and slept on his boat that night, not with them as he had the nights before. They did not blame him; the mountains filling the land as far as they could see inland and to the west were dark, brooding hulks.

The land leading up to the mountains had grown dryer, the trees had given way to scrubby bushes, and then even they had died out. Little grew on the land here but rocks and enormous oddly-shaped anthills, the ground barren to the southern horizon. On this eastern side of the mountain range, strange creatures were said to inhabit the craggy heights and shadowed canyons; creatures who lived deep beneath the ground, others who scaled the stony peaks feasting on the meat of goats and huni deer. Further to the west the mountains were the domain of the drell, their homes, unknown and unvisited, hidden somewhere within the craggy ugly mountain range where no other race roamed.

Chessy woke them before sunrise again next morning, and after a hurried breakfast they left. By first light the mountains to their left had grown huge, crowding the horizon with dark ugly heads and valleys filled with fog as thick as the smoke from old men's pipes. They began to see the shapes of three islands ahead and Chessy headed out to sea. It was clear he meant to take a wide berth around them.

The three islands stood sentinel around the mouth of a river that flowed from the centre of the Drell Mountains, and Shaeli fancied she could see the shapes of broken figures in the silhouettes of the giant islands. They were towering, treeless shapes jutting from the sea, the water around their bases writhing and slapping at the sides of the dark rock as if in punishment for a long-past crime. A few birds rode the air, calling to each other in plaintive voices and diving into the sea to catch small fish.

When the islands and the mouth of the Drell River were past, Chessy headed the boat back in towards the coast where the brooding mountains waited. Flin was glad of it. The swell further out was reflected in the rolling of his stomach, and he thankfully passed the rest of the day merely feeling queasy.

That night, they slept with the mountains behind them, just as Chessy had hoped. The mountains had crowded the coast, their dark feet almost in the sea, and they had seen little but bird-life along the shoreline. Chessy agreed to take them a few more days to the west, and then he would journey home. He would fish on the way, he said, and hoped for a good catch to take back to his wife.

"She has the knack of smoking fish like no one else, does my wife," he said. "But she does not like it when I'm from home for more than a Full. Besides," he added, "tomorrow should take ye within a short walk of Trilby, and ye should easy find a ship there to take ye across to Romynn. Or, mayhap a Trader."

"Perhaps we shall," said Flin, looking at Shaeli. "That sounds perfect."

* * *

CHAPTER ELEVEN

Chessy left them one afternoon three days later at the end of a long spit jutting like a sandy arm into the sea. He gave them several of his wife's smoked fish to add to their provisions and told them to hurry to solid ground, for when the tide rose the spit would be covered by water. They thanked him and waved as Tarkoda pushed the boat back out to deeper water, watching as he filled his sail with wind and headed out to sea. The boat quickly grew small, and by the time they reached the land at the end of the spit, it was gone.

"Chessy said Trilby is about a day's walk," said Flin.

Tarkoda looked at the sun. "There is not that much daylight left," he said. "Though we can walk after moonrise. There should be enough light, and we've had plenty of rest."

Flin nodded his agreement, yet Williver stopped him.

"We cannot," he said. "There is something I must do before we reach our destination. We need to find somewhere secluded to spend the night hours, where I shall not be disturbed."

He would not be drawn on his task, and they did not press him; they would know soon enough. They shouldered their bundles and headed west.

* * *

They found somewhere just before sunset. The land was filled with low foothills, and scrubby, pale-barked trees cluttered the coast, all leaning inland, their branches twisted by strong sea winds, the bark torn and ragged as old paper. The sandy soil beneath them was covered in low grasses, faded green and sharp as needles, but soon the trees petered out and there was only the spiky grass. They saw no people, nor distant towns, and as they began to despair of finding any proper shelter, they saw a small copse of trees a short way inland. They had travelled close to the coast, but they left the salty breeze behind and hurried to the stand of trees. They found a small clearing in its centre, with a spring pooling on one side, and they built a tiny fire that smoked very little. They felt sure they had left the guard far behind, and no one knew where they were.

Williver waited until the moon was high in the sky, and then he looked at them each in turn across the flickering of the flame. They now knew what he was planning, and why, but had no idea how he would achieve it.

"The hour is almost right," he said. "I will enter the dreamworld for only a short time, if all goes well. You four must help me while I am there. You must keep watch on the fire, and ensure it does not go out. Shaeli," he smiled at her, "you will stand behind me, on my right. If, for any reason, I need to return before my task is complete, you are to tap me three times on the shoulder. Alright?"

Shaeli nodded. "I suppose so, Williver," she looked puzzled. "But what could happen?"

"Not a great deal," he answered. "Though it's unlikely the guard will find us, if someone should happen upon us, it might look a little strange. Flin, Tarkoda, keep watch, and warn Shaeli if anyone approaches." They nodded and Williver looked at Kirrit. "It will be left to you to feed the fire. Do not let the flame die, yet use only the smaller kindling."

Kirrit nodded too, and moved to the pile of wood they had collected earlier. She began sorting it, moving the bigger pieces to one side and stacking the smaller branches beside her. Ebony liked the look of the game and began to stack the tiniest twigs into a neat pile next to Kirrit's.

"Have you ever been interrupted when we were talking, Williver?" asked Shaeli.

"Yes, once," he said. "Remember the time at the Autumn's Eve Hunt as you drowsed in the sun?"

"Of course," she smiled. "It was my first performance." She looked at Flin. "I'll never forget *that* night. I was so nervous."

"Yet you did an admirable job," said Flin. "As always."

She grinned, then looked back at Williver. "That was the day you told me to be careful, and about the little rose quartz in the custard."

"In *custard*?" said Kirrit. "You found a gem in custard?"

"Williver told me it was there," Shaeli said, shrugging her shoulders. "You never told me how you knew, Williver. Or how I could dream of you in such a tiny nap."

"'Tis possible for me to travel in the dreamworld at any time," he said. "In my own dreams I am free to roam anywhere in the dreamworld. These are the times I usually visit you, when we are both sleeping and free to roam our dreams as we please, yet for a specific task, I find it best to consciously travel. Then I am not subject to the usual whims of sleep."

"What's it like?" Shaeli asked. "The dreamworld?"

"It looks very much like this one," said Williver. "Only a shadowed version, eternally grey, as if it is almost night. One can fly through the skies and see the ribbons of dreams, if one knows how."

"The ribbons?" asked Shaeli.

"Yes. As each person dreams, the patterns of the dream coils up, like ribbons unfurling, ribbons wispy as smoke. Within a dream, anything is possible, as we all know, and the dreamworld is the place where these things happen, but each dream is contained to a single person, a single ribbon of dream." Here he looked at Shaeli. "Usually anyway, unless like me, one has the ability to roam between the ribbons, to enter the dreams of others. As each person dreams differently, so the patterns of the dreams are different. Many dreamers have dreams that are small, with ribbons that unfurl only a short way and have pale, muted colours; some have dreams that reach further and their colours are brighter. Occasionally, there will be a ribbon unfurling high into the sky, shining like a rainbow."

"There must be a lot of them at night," said Flin. "How do you find a particular person, like Shaeli?"

"Shaeli shines differently for me, I can find her light anywhere, but yes, at night there are many, and unless one knows exactly where someone is, then 'tis almost impossible to find them."

"Are there ghosts there?" asked Kirrit. "In the dreamworld?"

"No," smiled Williver. "The dreamworld lies somewhere between the waking world and the spirit world. It is possible to see memories, imprints of people who have passed over to the spirit world, even to receive messages, but no, there are no ghosts."

"How do you *know* it's between the waking world and the spirit world?" Kirrit said.

"Sometimes a tiny window opens between the dreamworld and the spirit world, or the dreamworld and the waking world, through which one can see things, yet it is not possible to pass through that window."

"But you can find the dreamworld awake or asleep?" said Shaeli.

"Yes. *You* must be asleep to see me, little one, but I can submerge myself in the dreamworld at any time. It is a matter of the mind removing itself from the body, and, with a clear destination, distance is irrelevant." He thought for a moment. "As I said, to enter a specific person's dream one must know where they are in the waking world, and the dreamworld lies somewhere *between* this world and the spirit world. You know that when someone sleeps, their dreams spiral up into the sky of the dreamworld, filled with the patterns of their dreams, the ribbons. The ribbons are a guide, so the dreamer knows their way back to themselves, to the waking world. When I consciously travel the dreamworld I *have* no dream spiral, and it helps to have a fire near me to guide me back."

"That's me, tonight," said Kirrit.

Williver nodded. "That's you."

"And you need the fire to guide you back?"

Williver nodded again. Kirrit looked nervous.

"But how did you find *me* the first time?" said Shaeli, changing the subject a little, to distract Kirrit, but also because she wanted to know. "I must have only been tiny because you've always been there."

Williver smiled warmly at her. "Your spirit has always been as a beacon for me, little one, whether you are asleep or awake. A certain light surrounds you, an aura that is called a *shenwa* in some places. The day you were born it shone as a lighthouse in my mind, and I was not able to resist seeing from where it came. I have been able to find you always." He reached out and cupped her face. "I know not why it is so, yet it is a great gift."

She covered her hand with his, and squeezed it before he took it away. "I agree," she said, her cheek warmed by his hand and her heart by his words. "But what about that day at the Hunt?"

"Well, I just felt a need to warn you about who you revealed your magic to. It was an urge not to be denied. I thought I would not reach you until the night, yet I tried several times during the afternoon, just the same. One of these times, just before you slept in the sun, I saw the lad helping at the custard stall fill the vessel with more prizes, through one of those windows I told you about. He spied the eroscia and took a fancy to it. He pushed it far down in that corner, for he had been promised whatever prizes were left at the end of the day. Unhappy he was when you took it away, I imagine."

"I used it accidentally that night, remember, Flin?"

"I remember," Flin said. "I also remember it was the next day we discovered the depth of your magic."

"Yes," she laughed. "And *I* remember the look on *your* face when I told you about stopping the rock from hitting Taffka."

"Didn't they know you could lift things?" asked Tarkoda.

170

"No, not then," she said. "It was only an accident when I *did* tell them."

"And poor Shaeli had no idea what it meant or how remarkable it was," Flin grinned at her. "Speaking of looks on faces."

"I know," Shaeli smiled back. "I didn't have any idea of what it meant until you and Qiren told me. It was lucky Williver had told me to be careful."

"It was luck indeed when I found you resting alone in the middle of the Hunt. Yet I *was* interrupted."

"I remember you seemed in a hurry," said Shaeli.

"An unexpected visitor, yet I had left someone to warn me, my friend Llianas, and I spoke with you, so it all ended well."

"But you knew I was safe with Flin. You sent Qiren to him, to take me as apprentice."

"To persuade him, yes, and I knew they would protect you, and keep secret the extent of your gift. I had not told Qiren of the strength you held, I only suspected it then myself, yet I knew that you had great potential, and needed proper guidance." Williver shrugged. "As I said, I know not why I felt so compelled to add my warning, yet so it was."

"*And* you also saw where I could find the eroscia," added Shaeli.

"A happy coincidence indeed," said Flin.

"There is little real coincidence in the World, I believe," said Williver. "The gods guide all things, coincidence and good luck included."

"I think so, too," said Shaeli. "There's something else, Williver," she looked at him. "Something you never told me."

"Only one thing?" he asked, grinning.

"Well, no, there are a lot of things you haven't told me, it seems," Shaeli said. She tried to purse her lips, but the smile broke through, just the same. "But, what I mean is, why didn't you tell me you could do it too? I've been wanting to ask you since we left Pa'laidiz. Why didn't you tell me you could throw? That you had a wand?"

"At first, the thought merely did not occur to me. My talent is small and not something I can sustain for long. My true gift is travelling the dreamworld," Williver said. "After your gift showed itself during your year at the Cave of the Traders, I was unsure what to do, or what it meant. I decided to leave it in the hands of the gods."

"But you sent Qiren anyway," said Tarkoda. "And Shaeli *was* apprenticed to Flin. *You* did that, not the gods."

"Yes, but it was not my idea," said Williver.

"Not yours?" Shaeli asked. "Whose was it then?"

"It was decided, after it was confirmed the wand was truly Shahlita's, that it would be wise if you were properly trained. There was no one in your Lands who was considered gifted enough but Flin. I knew Qiren had worked with him several times, and it was I who persuaded him to go to Palveron, and convince Flin to take you." The elf looked at Flin. "Though reluctant, in the end, he agreed."

"I admit it," said Flin, looking abashed. "The thought of having a young girl in my house and having to give basic training was tiresome indeed." He looked at Shaeli. "But I had not met her then. My mind soon changed."

Shaeli blushed slightly, and hoped the others could not see it in the firelight. "Thank you, Flin," she said. "But, Williver, you said 'it was decided'. *Who* decided?"

"That is too long a story," he replied, the question batted away with a wave of his hand. "And we have not time for it. The hour is late enough for my task and I should begin. Flin, Tarkoda, would you please go and make sure all is safe. Kirrit, the fire is yours."

Shaeli had to curb her curiosity. As Williver had said, there was more than one thing he hadn't told her, and while she wondered at his secrecy, she was not disturbed by it. She trusted him implicitly.

She watched as he pulled a small pouch from his pack, and gave Kirrit a few final instructions. The firelight was reflected in the russet and gold of her hair, and she now looked rather more than nervous at her responsibility. Shaeli tried to smile reassuringly at her, and then she gathered Ebony into her arms. The jevvi had tired of Kirrit's stick-stacking game, and was looking longingly in the direction Koda had gone. Tarkoda and Flin were both back before long, reporting they could see nothing but empty land around them.

"Good," said Williver. "Keep watch, then. This should not take long."

"Koda," said Shaeli. "Take Eb with you. She wants to explore."

"Alright," he said. "Come on, Ebony."

The jevvi looked up at Shaeli, and Shaeli gave an almost indiscernible nod. "It's alright," she said. "You can go with Koda, but don't wander off."

The jevvi nuzzled her cheek, leapt from her shoulder, and, arms and legs outflung, she glided to the ground. She dashed across to Tarkoda, and scrambled up his leg. She looked back at Shaeli as Koda put her on his shoulder, the strange jevvi smile on her face, her tiny hand waving. Shaeli laughed and waved back as they disappeared into the trees. Flin was laughing too as he went out the other side of the clearing.

"Will you be able to find her?" she asked Williver, as he sat down before the fire.

"Yes," he said. "The box she holds sends out a clear signal in her dreams. I have seen it before and I know her house. Remember, now, three taps on my right shoulder if I am to return."

"Three taps," she repeated.

He turned to face the fire. He sat cross-legged and he nodded at Kirrit, and Kirrit nodded back.

Williver took something from the small pouch he held, and sprinkled it on the fire. It was some kind of powder which crackled into bright blue sparks when it hit the flame. A sweet, pungent odour drifted up with the pale blue smoke, and Shaeli was reminded of the drell, Blenny, and the way he had thrown a strange red powder on the fire in Orrellis many years ago before bewitching the crowd with his omens. That had been the year she had found Nol's family and he had given her the first bangle. It seemed strange she should be reminded of that now.

Williver put the pouch back in his vest, and lay his hands on his knees, palms upward. After a while his breathing slowed, and Shaeli looked at Kirrit, her brows raised in question. Kirrit looked at the elf, then back up at Shaeli, and shrugged. She mirrored Williver's position, and closed her eyes for a moment. She opened them, shrugged again, and went back to feeding the fire, grinning broadly.

Shaeli almost giggled. It was clear from Kirrit's parody that Williver's eyes were closed and Kirrit didn't know what was going on. Neither wanted to talk aloud. They had forgotten to ask if it was alright.

They waited and waited, and after a very long time, Williver began to speak. Kirrit and Shaeli had grown bored as the time passed, stretching their limbs to stop them from cramping. Once Flin had come to the edge of the firelight, eyebrows raised, and Shaeli had shrugged at him and he'd disappeared back into the shadows. When Williver finally began to speak Shaeli and Kirrit looked at each other. Neither felt like laughing any more.

Williver's voice was urgent. His words, though spoken quietly and quickly, were full of compassion. They could make little sense of what he said.

"Why are you here?" were his first words, and then silence for a few moments.

There were a few mumbled sentences that they could not make out, and then Williver was silent again for a long time. When he spoke again the words were clearer. The sentences came in rapid succession, with short breaks between. It was clear they were hearing one side of a conversation.

"When did this happen?"

Silence.

"How many?"

Silence.

"And you left it there?"

Silence.

"I understand. It is not your fault."

Silence.

"Where?"

Silence.

"So you think it is still there?"

Silence.

"No, no. Do not blame yourself."

Silence.

"As long as you are safe."

Silence.

"You're *sure*? The gods be with you, then."

Again there was silence, but this time it went on and on.

Williver spoke no more. Kirrit kept feeding the fire. After a while Williver's breathing grew normal. Shaeli saw his fingers twitch, and then his hands left his knees, and he stretched his arms.

"Well done, Kirrit," he said. "Will you fetch the others for me?"

Kirrit nodded and went into the trees. Williver turned and looked up at Shaeli. His eyes were dark.

"What is it?" she said. "What's happened?"

He passed a hand across his brow. "Wait for the others," he said. "Bad news is best told only once."

* * *

Williver said nothing until Kirrit brought Flin and Tarkoda back to the clearing. Shaeli had waited impatiently, her heart beating against her chest and questions beating against her teeth. When they were again gathered around the fire, the light chatty mood from earlier was completely gone. In its place was a tense silence. Everyone waited to see what Williver would say. It seemed he was unsure how to begin, yet after he had sat staring at the flames for a long while, he spoke.

"I could not find her in Trilby," he said at last, "and I could find only a faint trace of the box. The house where they lived is a burnt-out shell. It was still smoking when I reached it."

"*No,*" breathed Shaeli. "Where are they Williver? Are they alright?"

"I found Ellirra and her children in the hills to the south. Her dreams were not hard to find. Red and grey, they were, filled with fire and despair." Williver again passed a hand across his brow. He looked more exhausted than he had after two days of running from Virrisian's guard in the forest by the sea. "I'm sorry. 'Twas more tiring than I anticipated."

"Do you want to sleep and tell us more tomorrow?" asked Flin.

"No," said Williver. "'Tis best told now." He sighed and took a deep breath. "At sunrise this morning, armed guard entered Ellirra's house. Her husband was killed. Ellirra and her daughters were taken outside and forced to watch as their house was burned. They were taken to the edge of town in their nightdresses and told never to return. They walked all day to her sister-by-law in the south, and are now safe."

"But why?" asked Shaeli, horrified by the tale.

"For aiding rebels, she was told. An example to others who thought to oppose the queen. That was what she and her townsfolk were told, but she believes it was about the box. So do I."

"Why didn't they just ask her about it, then?" asked Shaeli. "Instead of burning her house?"

"Destroying it works just as well. As long as it is not reunited with the other, it has no power," shrugged Williver.

"And no questions are asked," added Flin. "Merely blame the rebellion again."

"Just like Purple Leaf," said Kirrit.

"So we've come all this way for *nothing*," said Shaeli. "And it's all my fault Ellirra's husband is dead and she has no home." Her lip wobbled, and she began to cry.

"It isn't your fault," said Tarkoda, putting an arm around her shoulders.

"Your brother is right, Shaeli," said Williver. "You cannot blame yourself."

"But they knew where to go because of *me*," she sobbed. "Because of the dream. Because of the black wind."

"You did not ask them to invade your mind, little one."

"We may as well have gone with Purple Leaf," she cried, not wanting to be consoled. "We could have gone *home*, and now we're stuck out here, and for nothing. *Nothing*." She buried her face in her knees and wrapped her arms around them.

Kirrit moved over and she also put an arm about Shaeli's trembling shoulders.

"'Tis not for nothing we are here," said Williver quietly. "There is a chance it is still there."

Shaeli looked up, her face shiny from her tears. "Still *there*? But how?"

"Ellirra kept the box beneath a hearthstone. It may be there still, untouched," said Williver.

"Is that possible?" asked Flin. "That it survived the blaze?"

"Ellirra thinks so," said Williver. "She said that at spring's beginning, a seer had warned her to protect her most precious possessions from flame, and is seems so strongly did she believe him that she dug out a space in the earth beneath a hearthstone and buried it. And I did see a trace of its presence in the air still. It may have been saved."

"Then we can find it?" asked Shaeli, her face shiny still, but now with hope as well as tears.

"Perhaps, yes," said Williver. "Yet how, I don't know. There are many of the guard in Trilby, and the house itself is watched, at least for now. We may have to wait and hope that we can retrieve it undetected."

"Surely though, if we must, we can take care of the guard," said Flin. "We could just go and take it by force."

"Yet then they would know that we are here, in the area," said Williver. "Even if they know we are headed for Trilby, it will not matter if we can retrieve the box without detection. And they will still think it has been destroyed."

"That's true," said Flin. "If we can go in and out again without drawing attention, they won't know where we are, or that the box survived. At the moment they can have no idea."

"We should be able to find a Trader closer to the lakes afterwards," said Tarkoda, eagerly. "Any of them will take us to Cave."

"So, what are we going to do?" asked Kirrit.

"For now," said Williver, stifling a yawn. "We sleep. Tomorrow we shall travel as close as we can to Trilby, and find somewhere we can watch in safety."

* * *

CHAPTER TWELVE

It seemed that Chessy hadn't been quite accurate. They walked until almost midday before they saw anybody, keeping within sight of the coast, crossing through another small, scrubby forest, and then onto a seemingly endless plain filled with taller sharper grasses, grasses that slashed at their legs and left their hands covered in fine scratches. When they saw smoke inland, Tarkoda volunteered to go and find out where they were; he thought, judging by the stars and the countryside, that they were still a fair way from Trilby. Flin went with him while Williver stayed with the girls.

They sat in the shade of the only tree in sight, where the grasses were thinner, and though the tree had few leaves it provided some respite from the sun. Ebony had spent almost the whole day perched on somebody's pack, obviously disliking the sharp grasslands, and she bounded up into the thin, brown arms of the little tree, watching Tarkoda and Flin disappear into the grass.

It was well into the afternoon when Ebony chittered their return. They had eaten sparsely as they waited – provisions were becoming scarce – and the girls had dozed through the heat. Williver stood and watched the two men approach. They were laughing as they came, and Koda carried a cloth sack in his hand.

Shaeli and Kirrit stretched the nap from their limbs as the others sat down. Tarkoda began laughing again as he lay the sack on the grass.

"You should have seen Flin," he said, shaking his head. "He pretended I was a rich, stupid nobleman from Marnissi, who'd decided to walk to Trilby for fun. 'Twelve companions he had, and all turned back within a Moon,' he says to the poor farmer and his wife. 'But this one is too stupid and too

179

stubborn to turn back. Just my luck to get a master like this one.' Oh, it was all I could do not to laugh out loud, but of course, I was also profoundly deaf as well as profoundly stupid. The poor farmer's wife almost yelled herself hoarse at me."

"Well it worked, didn't it?" chuckled Flin. "We have provisions *and* directions."

"That we do," said Koda. "And, as I thought, we are a lot more than a day's walk from Trilby. There is a small village we should reach before dark, and another within sight of Trilby that we should see in a few days. It may be a good place to head for. See what's going on."

He had been unwrapping bundles as he spoke, and soon he had a small feast laid out. Though the others had eaten while they waited, the fresh food and sweet cordial from the farmer's wife was too enticing to be denied, and when they had finished, they packed the remainder and set off. The farmer's directions proved truer than Chessy's, and before the sun had moved too far down the sky they saw the village in the distance.

It was a fair way inland, a thin river snaking into it, and down the coast they could see the place where the river ran into the ocean. They had encountered only small streams in their path so far, easily traversed, but the river before them, though not large, spread itself out in many arms before it met the ocean, its mouth studded with a dozen sandy islands. They would have to pass through the village, so they turned inland and walked a short distance to wait for dusk.

The plains of sharp grasses had given way to a more pleasant plain of short grass and small copses. Inland the grass became lusher, the trees sturdier, and when the village grew closer they settled themselves in the shade of a small copse where they could watch it as they waited for evening.

A road ran close to the river on this side, leading into the village and out the other side – they could see the line of it fading into the plains to the west – but they could not see the bridge that crossed the river. They decided to angle in to the road as dusk fell and follow its path to the village, so anyone seeing them coming would think they had come from further inland and not from the empty coastal plains. They pulled up their hoods and Shaeli tucked Ebony inside hers where she could sit on her shoulder and see out, but was hidden by Shaeli's hair and hood.

The village was not large, and it seemed most of the buildings catered to travellers. It was a picturesque little place, built on either side of the little river, with taverns, boarding houses and places to eat lining the road. Light and loud voices spilled out onto the road and the five walked through the village until they came to the river. They crossed over the arched stone bridge and began to look for somewhere to spend the night.

"We should find something off the main street," said Tarkoda. "Somewhere they won't notice Williver."

"Perhaps," said Flin. "But sometimes the best place to be inconspicuous is in a crowd." He shrugged. "But let us look down one of the quieter streets."

They turned to the right on the next corner. The street angled back towards the river and they neared the end thinking they would find nothing suitable, but at the bottom of the street they heard music and saw a large stately building overlooking the river, its garden awash with roses. Out the front hung a sign with a black swan swimming on a river and holding an umbrella.

"Just the thing, I'd say," said Flin. "Come on."

The building was two floors high, with wide verandas running around both levels, not unlike Flin's house on Pa'laidiz, painted deep green with white windows and railings. They mounted the stairs and at the top there was an open door with huge paned windows on either side. A sign above the door proclaimed the name of the place in flowery letters: the Sheltered Swan.

Through the window on the right they could see a bar and a few tables filled mostly with men scattered around a piano where a bright-suited gentleman sang gaily. There was also an abundance of beautiful young ladies in filmy gowns draped on lounges around the edges of the room. Through the windows to the left, diners sat chatting around white-clothed tables.

"Wait here," said Flin, taking off his hood and going inside. He was soon back, followed by an enormous woman whose hair was piled so high it seemed as if only magic kept it there. "This is our esteemed landlady," he said. "Madam … er…"

"Madagenta," said the good lady, her voice matching her stature. "Welcome to the Sheltered Swan."

"Madam… er… Madagenta insisted upon showing us to our rooms," said Flin, eyebrows raised.

"Of course," she boomed, peering at them. "I like to greet every guest. Two rooms wasn't it? Connecting?"

"That's right, yes," smiled Flin.

"This way, then," said Madam Madagenta, making room for them to go through the door.

The entry hall was a bright, fern-filled affair, the doors to the bar and dining room opening off on either side. A wide staircase leading to the upper floors was directly opposite the doors.

"You'll not be eating in the dining room, then?" asked Madagenta, as she led them up the stairs.

"Thank you, no," replied Flin. "We prefer to eat in our rooms immediately. We shall be leaving very early and wish to go to our beds."

"'Tis a shame," she said. "We have many fine guests in the house this evening. You'll be wanting breakfast before you go?"

"Thank you again," said Flin. "Just some fruit and fresh bread will suffice, if that's no trouble."

"None at all. Ah, here we are," she said, opening a door and squeezing herself through it. She waited until they had all followed her into the spacious room. "The other room is the next along, and I hope you'll be comfortable. I'll send a girl up to see what you want for your dinner and to light the boiler. The bath's through that door there," she said, nodding at a door to the left. She eased her bulk out the door and closed it behind her, a magnanimous "pleasant stay" as she left.

"Flin," laughed Shaeli. "Do we have our own bathroom?"

"I believe so," he said, pretending he didn't know she was teasing him. "I asked for one and expect to pay for it."

"But, Flin, it must be very expensive," said Shaeli, no longer teasing.

"Don't worry about it," said Flin, brushing her frown aside with a wave of his hand. "'Tis only coin and made for spending."

There was a knock at the door and Williver and Shaeli went into the other room with Ebony while the others ordered dinner. After they'd had dinner and bathed – something that was becoming a bit of a luxury – they went to sit on the veranda. The balconies were private, removed from those on each side by finely-laced trellises.

Their rooms were at the front corner of the building overlooking the gardens, the street, and a portion of the river. The moon hung high above them, its reflection rippling on the river's dark surface as they talked quietly of their plans for the next day. They had just decided to go to bed when loud footsteps in the street drew them to their feet. Shaeli picked up Ebony as Flin moved to the railing. A dozen soldiers marched up the path, their black-and-scarlet uniforms out of place amongst the roses. They could all hear the loud voice of one, presumably the head of the guard, and the answering voice of Madagenta.

"To what do I owe the pleasure, captain?" she said from almost directly below them. "Are you and your men thirsty, or perhaps you'd like dinner? Or something more... personal?"

"None of those, madam," answered the captain of the guard. "We are here seeking rebels. Our orders are to check anyone who has arrived recently. Every establishment in the village is being searched."

Shaeli drew a breath and shrank further back into the shadows. She looked at Williver, who motioned for her to be quiet and she nodded. Kirrit stepped back beside Shaeli and took her hand.

"What rebels are these you speak of?" asked Madagenta.

"Fugitives we have been tracking from the Starisles," said the captain. "There are five, one an elf. They have escaped from her majesty's guard and are wanted for aiding the rebellion."

"Good on them," shouted someone from the bar, and there was a small burst of laughter from those too drunk to care for consequence.

"There are no fugitives in *my* establishment, captain, I can assure you," said Madagenta, as if she had heard nothing but the captain's words. "I have had several parties of guests these last days, and I would have noticed if there was an elf with them."

"Nevertheless, madam, if you could show me to their rooms, so I can see for myself..." began the captain.

Tarkoda slipped into the room and began gathering their things and stuffing them into packs. Kirrit let go of Shaeli's hand and followed him.

"I shall do no such thing. I run a respectable establishment, sir, and I'll not have you interrupting my guests," replied Madam Madagenta. "I have told you, there are no elves in the Sheltered Swan, and if there were you'd be welcome to them. Nasty, furtive creatures, just like those drell."

Shaeli looked at Williver and tried to smile, but it felt more like a grimace.

"But, madam..." tried the captain again.

"*No*, sir. I have told you we have no fugitives here, nor elves, only travellers and those here for some mid-summer pleasure, if you know what I mean." At this there was some ribald laughter from the bar. "Now if you would care to join us, you would be most welcome, as members of our good queen's guard are always welcome. But if not…"

"Well," began the guard, and they could tell from his voice that he knew he was beaten. "Well, as long as I have your assurance…"

"You have it," said Madagenta. "With my blessing. Good evening, captain."

"Good evening, madam," mumbled the captain.

Flin watched until he had led his men back up the street to bang on the door of some other establishment, and then they went inside and shut the door.

"It's alright, Kirrit, you can stop packing," said Shaeli.

Kirrit appeared wide-eyed in the doorway to the next room. "I wasn't packing," she said, her arms full of bundled clothes. "I was panicking."

"Very funny," said Shaeli. "But you can stop whatever you're doing. They've gone."

"Good," said Kirrit, flopping down on a bed. "That was too close."

"I'll say," said Koda.

"They are much closer than we thought, by any reckoning," said Flin.

"It's obvious they know we're headed to Trilby," said Shaeli.

"Yes, but *they* don't know that *we* already know what awaits us," said Williver. "And therein lies our advantage. They think that what we seek has been destroyed but we walk blindly into their trap just the same."

"But they *are* waiting for us," said Shaeli. "If it *is* a trap, we *are* walking into it."

"Yes, little one," said Williver soothingly. "But a trap is useless if the quarry knows it's there."

* * *

Two days later, they hid in trees outside the village that hovered on Trilby's edge.

They had left the Sheltered Swan before dawn, the bar and dining room dark and quiet as they crept through, but when they'd walked out onto the veranda, a bulky shadow had detached itself from a chair.

"I thought you'd be out early," said Madam Madagenta, moving towards them. She thrust a bundle at Kirrit and then she looked at Williver. "I'd advise you to walk through the gardens beside the river until you reach the trees. Follow the coast. The guard may be out searching for those fugitives with the elf," she said. "Nasty furtive creatures," she added, and then she smiled.

Williver chuckled and kissed her on the cheek. "You have our thanks," he said.

"Well, we can't let the guard have an easy time of it now, can we?" she said, a blush spreading across her broad cheeks. "Off with you now, before the house wakes."

She had gone inside before they'd passed the last rose bush, and they had taken her advice and gone through gardens until they reached the edge of town. They'd walked all day, stopping only to eat the supplies given them by Madam Madagenta. They'd walked, slept beneath the trees beside a small stream and walked again all through the next day. They had barely seen a soul, and then only a few farmers in the distance.

The village now before them was a small place, its outskirts drifting into Trilby's far-flung cottages. In the distance rose the tall buildings that marked Trilby's centre, yet they were uncertain whether to seek shelter here in the tiny village or venture further into Trilby. They decided, in the end, that Tarkoda and Kirrit should go and see what the town held; whether the guard watched the ruins of Ellirra's house or whether it had been abandoned. If they had to, they would find lodgings until they were sure the way was clear to retrieving the box.

When Tarkoda and Kirrit had not returned by nightfall, the others did not worry. Koda had told them about a rowdy inn on Trilby's coastal edge, and it was there that they had arranged to meet. Flin, Shaeli and Williver had settled themselves into rooms above the noisy bar late in the afternoon, but when Kirrit and Koda had not returned by the second nightfall, Shaeli went straight to worrying. She could not contain herself.

"We have to leave," she said for the tenth time.

Flin and Williver sat at a table set with a fine dinner. Flin's hair was slicked back and his clothes were cleaner than they had been for a Moon.

"Shaeli, they said they may be a day or two," he said, plonking another piece of fish onto his plate. "If they do not return by lunchtime tomorrow, then we shall leave."

"He's right," agreed Williver. "Your brother and Kirrit are the least likely to be noticed and I'm sure they're safe. They shall be able to tell us if we are able to retrieve the bangle. But, as Flin says, if tomorrow does not see them return, we shall follow them into Trilby."

"But, Williver, what if someone has invaded Ellirra's mind, and they know about the box beneath the hearthstone. What if they were waiting and Kirrit and Koda have been caught?" Shaeli said, barely able to keep the panic from her voice.

"I'm sure no one has entered Ellirra's dreams, little one," Williver replied. "No one could know where she is or that the box could still be whole. They are safe. Now eat something. You need your strength."

Shaeli sat uneasily at the table, unable to shake the feeling that had been growing within her. She sat sullenly, answering them in monosyllabic grunts and poking at her food. Something was happening. She felt it. She tried to eat, and eventually tried to sleep, yet she was up well before dawn, looking to the shadow that was Trilby as the sun cast its first rays over the horizon.

They could make her wait no longer than midday. She had everything packed and ready long before the sun was overhead and would not be dissuaded from leaving. Williver donned his hood, despite the sun, and they followed the road into the town centre. Shaeli also kept her hood raised; to keep the sun from her face, and to keep Ebony out of sight. The jevvi sat poised on Shaeli's shoulder, her nose twitching at the smells that permeated the town.

As Mareesha had always maintained, Trilby was a vibrant, pretty town, its buildings and wide streets interspersed with parks and gardens, the houses rambling and storeyed, their balconies facing the coastal views. The streets were filled with people too busy to pay attention to the many travellers, and travellers too busy to pay attention to the many people. They reached the centre of the town, and in its square found a busy market and a big Landing with a Trader moored at it.

It was Blue Bird, traders Shaeli knew only barely, yet the sight of the Trader lifted her spirits. She wondered whether Tarkoda had spoken to them, yet as the thought formed in her head, she heard shouting from across the square. Ebony, hidden beneath her hood and hair, stuck her nose further into the sunlight. Flin took Shaeli's arm and pulled her into a side street. Williver melted into the shadows behind them.

Across the square came a contingent of the queen's guard. Ebony squirmed against Shaeli's ear, and she put a hand up to calm her. The guard had a man in their midst, and they dragged him to a post set in the ground opposite the Landing.

Three people watched from the Trader, a man and two women, and as Shaeli looked from the Trader back to the guard, she wondered at the names of those of her Fleet so close and yet so removed.

The post to which the guard dragged the man had a ring set in its top, and they tied his hands so he stood with them lashed high above his head. The head of the guard then read loudly off a paper he unrolled, stating those caught looting the queen's property would suffer the consequences, then they disappeared back into the streets.

The people around Flin, Shaeli and Williver muttered amongst themselves. Shaeli heard a woman nearby mumble something about "poor lass, she done no wrong".

An old man nodded back. "'Twas Iden's property a few days ago, not the queen's, and nothing left to loot, anyways," he said, and the woman hushed him.

The people had turned back to their business, ignoring the man tied to the post in the square, and the people on Blue Bird turned also and moved off onto the unseen deck of the Trader. Shaeli looked at Flin.

"Where are they?" she said, quietly. "How do we find them?"

"Perhaps those on the Trader have seen them," he said. "Or we check the inn Tarkoda spoke of."

"'Tis clear the ruins of Ellirra's house are still watched," said Williver, from the shadows. "Your brother must still be waiting, and as Flin says, perhaps those of your Fleet have seen him."

"I don't know," said Shaeli, doubtfully. "I don't know the traders on Blue Bird very well, and I don't think Koda does either. I think he's more likely to be at that inn." She shivered. "Unless the guard have them."

"I think it's clear what they do with looters," said Flin, looking at the bedraggled man tied to the post across the square. "And I don't think your brother is silly enough to try for the bangle with the guard around. I think it more likely he is somewhere close by, watching."

"'Tis only a street or two away, where Ellirra's house lay," said Williver. "We should find that inn." He looked around.

The flow of people moved like windblown leaves, their faces averted from the man tied to the post in the square. "I fear attracting attention."

"You're right, Williver," said Shaeli. "I'm sorry. I'm sure they're fine. I'm just worried."

"I know," Williver replied. "But I think your brother would have taken no risks. I hope only we have not missed them. Yet we must seek shelter and then Flin can make enquiries without attracting too much attention."

Shaeli nodded, and they began to walk across the square. Ebony again began to squirm under Shaeli's hood as they went, and again Shaeli put a hand up to calm her, yet before she touched her, Ebony leapt from her shoulder and ran down a street – the very street down which the guard had just gone. Shaeli dashed after her.

Ebony darted down the narrow street, leaping in and out between the legs of people who reacted with cries of surprise and delight. Shaeli had almost caught up when Ebony leapt into another street, this one broad and filled with carriages and a mass of people. Ebony's passage was easy to follow as screams and cries followed her across the road, but Shaeli saw with horror that the jevvi was heading straight into the waiting arms of the guard. She was scooped up by one of the soldiers and Shaeli was skidding into a sea of scarlet and black.

She had time to glance over her shoulder and see Flin and Williver slide into a crowd of passers-by, and then a tall soldier was pushing his face into hers. In one hand he held the struggling jevvi by the scruff of her neck, and with the other he grabbed Shaeli's arm.

"What have we here, then?" he said. "A girl with a jevvi. What luck. 'Tis just what we seek."

Shaeli pulled against the arm holding her. Across the street she could see Flin reaching for his throwing stone, and

Williver put a restraining arm on his shoulder. She looked back up at the guard.

"Let me go," she cried.

"Not likely," said the guard, a smirk on his narrow face. "My captain will have questions for you."

"I suggest you do as she says," said a soft voice from nearby. "This is not the person you seek, I can assure you."

Shaeli looked around, and with a shock of surprise she saw the Princess Crissita standing behind the guard. She was much as Shaeli remembered her, beautiful, defiant, her hair shorter, but her blue eyes as determined as ever. Beside her stood S'resh, her maid, with Minti the white jevvi in her arms.

Crissita pushed her way through the soldiers, and smiled condescendingly at their leader. "I fear you have caught no one but one of my servants, young man, out chasing after a wayward pet," she said.

Ebony at that moment struggled out of the soldier's hand, leapt to the ground, raced across to S'resh and scrambled up her skirts. She and Minti snuggled against each other, chittering and dancing in S'resh's arms.

"You see," said Crissita. "My pets are reunited. I beg you release my girl also."

"I beg your pardon, madam," said the man, tightening his grip on Shaeli's arm. "My orders are to look out for a girl with a jevvi, and I seem to have found one."

"Yes, perhaps," replied Crissita. "But they are *my* girl, and *my* jevvi, and when my husband, Sir Brudloc, regent lord of Romynn, returns this evening, he shall expect us to be ready to accompany him north in the morning. Servants, pets and all." She smiled a steely smile. "So if you would be so kind, I have some words to say to this stupid girl about letting the jevvi stray from our quarters in the first place. We stay right here," she said, nodding at a sign depicting an enormous pig with wings. "If you have any questions about the legitimacy of my servants, or my pets, you may see my husband in our rooms at

191

the Flying Pig this evening." Crissita moved forward and took Shaeli's other arm. "Now, if I may?" she said, and before Shaeli knew it she was through the crowd and the door of the inn, Crissita's hand still firmly about her arm.

Crissita began a tirade as they pushed through the people, and she continued as they went through the door and into a lofty hall. "Stupid girl. I told you not to let them out of your sight," Crissita ranted loudly. "Your master will be severely displeased, you mark my words. I've told you time and again to watch that one." She pushed Shaeli up a staircase, a hand still tightly about Shaeli's arm.

Shaeli looked back and saw S'resh following, the two jevvies in her arms. The head of the guard stood in the doorway staring up at them. Of Flin and Williver, there was no sign. Crissita pulled her upward.

"No point worrying about them now, you stupid girl," Crissita shouted. "S'resh has them well in hand. Wait until we reach my suite, and *then* you shall have something to worry about."

They reached the top of the stairs and turned down a broad hall, Crissita continuing to rant loudly. At the end of the hall a door opened, and Crissita marched Shaeli through, all the time telling her what terrible punishment awaited her.

S'resh came in behind them and closed the door. Instantly Crissita let go of Shaeli's arm and threw her arms about her, enveloping her in a tight embrace. She kissed her cheek, and held her back to look at her. It was then that Shaeli saw Tarkoda and Kirrit grinning at her from across the room. She rushed at them.

"Where have you *been*?" she cried, hugging them in turn. "How did you get here? How did you find Crissita?"

"I found *them*," smiled Crissita. "I saw Tarkoda in the street from the window, just as we saw you." She drew Shaeli to the window, and below was the broad street they had just left.

192

The guard was just disappearing around the corner, two of their number left at the door, and Shaeli looked for Flin and Williver in the crowd, but could not see them. She looked at her brother.

"Koda, did you see where Flin and Williver went?" she asked. "Were you watching?"

"I was," he said, moving up beside her. "They are in that ale-house on the corner, and now that the guard has gone, I'll go and fetch them." He kissed his sister's cheek. "I'm glad you're here," he said, before going out the door.

"It was lucky Minti started making such a fuss," said Kirrit. "Or we never would have seen you." She shuddered. "And the guard would have caught you."

"It was Ebony's fault I ran into them," said Shaeli. "She just dashed away before I could stop her." She looked at the jevvi sternly. "And I thought she'd gotten over running away."

"It's not her fault," smiled Crissita. "She knew her mother was near."

"I thought you gave Minti to Brudloc's mother," said Shaeli. "As a gift."

"I did, but I brought her over to... shall we say, introduce her to a very handsome gentleman jevvi who I thought would appreciate her charms," said Crissita. "He has wonderful markings. Luckily I did, for your little jevvi must have scented her. Minti certainly knew. You should have seen the fuss she made, and as Kirrit said, we would not have seen you otherwise."

"No," agreed Kirrit. "We were just getting ready to come and meet you. We would have been gone within the hour." She looked at Shaeli. "I thought you were waiting for us at the inn on the coast."

"I couldn't," she admitted. "I made them come and look for you."

"Typical," smiled Kirrit. "And we would have missed you, or worse, if not for Crissita." She looked at Crissita. "We were despairing of finding somewhere to watch Ellirra's. You should have seen Tarkoda's face when S'resh came up to us in the street."

"She was the last person he expected to see, I'm sure," smiled Crissita.

"What do you mean? Watch Ellirra's?" asked Shaeli.

"You can see it," said Kirrit, "Or where it was, anyway, from a window at the back of the suite. Crissita has let us stay here with her, and we've been watching, but there's been soldiers there day and night."

"And we leave tomorrow," said Crissita. "On the Trader moored at the Landing. I expect Brudloc back this afternoon, and we fly at first light. I have preferred travelling on a Trader rather than by ship since Purple Leaf took me to Romynn."

Shaeli smiled at her. "That was a long time ago," she said. "And so much has happened since."

"So I understand," said Crissita. "Ah, here are your other companions," she added, as they heard voices outside the door.

They were soon reunited, introductions were made, and then Tarkoda led them down the hall to the room that overlooked the site of Ellirra's house. Crissita accompanied them. Her rooms took up the entire wing; they passed several doors where maids were packing voluminous trunks, and another where a man was setting out bowls of fruit for a number of jevvi.

S'resh had followed them down the hall, Minti and Ebony still snuggling together in her arms, but when they reached the doorway where the other jevvi were, S'resh put them down and they dashed into the room. Minti took Ebony up to each of the four other jevvies – one brown, one white, and another two mottled grey and brown like Ebony, one with a baby peeking out from her shoulder – and they laughed as Ebony was smelled and chittered at by the others.

"It seems they've made their introductions," smiled Crissita. "S'resh will keep an eye on her for you, Shaeli, though I think she'll not be going anywhere."

They went on down the hall, and entered a dim room. The curtains were drawn, except for a small gap through which they could look out. Below lay a large open courtyard, several carriages parked on one side, and the roofs of the stables on the other.

Shaeli did not have to ask where to look. Beyond the courtyard and across the street lay the blackened shell of a once-large house. The remnants of two walls still clung together, a triangle of floor between them. A window in the face of one of the walls screamed soundlessly, and mounds of crooked burnt beams lay piled like blackened bones. The chimney stood like an accusatory finger pointing at the sky, its base crowded with ash and debris. Four of the queen's guard stood sentinel in front.

"Well, I don't think we're going to get in there without attracting attention," said Flin. "Even without the guard, it will take time to remove the hearthstone without someone seeing, even at night."

"That's what I thought," said Koda. "I wasn't sure what you'd want to do."

"Well, we'll just have to figure something out," said Shaeli quietly, her eyes still on the ruins of Ellirra's house. "Guard or not, be seen or not, it doesn't matter." She turned and looked at Williver. "It's too important not to take the risk."

Williver looked back at her for a long time, and then he nodded. "As you say, it is too important not to," he said, and then he smiled a thin smile. "But that does not mean we have to give ourselves away unnecessarily."

* * *

They talked the afternoon away planning what they were going to do. Crissita begged to be included and offered to do whatever she could. It seemed a fine game to her and they found as they talked that they did need her. When Sir Brudloc arrived and had gotten over his initial surprise at the unexpected reunion, he wholeheartedly vowed to help them, too. They had told Crissita as little of their mission as they could, and though Brudloc looked dubious at the sketchy details they told him, he did not push them, merely nodded as Crissita told him their plan.

Shaeli watched the two as they interacted, and saw an easy rapport between them and the way they touched each other casually. It seemed they had made a good marriage, talking of their two daughters fondly, and she hoped they were happy. She noticed Tarkoda watching them, too, and remembered the hurt he had felt when they'd left Crissita on Romynn, yet she could see no sign of that old wound on his face.

That evening, the servants began transporting baggage to the Trader, and before dinner, they were paid a visit by the guard who had accosted Shaeli earlier. Sir Brudloc saw them and assured them that he had known the girl and her jevvi for many Winters, which was true enough, and would personally guarantee them, and then he berated the guard for questioning his wife and servants. The guard mumbled apologies, and when they had gone Shaeli confessed she almost felt sorry for them.

Later, Sir Brudloc left with the last load of trunks to see the trader, and Tarkoda accompanied him, carrying baggage so he'd look like a servant – something he and Kirrit had pretended to be in the few days they had been staying in Trilby. Crissita had so many servants, and jevvies, that no one knew they had not arrived with the original party. It was well that he had carried baggage. When they returned they reported two guards had been loitering on the corner, and had followed them to the Landing and back.

"Oh, they tried to be discreet," said Brudloc. "But we knew they were there."

"It matters not," said Williver. "In fact it works quite well."

"And you talked to those on Blue Bird?" asked Shaeli.

Koda nodded. "Yes, they're all set," he replied. "They know Da well and know we would not ask unless we were in need."

"That's it, then," said Flin. "Everything's ready. Nothing more remains but to wait for morning, and we better try and get some rest as we wait."

"I suppose you're right, Flin," said Shaeli. "But I don't know if I can sleep. I'm much too nervous."

"'Tis just another performance, Shaeli," said Flin. "Think of it as nothing more."

"I'll try," she answered.

"You'll be fine, as always," he said, and then he looked at Tarkoda. "The horses are organised?"

"The groom will have them waiting on the outskirts," Koda nodded. "I told him we wanted one last stroll through his lovely town."

"Let's hope it *is* a stroll," said Kirrit. "And not a wild dash. The horses sound good though. No more walking."

"That's easy for you to *say*, Kirrit," said Shaeli. "But how many times have you actually *been* on a horse?"

"Well, a couple," said Kirrit. "At fairs and things. But it doesn't look hard."

Crissita snorted. "Oh, my dear," she giggled. "You have no idea. You just wait."

"Why?" asked Kirrit, starting to look alarmed. "You just have to sit there, don't you?"

Brudloc answered. He too, was laughing as he spoke. "Hardly," he said, politely trying to stifle his mirth. He looked at Tarkoda. "You asked for mild mannered beasts, I hope?"

Tarkoda nodded. "Oh, yes," he said, trying to keep check on his own laughter. "Specifically. Even the groom gave me a strange look when I told him two of our party had never been on horseback, but he promised to choose the animals wisely.

It's alright, Kirrit," he said, finally letting his laughter go at the look on her face. "You'll be fine."

"If you say so, Koda," she said. "But if anything happens, I'm holding *you* responsible."

"*Me?*" Tarkoda sputtered. "Why me?"

"I don't know," said Kirrit. "But I have to blame somebody." She looked stonily at him.

"Oh, stop teasing Koda, Kirrit," said Shaeli, laughing at the look on her brother's face. "I'm sure we'll both be fine. I once had three riding lessons on Romynn. I'll teach you. Come on," she said, hoisting Kirrit to her feet. "Let's try and get some sleep, we have a busy day tomorrow."

* * *

They were all awake while it was still dark, and after a hurried breakfast, Tarkoda, Williver and Flin left the Flying Pig by a shadowed side door. Sir Brudloc said his good-byes and he left also, with most of the servants and the last of the baggage, by the inn's wide front door. A short time later, as the sun began to turn the World grey from beneath the horizon, Crissita and her maids left with much unnecessary ado, carrying the jevvies, each in their little cages, also by the front door. When they reached the Landing they entered a flurry of activity.

Though it was early, the square was beginning to fill with people. Around the Landing stood Crissita's retinue, Sir Brudloc calling directions from the stairs. One of the traders was harnessing the Zoi, and several people stood on the deck watching. A small contingent of the queen's guard stood in a corner of the square, trying to look casual.

Shaeli stood with Kirrit, also trying to look casual, and trying not to look at the guard who was trying not to be seen looking at them. It was obvious they were watching the suspicious girl and her jevvi to make sure they flew to Romynn as Sir Brudloc had said they would.

198

When the Zoi were harnessed, the trader spoke to Brudloc, and Brudloc called loudly to his wife. The sun broke over the horizon and long rays poked between the buildings. Already the warmth of the coming day could be felt, and Shaeli began to sweat, yet it was not from the heat. It was time.

Crissita looked at her. "It has been lovely to see you," she said, quietly. "If you ever need us again, you have only to send word." She spoke louder. "Come girls, it is time we boarded. You there," she said to Shaeli. "Be sure that jevvi's cage is shut tight. You know she loves to escape." Her voice dropped again. "Good luck," she said, and then she turned and went up the stairs.

The others followed her, Shaeli and Kirrit last. They drew up their hoods as they went.

The trader was untying Blue Bird's rear mooring as they approached the stairs, calling to his partner on the deck. He nodded slightly when he caught their eye and then studiously ignored them.

Shaeli stopped and put the little cage she carried on the lowest step. She stooped as if checking the door of the cage, just as Crissita had told her. Kirrit stopped beside her.

"There's Flin," she said, her voice barely audible. "Go."

Shaeli slipped her right hand into her amulet, and with her left she undid the cage. Ebony poked out her nose.

"Find Koda, Eb," she said. "Quick as you can."

Ebony bobbed her head and sniffed the wind, then she was out of the cage and dashing across the square.

"Oh, my lady," Shaeli cried, loudly.

"Oh, stupid girl, what did I tell you?" wailed Crissita, also very loudly. "Fetch her quickly. You," she said to Kirrit. "Go and help her."

The guards had turned, several took a few steps closer. The trader stood near the forward mooring, the rope in his hands.

"You best hurry," he yelled.

Shaeli and Kirrit dashed across the square after the scrambling jevvi. People stopped to watch the spectacle. Half of the soldiers began to follow the girls following the jevvi.

Just then a ball of red light exploded down a side street. There were gasps and a few screams. Another ball, purple this time, erupted in the air behind the square. No one saw the amethyst Shaeli dropped back into her amulet.

Shaeli heard one of the soldiers yelling and turned to see some of them running down the street where the red ball had exploded, and others disappearing towards where the purple had been. Only three of the guard still followed them across the square.

Ebony leapt into a side street, Shaeli and Kirrit just behind her, the three soldiers perhaps thirty paces behind them. The people parted as they passed and a few laughed, but most were looking back to where the strange skylights had exploded.

The side street was still thick with shadow, untouched by the sun's rays, and ahead was the black skeleton that had been Ellirra's home and the four soldiers who were stationed before it.

Ebony dashed towards them. The eyes of the guards moved from the sky to the spectacle approaching through the gloom. One soldier seemed to deduce what was happening more quickly than the others and she stepped forward, into the jevvi's path.

"Oh, no," groaned Shaeli.

Yet she needn't have worried. Ebony side-stepped the woman easily and kept running, straight towards the blackened ruins. The others moved forward, all trying to block the jevvi, but Ebony stopped and sniffed the air. Shaeli and Kirrit were but a few paces from her when she moved again, dashing back across the road, away from the ruined building and the grasping hands of the guard.

"Please help us catch her," Kirrit called to the guard in front of the remains of the building. "The Trader is ready to leave and we must be on it." Then she ran after Ebony and Shaeli. The four guard, after a moment, followed. The three from the square were not far behind.

Ebony had run into the back entrance of the inn where Sir Brudloc and Crissita had stayed, the Flying Pig. Carriages were parked along one side of the large open yard, and from the other side came the smell of horses. The place was thick with the night still, the shadows pooling deeply around the parked carriages. When the soldiers entered the dusky yard, they saw the two maids disappearing amongst them.

"Please, check the stables," the tall one called. "We must hurry."

The seven soldiers dutifully began to look for the jevvi. None of them noticed the two figures moving in the shadows of the chimney in the burnt-out husk across the road.

A short time later, another ball of red exploded in the sky, but before the soldiers had barely raised their heads to look at it, the two maids were emerging from between the carriages.

"We found her," the shorter one called. "Thank you all for your help. We must hurry back to the Trader before my mistress leaves us behind." She carried the small brown jevvi in her arms.

"We shall escort you," said one of the soldiers. "You best get back to your posts," he said to the four who had joined the chase. They nodded and went to stand before the remains of Ellirra's home.

The three who had followed from the square escorted the maids back to the Landing. They were thanked, and watched as they were berated by their mistress all the way up the stairs and onto the Trader. They could still hear her harassing her maids after the Zoi had risen into the air. They felt sorry for the two girls, and returned to report their departure to their captain.

* * *

Inside one of the carriages behind the Flying Pig, Shaeli and Kirrit sat leaning into the shadows as the guard left the yard.

"Well, that went well," said Tarkoda, sitting across from them with Ebony on his knee.

"Let's hope so," said Kirrit.

"How long do we wait?" asked Shaeli.

"Only until the Trader leaves," said Koda, peering out the window. "And there it goes. Let's go." He opened the small door and stepped down. "Come on. We have to meet the others."

They left the carriage, went through the inn and out the front entrance. As they stepped out into the street, full sun stepped over the buildings, and they hurried through the streets until they found Williver and Flin waiting in a park to the south, their hands streaked with soot. Flin was smiling.

"A bit singed, but fine," he said.

Shaeli breathed a sigh of relief, but they did not indulge in their success. They still had to leave Trilby undetected.

* * *

As Blue Bird flew higher, leaving Trilby behind, Crissita turned to S'resh. "You and Wanda did well," she smiled. "It went as expected?"

S'resh nodded. "I believe so," she answered.

"And the guard did not suspect?"

"I don't think so. We exchanged cloaks in the carriage and kept our hoods up. None looked closely at us. We had the jevvi, and while I am a little shorter than Shaeli, Wanda and Kirrit are of the same height. 'Tis lucky Wanda did not mind becoming a redhead for a few days." S'resh shrugged. "We can only hope all is well, my lady."

Crissita nodded. "That we *can* do, S'resh," replied Crissita. "Hope, and pray the gods keep them safe."

* * *

The guard stood before their captain reporting on the departure of the Trader, suspicious girl and all, and the skylights that had been seen. Whoever had fired the skylights was a mystery. The captain was concerned little with the skylights; the girl and jevvi were another matter.

"And they found the creature where?" asked the captain.

"At the back of the inn at which they'd stayed," answered the soldier. "The Flying Pig. It lies across from the building we burnt a few days ago."

The captain's eyes narrowed. "The site was not entered?" he asked.

"No, sir. They were across the street. They never went near the site."

"And it was watched at all times?"

"Well, the guard on duty helped us look for the creature, but it was only moments, and..."

The captain took up his hat, and stalked to the door. "Fools," he said. "Come with me."

* * *

South of Trilby, Tarkoda was trying to educate the two girls on the finer points of riding – as they rode. Kirrit was not happy. She had been unprepared for the bouncing she was receiving, and was trying to learn to grip with her knees, keep a tight rein, and rise to the trot, all at the same time. Shaeli, though trying to master the same things, was laughing at Kirrit.

They had decided to go due south. Most of the things in Ellirra's singed box were her personal belongings and Shaeli wanted to return them to her. She felt it was a small thing to do when Ellirra had lost so much. Then they would head towards the Lakes' country and try and find a Trader to take them east.

They had looked in the box after the groom had left them with their horses on the outskirts of the town. The bangle was there, as bright as it was in Shaeli's memory, and for the first time she began to feel that everything might be alright. But she would be wrong.

In Trilby, the captain of the guard stood over a hole in front of the blackened chimney.

"Ready the horses," he said. "They cannot have gone far."

Shaeli watched from the trees as Kirrit and Flin took the box to Ellirra. Williver thought it would be safer for Ellirra and her family if she did not know who delivered the box to her, and Shaeli had to agree. Much as she wished to see Ellirra, she knew Williver spoke wisely.

Flin and Kirrit walked up the path to the farm where Williver had visited Ellirra in the dreamworld. They spoke to some children in the garden and one ran inside and returned with Ellirra. Her daughters were at her side as Flin handed the box over.

Ellirra looked at it. She ran her hands over the lid, opened it, and even across the distance Shaeli could see that she began to cry. Flin was talking. He was to say it was a gift from an old friend in Trilby, with apologies for those things that might be missing, and then Ellirra hugged them both and stood watching as they came back down the path.

As they reached the trees, though neither Flin nor Kirrit looked around, Ellirra raised one arm in farewell. Shaeli felt the tears spill over her lids and she raised one hand in return, even though Ellirra could not possibly see her. As they walked back to where the horses were tethered, Kirrit took Shaeli's hand.

"She'll be alright, Shaeli," she said.

"I know," said Shaeli, rubbing at her eyes. "I just feel bad for her."

"She said something funny before we left," said Kirrit, and she stopped.

Shaeli stopped beside her. "What?"

"She said," Kirrit began, looking her closely. "She said that she knew the thing that was missing would be gone, because it had been told to her in a dream, and then she said, 'tell her thank you, and to remember the prophecy'. I had the strangest feeling that, though we never mentioned anything, I think she knew it was from you. I don't know why I think that, I just do."

"Did she say anything else?"

"No, Shaeli," said Kirrit. "Just that. 'Thank her, and remember the prophecy.' What does it mean?"

"She's talking about King Tenelon, Kirrit," said Shaeli, quietly. "And the prophecy he made before he died."

"But he was mad, wasn't he?" asked Kirrit. "Hadn't the Fever taken him?"

"No, Kirrit," said Shaeli, her mind and her eyes far away. "No, I don't think it had."

* * *

It was well that they had gone south. The search fanned out along the coast, and it was two days before the searchers moved further southwards. Every post was warned to be on the lookout for a party of five on horseback, an elf and a girl who carried a jevvi amongst them.

* * *

CHAPTER THIRTEEN

Far to the south-east, Jarris saw the last cliff before the Long Lea rise up before him. Behind the Trader, the Valley of Stones shimmered in the heat of the day. He was filled with relief and exhaustion. He had barely slept these last days and he felt a strange urge to cry as the Trader rose up above the waterfall and the Lea spread out before them. Jarris had not seen it like this since his Cave year, and the unlooked-for tears fell without his permission. Jeth put a hand to his brother's shoulder before he went down to open the landing gate.

Jarris flew the Zoi up the line of the stream, upturned faces in the fields below, the roof of the hall above the tops of the trees ahead. There was a tiny Landing beside the barn and he brought Purple Leaf down to it in one smooth movement, and then Jeth and Andos were mooring them and there was nothing for him to do but breathe the air of safety. His shoulders slumped. Old ones and children were beginning to mill about the Landing, and Sahli'en, Navez, and the Warlocks were coming down the stairs of the hall, the questions already on their faces. He sighed and looked up.

The balloon had a dejected air about it and Jarris felt much the same. It was puckered with a score of holes, some with arrows still stuck in them, and a huge rent scarred one side. Three times they had encountered large contingents of Virrisian's soldiers intent on boarding, the last at Serrat, ever the safest of havens. If it had not been for the warning from his old friend Billitt, and Qiren's magic, he did not know how they would have escaped. He hoped the old baker was not suffering for his loyalty.

Mareesha came up behind him and put her arms about him, and he was glad of them; he had had little other comfort, lately.

"Come, Jarris," she said, her own face soft with weariness and relief. "'Tis time our tale was told."

* * *

It was very late that evening before the whole tale could be told. The children and old ones had gone to their beds thinking Purple Leaf had been attacked because of false claims of treason. The reason invented by Queen Virrisian seemed the simplest way to answer the questions thrown at them after their unexpected return. Yet later, after Shanna and Neesha had gone to their beds, they sat in the empty hall and told Almarnoch, Llevvis, Navez and Sahli'en everything. Jeth and Eenis were there, for it was time they also knew the truth. Qiren and Illen were also there, sitting quietly in the background with Wyshka and Olver.

Mareesha spoke quietly, Jarris added a detail here and there, and after they had finished there was silence. Navez studied the ceiling, Jeth the floor. Llevvis contemplated his hands. Illen and Qiren said nothing and their faces were unreadable. Wyshka's eyes were wide, Olver holding her hand. Almarnoch had sat through much of the story with his beard on his chest and his eyes closed. Sahli'en and Eenis stared at Mareesha, their faces constantly changing expression.

"And no one else knows of this, Mareesha?" said Sahli'en finally.

"Until this last Wintering, there were but three people in the World who knew," replied Mareesha. "Jarris, myself and Irinesta. Perhaps Irinesta's maid, E'Nith, who is in seclusion with her. Now..." She shrugged and shook her head. "Now, I'm not sure."

"Well," said Navez. "'Tis clear Taffka must be told."

"That is so," said Almarnoch, opening his eyes and raising his head at last. "Taffka must be told. But more than that, the World must be told. I fear this places the Fleet in danger, and the sooner this Land and the others are told, the safer we shall

become. Yet how we are to reach Taffka, I do not know. It is clear Purple Leaf cannot fly to Palveron."

Mareesha looked at him. Her eyes were dark emerald. "I think I know how we can tell him," she said. "I think I know how we can tell them all."

* * *

That night, in the tower of the Glade at Great Court, Irinesta was preparing for bed.

The day had passed as every day did – slowly. There was little for her to do but study the contents of her mind, yet she tried to fill the day with something. She sewed; their clothes were becoming threadbare and requests for new material had been constantly denied. She and E'Nith prepared their own meals with the few supplies they were given; essentials only, neither of them had tasted meat, tezz or wine since E'Nith had been denied the right to leave the tower. She and E'Nith tidied the already immaculate room, and she spent many hours standing on the balcony looking down on the gardens and the city or out to the bay, and she also spent much time gazing at the mural. The soft, painted grass and the towering trees hiding the scores of faces around the Glade seemed to mock her gently, taunting her with their beauty. She also wrote a great deal. Many of the drawers and cupboards of her room were stuffed with paper bearing her elegant writing.

Soft breathing came from the corner where E'Nith slept in her tiny bed. Irinesta braided her hair looking at the Glade, and then she sighed, turned, and went over to her bed. As she leant to turn off the lamp, a soft light blossomed to her right. She started, drew a sharp breath and slowly turned her head. On a shelf beside her bed were scattered a few trinkets, and one, a small hollow rock, its centre filled with tiny crystals, was emanating a soft light. Irinesta's eyes widened and she rushed to stand before the rock. She lit a candle and began to chant softly. An answer to her melody came from the small stone, and then a voice followed it.

"Irinesta?" said the voice. "Is it you?"

"Yes," Irinesta said. "Yes, it's me." Her hand went to her throat. "Oh, my dear, you take a great chance."

"It doesn't matter anymore," replied the voice. "Irinesta, they know."

"What?" she cried. "How?"

"There is no time, but they know. You must tell the Fleet leader, Irinesta. You must tell everyone. She is in danger."

Irinesta thought for only a moment before she answered. "It shall be done," she said.

* * *

Mareesha watched the light fade from the stone, and she turned to face Almarnoch.

"It shall be done," she said, repeating the words of King Tenelon's widow.

* * *

Taffka and Renn alighted from the carriage under bright skies and walked through the inner wall into the courtyard and the shadow of Great Court. In the centre of the enormous courtyard was the well, brimful as always, and typically sweet when Taffka poured a cupful for each of them. Renn looked up as she sipped at the water, a breeze from the south-east ruffling her dark hair.

"What's that?" she asked, pointing up.

Taffka's eyes followed her hand. High above, near the top of the castle, something was fluttering towards them. Something white. The one fluttering thing became two, ten, a score, and then hundreds of the fluttering white objects were falling from the sky. The breeze caught some, and they fluttered out over the inner wall and across the lawns. Others began to rain softly down into the courtyard. A few fell near the feet of Taffka and Renn. It was paper, the ones at their feet only a few of hundreds of pieces of paper drifting down from far above, from the balcony of the tower of the Glade.

Taffka and Renn both picked up a piece of the fluttering paper, read the words written upon them in the spidery, elegant hand, and they looked at each other. Taffka looked up at the tower. Sheaves of paper were still falling from it, drifting down into the courtyard inside the inner wall, floating on the breeze out into the gardens, into the courtyards of the Faunist and Warlock houses and still further. Many of the papers were floating on the south-east wind across the castle gardens and on over the high outer wall, down into the city.

Taffka saw a Romynnii lord pick up one, scan it, and stuff it into his vest before turning and stalking back out through the inner wall. He mounted his horse and took off at a gallop down the hill. Nearby, a party from Ashkanna were reading the pages, and then they too left the castle. Taffka shoved the paper he held into his vest and looked at his wife.

"Mareesha," said Renn, and Taffka nodded.

He opened his mouth to speak, but a scream across the courtyard stopped the words in his throat. He looked up in time to see the body of a woman crash onto the cobblestones, pieces of paper still clutched in her hand. Blood and bits of flesh splashed across the stones. People began to scream. Renn cried out and Taffka took her arm and steered her away from the shattered body, back out to their carriage. As they drove away from Great Court, scores of the white pieces of paper still fluttered on the breeze over Palveron.

Taffka did not see Almarnoch's former apprentice standing outside the Warlock house, a piece of paper in his hand, and he did not see the way Garrit's eyes moved from him to the castle, and then to where the Warlock Island lay serenely in the bay, to where Dari would soon be finished his training.

* * *

Queen Virrisian had been arguing with Orm of the Treasury again when one of her guard rushed into the room. The queen's eyes narrowed and she turned to berate the soldier for her interruption, yet the woman bobbed apologetically and thrust a scrap of paper at her. The queen scanned the page, crumpled the paper in her fist, and left the room without a word.

Sir Azeron, her master-at-arms, followed her as she rushed up the stairs of the tower of the Glade and helped his soldiers break down the bolted door at the top.

Inside the room, the old queen and her maid stood on the balcony, surrounded by drawers and boxes. Most were empty, but a few were still stacked neatly with sheath upon sheath of paper. The old maid kept throwing papers frantically over the side as the old queen turned to meet the new.

Queen Virrisian pushed Irinesta aside, and Irinesta fell to the floor as Queen Virrisian strode out onto the balcony. She grabbed the tiny old maid by the arm, leant over, picked up one of her legs, and then in one clean movement, she lifted her up and threw her over the railing. Azeron had a glimpse of the toothless, terrified face before the old woman fell out of sight, the papers in her hand fluttering as she scrabbled uselessly at the air. Irinesta screamed and flung herself at Queen Virrisian, but she was easily thrust back to the floor.

"Stay where you are, Irinesta," spat the queen. "Unless you want to follow your maid." She flung the crumpled paper in her hand at the old queen's face. "It will do you no good, Irinesta, no matter what you think. 'Tis easy to make them think you have finally succumbed to madness, for they will never see the child."

"Oh, but they will, Virrisian," said the old queen. "They *know* now. The rumours of this day will spread like grassfire. Tenelon's prophecy shall come to pass."

"That will never happen," said the queen. "He... *I* will not allow it. Azeron," she barked. "Get rid of these." She kicked at the boxes still holding the papers. "Remove the door. Station four soldiers inside the room and six on the landing. It seems the old queen has become a danger to herself. We must keep an eye on her." Before she left the room, she leant and hissed at

Irinesta. "Prepare yourself," she said. "You will soon have bad tidings. *Very* bad tidings. It may just be that you will *want* to follow your maid to the cobbles below."

* * *

Taffka waited until he was inside the Trader before he pulled the paper from his vest. He read the words again. The words on Renn's paper were identical. Others that he would see in the coming days would hold the same words.

The child of King Tenelon and Queen Irinesta is not dead, it said. *The child has been held safe by a loyal subject to keep it from harm. The false queen cannot be trusted. Tenelon's heir lives. Prepare for it. The child will rule.*

It was signed Queen Irinesta, wife of King Tenelon, and stamped with his royal seal.

* * *

As Irinesta had predicted, the papers and the news they contained spread quickly. Lady Arinola found one in her garden when she was cutting roses. She recognised Irinesta's handwriting immediately, and though she wanted to find Sir Vulcan right away, she had to take a few moments on a bench before she rushed inside, leaving her half-filled basket sitting forlornly in the middle of the garden.

* * *

When one of the crumpled pieces of paper reached Fezzik a few days later, he read it three times, his throat and chest swelling with its importance, its implications. He smiled to himself and went to find Verlie.

They were living deep in a thick forest far to the west of Boccra, where someone had discovered a few caves at the base of a rocky cliff. There was a creek nearby, shallow but running with clear water, and the caves were small and would be freezing in the Wintering, but while the year lasted, they would stay here. The cliff above the caves gave an overview of the land around, and they would not be taken by surprise by the guard that hunted them throughout the Land. Bekerra and her huge horse were still with them, for she had decided she rather liked being an outlaw. She had proved invaluable to his safety on a number of occasions.

When he showed Verlie the paper that had been brought to him by a runner from Palveron, her face grew pink. She thrust the paper at Pemba, who read it with widening eyes and then clutched the scrap to her breast, her eyes filled with more hope than Fezzik had seen in them for a very long time.

* * *

The papers spread further, to each of the Lands; one even found its way to a small island on the eastern edge of the Starisles. It was brought by the elves from their island nearby, and, as they had thought, the old woman was most interested. She stroked the paper, smoothing the creases that had been made during its passage. Zeb watched her, wondering at the look on her face.

"So, Tenelon's child lives after all," she said at last. "Tarkon's line continues."

* * *

CHAPTER FOURTEEN

Shaeli thought of her family a lot over the next days, but her concern for them was often overshadowed by a more urgent problem – her aching bottom, legs, and back. The others suffered too, but she and Kirrit were in agony for days.

They had kept travelling south through the low mountains that ran from the northern coast down to the Lakes' country. Tarkoda knew the route well, having flown it many times on Purple Leaf, and they steered clear of towns and villages, riding through only when it was not possible to go around. They stopped when their supplies ran low, and then only Flin and Tarkoda went in to a village to buy what they needed. Though they believed they had left Trilby and suspicion far behind, they thought it wise to take precautions. It was well that they did. Every post along the western side of Zirrus was looking for them.

They came out on a high ridge eight days after they'd left Ellirra's, the foothills fading away into flat green plains before them. The plains spread out around the vast network of lakes that ran from here down to the River Zerrin.

"Well, we can go further south, to Orrellis," said Tarkoda, referring to the town on the shores of Lake Oliss where they had rescued the twins years before. "Or turn east and see if we can't find a Trader around one of the smaller lakes inland."

"That seems like the most sensible thing to do," said Flin.

"And at least we'll be heading in the right direction," agreed Shaeli.

"Inland it is then," said Tarkoda, and he turned his horse down the hill.

As they had been assured, Shaeli and Kirrit had gradually gotten used to riding. Luckily the horses they had been given were the sturdy, mild-mannered creatures they had been promised, and they seemed to almost aid the girls in learning. Ebony was in her element, perching on Shaeli's shoulder, the pommel, or on the horse itself. Shaeli's horse seemed not to mind in the slightest, and would sometimes flick its tail at Ebony when the jevvi sat on its rump, snorting as it did so. Shaeli would almost swear it was laughing.

They camped that night behind the last hill before the plains began, taking the chance of lighting a small fire, and in the morning they headed east, into the vast fields and plains.

They travelled three more days without incident, out into the green plains, passing tall hemp fields ripe for harvesting, ready to be made into rope and paper and a hundred other things, and wide fields of corn and wheat. They met few people; an occasional traveller, a farmer's cart, and they saw small clusters of farmhouses far off the road amidst the green farmlands. They also saw the great leaping forms of the shy karabool in the distance, the giant doe-faced creatures that were common only around the great lakes, who pricked up their ears and bounded away before they ever came close enough to see them properly. They began to enjoy themselves, they grew lax and secure in their journey; the ride had become easy, almost pleasant.

Late one afternoon they rounded a bend in the road. Before them was a small village. Its streets were filled with two score of the queen's guard, half of them on horseback. They stopped in the road, looking at the guard. The soldiers, just a few, turned to look at them, and then they began to shout and point. Before they had turned their horses, the guard had begun to ride.

It was well the girls had learned to ride. They galloped back the way they had come, Tarkoda out the front, Flin and Williver behind them. The guard had not yet rounded the bend behind them, and before they did, Tarkoda led them into a thin pathway, no more than a strip between fields. The corn stalks slapped their faces like spiteful hands as they pelted down the row, and halfway along Koda turned to the right, down another thin space between rippling fields. After that it became a blur, left and right they went, riding as fast as they could between rows, twice stopped by fences barring their path. They followed the fences away from the guard, the only sounds the thuds of the horse's hoofs and the stalks slapping at their bodies. Shaeli realised at one point that they were going west, into the setting sun, and then the light was gone and still they went on, into dusk and then darkness. When the horses could go no further, they tethered them in a patch of grass and huddled together in a hollow, the three-quarter moon rising to the east.

"Well," said Flin, dryly. "I think we know they're still looking for us."

"I'd say that's a safe thing to assume," said Williver, with a grim smile.

"Obviously we weren't quite as clever in Trilby as we thought," said Tarkoda.

"At least we have the bangle, and they don't have us," yawned Kirrit, running her fingers through her russet hair and replaiting it. The freckles across her nose stood out starkly against her pale face.

"We just need to get to Cave," said Shaeli. "And then we'll be safe."

"Yes, but what do we do now?" asked Kirrit.

"Rest for a few hours, and then go on," said Flin. "There's nothing else we *can* do."

They dozed until sunrise began to pattern the sky and then they left. Morning found them at the edge of a lake, safe once more, but far to the south-west of where they had meant to go.

"I think this is Lake Oliss," said Tarkoda. "The northern edge. We can follow it around to Orrellis, or try going back east, along that side."

"I don't want to go back," said Shaeli, quickly.

"Neither do I," said Kirrit. "That was as close as I want to come to meeting any more of the queen's guard."

"My sentiments exactly, Kirrit," said Williver. "Yet we may encounter them wherever we go."

"Perhaps this is another time to seek shelter in a crowd," said Flin.

"There'd be more chance of seeing a Trader further south," said Tarkoda. "And if my memory is right, they should be holding the summer festival in Orrellis about now."

"Even better," said Flin.

"It seems that is the direction to go, then," said Williver.

"But what if we run into some more of the guard?" said Shaeli. "We can't rely on good luck forever."

"Do not worry, little one," said Williver. "We shall reach your Cave safely, I promise you."

"But how can you *know*, Williver?" she said, the chords of her voice hitting a plaintive note. "They could be anywhere."

Flin answered. "Shaeli," he said. He spoke gruffly, for him, his voice determined. "If we cannot outrun them, you seem to keep forgetting something." He looked at her through lowered brows. "We can fight them." His brows grew closer. "Fight them, and win."

* * *

They decided to travel at night. The moon was approaching the Full and it seemed safer, so they slept through that day by the shores of Lake Oliss and travelled throughout the night, skirting the lake's northern edge. As the day after their flight from the guard began to dawn, they looked for somewhere to rest through the heat of the day, saw a small grove of trees across a field, and turned their horses towards it. Just ahead, a squat figure stepped out from behind a clump of bushes.

"I would not do that if I were you," said a deep voice.

"Who are you?" called Flin, reining in his horse. "And why tell us what to do?"

"I am friend," said the voice. "And I know that if you sleep in that grove, you shall wake to find the guard at your throats."

A taller figure stepped out beside the first one.

"And what would you care?" asked Flin, his hand on his throwing stone.

"I told you, we are friends," said the voice. "And so we are."

Shaeli had been peering through the gathering light. She jumped from her horse and ran towards the two figures in the road.

"Shaeli, stop," called Flin, dismounting.

"It's alright, Flin," she called back.

Tarkoda was already down and following Shaeli up the road, yet by the time Flin reached them, Williver and Kirrit just behind leading the horses, Koda was laughing. Flin saw a pair of huge dark eyes, red-rimmed, through the dim dawn light, and he started. It was a drell. A drell and Shaeli was hugging him. Then he remembered Shaeli telling him how she'd met a drell, many Winters before, and he relaxed.

"*Blenny*. Spotjaw," Shaeli cried, after hugging each in turn and introducing Flin and Williver. "How did you get here? *Why* are you here?"

"We rode as you do, young Shaeli, so we did," smiled Blenny. "And we're here for you."

"For me?" asked Shaeli. "Why?"

"Because they're waiting for you in Orrellis and this road will be full of 'em soon, so it will," Blenny said. "And because they'd like to be catching you. Catching you all."

"Who, Blenny?" she asked. "Who's waiting for us?"

"Why, that false queen's soldiers, of course," replied the drell. "Yet there is little time to spare for explanations. By mid-morn this road will be filled with soldiers coming from Orrellis to search the Lakes' country. We must go back towards the east."

"Back?" said Shaeli. "We can't go back, they're behind us."

"Aye, lass, and they're ahead of ye, too," said Spotjaw, speaking for the first time.

"So, we must go back," said Blenny. "If we can't slip through their net, 'tis likely we'll have to break through it." He looked at Flin and Williver, bowing his head slightly. "And I think these two will make an easy task of that, if they must." The smile that crossed his face was slight but sure. "Am I right?"

"You are," Flin answered. "If we must, as you say. But why do you keep saying 'we' must go back. Surely you came from Orrellis?"

"Yes, lad, that we did," said Blenny. "But we'll not be going back there. We shall go with you."

"What?" said Shaeli, puzzlement creasing her brows. "Come with us? *Why?*"

"Because you may have need of us, young Shaeli, so you may," replied the drell. "But there is little time for talking. Fetch the horses, Spot, please."

Spotjaw went over to the copse for which they'd been heading and returned with a brown horse and a smaller grey pony. The others remounted, Spotjaw boosted Blenny up on the grey pony, and then he mounted the brown horse.

"Hurry, now," said Blenny, taking the reins. "We do not have far to go."

He kicked his horse and galloped off down the road, Spotjaw beside him, and they followed.

"Are they to be trusted, Shaeli?" asked Flin, pulling his horse in beside her.

"Yes," said Shaeli, watching the backs before them; one so lean, one so stubby and regal. "I have not seen them for many Winterings, but yes."

"It seems we may have little choice, for now," said Flin.

* * *

The sun had risen by the time they reached a crossroad, and Blenny stopped his horse. To the left the road to Orrellis began, and far down it they could see a great plume rising into the still morning air. At first Shaeli thought it was smoke, but then she knew it for what it was: a dust-plume. She could see it moving slowly towards them, and she shuddered to think how many horses it took to make that big a cloud.

"There they are," said Blenny. "But we go this way."

Ahead the road wound on towards the coast, but Blenny turned his horse towards the low hills they had descended from just a few days before, thinking they had escaped Trilby unnoticed. How wrong they had been.

They did not go far before Blenny turned his horse down a thin lane banked by shrubs. The shrubs grew high above, shading them from the sun, and after a while the lane went past an opening where the ruins of a farmhouse sat in a weed-choked lawn. The windows were glassless, the veranda roof had collapsed at one end, the wall beneath it sagging outwards. The lane thinned even more past the ruined farmhouse and became little more than a track, the shrubs lining it grew thicker and tall trees began to grow up around them. They were heading east now, into the morning sun, and though they were grateful that the thick foliage overhead kept the sun from them, the humidity was oppressive, for little breeze stirred inside the wall of trees and bushes.

Before the sun was far up the sky, Blenny stopped and dismounted. Spotjaw slid down off his horse's back, slipped forward, and took the reins of Blenny's pony. Blenny walked up the track a little way and fiddled about in the bushes to the right, mumbling incoherently, and suddenly a wall of bush was moving into the track. Spotjaw clicked to their horses and pulled them on, taking a sharp turn to the right behind where Blenny stood, and the others followed. Blenny somehow manoeuvred the bush back in behind them, mumbling again all the while, sealing them off from the thin track, and they dismounted and looked about.

They found themselves in an open space full of sunshine, surrounded by the same trees and thick bushes that had lined the track. On the far side of the glade there was a low building made of stone, with arched windows and carved gables. Beside the house was a small well, brimful of water, with a low trough next to it which Spotjaw began to fill for the horses. They unsaddled them and the horses drank from the trough and began munching on the thick grass of the glade. It was a quiet place, only the soughing of the wind through the trees and the calls of tiny birds in the bushes could be heard.

Shaeli stood holding Ebony in her arms, but the jevvi began to struggle, so Shaeli put her down. Ebony bounded across the grass to explore. "Don't go too far," she called, and then she looked at the drell. "What *is* this place, Blenny?" she asked.

"A sanctuary, lass, so it is," he said. "Built by the drell, it was, many hundreds of Winterings ago as a place they could shelter from the World. There were many such places once, when drell still roamed the Lands. There are still some, here and there, if one knows where to look, aren't there, Spot?"

"That there are," agreed Spotjaw, grinning. "And many times have we used this one."

"I believe there is one not far from my lands," said Williver. "My kin come from the northern mountains."

"You would be right then, lad," said Blenny. "There is one such place on the edge of elfin lands, for the drell never needed such a sanctuary within them." He smiled. "Elves and drell have ever been friends. But come inside. We have already brought supplies for the journey."

He opened the door of the building and went in. The others followed, and even Shaeli had to stoop to fit through the low doorway, but once inside they could stand upright, though Spotjaw and Williver's heads almost brushed the ceiling. It was cool inside, the thick stone walls keeping out the heat, and their eyes soon adjusted to the dimness. At one end of the room there was a hearth with a table and chairs before it. The other end of the room was filled with beds that lined the walls three high, pillows and blankets piled neatly at the head of each. Everything was small. The table and chairs were low, the beds short, the mantelpiece over the hearth was little higher than Shaeli's waist. The arched windows were also at waist height and Flin went to one and looked out.

"And this place is completely secure?" he asked.

"In a thousand years, no one has ever invaded the safety of a sanctuary," said Blenny solemnly. "We shall not take the chance of lighting a fire, but the guard could pass by out there and never know we are here." He looked at Williver. "We would hear them coming, so we would, even without elfin ears to hear for us, and besides, all sanctuaries have layers of protection spells woven about them." He looked over at his lofty companion. "Now, Spot, where are those supplies? Our guests must be hungry."

He and Spotjaw pottered about, producing meat and fruit and a few loaves of fresh-baked bread to lay on the table, and they all sat down, finding somewhere to stick long legs under the low table. Ebony bounded in, helped herself to fruit and bread, and then she climbed up on one of the beds and fell promptly asleep. There was silence as they ate, but afterwards Shaeli couldn't help but ask the question.

"Blenny, how did you know it was us the guard was looking for?" she said.

"I knew, lass," he said. "I knew it was you because I saw it in the smoke, so I did."

"You saw *me* in the smoke?"

"Yes," he said. "And these folk, too." He waved a piece of bread at Williver, Flin and Kirrit.

"You saw *us* in the smoke when you were in Orrellis?" asked Tarkoda.

"No, lad, not Orrellis," he said. "'Twas in Trilby I saw them. You I did *not* see."

"Trilby?" said Shaeli, startled. "When were you in Trilby?"

"Some Moons ago now, wasn't it, Spot?" Blenny asked.

"Yes," said Spotjaw. "Almost halfway through spring it were, after we sailed in from Romynn."

"That's right," said Blenny. "So it was. We did a show in the square before we headed down to Orrellis. That's where I saw you in the smoke. You and your friends. In Trilby."

"But, why...?" began Shaeli.

"I think I know," interrupted Williver. "'Twas you who told Ellirra to protect her possessions. *You* were the seer who warned her of a fire."

Blenny nodded. "That's right," he said. "Sad for her I was when I saw her house burning in the smoke. I knew I could not save it, yet I gave her a warning. But when I looked in the smoke again, I saw the burnt house once more, this time cold and guarded by the false queen's soldiers." He grinned, his round pudding-face lighting with mirth. "And then I saw the strangest thing. Two girls chasing a jevvi down the street, the guard helping them, while a man and an elf took a box from beneath a blackened hearthstone." His face grew serious. "Then I saw the captain of the guard standing over the same hole."

"So *that's* how they knew," said Flin, pounding fist into palm. "They found the hole beneath the stone, even though we replaced it."

"And you saw they were searching for us in the smoke, too?" asked Shaeli, sure she was right.

"No, lass," smiled Blenny. "That was mere eavesdropping. Spot heard them in a tavern, talking of the girl with the jevvi who can throw skylights that they were being sent out to search for. When he told me, I knew it was you, as I had seen you in the smoke. Three ships of soldiers arrived on the coast off Orrellis four days ago." He shrugged. "We thought the odds were unfair, and ye should have two more on your side."

"How did you find us, then?" asked Shaeli.

"That I *did* ask the smoke," said Blenny. "It showed you heading for that copse where we met this morning. We knew there was no one else to warn you and decided we had to try, didn't we, Spot?"

"That we did, Blenny," said Spotjaw, lighting a long pipe.

"So, we took our wagon out to some old friends and came with all speed. We left only a day before the guard," said Blenny. "The old friends send their greetings, Shaeli, by the way. They remember you with great fondness."

Shaeli frowned, wondering what he could possibly mean, and then her eyes lit up. "Nol and his family?" she asked, remembering the sad-faced man she had reunited with his wife and children.

"We saw them in Orellis several times after Purple Leaf was gone," said Blenny. "And we have visited every time we went to Orrellis since."

"Are they well?" asked Shaeli. "Where are they?"

"Still in the little house by the sea," said Blenny. "The sons married and with children. Our little wagon is parked beside their house and they lead a happy, quiet life."

"I'm glad," she said. "Remember, Williver?" she asked the elf. "You sent me to him. He gave me the first bangle."

"I remember," smiled Williver.

"You never told me about this," said Kirrit, shaking her head. "You're always keeping secrets, Shaeli." Though it was said in fun, Shaeli looked enormously guilty, but Kirrit did not notice. She was yawning loudly. "But I don't want to hear about it now," she said, when she had finished yawning. "This is all very interesting, but you seem to be forgetting we were up riding all night. I need to sleep."

"I'm with you, Kirrit," said Tarkoda, yawning too.

"You most certainly are not," Kirrit said, going over to a bunk, kicking off her shoes and curling up on the short mattress. "Find your own bed."

Koda laughed. "Very funny," he said dryly. "Those bunks look a little short though," he added.

"I find it best to pull the mattress down on to the floor," said Spotjaw, doing just that. "We'll sleep, too, won't we Blenny? We were also up most of the night."

"So we were, Spot," said Blenny. "So we were. Sleep peacefully. You are safe here."

Koda, Flin and Williver made up beds on the floor beside Spotjaw, while Shaeli, Kirrit and Blenny slept on the bunks. Shaeli just fit, but Kirrit's legs hung off the end a little way. It didn't seem to bother her. She was asleep before Shaeli had put her head on the pillow.

* * *

Shaeli woke to the sound of horses and the shout of voices. She sat up with a start, one hand going to her amulet, her head colliding with the low bunk above. She groaned, put the other hand to her head and staggered to her feet. Ebony bounded across the floor and scrambled up her skirt.

Koda and Spotjaw were still asleep on the floor. Of Kirrit she could see nothing but a mound of blanket and a splash of red hair.

Flin stood by the door, and he looked at her as she stood up. He put a finger to his lips, yet there was no need for his warning. She could hear the voices and the jingle of the bridles on the other side of the bushes where the track lay.

She crept to the door to stand beside him. The sun was low in the western sky, the shadows long around the trees. Williver and Blenny stood just outside. They both looked at her, and though Williver's face was full of concern, Blenny smiled at her.

"Why are we down this goat track?" said a sullen voice from beyond the bushes across the little glade.

"Because our orders are to search every grove, thicket, path *and* goat track between here and Marnissi," answered a woman's voice.

"They were spotted leagues away from here," said the first. "It's not likely they're anywhere around these parts. *And* it's almost dark."

"There's no sign of them down here, Captain," said another voice. It was another woman, her voice softer than the first, and it came from the other side of the bush that Blenny had moved that morning. The soldiers had stopped just outside the sanctuary. "There has been no one down this path for many days. There are no branches broken or any sign of prints, either horse or person. Not even a *goat* has passed this way."

There were a few laughs at that, and then the first woman spoke again. "Alright, then," she said. "Let's turn around. We can camp for the night at that abandoned farmhouse we searched back there."

There were the sounds of horses again, and then the voices and hooves receded back down the thin track. Shaeli breathed a sigh as the noise faded. Williver smiled at Blenny.

"Your protection spells still work well," he said.

"Drell magic is limited in its range, young elf," Blenny smiled back. "Yet what magic we do, we do well."

"What do you mean?" asked Flin.

"Well, there must be many signs of our passage on that trail," Williver said. "Prints, bent branches and blades. Yet their tracker could see none of them."

"The protection spell you spoke of?" asked Flin.

Blenny nodded. "That is one of them, yes," he said. "Now it's time we woke the others."

"But we'll have to go past the guard, won't we?" said Shaeli. "Back at that old farm."

"No, lass," said Blenny. "We follow the trail on. We go east."

After waking the others and eating a meal, they tidied the sanctuary, saddled the horses, and Blenny made the bushes move again. When they were out on the track he replaced them, making the trail seamless once more. The sun had set, the moon had not yet risen, and the track was not clearly visible, yet Blenny seemed to know exactly where he was going. He and Spotjaw went first, followed by Flin, then Shaeli and Kirrit, with Williver and Tarkoda at the rear. Ebony perched on Shaeli's saddle, sniffing at the cool night air.

When the branches and trees thinned, the track became merely a rut between scrubby bushes, and soon they came to a road. Blenny did not turn onto it, however, but crossed it, and they followed a thin line between tall hemp fields. The lines between the hemp fields were much the same as those they had followed through the corn fields when escaping from the guard, and they wandered past field after field through night-time silence, only the sound of frogs and crickets accompanying them. The tall, thin hemp plants were almost ready to harvest; here and there they passed fields already holding nothing but stubble. The moon rose over the fields in front of them, huge and golden, and they rode beneath it all night.

When the moon set behind them and the stars began to fade, Blenny led them to a rocky hill not far from the endless fields. At its base lay a cave big enough for them and all the horses. Its entrance was cunningly hidden, and though Blenny said it was not a sanctuary proper, it was secure and protected. There was a spring close by where they could fill their water bottles and water the horses, and food they had in plenty; there would be no need to approach any towns or villages for a while.

For three days they went on like that, Blenny leading them through leagues of farmlands, and then through natural grasslands, east and north and east again. Twice they saw karabool grazing in the distance beneath the moon-soaked sky, the mob of long-tailed, horned animals chewing their meal with their noses in the air, scenting for danger.

They followed the drell through the silent grassland, the plaintive cries of the occasional night-bird the only sound to accompany them. Each sunrise Blenny found a secure place to sleep through the day.

On the third day as the sun dipped into the west and they were readying the horses to leave, they saw in the distance a huge party of riders heading east, the last rays of the sun highlighting the tips of their spears and the scarlet and black of the queen's standard. They waited until moonrise before they left their hiding spot.

That night they passed through the neck of land that ran between the two lakes, Orrin and Odynn. Blenny smiled broadly when the thin strip of land was safely past without their seeing anyone.

"'Twas the only place that worried me," he said. "If there had been guard here we would have had to fight, so we would. From here it will take us eight or nine days to reach the edge of M'Zen'sclahr Forest, but the false queen's guards will not find the paths that we follow."

"You've said that a few times, Blenny, 'the false queen'," said Tarkoda. "Why do you think she is false?"

"Because there is one other than Virrisian," said Blenny. "One who truly has the right to sit on Zirrus' throne, so there is." He peered through the night, but it was Shaeli he looked at, not Tarkoda. "I have suspected something of it for years, but before we left Orrellis, the streets were abuzz with rumours of a true heir."

"Someone else has the right to the throne?" asked Koda. "Who?"

"I do not know," answered Blenny, looking at Koda.

Shaeli was relieved when he looked at Koda. Blenny's eyes had made her feel distinctly uncomfortable. Then she realised only one of Blenny's eyes had moved to Koda; the other stared at her still and her discomfort bloomed anew.

"Anyway, lad," continued Blenny, clicking to his horse. "Now is not the time for questions. The sunrise hours approach and we still have a way to go."

"That we do," said Spotjaw, talking as they rode. "And in a night or two we take the path through the Poisoned Marshes."

"You're not *serious*?" scoffed Tarkoda.

"What are the Poisoned Marshes?" asked Kirrit. "I don't remember hearing about them."

"Traders don't even *fly* over them," said Tarkoda. "We go around. There's nothing there."

"Aye, lad, everyone goes around," said Spotjaw. "And with good reason. 'Tis a nasty place."

"So it is," said Blenny. "But a safe one for all its nastiness, if you know what you're about. And there is something there, lad. A sanctuary lies in its midst."

"But *are* they dangerous?" Kirrit persisted. "These marshlands?"

"Aye, to some," said Spotjaw.

"Why? What's in them?" said Kirrit, her voice rising.

"Oh, not much," said Spotjaw. "Nothing much can live there. Bugs, mites, leeches. The danger lies mostly in not knowing the paths."

"There, Kirrit," said Shaeli, soothingly. "At worst we'll get bitten a bit."

"The bugs and mites aren't too bad," conceded Spotjaw. "But you want to avoid the leeches. They're a bit bigger than your usual leech and mighty hard to stop the bleeding. That's if you can get 'em off."

"Big?" cried Kirrit. "How big?"

"Oh, they're big enough. Makes 'em easy to see," said Spotjaw, mildly.

"We'll be alright, then," said Shaeli, reassuringly. "We'll just be careful."

"If you say so, Shaeli," said Kirrit, dubiously. "And that's *all* that's there, Spot?"

"Aye," he said. "Just them." He thought for a moment. "Oh, and them giant roaches. But they look a lot worse than they sting."

"*Roaches*," sputtered Kirrit. "*Sting?*"

"Aye. Huge ugly brutes," said Spotjaw, still mildly.

"Worry not, lass," said Blenny. "We know where their colonies lie, and not even a mite can breech the safety of sanctuary."

"How many days will it take to cross these marshes?" asked Williver.

"Oh, four, perhaps five," said Blenny.

"And there is but one safe place in there?" said Williver.

"So there is," agreed Blenny. "Yet there is no need to travel only at night. None will see us once we enter the marshes, and none will follow. Not even the queen's loyal guard."

"How far away is it?" asked Flin.

"The ground becomes barren beyond that ridge," said Blenny, pointing to a dark line cutting across the sky to the east. "In the centre of the Barren Lands lie the Poisoned Marshes. We shall reach the ridge before sunrise, with luck, and rest for the day in a cave on the other side. We must pass close by a village, and then we go where no road lies."

The village appeared as Blenny had said it would and they skirted its dark buildings. Only one light glimmered in a window, mirroring the glimmer of light that had begun to grow to the east. They went over the ridge and before them lay wasted rocky lands, long fingers of shadow reaching towards them across the colourless ground. Nothing moved.

They went down the steep ridge into the rocky land in single file. None of them saw the figure watching from the edge of the village behind them.

* * *

At the bottom of the ridge lay a few scrubby bushes, almost the only sign of vegetation in the Barren Lands. Blenny mumbled a few words and the shrubs parted. On the other side was an open area and a cave, small, but large enough to hold them and the horses too, with a tiny spring just outside the cave mouth. They let the horses crop at the pale, short grass growing in front of the cave while they ate a sparse meal, and then they brought them inside. They would rest for much of the day, for Blenny said it was best to leave mid-afternoon. They would have to travel all night and through the next day before they reached the drell sanctuary in the midst of the Poisoned Marshes.

They woke and ate after the midday hours had burned the worst of the heat from the day, filled their bottles from the tiny spring and watered the horses. They were just finishing saddling them when they heard voices.

Williver and Blenny went to the screen of shrubs that hid the entrance to the cave, thankful they'd brought the horses into the cave to saddle them. The others stayed back in the shadows as the elf and the drell looked through tiny gaps between the leaves.

Outside, two score of the guard were coming down the hill on horseback, creating a cloud of dust and noise. They stopped just past Williver and Blenny's line of vision, but close enough for them all to hear the conversation that followed.

"You're sure it was them?" asked a harsh voice.

"Oh, I'm sure, Captain," answered another thin croaky voice. "I saw 'em creep past in the sunrise hours and watched 'em go over this ridge. Where they're headed I can't say, there's nothing but the Barren Lands and the marshes out there, but I've earned my coin. I found 'em for ye."

"And you saw the elf clearly?"

"Aye. Him, *and* them girls. One with red hair, one with a jevvi. It were riding on her pommel. And there were something else."

"Something else?" asked the harsh voice. "What?"

"Well, I was looking for five, but there were seven horses, two that were leading them others. One was tall, one short. Short as a drell."

"Short as a drell, you say?" said the captain's voice. There was a long silence. "Very well, here is your coin. Take it and go back to your miserable village."

There was the clinking of coin and the croaky voice spoke again. "Thank you, sir," it said, and they could hear the grovel in the voice. "And may I ask what of these new rumours? Is it true Traders are being banished to their Cave? Does Tenelon's heir truly live?"

"'Tis true some Traders are *hiding* at their Cave," replied the first voice. "Their actions of late speak of treason, and they fled rather than answer the charges. Of this you may make what you will. Yet Tenelon's heir does *not* live. They are merely rumours. *I* advise such rumours should not be repeated amongst *loyal* subjects."

"No, no, I agree," said the grovelling, croaking voice. "The words will not pass these lips again. Thank you again, sir. With your permission, I shall return to my home."

"You have it."

There were sounds of someone scrambling back up the hill, and then the captain's voice spoke again.

"We shall have to search the area. Mount up."

"But, Captain," said a woman's voice. "The afternoon wanes. There are only a few hours of daylight left."

"We shall search until there is none," said the captain. "They cannot have gone far. We shall split into two groups. One shall search north. The other shall go south. With luck, by the time the reinforcements arrive we shall know which direction they have gone."

"You think they have not continued to go east, sir?" asked the woman.

"Into the marshes? I think not," said the captain. "Only fools would enter the Poisoned Marshes. And if they do," they could almost hear him shrug. "If they do, they'll not come out again."

"It's that dangerous?"

"That and more," the captain scoffed. "The Barren Lands circle the Poisoned Marshes, and 'tis nearly impossible to survive those. No water. Only snakes and vermin. 'Tis not called the Barren Lands for nothing. The Marshes are even more vile. Stench-filled and ugly. I went to the edge of them once and saw the giant, stinging creatures that inhabit them. I never want to look on them again." He was silent for a few moments. "Take fifteen soldiers and go north. I'll take the rest and go south. When night falls I'd advise you cross the ridge again before you make camp. You should have reinforcements by morning, then you can ride south and join us."

"Yes, Captain," said the woman.

The sound of horses came again, and then a group rode straight past the entrance to the little cave. Williver took a step back, but not one of the guard looked their way. Hoof beats receded slowly in both directions, and when they could hear them no more, Blenny waited at the entrance for a long time, looking out.

"Well," he said, when he finally came back. "We shall have to delay our departure for a short time, so we shall." He seemed unperturbed by the arrival of the soldiers.

"Shall I unsaddle, Blenny?" asked Spotjaw.

"No, Spot," said Blenny, making himself comfortable on a rock and beginning to stuff his pipe. "It won't take long for them to get out of sight."

Shaeli felt panic fluttering in her chest. Every time she thought they'd escaped the guard, they were found again. It was only a matter of time before they were caught. And what that man had said. About the rumours. It seemed Tarkoda was also thinking about the same thing.

"He said Traders had gone to Cave. Not just one. Not *just* Purple Leaf, but others," he said. "I wonder who, and why."

"I hope everything's alright on Red Arrow," said Kirrit. "And what about what they said about King Tenelon's heir. That it still lives. Do you think it's true?"

"Probably not," said Flin. "Probably just a rumour started by the rebellion to create more unrest."

"That's what the guard were saying in Orrellis," said Spotjaw. "But others said the rumour had come from Palveron. From Great Court itself, some said."

233

Shaeli could stand it no longer. She looked at Williver, and he nodded imperceptibly, his eyes filled with compassion. Blenny's eyes were deep, unreadable pools.

"You're wrong, Flin," Shaeli said, her voice dull. "The rumours *are* true." She took a deep breath. "Tenelon's heir *does* live. It's just that she doesn't know who she is. Nobody does."

* * *

Shanna and Neesha sat by the pool that had been their favourite swimming place during their Cave year, and their sister's favourite during hers. Though they did not know it, they sat on the rock where Ishaan had seen Shaeli dripping wet and in her underclothes.

They were wet, too. Although they did not have to, they had begun to help the children having their Cave year. They knew many of them and there was nothing very much else to do anyway. They'd come down to the fishing hole for a swim after a hot day harvesting fruit.

"Fancy having to have *two* Cave years," said Neesha, squeezing the water from her hair. It was not the first time she had said it, and her sister's eyes went skywards.

"It isn't quite what we expected, no," said Shanna, patient as ever. "But it's not so bad. At least Purple Leaf is here too."

"Yes, but not Koda and Shaeli."

"No, not Koda and Shaeli," agreed Shanna.

"Where do you think they had to go?"

Shanna sighed. It wasn't the first time Neesha had asked that question, either. "I don't know," she said. "You know as much as I do."

"Well, it must have something to do with the wand."

Shanna sighed. The conversation was following its usual pattern. "Yes, Neesha, it must."

"Well, I wish they'd hurry back."

"Me, too."

"And two more Traders back early, accused of helping the rebels. Just like us."

"I know," replied Shanna. "Taffka won't be happy about it when he gets back. Da says there might be more."

"Things are getting bad, aren't they?"

"Yes," Shanna said. "Yes, they are."

They sat without talking for a while, until Neesha spoke again. "Shanna?"

"Mmm." Shanna's eyes were closed against the sun.

"Have you noticed anyone looking at us funny lately?"

Shanna opened her eyes and looked at her sister. "Like who?" she asked, quietly.

Neesha was not looking at her, but out across the water. "Oh, Sahli'en. Navez."

"Llevvis? Wyshka, even?"

"*Yes*," Neesha exclaimed, turning to look at her sister. "Jeth and Eenis, too. You *have* noticed."

Shanna nodded.

"Oh, thank goodness," said Neesha. "I thought I was imagining it."

"I thought *I* was," said Shanna.

"*Why* are they, do you think?"

"I don't know," said Shanna. "But it's strange. Definitely strange."

* * *

Shaeli spoke quietly, her eyes on the ground most of the time, yet every now and then she looked at Williver and seemed to draw strength from him. She would take a deep breath and go on, her hands clutching her amulet as they had when she was a frightened child. When she had finished, no one spoke for a long time.

Spotjaw stood with his back to them at the cave's entrance. Blenny sat on his rock smoking his pipe, the red rims of his eyes glowing like the ember in his pipe. Flin leant against the cave wall. His eyes had not left Shaeli's face the whole time she had been speaking, his hands aching to take some of the burden from her shoulders. Williver's eyes had stayed on

Shaeli's face too, but he knew that the telling of her burden would be enough to lighten the load. Kirrit and Tarkoda had sat on either side of Shaeli; both had pale faces and round eyes. At last Koda spoke.

"And you had no memory of this?"

Shaeli shook her head. "Not until Williver came, no," she said. "I don't think I would have remembered anything if he hadn't come, not even myself. And I don't think I would have *ever* remembered anything about that night if it wasn't for that... that *thing* in my head."

"And you didn't tell Mam and Da that you had remembered this?" asked Koda.

"Yes, I did," said Shaeli. "I spoke to them before we left the Trader. The night Williver came to Flin's and told us about the wand, I said it had invaded my memories and I think Mam had guessed at some of it, but I felt better after I spoke to them. Everyone else thought it was about the wand."

"The *wand*?" cried Kirrit. "The wand is *nothing* compared to this."

"Oh, the wand *is* something, Kirrit," said Williver quietly. "Why do you think the guard seeking us is so vigilant? And why there are so many?"

"But *that's* why they wanted Purple Leaf in Palveron," said Tarkoda. "It's not *just* Shaeli and the wand. It's the twins, too." He looked at his sister. "One of them anyway."

"Why *your* family, Shaeli?" asked Flin. "Why hide the child at all?"

"I don't know *why* Queen Irinesta hid her," said Shaeli. "But our Mam lived a long time at Great Court when she was young, and she and the old king and queen were very close. They must have trusted her a great deal."

"So they must, lass," said Blenny from behind a thin cloud of pipe smoke. "And the old queen must have feared for their child's life a great deal also." He knocked his pipe against his boot. "I am sorry to say 'tis time we were leaving, and more talk will have to wait, so it will. The guard should be well out of sight by now."

He went to the entrance and mumbled a few words, opening the branches of the shrubs at the front of the cave, and they led the horses outside. Blenny moved the shrubs, thin of leaves but strong with ancient drell magic, back into place. There was again no sign of the cave, nor were any of the guard in sight. They mounted and turned to ride on. A voice spoke from their right.

"Go no further, unless you want an arrow through the girl," it said. It was the same harsh voice they had heard earlier. The voice of the captain of the guard.

He stepped from behind a boulder fifty paces down the ridge line. His face was craggy, weather-beaten, and smug. Behind him came three soldiers, two women and a man. Another rose up atop the boulder above them, and yet another stood halfway up the ridge. All had their arrows aimed at Shaeli.

"Well, it seems waiting to give the reinforcements direction has paid an unexpected bonus," said the captain. "Keep your hands where I can see them," he barked, as Tarkoda's fingers inched towards his belt. "All of you, keep your hands where I can see them. Get them up."

Spotjaw and Kirrit raised their arms straight away, Tarkoda and Williver followed more slowly. Flin also stuck his fists begrudgingly into the air. Shaeli put her hands on her head as Blenny raised his stubby arms from the reins.

The captain began to walk forward, drawing his sword. The three soldiers followed, keeping their arrows trained on Shaeli. Her chest felt heavy with the weight of them. She whispered to Ebony, who was sitting on the saddle between her knees, behind the pommel.

"So now a drell has joined the fugitives," said the captain, moving closer. "One at a time, down from your horses, the tall one and the drell first." He stopped twenty paces from them.

"And remember, with one wrong move the girl's life ends here."
He barked a laugh. "We are under no orders to take *live*
prisoners."

Spotjaw lowered his arms slowly and slid off his horse. He
turned to help Blenny.

Ebony scrambled up Shaeli's bodice and disappeared
beneath her hair. The soldier's arrows were trained on her
chest still, ready for flight, yet their eyes were on the tall man
and the drell. She would have to be quick.

Small hands pushed a long cool shape between sweaty
fingers, and Shaeli ducked as she threw. She did not veil her
magic. There were no soft, pretty skylights. There was white
fire and burning hands.

Four lights streaked at the captain and the three archers
beside him. Three bows exploded into flame beneath fists. The
captain's sword turned white and he dropped it, screaming.

Another bolt flew at the soldier atop the rock, and
unhappily for him, his arm was enveloped in white flame along
with his bow. He flailed and fell, screaming and on fire, out of
sight behind the rock.

Shaeli felt something whistle past her ear, and moved her
hand to aim at the last soldier standing on the ridge, the only
one who had had time to loose an arrow, and the only one not
screaming. Yet she did not have to fire. A stone from Tarkoda's
sling thudded off the man's forehead. A blue bolt flew from
Flin's fist and slammed into his chest. Another bolt hit his bow,
thrown from Williver's wand. The man fell without a sound and
slid with a clatter of rocks and dust to the base of the ridge.

Shaeli looked at the three beside the screaming captain.
They did not look too badly hurt, their hands were singed but
they no longer screamed, yet the captain was on his knees, the
skin of his right hand peeling off like the skin of a blackened
fruit, and she looked away. She dropped her quartz back into
her amulet, took Ebony from her shoulder and hugged the jevvi

to her chest. Then she started to cry. She looked at Williver, her face ashen beneath the grime.

"I had to," she said, around hitching breaths. "I... We can't let them catch us."

"I know, Shaeli," Williver said. "It's alright. You did what had to be done."

"Williver's right, Shaeli," said Flin. "I was ready to do the same thing, but I would not have left them with mere burns."

"Hurry now," said Blenny. "We must go before we lose any more time."

Shaeli wiped at her face, held Ebony up and looked into the rich black depths of her eyes. "You are a treasure," she whispered, and she held the warm soft creature to her cheek for a moment before she put her back on her shoulder. She gathered up her reins and took a deep shuddering breath.

Spotjaw had remounted and Blenny kicked at his horse and they took off, a pale-faced Kirrit behind them. Tarkoda looked at her, eyebrows raised, and she nodded at him and he rode off too. Williver and Flin moved their horses either side of her, and as they passed the boulder where the soldier had fallen, she saw that his clothing was still on fire, yet that barely mattered. His head was twisted at an unnatural angle and blood seeped from his ear and mouth. His eyes stared sightlessly at the sky.

They galloped after the others, away from the screaming captain and his dead and wounded soldiers, into the Barren Lands.

* * *

CHAPTER FIFTEEN

Shaeli did not look back over her shoulder until dusk turned the world grey. All she could see behind them was the black line of the rocky ridge, small and distant, and the high pale sky.

The tears had subsided quickly but the feeling had not. She felt sick, horrified by what she had done to those soldiers, but she had also realised something. She would, more than likely, have to do it again. She had known she was not sending out mere skylights when she'd thrown those lights – had known their potential – yet she'd also known that she *had* to. She rode with her head bowed through the desolate land.

They had not been able to gallop far across the Barren Lands, the stony rubble on the ground gave way to increasingly uneven terrain, and soon the horses were picking their way between jagged boulders across pock-marked ground. The only life they saw were lizards, red-tongued and hissing, jagged spines along their backs like miniature Qotarr, and the occasional snake, these longer than the horses. And there were the ants, giant red beasts that built mammoth nests and attacked anything that came within their territory; the horses legs were targeted in moments whenever they stopped. The ants bit with ferocity, leaving large red welts, and all of them had sustained bites when they'd ducked behind a boulder to relieve their bladders.

And it was hot. The sun fell huge and golden into the western horizon, but even after a red-streaked sunset there was no respite from the heat. No breeze blew across the dead plain, and the heat that had been baked into the ground through the day rose up until long past the midnight hours. They stopped only once to rest, atop a mammoth slope of rock where the ants could not reach them, to feed and water the horses and themselves, dozing through the small hours of the night, and then they went on, into the sunrise. Shaeli rode in near silence, her shoulders slumped, lips pursed against the tears that still threatened, and when she did speak it was in terse, short words.

With the light of day they could see how close the marshes had grown, yet it still took most of the morning to reach the outskirts. They had smelt it long before that.

Blenny had advised them to tie a cloth around their noses, and they were glad of them, for the stench *with* a mask was almost too much to bear. Breathing through the mouth gave the even more revolting sensation of tasting the vile smell. Tarkoda muttered that it smelled like old privy, dead animal and rotten eggs all mixed together. Kirrit forbade him from ever trying to describe it in her presence again. Shaeli laughed, despite the disgust she felt at herself and an overwhelming desire to gag; there was a touch of hysteria in the sound and she realised she must be very tired.

The wall of the Poisoned Marshes grew until it filled their vision as fully as its miasma filled their nostrils. The ground began to grow spongy, the horses hooves made slippery sucking sounds as they neared the grey-green wall. They dismounted to rest the horses for a while between the biting ants and the marshes proper, surveying the way ahead.

The marshland was full of reeds and rushes like all marshes, yet these were as tall as small trees, their stems thick, their leaves jagged and spiteful. Between the thick clumps of overgrown reeds the water was dark and filmed with an oily substance. No birds stalked long-legged through the shallows; no frogs burped and croaked from lily pads; nothing moved but a cloud of mosquitoes, these too, overgrown, legs hanging like hair and wings flapping erratically.

"I can see it has earned its reputation," said Flin, adjusting his cloth mask. "And it will take *how* long to reach the other side?"

"Two days to cross the Poisoned Marshes themselves," said Blenny. "Another to cross the Barren Lands on the other side."

"More Barren Lands?" groaned Kirrit. "Great."

"The Barren Lands circle the Poisoned Marshes, young Kirrit," said Blenny. "One must go through them to reach the good lands beyond."

"And there is solid ground in there? A pathway through?" asked Tarkoda, eyeing the dark water.

"There are many paths, lad," said Spotjaw. "The trick lies in knowing which to follow. *Our* path is wide enough to take our wagon."

"You bring the wagon through here?" said Tarkoda, incredulous.

"Aye," said Spotjaw. "Every two or three year we go east. This way is smelly and ugly I'll grant, but it's a dozen days journey at least, going round."

"So it is," said Blenny. "And we must hurry or we'll not reach sanctuary until after midnight."

"After midnight?" said Spotjaw. "But…"

"It'll be fine, Spot," said Blenny.

"But won't they…?"

"I don't know," Blenny interrupted. "But 'tis pointless to worry now."

"Worry about what?" said Kirrit, already nervous about going through the marshes.

"Nothing lass," said Blenny, reassuringly. "We'll be fine. Come on now, we best begin, so we do."

The path they followed was boggy, in some places tufted with thick stubby grass, in others almost disappearing beneath the black water. In many places the path forked, other ways leading between the giant reed-clumps, and Blenny had turned right and left so many times by mid-afternoon that only the sun gave them a clue as to their direction. It was plain to see how easy it would be to get lost.

Spotjaw had pointed out several of the giant leeches, black and shiny and thick as rope, with a bright blue streak running down each side, but they were as sluggish as snails and were passed before any had even begun to crawl from the black ooze beside the path.

By afternoon they were exhausted, hot, hungry, and almost mad with the merciless attention of insects. The huge mosquitos were slow and easy to bat away, if one were eternally vigilant, but there were tiny biting creatures, mere dots that hung in a cloud around each horse, and these were almost impossible to repel. Ebony had long before taken refuge in Shaeli's satchel, and they all wished for such an escape as the insects swarmed around, biting any exposed flesh, persistent and painful, yet the riders could not stop, could not eat, could not take off hoods and masks, could find no respite from the swarms or the heat. Then Shaeli had an idea.

"Flin," she said. "Do you think if we sent up a skylight, a soft one that rained around us, do you think it would help?"

"It's worth a try," he said, already pulling his stone from his pocket.

Flin sent a skylight up. It blossomed not far above their heads in a wide umbrella, falling in a white circle about them. The insects buzzed and flew a short distance away, and those that were struck by the skylights fell to the ground or into the water with the white drops. Before the insects advanced again, Flin sent up another light that burst umbrella-like above them, and within the bubble created by the white light-drops, no insect flew.

They breathed a sigh of relief, and as Flin and Shaeli took turns throwing protective bubbles around the horses, they removed hoods and pulled up sleeves and felt air on their bitten limbs. Ebony ventured out from the satchel and one of the horses even neighed in appreciation. Soon they could judge how long they had to wait between throws before the swarm came back, and after nightfall the skylights also helped light their way, even making the ugly marsh water look almost pretty.

Yet it was tiring, they had not eaten or rested all day or much of the previous night, and Shaeli, too tired now to brood, began to wonder how much longer she would be able to go on. She was just about to say so when she heard an odd sound.

"What's that?" she said instead.

The sound was like rats scratching on the other side of a wall.

"'Tis a colony," said Spotjaw. "Them roaches I told you about."

"The giant ones?" said Kirrit, her voice rising. "The ones that sting?"

"That's them," said Spotjaw. "We should've been past them by now."

"Why?" asked Kirrit.

"They're active at night," he said. "'Specially in the midnight hours." He looked over his shoulder at Kirrit. "We come through once, real late. Swarmed us they did, just like them insects. Had to beat them off with sticks and a flame." He turned forward again. "No fun, it were," he added.

"With *sticks*, Shaeli," said Kirrit. "They had to beat them off with sticks." She swallowed hard. "I think I'm going to be sick."

"Don't worry, Kirrit," said Tarkoda, coming up beside them. "I'll find you a good stick if you need one."

"Funny, Koda," said Kirrit, taking a swipe at him. "You're always *so* funny."

"You'll want to have better aim for the roaches," he smiled, easily ducking her hand.

The odd noise had grown louder; now it sounded like a thousand rats scratching. And there was a clicking sound.

"We best all be quiet from here on," said Blenny. "And we should don our hoods, in case they fly at us."

"Fly at us?" Kirrit groaned. "They're going to *fly* at us?"

"Maybe," said Blenny. "Depends whether they have young to feed."

"Aye," said Spotjaw. "They like fresh meat for their babies."

"What do they usually eat?" asked Flin.

"Oh, the slime, the leeches, the insects," said Spotjaw. "Each other."

Kirrit groaned again.

"What about the skylights?" said Flin. "Should we stop?"

"No, they're practically blind," said Blenny. "But they can hear us it seems, and sense movement." He lowered his voice. "Quiet now. Their island lies across the water. We shall pass it as swiftly and quietly as we can, so we shall."

The water spread out into a wide lake, the giant clumps of reeds few and far between, and in the erratic light of the skylights they could see an island, black against the night. It seemed to change shape as they watched, and after a while they knew why; the surface of the island was moving, writhing and boiling above the line of the black water, moving with the bodies of the giant roaches climbing over the island and each other. Now and then, one of the roaches would flutter up into the night sky and fly about before settling back onto the shuddering island.

The path ran around the edge of the wide marsh-lake and they followed it silently, the writhing mass of the roach island on their right, a few misshapen trees growing between the path and the lake, their limbs gnarled, their leaves hanging like old men's beards. They were almost past when it happened.

The path narrowed at the end of the lake, and a few of the twisted trees grew on either side, their deformed branches overhanging it. Blenny had no problem with the hanging branches, but Spotjaw had to duck as they passed, Williver also as he followed them through. Shaeli was just behind him, Ebony again sleeping in the satchel hanging from her saddle. Kirrit and Tarkoda still rode side by side behind her, with Flin last. He had just fired another insect deterring umbrella into the air and the drops were falling slowly to the ground. Tarkoda ducked beneath the branches, there was a soft *plop*, and then Kirrit was screaming.

"Koda. Shaeli, *help*. Get it off me," she cried, panic clear in her voice. "Help. Get it *off*. Somebody get it *off!*" She screamed again, slapping at her arm.

A leech as long as a snake hung from just beneath her left shoulder. It writhed against her sleeve and the blue lines on its sides began to pulse. They turned first purple and then began to throb dark red.

"Get it *off*. It hurts," Kirrit screamed. "Shaeli, help. It *hurts*."

Her cries began to grow fainter. The hand flailing at the leech grew feebler. The leech began to grow fatter. The pulsing red light down its sides throbbed faster. Tarkoda grabbed it and pulled. Kirrit screamed.

"No lad, don't," yelled Blenny, and Tarkoda let the creature go.

Kirrit began to sag in her saddle. She slipped sideways against Tarkoda, her eyes unfocussed, and Koda grabbed her before she slid to the ground. Blenny and Spotjaw were getting off their horses, Shaeli and Williver were already down on the muddy path, and Tarkoda let Kirrit slide into Williver's arms. Her eyes were closed, her face white against the dark red of her hair.

Blenny was beside them, and he put his long fingers into a pouch at his belt and threw clumps of white powder on the leech, which was growing fatter before their eyes, and it began to writhe and the pulsing red light down its sides stopped. It buckled but did not loosen its grip. Kirrit moaned.

"They're coming," yelled Flin.

At first Shaeli did not know what he meant, but then she heard it. They'd grown used to the clickings and scratchings that came from the roach island, but now there was another noise. A dull flutter. A whirr. And then they were all around, and everyone was yelling, and Kirrit was lying in the mud with the fat black leech writhing and squirming on her shoulder as winged black shapes flew at them, big as crows, with fat bodies and thick jagged legs. From their tails swung a long spike, dripping venom. They were the first of a dark swarm that was rising from the island.

Flin had not dismounted and was still throwing from his saddle, but he no longer aimed at insects, but at the roaches. Scores of tiny balls were blurring from his stone, and these were no harmless skylights, but lethal drops which exploded when they hit a roach. Every one hit a roach.

Spotjaw had gathered the horses a short way down the path, and he stood before them with a stout branch in his hands, swiping at the air. Williver had his wand out and was firing at the closest of the creatures, and Tarkoda stood over Shaeli, Blenny and Kirrit, his sword whirling about his head, but the roaches were becoming thicker, more and more were leaving the island and flying across the inky water towards them. A score of the creatures buzzed overhead, and as Williver and Tarkoda hit one, they were replaced with two more. The air vibrated with the dull whirring of wings.

"The leech is dying, but it will take time," Blenny yelled above the noise.

"We don't *have* time," said Shaeli, fumbling in her amulet. She peered through the darkness at the stone she held, the verdena. "Hold it away from her," she said to Blenny, and he grabbed the squirming leech and pulled it away from Kirrit's body.

Shaeli leant back, studying the distance. If only she could see better.

Tarkoda slashed at the air above them and two halves of a roach's body fell either side of them, the legs twitching, the tail spike still searching for a target.

"Shaeli. I need you," called Flin, and she glanced at him.

Roaches swirled about his horse and his lights still flew, but more slowly. The red of Williver's wand was paling to pink, and although the lake's surface was littered with black bodies, some still burning, the air above the island was filled with a churning black mass.

"Coming," yelled Shaeli, and she turned back to Blenny. "Hold it as still as you can."

She held the green triangle between her fingers and aimed at Kirrit. A thin green line leapt between the stone and the place where the leech met Kirrit's shoulder, there was a wisp of black smoke and the leech fell away, gushing blood and foam and still writhing. Kirrit did not move, but her lashes flickered.

"Koda. Help Blenny with Kirrit," she said.

Tarkoda nodded grimly, his arms swinging at the fat bodies that fluttered about their heads. Three more halved roaches fell into the mud.

Shaeli ran to Williver's side, dodging dark wings and thick black bodies. She dropped the stone back into her amulet and her fingers searched for the smoothness of the amber. She wanted heat.

Williver shot long streams low across the lake's surface. Flin, still astride his horse, shot higher into the air, destroying hundreds of the black, flying shapes. And still the roaches came.

Flin called to her. "The island, Shaeli."

She looked at him and nodded. "Williver, help the others," she said, and he ran back to where Blenny and Tarkoda were struggling to get Kirrit to the horses, fat roaches swirling about them.

Shaeli held out her arm and took a deep breath. She glanced at Flin and he nodded. Together they threw their beams at the roach island.

Shaeli threw as hard as she could. Molten gold flew from her fist beside the bright blue of Flin's beam. Together they struck the churning island of roaches and it exploded in a ball of blue and gold.

The noise was hideous, the sky filled with fat flaming bodies that rose up and then fell back into the flaming pile or the lake, their wings burning like paper. The roaches already in the air seemed confused by the noise and flew back to investigate, most to be consumed in the flames. A few fluttered uselessly at the edges of the conflagration.

Shaeli ran to the others standing beneath the deformed branches that had harboured the black leech. Flin rode behind her, looking back at the burning island.

The roaches cries were becoming fewer as she swung up into the saddle. The sky and the marshes around them were brightly lit, the ash from dead roaches floating into the air.

"We have to hurry," said Tarkoda. "Kirrit's still bleeding."

* * *

It was well they did not have far to go before they reached the drell sanctuary. No one knew what hour it was. The sky had grown overcast and it was very dark. They barely noticed when the cloud of insects again descended on them; they seemed inconsequential now.

Shaeli rode beside Blenny, a soft beam from her quartz lighting their way. Flin's energy was almost spent, Williver's too, and while Shaeli could barely see for exhaustion, she was still more than able to throw light. Spotjaw rode behind them leading Kirrit's horse.

Kirrit sat slumped against Tarkoda's chest, blood slowly oozing from beneath the cloth they'd hastily wrapped around her arm. Shaeli knew Kirrit was alive only because she moaned faintly every now and then.

They came to a fork and followed the boggy path to the left, but soon the path stopped and a wall of rock rose high into the air, its face flat and bare except for a few strange symbols carved into it. Blenny slid off his horse and walked to the rock. He mumbled words they did not understand, his hands moving over the carved symbols. The rock face split. A space opened into darkness.

Blenny stood back so they could enter, and when they were inside he mumbled more of the strange words and the rock wall slid back into place behind them.

"Ye can take off your masks in here," he said. "The stench of the marshes does not reach into sanctuary."

They removed the cloths from their faces, breathing musty, but clean air, and by the light of Shaeli's stone they could see they were in a great cavern, vast and high-roofed.

Blenny remounted and led them across the dry sandy floor to a ramp that rose up above the cavern floor. The ramp went up into a tunnel large enough to fly a Trader through and they went on, past other tunnels and beneath carved arches, up more ramps, climbing higher and higher until they came to a wide chamber. They slid off their horses wearily, Tarkoda passed Kirrit down to Flin and Williver and they carried her across the cold floor. Shaeli went beside Blenny lighting the way, and they went through a small archway into a room with mattresses lining the floor against one wall. They laid Kirrit on one while Spotjaw lit several lanterns. They could all see how pale Kirrit's face was and the dark stain that covered her sleeve.

"Koda," said Shaeli. "Mam gave me a little Faunist pack. It's in my satchel. Under Ebony."

Tarkoda nodded, went out the door, and was back in a moment, his face almost as pale as Kirrit's. He held a small cloth bag in one hand and Ebony in the other. They had removed the sodden bandage and cloak, and Blenny used a small knife to cut the sleeve away. The wound oozed blood, and when Shaeli wiped it she saw it was made up of tiny puncture wounds, each slowly seeping.

"Good," said Blenny. "It did not have time to destroy the skin entirely. Yet we must stop the bleeding, she has lost too much already, so she has."

Shaeli had been pulling things from the cloth bag. "I need a metal bowl," she said. "There's no time to light a fire."

Blenny went over to a cupboard and came back with a metal bowl, dull with age, and Shaeli filled it with water. She took out her quartz and threw a beam at the bowl until the water bubbled, and then she dropped some herbs into it. A sweet, pungent smell rose up from the bowl. Blenny found her some clean cloth and she bathed the wound. The bleeding slowed, but did not stop.

Shaeli rummaged in the little cloth bag again, searching her memory for the right treatment. She found a twist of powder in a paper, smelt it, and sprinkled it on Kirrit's arm. The flow of blood slowed even more and then finally ceased. Blenny smiled at her.

"It seems you have something of the Faunist in you as well as your other gifts, lass," he said.

"It's just from Mam, I guess," Shaeli said.

"Yes, Shaeli," said Tarkoda. "But my Mam is yours, and I have no idea which herbs to use."

Shaeli looked at the tiny parcels she had pulled from the cloth bag. There were at least two dozen, and she had not thought hard about which ones to use. It seemed she had just known.

"Anyway," she said. "We need to bind her arm tightly. When she wakes she'll be weak. As Blenny said, she's lost a lot of blood."

She tore up more cloth, made a pad and bandaged the arm, and then they covered Kirrit with a blanket and let her sleep. There was nothing more they could do for her until she woke.

Shaeli sat back on her haunches when she'd finished and looked about. The room was large, wide benches on one side with all manner of cupboards and drawers beneath, and a score of mattresses on the other. A hearth lay against the wall at the end and Spotjaw soon had a fire going in it. Despite the heat of the marshes, it was cool in here, and the fire was a comforting sight.

"We'd best see to the horses," Spotjaw said, taking up one of the lanterns.

Tarkoda grabbed another and they all rose slowly to their feet. Now they were safe – Kirrit was safe – exhaustion swamped them.

Back out in the long chamber the horses stood, ears and tails drooping, patiently waiting to be unsaddled. They pulled bags and saddles from sweaty backs and piled them in a corner, then they led the horses down to the end of the hall where a wide trough sat beside a well. Spotjaw and Tarkoda filled the trough and the horses drank noisily.

"Shaeli," said Tarkoda. "Can you have a look at this?"

She went over and saw a wound on one of the horse's rumps; a puncture wound covered in dry blood. Blenny inspected it with her.

"Looks like a roach sting," he said. "We'd best treat it and check the others. There's not much venom in them, but the spike goes in a bit. They'll be fine in a day or two."

"Well, you best have a look at this too," said Tarkoda, pulling off his shirt. He turned around and on his shoulder there was a large welt, a dark wound in the centre, angry red skin surrounding it.

"Oh, Koda," said Shaeli. "Why didn't you say something?"

"I was more worried about Kirrit," he said. Then he smiled. "But don't tell her I said so." He looked over his shoulder, trying to see the wound. "Smarts a bit."

"Aye, lad," said Spotjaw. "I know what you mean." He pulled up the leg of his trousers, showing the same angry puncture wound on the calf.

Shaeli sighed and went to get some fresh water, bandages, and her mother's herbs. She treated Spotjaw and Tarkoda's wounds with a thick cream she made with the herbs, and then she treated the horse. Three other horses had the same wound and it took her some time to treat them all.

"We'll have to keep an eye on them," she said. "But they look alright and there's no heat coming from them." She patted the horse she'd just treated on the neck and it tossed its head and whinnied. "I guess they're hungry. I know I am."

"I can fix that, lass," said Spotjaw, and he pulled a bale of hay from a corner. The horses whinnied their appreciation. "A bit dry," he said. "But better than nought."

"How did that get here?" asked Flin, as they walked back to the room where Kirrit lay.

"We always lay in supplies when we bring the wagon through," Spotjaw answered. "Blenny always brings more than enough to last our horses a few days, and wood for the fire. Just in case."

"But how is it there is fresh water in the middle of the marshes?" asked Williver.

"I know not," said Blenny. "The drell found this place centuries ago when they were still hunted by the People. The cavern, the halls, the well; all were here as you see it now, we were merely lucky enough to find it. It needs barely any magic to protect it. It is its own fortress."

"It seems huge," said Williver.

"Aye," said Blenny. "So it is. There are many levels, scores of tunnels and lofty halls, shafts that run far below the ground. There is one shaft so deep even the drell will not explore it. 'Tis not known how deep it is, or if it leads anywhere but down."

"Where is it?" asked Koda.

"We shall pass it as we leave," said Blenny.

"Aye, and an eerie place it is too," said Spotjaw. Given his predilection for understatement, they knew that if Spotjaw found the place eerie it must be truly so.

"A quick bite and then to our beds," said Blenny, pulling provisions from bags and plates from cupboards. "I think we might have... yes, here it is. I've been saving it, so I have."

In his hand he held a small parcel of tezz, and soon they all held a steaming cup in their hands. It had been many days since they'd had any.

They ate only sparsely, they were too tired, and then Blenny found blankets and pillows and they each made a bed on one of the mattresses. Shaeli made hers next to Kirrit, and Ebony was asleep beside her pillow before she put down the blankets.

"Should we watch her?" asked Shaeli, looking at Kirrit.

"No, lass," said Blenny. "She will sleep for many hours. The leech's spittle holds a poison to make its victim sleep, yet she was not exposed to much. She will wake, weak and thirsty, but she will wake. Sleep without worry."

"Alright, Blenny," Shaeli yawned. "As long as you're sure."

She did not think she *could* have stayed awake, really. Already Spotjaw was snoring softly, and Flin's eyes were closed. Blenny turned out the lanterns, all but one, which he carried to his bed. Shaeli said a sleepy goodnight and heard Tarkoda and Williver answer her, but she did not hear Blenny, nor did she see him turn out the light.

* * *

How long she slept, she did not know. For a long time there was nothing, and then she was plagued with strange dreams; dreams of being in a carriage with no horses, hurtling down a road with no control of the thing, pulling at reins that went nowhere; dreams of endless tunnels where she could find no way out; dreams of great winged shapes following her across grassy fields; dreams of the captain's blackened skin peeling away from his ruined hand. Then there was nothing again, until another dream brought her to the edge of wakefulness. She could hear Koda. He was in the big room on Purple Leaf talking to Mam and she was frying bacon, and Shaeli was hungry. Really hungry. She woke up confused at not being in the bed in her little room. She could still hear Koda, but Mam wasn't there. She wasn't on Purple Leaf.

She sat up, yawning and stretching and screwing up her nose at the smell of herself. She smelt of dirt and horse and sweat and the marshes. The sun poured in through high windows, no insects or marsh-smell accompanying it.

Tarkoda was over beside the fireplace with Williver and Spotjaw, and Spotjaw, amazingly, was frying the bacon that had pervaded her dreams. Blenny was brewing another pot of tezz and Ebony was watching him, and when Shaeli sat up, the jevvi leapt from the bench and came over to nuzzle her hand. Flin walked back in the door just then, rubbing his hair, smelling of soap, with a pile of wet clothes in his hand.

"Let me guess," said Shaeli. "You found the bathroom."

"I did," he said loftily. He wrinkled his nose as he passed. "Perhaps you should do the same." He pulled a bench into a patch of sunlight and began to drape the clothes over it.

"I will," she said. "As soon as I've had some of that tezz." She looked at the bed beside her. "How's Kirrit?"

"Sleeping soundly," said Blenny, bringing her over a mug. "The wound is dry and her brow cool. I have saved the last of the tezz for when she wakes."

"Good," said Shaeli, relieved. "Do you know how long that will be?"

Blenny shook his head. "No, lass. But we'll not be travelling this day."

"What time is it?"

"It's halfway through the afternoon already," said Tarkoda. "We slept the rest of the night and most of the day."

Shaeli stretched. "I feel like I could do it all over again," she said. "The sleeping part, I mean. The rest of it was horrible."

"I don't know," said Koda. "It looked pretty amazing when you burnt the roach island."

"And at least they'll not be there next time we come through," said Spotjaw. "Now, who's for bacon and stale-bread toast? No eggs, I'm afraid."

After they'd eaten, Flin showed Shaeli the bathroom where a small fire heated a boiler that drained directly into a short, deep bath. She washed slowly, soaked herself thoroughly, and then washed her clothes in the water before she let it drain. She was revolted by the colour of the water and rinsed them several more times before she found somewhere to hang them.

They rested through the afternoon and fed the horses again. Shaeli made a poultice to sooth the bites they all had – the ant bites from the Barren Lands in particular were beginning to itch horribly. The horses were also washed down, for they had had their fair share of ant bites too, and she checked the wounds from the roach stings. The wounds on the horses were no longer raised and seemed to give them no pain, so she smoothed some of the poultice on each of them, and then checked her human patients for the same thing. The angry red surrounding the puncture wounds was fading, and although Tarkoda confessed to a headache and Spotjaw limped a bit, they seemed to be healing well. Then she brewed a soup from the rest of the bacon and some dried grains Blenny found for her, and as the light faded from the sky they sat down to eat. They had almost finished when Kirrit woke up.

"Where's mine?" she said groggily from her pillow. "I'm hungry, too. And thirsty."

She tried to sit up, couldn't, and fell back against the pillow, looking cross-eyed at the bandage on her arm. She blinked as if she couldn't see very well.

"What the...?" she began, and stopped. Her eyes grew wide and she looked at Shaeli. Her lip trembled. "I knew you'd get it off," she said, and then her eyes filled with tears.

Shaeli put down her bowl and went over. "Of course we did," she said, taking Kirrit's hand. "I couldn't let that disgusting thing have my best friend for dinner."

"Did I make the roaches come?" Kirrit asked, shutting her eyes. Tears rolled fatly down her cheeks.

"Well, yes," said Shaeli, slowly. "But we got rid of them alright."

"Good. I'm glad I missed that bit." Kirrit opened her eyes again and swiped at the tears. "Did Koda have to use a stick?"

"No," Shaeli smiled. "His sword worked much better."

Shaeli helped her sit up and propped her with pillows while Tarkoda brought her over a bowl of soup. She ate slowly, drank two glasses of water, had a cup of tezz, and went back to sleep.

She did not wake again until midday the next day, when she drank more water and Shaeli helped her to bathe. After she'd eaten again she seemed to regain some of her strength; the fuzzy look disappeared from her eyes, and she began to tell them they should be thinking about going.

Shaeli unwrapped her arm. The tiny puncture marks had dried and there was none of the angry red of infection surrounding them. She made a paste of some more of her mother's herbs, spread it over the marks and wrapped the arm again.

Despite Kirrit prompting them to leave, she slept again soon after she'd eaten. They washed and fed the horses, filled all their water bottles, and ate as the sun went down. Despite a sense of urgency, they fell asleep one by one, and next morning they woke with the sun already high in the sky. Kirrit slept until early afternoon, stumbling from sleep ravenous and thirsty, but then she fell asleep as they began again to think of leaving. They drowsed until Kirrit woke in the midnight hours, and although she moved slowly and her arm felt numb and moved awkwardly, she was ready to travel. Shaeli had made a sling for her, and although her face was still pale, her lips were pink and her eyes clear.

They left the room as they'd found it and rode out of the chamber, the horses well rested and tossing their heads. Ebony was as skittish as they, sitting up between Shaeli's horse's ears as they rode, and Kirrit managed well after they'd helped her mount.

They travelled through dark tunnels and vast halls, and wondered how such a place came to be here in the middle of the ugliest spot in the World that any of them had ever seen. Strange carvings covered the walls in some places, and Blenny told them the drell had no memories of this place other than as a sanctuary. It must have been built eons before the land had turned bad around it; before the memories of any of their races had begun.

They knew when they came upon the place Blenny had spoken of; the place where the shaft lay. They entered an immense cavern and Shaeli and Flin both shone light into the space, yet it did nothing to extinguish the cold, dead feeling of the place. The ceiling was a perfect dome rising high above their heads, the walls carved, deep recesses hiding in the shadows. The shaft lay in the middle of the floor, an icy blast of air flowing from its depths. They skirted it in a wide arc, but Tarkoda fired a rock from his sling as they passed. It fell into the mouth of the shaft, bounced a few times, but it was a long time before they heard a distant *clack* as it hit bottom. They shuddered and hurried on.

Through more halls they went, down now, and then along a tunnel which grew smaller, yet was still easily wide enough to take a wagon. This last tunnel had no more branches coming off it, and at the end there was another cavern with the same smooth wall through which they'd entered on the other side of the vast, inexplicable sanctuary. Blenny slipped from his horse, told them to don their masks, and then he opened the door back out into the Poisoned Marshes.

* * *

They rode through the night and the next day, stopping for a few hours at the edge of the marshes before heading out across the rocky terrain. The day after that, long after the sun had fallen into the western sky, they reached the high ridge that heralded the end of the Barren Lands. They went up the steep ridge, the ground beneath them leaning outwards as if drawing back in horror at what lay in its centre.

The trip through the rest of Poisoned Marshes had been uncomfortable and tiring, the clouds of dim-witted mosquitoes and their biting, tiny cousins kept away with the skylights, the black oily waters traversed successfully, and the Barren Lands had looked almost home-like when they reached them. Now the Barren Lands were also behind them, but the queen's guard were no doubt ahead. It was almost midnight, but they would travel by night again now that they were back in the World. Tarkoda squinted at the stars.

"We should head south-east. Skirt M'Zen'sclahr Forest and go to Marnissi," he said.

"I have many friends there," agreed Flin. "Any of them would shelter us."

"I suppose we have little choice, though I'm sure that's the path they expect us to take," said Williver. "Unless anyone has a better idea." He looked at Blenny.

The drell smiled. "Yes, young elf," he said. "I have a much better way."

"Where then?" asked Koda. "We can't go through the forest unless you have a sanctuary there too."

"No, lad," said Blenny. "No drell has entered the Ancient Forest for centuries. But there's the best sanctuary of all to the north-east, so there is. In the mountains. Our mountains."

* * *

CHAPTER SIXTEEN

A few nights later, as dawn broke over the eastern horizon, they rode into the foothills at the edge of the Drell Mountains. As they had when they'd sailed past with Chessy, the mountains looked dark, forbidding hulks, bleak and lifeless. Small pockets of forest grew in clumps between treeless mountains, the dark sides sheer and ragged, and a shallow river ran lazily towards them. The mountains were not nearly as lofty as the mountains surrounding Zerrinius, but the craggy heights looked grim and impassable.

They had seen many of the queen's guard patrolling when they'd first left the Barren Lands and had managed to avoid them, but the further north they went, the less they'd encountered. Not only was the guard here fewer, so were the people. They passed only a few villages, their houses all huddled together. For the last part of the journey, the brooding trees of M'Zen'sclahr Forest had soared to their right, the shadowy trunks creating a dark silent wall, and there had been no more villages.

Now, with the mountains before them and a night's ride behind them, they stopped beside the river to eat, water the horses and rest for a while. They planned to ride on through the morning, for once they were in the mountains none would follow them – so Blenny said.

Tarkoda stood contemplating the mountains as he ate. He shook his head and sat down, now contemplating Blenny.

"So," he said. "How do we get over those?"

"There is no way *over*," said Blenny. "But through, there is a path, so there is."

"And tonight we shall have a fire," said Spotjaw. "We'll see if we can't catch us a few birds to roast."

"And we'll be... welcome among your people?" asked Flin.

"If I were not with you, you'd not be," said Blenny. "But I *am*, and we shall be fine, so we shall. I look forward to seeing my home. 'Tis many Winters since I was last here."

"Have you ever been there, Spot?" asked Koda.

"No lad," the tall man answered, around a mouthful. "We stopped once, though, on the other side where the river meets the sea, and I met some of Blenny's kin." He looked at Blenny. "Five Winters ago, were it?"

"So it was," Blenny nodded.

"How long have you been travelling the World?" asked Kirrit. Her wound was healing nicely, and though her shoulder was still a bit stiff, she had regained her strength.

"Oh, about ten Winters," said Blenny.

"Eleven," said Spotjaw.

"You haven't been home for *eleven* Winters?" asked Shaeli, thinking of how long it was since she'd seen Cave. "You must have missed it a lot."

"Aye, lass," said Blenny, one eye on her and one on the mountains. "Aye, I have."

"Why did you leave?" she asked.

"That I will tell you when we reach our destination," he said. "But we still have a way to go, so we do. 'Tis time we went on."

Shaeli said no more, but wondered again why this drell would be out in the World when others of his kind were rarely seen, and none she had heard of had ever chosen to live among the People. She vaguely remembered the old drell woman she had seen when she was very young, the one who had told her to learn how to swim. She had no idea where it had been or how old she was, but she knew it had been before the twins were born.

The twins. She would always think of them as that. No matter what the future may hold, they would always be her sisters.

261

As they passed through the foothills, the vegetation thinned and then almost ceased. The ground was rocky, but not uneven as it had been on the Barren Lands, and the horses picked their way easily between the rocks. Here and there a few trees clumped together, their branches intertwined, but the hillsides became steeper and eventually they were riding between gorges bereft of any green, the ridges high above. The sun, white and high in the sky, beat down on their heads. They turned down a cleft between two rocky faces.

"Beyond this gorge lies the beginning of Drell Lands," said Blenny, and they could all see the eagerness on his face. "Tonight we shall camp within them, and in a day or two we will reach the city."

He clicked to his horse and entered the canyon, the others right behind. Williver looked up at the line of cliffs surrounding them, suddenly uneasy. His scalp prickled and his heart fluttered in his chest.

"You're sure no one ever comes this far into these mountains?" he said.

"The People are not usually seen this close to Drell Lands," Blenny answered. "Why?"

"Perhaps it's nothing," said Williver, his eyes still on the high ridge. Then he saw it. A glint. A mere flash of light, but it was there. "Blenny," he said, quietly. "There are soldiers up on the ridge to the left." He heard a pebble roll. "And more behind those boulders ahead on the right."

Blenny swung one eye to Williver, and the other moved slowly along the ridge. He nodded slightly. "What do you want to do?"

"Keep going. Slowly. I don't think there's many, and we cannot go back. Tell Spotjaw, Koda and Flin."

Blenny nodded and dropped back.

"Shaeli," said Williver. "Come here."

Shaeli moved her horse up beside him and he mumbled a few words to her. Her brows rose, her face paled beneath her tanned skin, but she merely nodded, gathered Ebony in behind the pommel, and dropped back beside Kirrit. Tarkoda came up on Kirrit's other side. Flin, Spotjaw and Blenny were behind them. Williver rode just in front.

The end of the canyon was only a few hundred paces away when they struck. Ten archers rose up from the ridge to their left. With a yell, a dozen more appeared from behind a mound of boulders fifty paces down the canyon. Yet they were ready for them.

Only three of the archers had time to loose an arrow. Two bounced harmlessly to the ground, the third flew over Williver's head. Above, the archer's bows turned to balls of fire in their hands and they dropped them, shouting, their hands burning.

The soldiers ahead fared little better. Three fell with Williver's arrows through their throats, two more by sharp rocks from Tarkoda's sling. The rest lost their weapons by blasts from Flin and Shaeli's gems. Their yells of surprise turned to yells of pain, and they fell to their knees on the rocky ground pleading for mercy.

They rode slowly past the fallen men and women, their weapons still trained on them and the others, useless and burned, on the ridge above. The end of the gorge was before them, and behind the soldiers were still on their knees among the rocks, yet they did not lower their weapons for a long time.

* * *

They made camp late in the afternoon beside a stream that trickled from a spring in a rock wall. The spring had formed a pool beneath the wall, and though it was not deep enough to swim, they could wash well enough even for Flin's liking.

They were in a valley between three of the bald-faced mountains. Here there were trees and soft grass. Birds twittered from treetops and bushes.

They had found the Drell Mountains full of life. Despite its dark rocky look, the stony gorges teemed with life. Lizards of several varieties they had seen; one species as long as two of the horses together, yet they were skittish creatures that ran off to hide between rocks or up the nearest tree, making a harsh hissing sound. In the rocky canyons they had also seen small leaping mice, and once in the distance three jenka, the small sharp-toothed cats. In some of the rocky gorges they found deep pools fed by glass-clear creeks and gushing falls, some empty, some filled with the shadows of fish or the long, predatory lines of qayters, a water-dwelling lizard, cousin to the dragon and the Qotarr. These pools they steered well clear of; the qayter was not a happy creature and it was a hungry one.

In this small pocket of forest there were spiky bushes covered with delicate blue flowers, and tall grasses, their stems topped with flowers soft as velvet, in deep shades of red and gold. One tree, the only one of its kind, stood proudly in the middle of the others, covered in vivid red blossoms, and it was filled with loud-voiced parrots feeding on the flowers. The blue and crimson birds were only one of the dozens they had seen, from tiny wrens to the enormous, flightless erk, a bird as foolish as its name suggested, but with a wicked spike on its heel which it would use if cornered. The mountains were filled with extraordinary wildlife, and Ebony ran around the edge of the camp, her tiny nose sniffing at the fragrant air. From the inside, the Drell Mountains were anything but dark and imposing.

Spotjaw, Tarkoda and Williver went hunting as soon as they'd unsaddled the horses, and they came back with four plump pheasants and one of the giant lizards, albeit one of the smaller ones. Spotjaw assured them it was good eating, Blenny confirmed this, and when they tried it they found the meat even sweeter than that of the birds.

Night had grown thick about them by the time they'd finished eating, and they sat, not talking, not sleeping, some staring at the flames and some into the sky. The quiet respite in the journey had given them all time for contemplation.

"When will they give up, do you think?" Shaeli said at last. She seemed to be speaking to the flames.

Williver answered her. "When they catch us, little one," he said gently. "Or when we reach the safety of your Cave. Whichever comes first."

"They won't be catching us," said Flin, firmly.

Williver smiled. "I hope you're right, my friend," he said.

"But how do they keep *finding* us?" Shaeli said, her voice curdled with despair. "How did they know we would come this way?"

"The ones on the other side of the Barren Lands," said Blenny. "They saw me, and must have thought there was a chance we may come through this way, though only a small chance."

"That's true," said Williver. "Else there would have been more soldiers than the few we encountered. They probably thought we'd go to Marnissi. As we would have without Blenny."

"We should have left none alive when they surprised us before we entered the marshes," said Flin. "I thought it at the time, but..." He looked at Shaeli.

"We couldn't, Flin," she said. "It wouldn't have been right." The wounding of people was still a raw place inside her; the thought of actually killing someone on purpose abhorrent. The picture of the soldier she had left laying beneath the boulder with his neck broken came to her often.

"I knew you'd say that," Flin said. "That's why I only thought it."

"It doesn't matter," said Spotjaw. "We're safe now. They'll not follow us into the mountains any more than they followed us into the marshes."

"Yes, Spot," said Blenny. "But they'll be waiting for us when we leave, so they will."

"Then we'll go round them or fight," said Flin, far too strongly. He looked at Shaeli. "We'll make it to Cave."

"'Tis best not to dwell on what has not yet come to pass," said Blenny. "We shall reach the Cave of the Traders when the gods deem it fit, but for the moment we are safe, as Spot says."

"But when we leave, they'll be waiting for us," said Shaeli flatly.

"It'll be alright," said Kirrit. "We've managed to avoid them so far."

"But how long can we *keep* avoiding them?" said Shaeli, her eyes still on the flames. "How long until we can't fight our way out?"

* * *

"At the end of this valley lies the entrance to the city. It will be watched, but worry not, we shall be fine, so we shall."

The valley Blenny spoke of was lush and broad. To their right, a deep rambling river ran from somewhere ahead, and they followed its path through long soft grasses scattered with flowers. On every side the mountains reared, their faces still dark and forbidding, patterned with red and grey, but here in this hidden valley the sun shone brightly. It reminded Shaeli of the Long Lea, and Kirrit and Tarkoda wistfully agreed with her. They rode together, admiring the day and the view, until they saw what lay at the end of the valley.

Like the waterfall at the end of the Long Lea, the river flowing through the valley fell from a waterfall on the mountainside, but this waterfall was a hundred times the size of the falls that fell from the Lea into the Valley of Stones. It was boiling with water as it fell down the cliff, yet it was not the waterfall that widened their eyes, it was the sentinels that stood on either side of it.

Two towers stood on each side of the torrent, both topped with a soaring dragon, wings spread, mouths open as if ready to devour them. Rainbows danced in the spray beneath their wings.

"A grand sight, so they are," said Blenny proudly. "Drell built to last ten thousand years. But here now, let me go first. They're watching us."

"Who?" asked Kirrit.

"My kinsmen," said Blenny.

They stared at the dragon towers riding the waterfall's spray.

"I can't see anything," said Shaeli.

"Neither can I," said Tarkoda.

"They watch from the eye of the dragon on this side of the falls," said Williver.

"Elfin eyes see true," smiled Blenny.

Though they squinted through the midday sun, they could not see what Williver did, even when they neared the base of the tower, though they all felt the eyes watching them. The roar of the waterfall drowned all sound, and they had to shout to be heard.

Across the frothing torrent of the waterfall, the base of the eastern tower was obscured by spray, the dragon atop it floating on mist and shimmering rainbows. The western tower rose up before them, its sides wet and unbroken. The dragon soared above, its outstretched wings creating huge shadows. The valley ended here. Before them there was only the tower and a blank rock face, to the right an impassable torrent of water. A breeze swept a wave of mist from the falls onto them, cooling their hot faces.

"What do we do now?" asked Flin.

"We wait, so we do," said Blenny. "For them to let us in."

"In where?" asked Shaeli.

"Into the tower, of course," smiled the drell. "And then to the city."

Shaeli looked up and down the face of the tower, and could see nothing, but she remembered the seamless door in the sanctuary in the marshes and the drell's many protection spells, and she wasn't surprised she couldn't see anything.

They dismounted and waited in the shadow of the dragon's wings while the horses cropped at the grass. Ebony ran around, but did not venture far. She kept looking up at the stone dragon perched high above. Every now and then, the breeze would cover them in fine mist, and Blenny said that it was lucky there was not a stronger wind blowing, else they'd all be wet as they waited. They ate something, and Shaeli began to drowse.

She was roused not by a sound, but by a feeling. The sensation that she was being watched had been with her since they'd first sighted the towers, but now it heightened. She opened her eyes and sat up, gathering Ebony into her arms. A seam was opening in the side of the tower, and before she was on her feet, the seam had turned into a door. Three drell stepped from the opening. The two at the rear bowed, the one at the front came towards Blenny, hands outstretched.

"'Tis too long since we have seen your face, Lord Blenn," he said.

They clasped hands and then embraced. This drell was younger than Blenny, his round face topped with a thatch of dark hair. He was a trifle taller than Blenny, his features less puddled, and he was a great deal thinner.

"Glad I am to see your face also, Wendll," replied Blenny. "And glad to find you on duty this day, so I am."

"Come. Word has been sent and they will be awaiting your arrival." One of his eyes took in the group standing behind Blenny. "We thank these folk for returning you to us, so we do. Do they travel back down the valley, or do they wish to spend the night beneath the tower?"

"They do not *leave* me here. They travel *with* me, Wendll," said Blenny. "They go to the city. My quest is not yet over."

Wendll looked at Blenny for a moment and then nodded. "As you say," he said. He looked again at the others and smiled, if a trifle grimly. "Come then. Bring your horses and enter the First Tower of the Dragon."

He took Blenny's arm and they walked to the tower and through the door. With only the slightest of hesitations, the others followed.

The door was wide and high enough to easily accommodate the horses, and when they were inside, the two other drell followed them in and the door slid seamlessly shut behind them. The roar of the waterfall was instantly dulled. They were in a lofty hall, lit somehow with a warm golden glow.

"This way, please," said Wendll. "The horses shall be taken to the city by another route. Do not worry, they shall be in good hands."

They gathered a few belongings and left the horses in the hands of the two silent drell. Wendll led them across the floor. On the left side of the hall was a broad ramp, but they went past this and through a door on the far side. The room they entered was small and round, the ceiling too high to see through the shadows. There was a table in the centre, several small couches against the walls, and when Wendll shut the door, the only light came from glowing rocks set in the floor.

"You may want to sit down," said Blenny. "Some find the levitator disturbing."

"Levitator?" squeaked Kirrit, taking Shaeli's hand and pulling her down onto a couch. "What's a levitator?"

Spotjaw folded himself onto the couch beside them.

"Ye shall see, lass, so ye shall," smiled Blenny. "Worry not, some love it." He sat down between Williver and Tarkoda, smiled at Wendll, and began to stuff his pipe. "When you're ready, lad," he said.

Wendll moved to the table in the centre of the room. Its base was one thick column, its surface not much bigger than the base; upon it was what looked like a tray covered with a domed lid. Wendll removed the cover, and Shaeli was amazed to see a ball of vistrella almost as big as her fist half embedded in the table. She looked at Williver and he returned her surprised gaze with a shake of his head.

269

Wendll covered the vistrella with his hands, and closed his eyes. Beneath his fingers the ball began to glow, brighter and brighter, the rocks set into the floor begun to pulse slowly, and then the little round room began to move.

At first they weren't aware of it, the slight sensation in the pit of their stomachs was odd, but then it grew stronger and somehow they all knew they were going up. The rocks in the floor pulsed more quickly, the room rattled slightly and the walls above were sliding past the walls of the round room. The falling-stomach sensation grew, the walls moved faster, and they kept their eyes up, wondering when the ceiling was going to come crashing down on them.

A light grew above them, soft and warm at first, and then brighter. The passage of the room slowed, the rocks in the floor stopped pulsing and shone with a weak constant light once again, their stomachs rose back to their proper places, and they stopped. Bright light spilled over the walls of the round room, and far above they could see a rocky ceiling.

"How did you do that?" breathed Shaeli, her eyes full of admiration.

Wendll looked at her. "'Tis merely levitation," he said, as if he had only boiled water. He covered the vistrella again and moved across to open the door.

They followed him into a vast, odd-shaped room. The light came from dozens of lamps lit with what looked like Warlock light. A dozen drell stood in formation outside the door. They were obviously soldiers, and they bowed formally as the group came from the round room. Blenny bowed back to them. It was plain that Blenny held a high rank in the drell world.

They looked around and realised they were in the dragon atop the tower. The ceiling was roughly domed, to the right a corridor opened out – the neck of the dragon – and they could see two large leaf-shaped windows at the far end. Wendll led them along the corridor, and from the eyes of the dragon they looked down on the valley. It was like a picture, the river and trees like miniature versions of themselves. Apart from a few birds floating in the air beneath them, only the waterfall moved, a churning white mass, its mist touching their faces, and they could also see the wide river that fell into the foaming falls. Across the top of the falling river, the other dragon stood atop its tower, yet they could not see what lay beyond. Shaeli stood well back from the openings, clutching Ebony, her heart pounding until they went back down the corridor.

Wendll spoke to one of the soldiers for a few moments, and then he led them from the dragon room. A staircase led down, curving as it went, down into the belly of the dragon statue. They came out in another long hall.

"There lies the long way down to the base of the tower," said Blenny, pointing to a tunnel. "Our horses will be brought up that way." He pointed to the left. "We go this way. To the second tower."

"But, Blenny," said Shaeli. "Isn't the waterfall that way?"

"Aye, lass," he answered. "So it is."

"But how do we cross it?"

"We don't cross it," he said. "Our path lies beneath the torrent. Come."

They went down the tunnel lit by a few small lamps, these also like Warlock flames, and at the end lay an archway. Past that, there was only darkness and the sound of thunder. Wendll moved to take one of the lamps from the walls, but Blenny stopped him.

"No need for that, lad," he said. "My companions will light the way much better." He smiled at Flin and Shaeli. "If they would be so kind."

Shaeli shrugged and pulled the quartz from her amulet. She pointed it through the archway. "In there?" she asked.

Blenny nodded, and she fired a soft white beam a short way into the tunnel beyond the arch. It glowed instantly, lighting the tunnel for twenty paces. Wendll looked at her with all the amazement she had given him after the trip in the round room. She smiled at him and shrugged.

"It's only a skylight," she said, stepping forward. "Shall we go on?"

Wendll blinked, nodded and they went through the archway.

The floor on the other side of the archway was sandy, the walls damp, the sound of the waterfall groaning through the tunnel. Its rumble grew louder as they went beneath Shaeli's beam.

Wendll stopped before a bend in the tunnel where dull grey light shone round the curve. The sound of the falls had grown so loud he had to shout to be heard.

"Stay close by the left side," Wendll shouted. "The way is wet, but there is a rope to steady yourselves." He went to an alcove and returned with a hooded cloak for each of them. "Put these on. They will be a little short, but will keep most of you dry."

They donned the capes, which were obviously made for the drell, pulled up the hoods, and Shaeli tucked Ebony inside her shirt. She had no idea what they were about to do, but she was fairly sure she wasn't going to like it much.

"Ready?" yelled Wendll, and when they nodded he pulled on his hood and turned forward.

Shaeli found that she had been wrong. It turned out to be an amazing experience. As they rounded the bend, the noise of the falls became deafening. Their faces were wet in moments, their legs below the short capes became more drenched with every step. Ahead, the right side of the broad tunnel disappeared, and in its place was the waterfall. The underside of the waterfall.

Shaeli had been under falls before, little ones at Cave and on their travels, but this was like nothing she had ever seen. The white wall boiled downwards at a staggering rate, the power could be felt in their feet, their very bones. The noise was almost too much to bear, and she dragged her eyes away from the seething mass and saw the tunnel floor had widened considerably. The sandy path ran close to the remaining tunnel wall, a rope bolted along its length to help steady them, but they barely needed it. The floor was even, though very wet, and they had no trouble crossing the vast expanse.

The walk past the churning torrent was not short, but they did not begrudge the length, the noise, or their saturated legs. The sight of it was worth it, the power in its thunderous fall intoxicating, and when they reached the other side, the tunnel curved and became solid once more. The sound had faded enough to speak when Wendll stopped and they removed their cloaks, yet they did not speak, they merely grinned at each other. They had just walked beneath the greatest waterfall that any of them had ever seen.

Wendll led them on, the tunnel winding upwards, and eventually they came out in a long hall, identical to the one in the western tower. Here their smiles faded, for this hall was not empty, but crowded with drell. None stood higher than Shaeli's shoulder, some were little taller than her waist, and all bowed as the group came beneath the arch that led from the tunnel. Soldiers stood at the front and behind there were dozens of others. All were hailing Blenny. They stood dumfounded as voices called out to Lord Blenn. Blenny held up his hands and thanked them.

"I wish I had time enough to linger and speak with you," he said. "But I must go to the city."

He bowed and then pressed ahead through the crowd, which parted begrudgingly. The six following Blenny and Wendll across the room drew many curious eyes, though mostly only one eye per drell, the other they all kept on Blenny.

The drell followed them down the hall and on through the tunnel beyond. Blenny spoke to many of them as he passed, calling most by name and clasping hands, and they followed until they came to another wide arched opening. On the other side of the arch lay bright afternoon sunshine and a grassy courtyard where an extremely elaborate open carriage waited. Eight ponies tossed their heads and pawed the ground before it.

Above soared the second dragon tower, its tail above their heads, the great head pointing south, and as they walked to the carriage, still trailed by the crowd of awed drell, they could see back across the river they had walked beneath to where the first tower stood sentinel.

Blenny again thanked the crowd from the carriage as the others found seats. Williver, Tarkoda and Spotjaw looked particularly comical sitting on the low seats, their knees somewhere up around their ears as Wendll took up the reins and they left the waving crowd behind. Beyond the courtyard lay a small village, completely deserted, its inhabitants the waving crowd they had left back at the dragon's feet. As the last buildings fell behind them, the view ahead opened out like a tapestry unfurled on a castle wall.

Behind soared the dragon and the small village, both standing at the top of a high ridge of mountain, the river flowing within the embrace of the ridge before it fell into the valley behind them. Here and there, the river spilled over the ridge on its way to the great falls like water spilled from a cup, thin lines falling to the floor of the valley below. The valley itself was encircled by mountains and tall ridges, much as the Long Lea was, but there the resemblance ended.

Below were fields and small villages, streams and clumps of forests, but further on the valley narrowed and they saw what could only be the city Blenny spoke of. Yet they had little chance of seeing details for Wendll drove the carriage beneath a line of trees, and the view was gone.

When they saw the valley again they were down on its floor, the mountains surrounding them, and the afternoon was waning. To their left, across the valley, the thin lines of waterfall fell from the river high above and the falls became streams they crossed as they travelled north up the centre of the valley. Everyone they passed waved and bowed and called out to Lord Blenn, and all stared curiously at his companions.

They passed many fields full of curling vines and high trellises. The trellises seemed built very high for the diminutive drell, and Shaeli wondered how they picked from the tops. They passed through one of the small villages, the houses squat but elaborately carved, many with statues gracing the tiny gardens, and on the far side of the village there were more fields. Here and there, at the sides of the fields, were metal discs with little railings around the edges, and she wondered aloud at them, but Blenny evaded the question, speaking to the drell standing respectfully beside the road, their hats in their hands.

To Shaeli, there was something odd about the picture of smiling drell groups, and after a while she knew what it was. There were no small children, no babies. Young drell, certainly, for these were as high-spirited as the children of Shaeli's Cave year – they had come upon one group laughing uproariously beside one of the metal discs, the joke unclear to the travellers – but there were no toddlers clutching at knees, no babes-in-arms. She wondered at this, but then the wondering was taken from her as they approached the gates to the city. Ahead the valley narrowed, and the fields ended abruptly beneath the walls of two more towers which mirrored those that guarded the valley below the waterfall, but they were much smaller and much more elaborate, the dragons more fiercely beautiful than those at the great waterfall, much more intricately carved.

The sun was beginning to set as they entered the gateway. A fanfare echoed across the valley, and Blenny mumbled something about "a lot of fuss and bother", and then the city of the drell lay before them.

The space between the cliff walls was perhaps two fields wide, carpeted with fine grass and studded with gardens bursting with colour. Fountains spouting water from fabulous statues were scattered about the gardens, but there were no buildings; no houses, no huts or cottages, no castles. There was only the walls of the valley carved into a towering city. Shaeli had never seen anything like it. Instead of cutting the mountain into blocks to build the city, the city had been carved from the very mountain, *into* the mountain; the castles and towers growing within the rock. Surrounding the gardens the city rose in a half-circle, the stone glowing with soft gold-and-russet tones, windows and archways patterning it. They saw bridges spanning between towers, balconies thrusting from turrets, tall columns framing lofty doorways. Unlike the dark ragged slopes of the rest of the Drell Mountains, the stone of the carved city was warm and smooth, the buildings hewn from it rich in detail. Yet for all its magnificence, it was very quiet. Drell in fine clothes began to gather in the gardens, but only scores, not hundreds as one would expect in so large and grand a place.

Wendll drove the carriage on and Shaeli saw the city was made of sections. The towers and arches nearest the dragon gates seemed ancient, the stone dull and weather-beaten. In places some features had even crumbled from carvings, but as they drove further on the stone seemed fresher, the carvings crisper. When they reached the end, she saw the carven city did not extend all the way around the half-circle. At the very back, in the centre, there was only a blank cliff face like an unfinished canvas.

They had gained little information from Blenny as they'd driven to the city. Shaeli in particular was wildly curious as to why he was treated with such deference, but despite their questions and the fervour of the small crowd that followed their carriage he would tell them nothing. He happily talked about what grew in the fields, about the people and their lives, but he would not be drawn on his obvious status. Now as they drove into the city, he told them that drell royalty had begun its construction at the dawn of their civilisation, and throughout the centuries new kings and queens had carved palaces into the mountain, and it had often sheltered the population from extinction.

"Once the drell thrived. Their villages went as far as the valley outside, at the feet of the dragon towers," he said. "The towers were built to deter the dragons themselves from scouring the valley."

"And did they?" asked Kirrit. "Keep the dragons away?"

"Oh yes," said Blenny. "The towers are twice the size of a real dragon."

"Why doesn't anyone live on the other side of the towers now?" asked Koda. "The valley seemed a fertile place."

"Aye, lad, so it is," said Blenny. "But long ago we had to move back into this valley. Our numbers grew small," he added quietly.

They all knew this had been when the drell had been feared and hunted as primitive beings. They were obviously far from primitive.

"We did still go to the valley in recent times, when it became safe again," Blenny continued. "There is good hunting, special herbs that grow only there. Other things…" He stopped and was silent for a while. "But none go there now, not without armed escort."

They had no time to ask why, for Wendll had stopped the carriage in front of the last part of the sculptured city before the blank mountain face. They could see scaffolding through a gap between towers, and upon it the drell who had downed their tools to watch the carriage's arrival. On the ground nearby were several more of the flat metal discs, more workers standing watching their arrival beside them.

The stairs at the front of this last edifice grew out of the earth, and led up to a wide platform. Statues of noble drell in long robes stood either side of the huge double doors, each taller than ten drell. The doors themselves were wooden, but still elaborately carved, and were wide open. Before them stood three drell, two men standing either side of a woman. All three were as noble and regally dressed as the giant statues guarding the doors. The woman had many jewels on her robes and her long gloves. None of the three smiled.

Blenny went up the steps and bowed deeply, but the others stayed where they were, suddenly unsure.

The two male drell had ancient pious faces. The woman was tiny, shrunken and wrinkled as a walnut. When Blenny rose she looked at him sternly. The last golden rays of the sun shone upon her face.

"Too long have you been gone from your home," she said, and then suddenly her face crumpled into a smile and tears filled her muddy eyes. She opened her arms and drew Blenny into them. "Too long, my son," she said, as she hugged him and cried. "Far, far too long."

* * *

CHAPTER SEVENTEEN

"You don't come alone, I see," said Blenny's mother when she'd released him. For her diminutive size and obvious age, the eyes she turned to the group standing behind her son were keen and bright. "Yet the one you seek is not among them."

"No, Mother," said Blenny. "But allow me to introduce my companions."

The others stepped forward, but the old drell to the right of Blenny's mother spoke first.

"Surely this can be done in the throne room, your majesty," he said. "You should sit down."

The others looked at each other. Throne room? Your majesty?

"I'll not go and sit in the throne room, Bergamoll," said the tiny woman haughtily. She drew herself up. "I shall greet the first outsiders to enter the City of the Drell in more than half a century as is proper. At my door."

* * *

They sat with Blenny's mother late into the night.

They had been given rooms after their introduction to Queen Orbanna, high up, overlooking the gardens and the valley beyond the walls. Every ceiling, floor and wall was stone, yet it was not dark, nor cave-like, even within hallways, for everywhere candles and magic light reflected off the golden walls, and there were many windows and skylights cut through the thick stone. It was cool inside, but there were thick rugs underfoot and plush furnishing to soften the hard stone.

They had all been given fresh clothes, surprisingly in their proper sizes, courtesy of some ancient shipwreck whose debris had washed up on drell shores, and then they were given a huge feast. Ebony delighted Blenny's mother as she delicately dined on fruit and bread, and after they'd eaten they closed the doors and began to talk.

They told Queen Orbanna something of their mission, and of meeting Blenny and Spotjaw. Orbanna, who was dressed in even more immaculate robes and longer bejewelled gloves than she had worn to greet them, the sparkle of vistrella at her throat, listened carefully. Then they spoke of the journey from the west through the Poisoned Marshes and the Badlands. Williver said with a smile that they'd had no idea that they were travelling with a prince of drell.

"My son is ever the modest one, so he is," said the old queen. "And not inclined to give much away." She smiled. "I suppose you know nothing of his reason for walking your lands instead of his own?"

"No," Shaeli smiled. "Though it's not from wondering."

"Shaeli is a very curious lass, Mother," said Blenny with a wry smile.

"I know," said Orbanna. "And an excellent swimmer, I'll warrant." She smiled back at Shaeli, a hint of slyness creasing her eyes. "I thought she'd not remember me."

Shaeli looked at her closely and suddenly she knew. Queen Orbanna was the old drell woman who had told her to learn to swim when she was very small, long before she had saved the twins in the barrel at Orrellis.

"You?" she breathed. "*You* were the old woman I met when I was...?"

"Four, lass, so you were. You told me yourself, ever so politely."

"*I* told you?"

"Aye, so ye did. We had a nice chat, though you were a bit shy."

"Shy? Shaeli?" scoffed her brother. "You're lucky she didn't ask you a hundred questions, once she started."

"Oh, I could tell she was a curious lass," said the queen. "But we didn't speak for long. I asked for her promise, she gave it, and I returned to my own lands."

"What promise?" said Shaeli.

"Why, that you learn to swim, of course. And swim well."

"Do you mean," said Flin, leaning forward. "Do you mean to say that you went into the World to find Shaeli and ask her to learn how to *swim*?"

"Aye, lad," said the old queen, as if such a thing was an everyday occurrence. "I took the opportunity of visiting an old friend in the Starisles also, but yes, I travelled into your lands to seek out the daughter of the trader."

"But, why?" asked Shaeli, completely baffled. "*Why* would you do that?"

"It was given to me in the smoke, so it was," Orbanna answered.

"You also see into the smoke?" asked Williver. "Shaeli has told me of Blenny's skill with that magic."

"'Tis not a difficult thing for drell to see into the smoke," said Blenny. "Most see something, if they care to look. It is one of our kinds of magic."

"Is it like the dreamworld?" asked Kirrit. "Looking in the smoke?"

"Not unlike it, lass," said Blenny. "But images in the smoke are always real, real and brightly coloured. In the dreamworld anything can happen. Within the smoke there is only truth."

"But why would you see *me* in the smoke?" Shaeli asked Orbanna.

"I know not," she said. "But I saw myself speaking to you, and asking for your promise to become the best swimmer you possibly could, so I determined I should have to go into your lands and find you."

"Swimming once saved my sisters' lives," said Shaeli, glancing at Tarkoda. "But how did you know where to find me?"

"'Twas no trouble. The smoke had shown me the town, your Trader, the season almost to the day. I merely had to *be* there to speak with you."

"She says it was no trouble, but I remember it differently, so I do," said Blenny, one eye on his mother, the other winking at Shaeli. "It seemed there were a great many arguments and a good deal of bother to see she was escorted safely."

"Well, that's only because your father was a stubborn old fool," Orbanna said, a fond smile belying her words.

"I miss him, too, Mother," said Blenny, patting her hand.

"He is with the gods?" asked Spotjaw.

"Aye, Spot," said Blenny, his face pained. "He was killed the autumn before I joined you in the lands of the People."

"Killed?" said Tarkoda tentatively.

"Yes, lad," replied Blenny. "Killed by raiders in the valley."

"People killing drell?" said Flin. "I thought that had been stopped a century ago."

"Aye," said Blenny. "Not quite that long, but stopped it had been. It had been frowned upon, but old King Tarkon outlawed it more than fifty years ago. Yet these were not here to kill." He looked at his mother and she nodded. Blenny passed a hand across his eyes before he went on. "They were here not to *kill* drell," he repeated, "but to capture them."

"Capture them? Why?" said Shaeli, appalled. "What for?"

Blenny thought before answering. "We know not. At first we did not even know that our people were being taken. A dozen or so disappeared over a decade. Young men travelling the mountains, girls out walking alone." He shrugged. "Many Winterings passed between each disappearance, and at first we thought they had met with some accident or other."

"But they hadn't?" said Flin.

"No," sighed Blenny. "One day, a young girl returned to her home, dazed and bleeding. She had been picking berries, she told her mother, with the lad from the next farm. They were apart when the girl heard yelling, and she ran to where her friend had been. She saw the lad being wrapped in a net, struggling hard, she said he was, but he was no match for six men with a net. The lad saw her watching, yelled at her to run, run for help. And so she did, but the men gave chase." Blenny stopped to take a drink. "She managed to escape them and reach her home, but the lad was never seen again. That was when we knew they were hunting us, but still we did not know why."

"When we realised what was happening," said Orbanna. "We kept all the people from the valley of the falls. It was forbidden to go there without armed escort."

"But why go there at all?" asked Flin. "Why not just stay on *this* side of the dragon gates?"

"There are certain things that can only be gathered from that valley," Orbanna said. "Herbs, game, the rocks that warm us during the Winterings. Other things."

"Oh, we use those rocks at Cave," said Kirrit. "Gathering them isn't much fun."

"No lass," said Blenny. "And it was on one such expedition that my father was killed. He and a dozen others."

"A *dozen* others?" said Tarkoda.

"Aye," said Blenny. "And great as the loss of them and my father was, something far more precious was lost that day. They captured our greatest treasure. My wife."

"Oh, Blenny, *no*," said Shaeli. "That's terrible. So *that's* why you're in our lands. You're looking for your wife."

"Aye, but not for the reason you think," he said, and then he sighed. "At least, not *only* that."

Orbanna covered her son's hand with her own tiny gloved one. The jewels upon them glittered in the lamplight. "When my son speaks of his wife as our greatest and most precious gift, he does not use such words lightly," she said. "He loves her dearly, this I know, but Mahra is much more than just Blenny's wife. She had been crowned queen, and so had become the life-blood of the drell."

"But aren't *you* the queen?" asked Kirrit.

"I only rule by default, my lass," smiled Orbanna sadly. "In the place of my son and his queen."

Shaeli looked at the bowed head of Blenny. "So, he is not just a *prince* of drell?" she said. "He is the king."

"That is so," Orbanna nodded. "Though he is called Lord Blenn, for the queen is ruler of the drell."

"But why do you call Blenny's wife the life-blood of the drell?" asked Williver. "The drell seem to do well in this valley, though 'tis obvious their numbers are fewer than they once were. Even if the worst should happen and she never returns, surely in the future... "

"Mahra is *queen*, Williver," interrupted Blenny. "And without her there *is* no future. I know it is difficult to understand, but the drell need their queen to survive in the same way a hive of bees depend on *their* queen. She gives direction, sustenance, but most of all, she gives life."

Shaeli remembered something she had noticed on their way to the city, and suddenly she *did* understand. "Is that why there are no babies, Blenny?" she said. "No little children?"

"Aye," he said. "There are no babies, and will be none until I return the queen to her throne." He looked at them. "Without the queen, the drell will cease to exist."

There was silence around the table until Spotjaw spoke. He had made few comments as the evening passed, sitting with his long legs stuck awkwardly under the low table. "And have you had a sign of her, my friend, on our travels through the World?" he asked. "Did you find her in the smoke?"

"*That's* why you look in the smoke?" cried Shaeli.

"So it is," Blenny smiled. "And yes, Spot. I have seen some things, a few clues."

He would say no more on the subject, and soon they went to their beds.

* * *

Blenny and his mother watched them go, and then the tiny woman turned to him.

"You know where she is, my son?" asked Orbanna.

"No, mother," said Blenny. "Not *where* she is, but I know she still lives. And I think I know why she was taken. Why they were *all* taken."

* * *

They had gone to bed very late, and the sun was high when they woke the next morning. They luxuriated in their surroundings and the feeling of safety. The sense that they were being pursued did not leave entirely, but it was almost possible to ignore it.

There was a light breakfast ready for them, and then Orbanna told them she had a picnic prepared, and they went down to where a carriage waited, young Wendll again at the reins. He took them on a tour through the valley, down dusty roads between rustling fields and towering trellises, and it seemed that the people were waiting for them, for no one worked the fields. Everywhere the drell stood outside their squat, carved homes, ready to wave as the carriage went by. Blenny and Orbanna waved back, Orbanna's bejewelled gloves glittering in the sun.

They ate on a hill overlooking one of the tiny villages, the late-summer sky high and giddily blue, studded with pristine clouds. They lazed through the heat of the day, and then Wendll drove them along the valley floor to a place where the cliffs narrowed around them and nothing green grew between them. They passed no more houses, no more waving drell, but drove down the rocky gorge, the cliffs growing higher and uglier around them. The sun was hot and bright on their backs when Wendll stopped the carriage before a massive gaping hole. They alighted to silence and sun-baked ground. High above, a pair of eagles circled. They were the only thing that moved.

"This is the entrance to the drell mines," said Blenny. "I thought you might like to see it."

"It's huge," said Tarkoda, staring at the yawning hole.

"Aye, lad. So it is," said Blenny.

"What kind of a mine is it?" asked Flin.

"Several things are to be found in these mountains. Gold, crystal, the occasional pocket of diamonds," said Blenny. He shrugged. "Several other gems and numerous metals. Inside there are tunnels that go many directions to many different veins. There is also the metal, drell metal, we call it, for want of a better name."

"Like the slingshot you gave me?" asked Tarkoda, pulling it from his belt. The dark metal did not shine in the sunlight; nothing reflected off its dark surface.

"That's right," said Blenny.

"That's what those big, flat discs are made out of, too, isn't it?" asked Shaeli. "The ones we've seen in the fields?"

"Aye," nodded Blenny.

"Vistrella is also found here, is it not?" asked Williver.

"No, it is found outside. In the valley beyond the dragon gates," Blenny said. Begrudgingly, Shaeli thought.

"Outside," said Shaeli. "Then that's one of the reasons you go there? To find vistrella?"

"It is," said Blenny, again with that begrudging tone. He shifted the subject. "Would ye care to look inside?"

He took his mother's arm, and without waiting for their reply, they walked across to the enormous mouth. Inside, the air cooled instantly and it took their eyes a moment to adjust to the gloom. The roof was high above, the rock rippled like a giant wave. Dozens of passageways led off the main cavern, the mouths of each black and sullen. They made various noises of appreciation, commenting on the vastness of the cavern and the eeriness of the tunnel mouths. Williver walked over to peer into one.

"Are they all in use?" he asked, his voice echoing down the tunnel.

"Most are," said Blenny. "Yet we only mine when we need. There is no need to take something from Merrom and Ettorr that one does not need to use. For the moment, none work here."

"I'm going back outside," said Kirrit. "It's spooky in here and I'm not partial to spooky. Or scary tunnels," she added.

Shaeli took her arm and they walked back outside in time to see one of the eagles swoop down and pounce on some tiny quarry which it carried squirming back to its nest. The other eagle still circled slowly above.

As they drove back towards the first of the villages, Shaeli saw something hanging in the sky out in one of the fields near some of the trellises. It looked like some drell standing on something beside the vines, and across the field below some other drell were waving at them. She nudged Williver and nodded her head towards the sight just as the thing began to drift back down towards the ground, and though his eyebrows rose just the tiniest bit, he said nothing, but met Shaeli's eyes with a slight shake of his head. When they neared the field where the thing had been, an older drell was berating a group of youngsters who stood before him, heads hanging, eyes on the ground. Beside them was one of the drell-metal discs, with a few half-full baskets on its surface. The older drell held out his hand to one of the youngsters as they passed, and the girl gave him something that shone in the sun. Shaeli caught Williver's eye. He shook his head again and they both knew they had seen something they were not supposed to see, so they pretended they hadn't. The others had seen nothing, they were busy discussing the city with Orbanna, and Shaeli shrugged at Williver and they went back to admiring the view and listening to the others talk, but they would discuss it later, and wonder over it.

It was late afternoon when they returned to the castle in the cliffs to find a sumptuous meal waiting for them, accompanied by ruby-red drell wine.

They spent five days in the city, discussing over and over what they would do next, what they might expect when they left the safety of the Drell Mountains. They ate and slept a great deal, and then talked some more.

They decided that they would not leave the mountains as expected of them. They would not travel across the land, but leave by sea. It had come as a great surprise to learn that the drell knew anything about boats and it took little time to plan, once the idea had taken hold. Wendll had suggested it one evening and even Flin thought it a good idea, yet when it came to sailing the vessel, only Spotjaw had any experience. Blenny and Williver knew a few things, but the others knew nothing. Flin, of course, knew a great deal, but he also knew he would be near useless if he became ill, so Wendll offered to accompany them. He was an adept sailor and Spotjaw confessed he would be happier if he had a crewmember with some idea of what was going on. Queen Orbanna gave her permission and she sent a party to the coast to prepare a vessel. They would take a boat across to the northern tip of Zirrus and sail down through Nebillonia Straits to Meoro Pass, and go to Cave by that route. They knew there would be many of Virrisian's guard searching for them, and none relished the thought of the journey through the daunting eastern side of the mountains and the dry lands beyond.

Wendll, looking forward to the unexpected adventure, became quite excited as the preparations were made, while the others became more sober.

Finally they gathered to say goodbye. They'd met many of the drell as they'd explored the amazing carved city, and everywhere they had met with kind words and good wishes. Most of the drell were there to see them depart, including the horses that had so patiently carried them from Trilby.

They took leave of Queen Orbanna as night took leave of the World. Dawn found them looking down on the city from a ridge high above the valley, and while Wendll looked eagerly forward, Blenny's shoulders were heavy as he sighed and turned his back once again on his home. Beside him, Shaeli's thoughts were on her own home, on the Long Lea and Cave.

* * *

On the Long Lea, there were many who thought of Shaeli and the others. Summer was passing swiftly, and Mareesha looked a dozen times each day down the Lea to the Valley of Stones in the hope some Trader bearing her children would fly into sight. Yet the long days passed, and though two Traders had returned – both sought by the guard for supposedly aiding the rebellion – there had been no word of her children, and so she spent her time helping in the fields or the kitchen, or tutoring one of the girls who showed the promise of Faunistry.

Jarris' eyes often followed his wife's down the Lea, his thoughts on his children almost as much as Mareesha's, yet his practical nature saw him filling his time on the Trader, repairing the damage to the balloon and making repairs to the old one's year huts. When the time came to fly again he wanted to be ready.

Shanna and Neesha mentioned their siblings every day. Neesha constantly wondered where they were, and Shanna grew used to the pattern of the conversation, often answering automatically. They talked of Shaeli's wand, why anyone would want a broken old thing like that, and Neesha once asked Almarnoch if they could see it. He had shaken his head, smiled, and sent them off to "do something useful". Shanna had asked him if he knew how someone had known Shaeli had the wand, otherwise why else had that thing looked in her mind? Almarnoch had shaken his head at that too. He knew when Shaeli returned that the two would be told what else "that thing" had found in their sister's mind, yet Shanna's question had echoed in his ears as they'd run off to find their grandmother.

It was a question Almarnoch wondered about often; how they had found out about the wand. He hoped he was wrong about who he suspected, he hoped it most fervently, but his suspicions were not lightly dismissed. He was certain he knew where Shaeli had gone, for he had seen the glittering bangle in the bag with the wand, and seeing it had confirmed what he had long thought: that the wand Shaeli had found on the shores of Lake Marnis was the lost wand of the elf Shahlita.

He had heard it spoken of only a few times over the years, but once he'd met a Warlock who had lived most of his life on the edge of elven lands in the northern mountains. The Warlock had come to spend his final years on the Warlock Island when Almarnoch had resided there for only a few years. The old Warlock had shown him drawings of the elf Shahlita and her dragon, who he had known before the dragons went from the World. The drawings had been made as a very young man, and the papers were thin and dry with age, but the young Almarnoch had been fascinated by them and he'd had many talks on what had happened to the dragons with the old man before he died. It had been the old Warlock's speculation that the Lady Shahlita had been somehow involved, for he had never seen her again after the dragons had disappeared from the World. Though he had asked about her, it was not until many Winterings later that one of the elves told him that she was dead, her wand missing. The elf had partaken of too many wines and denied the comment the next day, but the old Warlock had grown more suspicious as the years had passed. The drawings were left with the keeper of records on the Warlock Island, but Almarnoch's memory was good and he had often compared the wand to the pictures in his mind. When he had seen the bangle wrapped up with the wand he knew he had been right, for he also remembered the bright bangles worn by the elf Shahlita that he had seen in the old Warlock's drawings. How Shaeli had come across the bangle he did not know, and he was anxious to ask her about it, yet he was sure she had gone now to seek the other. He would have many questions for his young friend when he saw her next, but the questions that troubled him most he knew she would be unable to answer.

Who had invaded Shaeli's mind, and who had the power to do such a thing? And how did they know of the existence of the wand?

* * *

Far to the south-west, Dari stood beside the water of a small bay, pulling tiny spouting geysers from the water with a group of other apprentices. He was laughing as the waterspouts chased each other around the bay. The old Warlock instructing them was smiling benignly as he sat on a nearby stump, his robe stretched across his rotund belly.

Dari loved the Warlock Island. It was a huge place, dotted with buildings housing Warlock tutors, retired Warlocks, and the many young Warlocks who came from every Land to train for their final years. Apprentices spent their first years learning with a mature Warlock, and when it was time they were sent to train in the Bay of Islands, for none were deemed a true Warlock until the elders of the island made it so and gifted each young Warlock a staff designed for them alone. The buildings, turreted, many-winged, and initially impossible to negotiate, were home to hundreds of lads at any time, occasionally a girl or two; though this was unusual, it did happen, and there were several female Warlocks who were tutors on the island. There were protected bays and a long beach facing out to the Bastinian Ocean where they swam when the weather was warm, and a lofty hill crowned by a forest of terrezza trees where they could see in every direction. There were numerous orchards where they practiced their craft, as well as dozens of gardens, for the island was largely self-sufficient. In a low field surrounded by tall trees they learned to dissipate mist; in a glade they learned to colour smoke that would influence the clouds to rain, or stop raining as the case may be, and in another long field they practiced pushing energy through their staffs at targets set at increasing distances. The staffs were presented to each Warlock during their final year, and Dari had been the happy recipient of his when he'd returned from the Wintering at Great Court.

The year before, he had soaked up knowledge as if it was liquid and he was a sponge. Small things, lighting lamps or fire-rocks, he had learnt at Cave. Almarnoch had shown him many things during his years on the Lea, but the extra knowledge which was learned only on the island had fascinated him. This year he had learnt how to turn the course of a stream, how to protect plants from the harshest Wintering, and how to sustain the life of a plant beyond its usual span; the only thing tedious about those lessons was the continual rhetoric about the dangers of using such magic on living creatures, something entirely forbidden and against every Warlock principal. Yet he enjoyed bringing wilted flowers back into bloom as much as he enjoyed making new buds blossom into flower, as he had done during the Wintering at that ball where he'd seen his cousin.

He had enjoyed his time there, too. He had learned a great deal in the vast gardens and the Warlock house beneath the walls of Great Court, and it had been good to see Garrit again. Garrit had taken up a position in the Warlock house, and it was clear he revelled in being in such a prestigious place, surrounded by powerful men and glamorous women. He spoke of the few times he had seen the queen, escorted usually by her master-at-arms, Sir Azeron of Maxx, and how she had once spoken to him at a ball. Dari had seen Queen Virrisian himself once, in the distance, sweeping down a hall followed by two dozen courtiers. He had thought the sight quite amusing, the scurrying people like a flock of nervous chickens waiting for scraps to be tossed their way, but Garrit had been in awe; he thought the queen magnificent and spoke longingly of being in her favour.

It had been Garrit who insisted they go to the ball at the house of the old noblewoman; Dari would have much rather stayed at Court, but he had begrudgingly accompanied his friend. When Garrit had also insisted Dari ask his cousin about the wand, he had resisted, but in the end he had agreed. Though he could not see the point in the broken old thing, he remembered how Garrit had always coveted it.

The memory of taking it from Shaeli's room the night before they'd left him for Cave year made him squirm a bit, but he had so wanted to please his friend then, as he still did, he had done as Garrit had asked. How she had retrieved it he did not know, perhaps she had seen him from the window of the privy as Garrit said.

He had often stood on the seat and peered out the window as a child, for he enjoyed the feeling of watching others unseen. The night he had seen the shrouded woman carry the baby onto the Trader was the most interesting thing he had ever found with his spying, and the thought that one of his so-called "twin" cousins was nothing of the sort was highly amusing to him. He imagined her to be the bastard of some unwed woman from the pious town of Zuen who his soft-hearted aunt had taken pity on. He thought Mareesha far too soft, far too undisciplined, and felt smug inside himself when he thought of the night they had allowed the stumbling woman to leave her baby behind. He had seen her come aboard and waited a long time shivering in the privy before he'd seen Jarris escort her from the Trader, and he had kept the knowledge to himself for many years. He'd told Garrit during his Cave year, and Garrit had shrugged and said it was just another example of the false pride exhibited by most of the Fleet. It was Garrit's feeling that the traders thought far too highly of themselves, felt that they were above most others, and there were many times Dari had to agree. His cousin, Shaeli, in particular had always showed these traits, and though she had pretended to be happy to see him and made a fuss of him the whole time he had been in that boring old woman's house, he knew it was false; she'd barely taken the time to speak with him when they had lived together, and he was sure she had been overjoyed when he was left behind at Cave. Typically, he could tell she thought that her gift with the stones was far more important than his own magic, and he still bitterly resented the fact that she possessed any magic at all. Finding he had a gift for Warlock magic had been the best thing that had ever happened to him, and coming home to Cave and finding Shaeli had light talent had incensed him. It was all he could do not to shout about the unfairness of it. *He* was the one who had magic; *he* the one who was found to be special, at last. Still, he had managed to conceal his feelings, as he ever had – as he had seen his mother do so often – and when Garrit had asked him to find out about the wand he had done it, even finding it amusing to let Shaeli think he liked her, yet the mission was fruitless and Garrit had bid him to forget the matter. Even after Dari had insisted on knowing why Garrit wanted it so much, he still could not see the use in it. Dari had much preferred to worry about the excellent wine served in the house, and when the Wintering was over he returned to the Warlock Island to continue his studies. He had not bothered to see his cousin again, and he could not think that she'd care very much.

* * *

CHAPTER EIGHTEEN

Midday found Shaeli and her companions on a ridge overlooking the division of a river rushing between the cliffs of a broad valley. They stood on a v-shaped promontory at the point where it thrust out into the river, the waters split with unerring force, each side becoming a mighty river in itself. One branch led back to the south, to fall from the dragon gates into the valley far behind; the branch they had followed from the drell city. The other branch of the broken river led north, and they shouldered their burdens to follow it to the coast.

They walked all day along the top of the ridge, the river on their left sometimes far down between steep-sided cliffs, and sometimes so close that they could see the fish swimming in its depths. As dusk began to fall, the ridge above the river became merely a bank, and a few trees began to grow at the edges. They looked for somewhere to camp for the night, and Blenny led them to a ring of trees on a rise overlooking the river. The water flowed slowly here and Wendll and Tarkoda threw in a line. Spotjaw boiled water and made them all a cup of tezz while the others rested their legs and rolled out capes to sit on. Ebony wandered around sniffing the air, and then ran over to where Wendll was pulling in his first fish. Spotjaw pulled out a pan and soon four fish were sizzling in its bottom.

They ate as the sun was setting. Crimson and pink clouds hung over the horizon, thin, high clouds that faded to grey as the sun turned its face from them. As they sat talking, from somewhere far off in the distance there came a long, mournful howl. Voices stilled as the eerie sound wafted through darkness, eyes grew huge.

"What was that?" said Kirrit.

Wendll peered at her, the rims of his irises as red as the fire. "'Tis one of the creatures that live in the mountains to the east," he said. "A great ugly beast with fangs made for tearing flesh. The gondaag, we call it."

"Do they come over here?" asked Shaeli.

"Fear not," said Blenny. "The gondaag stay with the other creatures to the east, and the drell stay to the west. There is a mighty gorge which separates the two, running almost the whole length of the mountains, north to south, with a watercourse in its depths. The creatures on either side are amazingly different, the land, too." He grinned. "The mountains there are not as... pretty as they are over here."

Something leapt in the trees nearby, and Kirrit and Shaeli jumped. Blenny laughed.

"'Tis only a jindi," he said. "They are a cousin to your jevvi there, though a little bigger. They come out at night to feed on fruit and insects. Pretty things. They use the trees like pathways. We should see a few, so we should."

There was another shadowy figure leaping between the trees almost before the words were out of his mouth, and then another, and another. Soon the trees over their heads trembled as jindi after jindi leapt past on their way to find a meal. Several stopped to look curiously down at the group gathered around the fire, and Shaeli could see something of her jevvi in their big eyes, pointed ears and long fluffy tail, but the jindi was a merciless hunter. They saw one pounce on a long insect, its twig-like camouflage doing nothing to hide it from the big-eyed jindi, which munched hungrily on the still-squirming insect as it looked down at them from its perch. It devoured every bit of the insect and then suddenly bounced off into the night, the speed of the creatures amazing to see, as if their legs held tightly coiled springs. Ebony sat watching from Shaeli's lap as her distant cousins leapt through the trees, and she huddled beneath Shaeli's cloak when they lay down to sleep. They were woken by soft rain before sunrise and it continued falling sporadically throughout the day.

They followed the river for several more days until they could taste the salt on their tongues. Late one afternoon they crested a rise and were met with the sight of a house on the bank in a bend of the river below. Half a dozen boats with curved prows were moored at a small wharf, their sides bumping together, and several figures moved about on the largest boat. The house was similar to the first sanctuary they had stayed in, a long, low stone building, its door open and smoke coming from its chimney. Behind it was a high bluff, and beyond the place where the river met the waves. The bay, boats and house were all out of sight of the sea, protected by the high bluff from the sight of passing ships.

As they made their way down to the house, Shaeli noticed that autumn was beginning to show its colours in the russet curls of the leaves on some of the trees, and she suddenly felt a great sense of urgency; the Wintering was not far off, and they must be at Cave before first snow. Yet she calmed herself; the autumn days still stretched ahead, and it would surely not take many days to reach Meoro Pass.

They spent one last, comfortable night in the low stone house, and when the tide turned the next morning, they went with it.

The passage from the river to the sea was done with ease. Spotjaw and Wendll fell into an easy pattern of sailing the vessel, and Tarkoda was eager to learn all he could. Behind them the coastline blurred, and the bluff that hid the house and bay from sight blended into one dark mass. Ahead lay the three towering monoliths that stood in the sea outside the river mouth.

When they had passed this way with Chessy, summer had been bright upon the water and the Drell Mountains were things to be feared. Chessy had taken a wide berth around these tall stone edifices, muttering under his breath and peering at them from the corner of his eye, but now they knew the Drell Mountains were not to be feared, and so they looked on the towering islands with curiosity rather than with superstition.

From out to sea, the islands had looked dark and barren, but as they sailed beside them they could see a few gnarled bushes clinging to life in gaps high above the tide line and scores of birds wheeled about overhead, screeching at the intrusion. The sea slapped heavily at the bases of the rocky islands, churning and swirling and sucking.

The boat was twice as big as Chessy's, with a dark hull and patterned blue sail. Both fore and aft were tall curved structures carved with creatures of the sea. The cabin was big enough to have a closet sized bathroom and a small cooking space, and they had been well supplied by the drell. There were several padded benches inside, and a few more on the deck, so there was ample space to sleep, albeit they would have to take turns sleeping inside. They could sail long stretches without needing to stop, and unless they ran into one of the queen's ships, they should be safe until they reached Meoro City.

All eyes anxiously scanned the horizon as they entered the sea beyond the three islands, but there were few other boats in sight, all mere dots against the blue. A pod of dolphins leapt playfully in the boat's wake as they headed east, yet the dolphins' antics did not amuse them, for they were all scanning the coastline, fearing to see what they knew would be there. And so it was.

The eastern mountains passed too quickly, and as they shrunk down onto the dry plains, distant though they were, they could all see the encampments, the smoke of the fires coiling into the air, the peaks of tents against the line of the horizon. Williver's face grew grim.

"There is a lookout on that bluff," he said, pointing, and though none of the others could see, they did not doubt the elf could. "And I fear I hear the echo of a horn."

"Then they've seen us," said Shaeli.

"Yes, little one," replied Williver. "Yet you knew it would probably be so. More than likely they will send riders east. We may find a ship or two ahead of us."

"It doesn't matter," said Flin, shortly. "Guard or ship, I'll not let them capture any of us."

No one disagreed with him – his face did not permit argument – but they all doubted they could avoid capture forever.

* * *

It was three days later that Flin's words were tested.

They had sailed almost constantly, stopping only once to take on fresh water in the small hours of the night, and though Flin had had a couple of bouts of sickness, the seas had been calm and he had coped well. It was lucky it was so, because even he admitted later that he didn't know if he would have had the strength if he had been really ill.

It began as a speck on the horizon, and before they could see its masts, Williver had told them the details. The ship was huge, flying an enormous scarlet-and-black emblem, and it was accompanied by three smaller ships. Archers lined the rails. The three smaller craft had soldiers wielding grappling hooks and spears. There was little point in trying to avoid them, and so Wendll headed the boat straight at the larger ship.

Flin, Williver and Tarkoda went to the prow of the ship. Flin held his throwing-stone, Williver held his bow – he had no great reach with his wand – and Tarkoda stood with his sling in his hand, a bag of rocks at his feet. Shaeli knelt above them, on the roof of the cabin, the mast at her back. She looped one arm through a rope to steady herself, her other hand holding the long finger of smoky quartz. Behind her, Spotjaw and Kirrit stood on the deck, each clutching a bow. Usually neither had much use for the weapon, but both knew how to use one. Wendll sat at the tiller, his face frozen, his dream of adventure turned so quickly to nightmare.

They had talked of such an event and discussed their best defence. Each knew their task. Each felt their heart pounding as the moment approached.

Shaeli could see each individual lining the rails of the ship when Flin fired his first bolt. They were not close enough yet to fire arrows but they were more than close enough to throw light. Flin's first bolt hit the wheel on the bridge. Men leapt away as the wheel leapt into flame. The straight course of the ship wavered, its rudder now unguided.

Shaeli's beam hit high up in the sails. One, two, three beams flew from her fingers, one, two, three sails burst into flame. Instantly the ship lost momentum. Men scrambled about on the deck, yelling and frantically trying to douse the flames spreading through the sails. Bits of rope and sail began to fall onto the deck and the soldiers milling upon it.

The wheel was extinguished before the bridge caught fire, yet it was a useless blackened mass, and those on the bridge had no way of guiding the ship. It had been deprived of both impetus and direction before it had drawn close enough to even fire a shot, yet they still had to pass it, and though Wendll headed their boat in an arc around the hulk, they would still come closer than they cared to.

They came within bow range and a shower of arrows flew towards them. Some did not make the distance and fell uselessly into the ocean, others turned to flame and burnt as they flew, courtesy of a bolt from Flin or Shaeli. A few drove into the deck and the sides of their boat and one thudded into the mast beside Shaeli's head. For a moment she was unable to comprehend the haft quivering beside her face, then her eyes narrowed, and she threw a shower of sparks among the archers on the ship. Dozens of bows burst into flame.

Flin was busy with one of the three smaller ships that was bearing down on them from the left, its prow cutting white foam through the water, a man with an enormous pronged hook standing in its peak, a dozen others with similar weapons ranging its sides, and Flin quickly dispatched the man in the prow, but another took his place just as swiftly. This one also suffered a bolt from Flin, but again he was replaced. The smaller ship was now so close Shaeli could see the rope coiled in the man's hands.

Wendll took evasive action. They swept to the right, but in doing so they went precariously close to the large ship. The side of the vessel loomed above them, and Wendll veered again to avoid running into it. Those on the deck with their wits and their weapons still intact fired down at them as the back corner of the ship flew by a mere arm's length away, yet they were too swift or the archers too slow, for most spears and arrows fell into their wake, but still they were in range and the archers who still had bows above notched their next round of arrows. Flin dealt with them with a stream of burning fire.

Behind them the other vessel had followed Wendll's evasive move, yet their captain was slower to react. The prow of his ship mowed into the side of the hulk above, splintering wood and sending the crew diving for their lives.

The larger ship was now behind them, unable to pursue. One small ship lay upon the waves, pounded into kindling, its crew floundering in the water, but two more were now bearing down on them. These two smaller ships swept towards them as they went around the back of the larger ship, their crews leaning forward, urging their vessels on. A few arrows still flew at them from above, and Shaeli saw a wicked spear smash into the deck beside Tarkoda's foot. He spun around and launched a stone at the thrower, wiping the grin from the man's face with a blow to the temple. Beside him, Williver's hands were a blur as arrow after arrow flew from his tall bow.

Flin easily took out the mast of one of the remaining ships, causing it to wheel in its course. Shaeli was frantically trying to stop the rain of arrows from the third small ship when one hit Wendll in the arm and he crumpled. She yelled to Spotjaw and he leapt over to Wendll, pulled him to the deck and grabbed hold of the tiller.

The second small ship was drifting away, its mast snapped, its crew unable to do anything but watch the last ship try and stop them. And try it did, but it was now sorely outmatched. Though it was bigger and faster, it could not contend with the forces that leapt from the deck of the little boat. As it came towards them, Williver despatched its captain with an arrow to the throat. Stones from Tarkoda's sling thudded into the soldiers. Shaeli saw one woman thrown out of sight by a missile hitting her squarely in the stomach, but the sight barely registered as she threw a long beam at the mast. The mast groaned and bent, falling slowly into the sea and covering the deck with folds of sail, empty of all wind. The crew fired off a few half-hearted shots as they swept past, and then the queen's ships were gone, left in their wake, smouldering, obsolete wrecks.

Their joy at defeating the ships was short-lived. Wendll lay unconscious and bleeding on the deck, his head in Kirrit's lap. Dozens of arrows and one great spear were stuck in the wood around them.

They carried Wendll into the cabin while Tarkoda and Spotjaw set their course. Blenny hovered as Williver tore open the young drell's shirt, and Shaeli inspected the wound, bathed it and wrapped it tightly. The arrow had passed cleanly through the edge of his arm, and though he would have a fine scar to show, it should heal well. He moaned and woke as they bandaged his arm, his face pale. He sighed when they told him the wound was not great, and he slept again almost instantly.

* * *

They rounded the tip of Zirrus a few days later without further incident, the city of Conroi on the northern peak sporting a haze of smoke above its pointed roofs.

They travelled past the first few islands, stopping late one evening to replenish their water, then skirting Argon the next day. Xenel Island was also passed, and though it was far away, a mere lump in the ocean between them and the unseen tip of Ashkanna, Williver saw three sails exit from its harbour. Before long they could all see the sails following them, and they prepared to fight again, yet the three ships did not venture closer. They merely followed until the sun began to set and then they turned back. Puzzled, they relaxed their tense muscles, realising they had been stalked and would more than likely meet opposition closer to Meoro Village. They decided they would land well before they reached the village, travel through the hills, and meet the Pass somewhere to the west of Meoro Village. Yet they would meet disaster long before that.

They sailed close to Zirrus, for the land from here to Meoro Pass was unpopulated, the mountains too rugged to traverse, their feet right in the waters of the straits. They would be less likely to see any other craft this close to Zirrus, for most sailed in deeper waters.

Harsh and uninviting this stretch of coastline looked. Waves smashed themselves against rocks, foam leapt high into the air, and on the ragged shores they saw nothing but birdlife and the occasional stalking troupe of jenka.

Night fell, and in the brightness of the almost-full moon, Shaeli saw the fins of dolphins again riding their wake.

The moon was at its zenith when the wind rose and white flecks began to dance on the dark waters. The stars disappeared behind thick cloud and the waves hitting the rocks on the shore pounded louder, the wind strengthened and became colder, the thick undersides of clouds overcame the sky. The world went black as the clouds covered the moon.

They tacked across the southerly wind directly into the storm, for there was nowhere to land, nowhere to take shelter, and when the rain began, it came across the water in an almost solid wall. None of them were able to stay inside the stuffy cabin, and so they were huddled outside beneath the cabin's overhang when the wall hit them.

Wendll and Spotjaw held the tiller. Tarkoda and Williver scurried about pulling sails and tying ropes. Kirrit and Shaeli sat huddled with Blenny, Ebony held tightly in Shaeli's arms. All Flin could do was groan in a corner.

The rain-wall passed quickly enough, yet they were all drenched by the time the storm swept further north. The sky grew clearer and they began to see stars ahead, and when the moon was uncovered they were bathed again in silvery light. Shaeli looked forward across the cabin. Tarkoda was standing on it and she looked up at him.

"I'll make some tezz," she said.

He nodded. "Good idea."

She saw something in the sky far ahead. Something odd. She stared at it for a moment, her head on one side, eyes narrowed. "Koda," she said. "What's that?"

"What's what?" he said, tiredly, looking down at her.

She pointed and his eyes followed her finger. "That."

It wasn't a star, though it was quite bright, but it was moving. A Trader? No, much too high. It reminded her of something. Something buried in memory.

"It's the dragon," she said softly, and then she shook her head. Things she had heard about a black ship followed the shake. Her parents had talked with Ellirra and her husband about a black ship. A flying ship.

"Williver," she called nervously. "Can you see what that is?"

They were all looking now, scanning the sky. Even Flin had dragged himself upright. When Williver looked back at her, his face was grim.

"I know not, little one," he said. "But I fear it does not bode well."

It came at them with amazing speed. They stood dumfounded as it came closer and lower. Blenny's voice moved them into action.

"Spotjaw," he called. "As close to the rocks as you dare."

They held on as the boat swerved and the rocks grew closer, silver-black teeth dripping foam, and then it was above them, blocking out a shape in the sky, but resembling nothing. Its surface did not reflect light, or hold it; it seemed to *swallow* light.

The strange craft hovered uncannily above the waves, soundless and huge as they squinted up. Beams shone from it, one that had a reddish hue at the front and one from the underside, so bright they had to cover their eyes. They could not see its outlines, its true shape was lost in the glare of its lights and its odd surface.

Shaeli stood terrified, willing their boat to go faster, to escape the monster, yet it hung above them like a second moon. Drawing a stone from her amulet did not occur to her.

The vessel hovered overhead until Spotjaw turned for a sharp tack – it was either that or hit the rocks on shore – and as the boat swung around, a bolt of red light flew from the front of the thing and hit the mast, pulverising it instantly.

They dived for cover as the mast exploded. Spotjaw hung on to the tiller as the sail fell. The boat floundered, rocked by the blast.

Everyone was yelling and Shaeli could not make out a word. She saw Flin pull out his throwing stone and fire at the thing, yet it made no impression, bouncing harmlessly off the strange black surface.

"No, Flin. Stop," she heard Blenny yell above the others.

She had just staggered to her feet when the second bolt struck. The pretty, curved prow of the ship disappeared and in its place bright flames grew. The boat lurched and then a strange gurgling sound began. Ebony clung beneath her hair shivering as Shaeli looked up, waiting for the next bolt, then Williver and Flin were dragging at her.

"Jump, Shaeli," Flin was yelling. "We have to jump."

She knew then that the boat was going to sink.

Spotjaw and Wendll leapt over. Blenny grabbed a couple of small buoys off the deck and jumped after them. Tarkoda pulled a screaming Kirrit over the side, but Shaeli pulled at the arms urging her towards the edge.

"The bangle," she cried, trying to go back to the cabin. "I have to get the bangle."

"I'll get it," said Williver, letting go of her arm and turning back. "Go with Flin. *Hurry*," he yelled, but before he had taken a step, another bolt hit the centre of the cabin.

Instead of jumping into the water, they were tossed overboard as if blown by hot breath. They fell with the splintered remains of the cabin into blackness.

Cold water closed over Shaeli's head. Flin still held her arm and Ebony still clung to her hair, and she pushed off her shoes and kicked up. She broke the surface and heard Ebony gasp in her ear. She spoke quietly to her and told her to hang on. She felt for the familiar weight of her amulet on her hip, and knew that, at least, was safe.

"Alright?" said Flin. His face was pale and black circles hung beneath his eyes.

Shaeli nodded and looked around.

The boat was well alight now and another bolt hit it as she watched. Pieces of their little boat flew through the air, showering them with burning kindling. She ducked as a large chunk slammed into the water beside her.

Williver was not far away and he swam towards them. Tarkoda and Kirrit bobbed nearby, Spotjaw and the two drell – both hanging on to one of the buoys – floated just beyond them.

The strange craft hovered above them still, the great bright eye in its underbelly scanning the sea. Yet it was not content with merely destroying their boat.

Thick red bolts began to hit the water around them, thunking like rocks into the waves. The water hissed and boiled in a wide ring around each bolt, sending up great clouds of steam.

They swam over to Spotjaw and the two drell, clinging together in a group. They began to swim away from the deadly eye, pulling the drell along with them, recoiling every time a bolt slammed into the sea.

The tide was slowly pulling them out into the straits, but it seemed the craft above would never stop showering the water with bolts. The light in the underbelly scanned the water as they kicked and swam with the tide, drawing slowly away from the boiling waters. Then Shaeli felt something brush her ankle. At first she thought it was Williver, but then Kirrit screamed.

"Something touched me," she cried, turning and back-peddling into Tarkoda.

"What was it?" he said, looking around at the water. The exercise was futile. No one could see a thing.

"I don't *know*," she cried. "*Aaah*. There it is again."

"Something just touched me, too," said Spotjaw, for once sounding slightly nervous.

"What *is* it?" cried Kirrit.

"Don't panic," said Flin. "It's probably just seaweed or..." He stopped as another searing bolt slammed into the water, far too close.

The ship with its great light moved to hover just at the edge of the bobbing group. It was searching for them, Shaeli knew that now, and it wanted them smashed into pieces, the way it had smashed their boat.

They swam harder, pulling with the tide, kicking frantically, dragging the two drell, and still the bolts flew at the sea from the black ship above.

Then each of them felt something touch them. Something that grabbed them by the waist. Something that began to push them through the water. Through the water and back into the light.

Shaeli felt her waist. Touched the thing that was pushing her.

Fingers? *Hands?*

307

They yelled, struggled, pulled at each other, but they were inexorably pushed back, back towards the black ship and the light and the red bolts that made the sea boil.

"Don't struggle," she heard Williver cry. "Help is at hand." He sounded happy.

The water beneath them was churning as they went back towards the still-burning hulk of their boat; back towards the jagged shoreline. Back into the path of the light.

Then they were in its glare, directly beneath the great shining eye, passing through it, *rushing* through it.

When the next beam flew from the strange flying craft, it thudded into the water just behind them. They were swept through the wreckage of their boat, its sorry remains now sinking beneath the waves.

"The rocks," yelled Wendll. "We're going to hit the rocks."

They could see them now, looming up through the silvery light. Edges sharp as knives, a vast cliff rising above, the waves throwing themselves in fury at its base. They struggled against the things that pushed them, but it was useless, the wall of rocks grew huger and uglier. Williver called again, urging calm, yet they were far from calm.

Shaeli put a hand to the terrified jevvi clutching her hair and looked back. The last of their boat disappeared beneath the waves as she turned, as if it had never been. The black shape that had so easily destroyed their quest was rising now. It fired no more bolts, but followed them with its light, content to watch as the sea smashed their bodies into the rocks.

Shaeli turned away from the shapeless craft watching them, facing the rocks with their black faces and their edges like raised knives. Above the rocks, an enormous ragged cliff stared blackly down at them, its face still running with rain from the storm. She struggled half-heartedly, knowing she could not break free, saw Kirrit and Tarkoda also struggling uselessly. Spotjaw, too, writhed in the water, Flin struggled feebly, the drell beside him, clinging tightly to their buoys. Only Williver seemed resigned to his fate.

Shaeli felt the water grow warmer against her legs, a vague current trying to push her back into the straits, but on they went, closer and closer, the rocks and the cliff wall in front of them growing huger and blacker. She turned her head again as the rocks came within arms-length, and saw the black ship rising into the air. It turned and headed south at an incredible speed.

Forward again, expecting the slam of hard rock against her body. The water rushed past but the black rocks were all she could see. A wall of them, knives raised, dripping foam like silver blood.

And she saw a black... *blacker* space within the wall.

There was a space in the rocks. A low, arch-shaped space. She felt the water pulling at her, but the thing holding her tightened its grip as they slammed into the shore, yet they hit neither rocks nor cliff, they were swept into a black tunnel where darkness was absolute and the roar of the sea was all she could hear. On they went through the tunnel, and suddenly they were out the other side, the moon again bright above them, the water suddenly calm. The things that gripped their waists relaxed, but still they were pushed on.

The cliffs on either side opened out. They were in a lake, enormous and studded with dozens of towering islands. The sides of the islands reached high above the water, the tops thick with trees. Through the moonlight, Shaeli could see waterfalls dropping into the lake from the surrounding cliffs, and thin bridges like hanging vines spanning the gaps between the islands.

The water grew warmer and calmer still as they were pushed on through the silent lake. When they reached the base of the closest island they gratefully felt the sand beneath their feet, and as their feet touched land, the things that held them let go.

Shaeli pulled Ebony down from where she had been clinging in her hair and soothed her. She could feel the jevvi's heart bumping against her own as she turned. The water behind them bubbled. Ten heads broke the surface. Ten smiling faces rose beneath them, shoulders, arms, bodies. Ten figures stood before them, the one in front grinning more widely than the rest.

His smile was slightly crooked, his dark hair plastered to his forehead, the line of a thin scar upon it. His eyes were the greenest she had seen since...

"*Ishaan*," Shaeli cried incredulously. "Ishaan? Is it really you?"

"Yes, Shaeli," he smiled. "It is me."

"Then...?"

"Yes," he said. "Welcome to the city of the Ammerr. Welcome to Qorientae."

* * *

CHAPTER NINETEEN

Shaeli stared at Ishaan, dumbfounded. Thunderstruck, her father would have said.

"You are *Ammerr*?"

That he and his companions were of the legendary race of sea-people long thought lost to the World was unbelievable, yet here they were, and none of her race could have done what they just had.

"Yes, Shaeli," Ishaan smiled. "I am Ammerr." He raised an arm, standing thigh-deep in the water. "This is our city, Qorientae, and pleased I am to welcome you and your companions to it. Those unmet, and those already friends."

"Hello, Ishaan," said Kirrit, wading across to Shaeli and taking her arm. She knew nothing about Ishaan going into the Zoi cave at the end of their Cave year and thought of him fondly, as a handsome, unusual addition to their year. "If I'd known it was you, I wouldn't have kicked so hard."

"Greetings, Kirrit," Ishaan smiled. "Cheval was guiding you," he said, indicating a tall, blonde woman to his left. "But I think she suffered no damage."

"Only a bruise or two," Cheval grinned.

Ishaan came forward, kissed the two girls' cheeks, and then he looked at the others.

"Greetings," said Williver, coming forward.

Ishaan turned to Williver. "Well met, my friend," he said. His smile widened, and then he and Williver embraced as warmly as if they were brothers.

He and Ishaan kept hold of each other's forearms as they grinned at each other and Shaeli and Kirrit goggled at them.

"You *know* each other?" said Shaeli.

"Yes, little one," smiled Williver. "'Tis many Winterings since Ishaan and I first met. I knew we would need the

311

Ammerr eventually, yet I never imagined it would be so soon."
He grinned at Ishaan. "Nor with such fortuitous timing."

"Not quite as fortuitous as you would imagine, my elfin
friend," said Ishaan. "You have been watched since you left the
Drell Mountains."

"But..." began Shaeli.

"Further questions can wait," said Ishaan. "You are wet
and no doubt tired and hungry. Let me show you the same
hospitality you showed me at the Long Lea of the Traders.
Come. We shall go into the city."

He led the way, smiling and shaking the hands of the
others, introducing himself as he went. Tarkoda managed to
close his mouth enough to speak. Flin and Spotjaw managed
better. When Ishaan spoke to Blenny and Wendll, it was with
great deference.

"Honoured indeed we are to have two of the most ancient
race in our city," he said. "You are welcome Wendll, Blenny."

"Ammerr and drell have ever been friends, though it is
many generations since we have seen them," Blenny replied,
bowing and looking regal, though the water was near his waist.
"And I shall be pleased to follow you to higher ground," he
added.

They followed Ishaan up the sand. The other Ammerr
waded up behind them and Ishaan turned as he left the water
and raised an arm. The heads of three dolphins broke the
surface nearby, they leapt into the air, and then disappeared
under the water.

The line of sand ringing the tall island was thin, and at the
base of the rocky tower was an opening. Stairs led up through
the rock, and before Shaeli went in she looked up at the fat
moon, still riding high above.

Little time had passed since she'd first sighted the flying
ship, but everything had changed. Again. They were safe, and,
despite the mixture of emotions associated with Ishaan, she
was happy to see him, but, amazing as his appearance was – as

312

safe as they were – she had lost the bangle. It was Trilby all over again, but much, much worse. She sighed, hugged Ebony to her chest and followed the others up the stairs.

They came out at the top of the island tower into a dark room. They stopped as one of the Ammerr, a tall, broad-shouldered man, looked outside, and then he motioned to the others before he went out. They stepped from a low building into a lush garden, the moonlight shining silver on the trees.

Ishaan spoke quietly to the other Ammerr. All but Cheval took their leave, and then she and Ishaan led them through the garden and into a nearby house, a stone building gleaming in the moonlight, its sides rounded, its roof domed. Inside the entry hall, a wide pool sat in the centre of the room. Arms like tiny tributaries ran out across the floor, and when Shaeli walked over the little bridge spanning one stream, she saw tiny fish swimming in the water, yet Ishaan gave them no time to admire the room. He led them on through it and up a broad staircase, opening the doors to a large room. As Cheval went around lighting lamps, he showed them doors that led to bedrooms and bathroom.

The suite was large, with round windows that overlooked the lake, and in the moonlight they could just see the place where the low tunnel led through to the seas of the Straits.

"I must leave you now," said Ishaan. "Cheval will see to your needs."

Shaeli turned, surprised. "You're *going*?" she said. "But... but I thought we would talk." She swallowed. "There is so much to talk *about*."

"Forgive me," said Ishaan. "There is a matter I must attend to immediately, and I know you are all tired. Dry yourselves. Cheval will find you robes and food and we will talk in the morning, I promise."

Shaeli didn't know why she felt like crying, but she did, and she supposed Ishaan was right. She *was* tired. She said no more as Ishaan left, but Kirrit did not let it go so easily.

"I wonder what he had to do at this time of night?" she said. "And we didn't even have time to thank him, and you, of course, Cheval, for saving us from that... whatever it was."

"You must forgive him, as he asks," Cheval said. Like Ishaan's, her eyes were also an unusual colour; blue-green and amazingly clear. "I believe he has gone to ask the permission of the Elders."

"Permission?" asked Shaeli. "Permission to do what?"

"Why, to save you all," she said. "To save you and bring you to Qorientae."

They all stopped what they were doing and stared at Cheval.

"We are here without the knowledge of your Elders?" asked Williver.

"Well, yes," said Cheval, with a small shrug. "There was not time to consult them, but I'm sure it will be fine." Though she smiled cheerfully, she did not look as if she believed her own words. "Now, *you* must rinse off, and *I* must find robes and food."

She left the room and they took her advice, washing the salty water away and donning the soft robes she brought them. Tarkoda mumbled something about having to wear a dress, but put on the soft robe anyway – it was either that or his own sodden clothes, for few things had survived the wrecking of their boat. Shaeli and Flin had their throwing stones, Tarkoda had his sling and Williver had his small wand, but he had lost both bow and arrows. Nothing else remained.

When they had eaten, they tried to draw a few answers from Cheval, but she would tell them nothing except that she and the others had been asked by Ishaan to help him. They had not questioned his reasons, she said, nor if he'd sought permission, though she admitted she'd assumed he had not. She would not say anything further, but again she urged them to their beds, and in the end they went, too tired to protest very much.

They slept until mid-morning, waking within the same hour and meeting in the central room. Of Ishaan and Cheval there was no sign, except for a basket of fresh rolls and fruit, and they pondered the silence in the house as they ate.

They went over what had happened the night before, asking each other what had it been that had come so swiftly out of the night; what kind of craft flew so high, so quickly? And what, who, had fired the deadly bolts that had destroyed their boat? Shaeli told them of the time she and her father had seen the "dragon", and the things she had heard about the black ship that flew, long before in Trilby. Tarkoda's face puckered when she mentioned her father suspected a Trader had been lost to the black ship, but he had heard nothing of it. Shaeli told them also of those who had gone mad soon after seeing it.

"Well, we've all seen it now," said Tarkoda. "Maybe we'll go mad, too."

"I think you've started already, Koda," said Kirrit, deadpan. "Need I remind you you're wearing a dress?"

"Oh, Kirrit," said Tarkoda, shaking his head. "You try *so* hard to be funny. Unsuccessful as you are."

"I think Tarkoda is on the right path," said Williver.

"What?" sputtered Kirrit.

"You're not serious, Williver," said Flin.

"Oh, I don't think we are likely to be driven to insanity," said Williver. "But a connection between the black ship and..."

He was interrupted by Cheval bursting through the doors. She was dressed in a loose, flowing gown, but her feet were bare. They were very big feet, for a girl, and Shaeli remembered then that she'd noticed Ishaan also had very big feet, but she'd never seen him barefoot.

"You must come," Cheval cried, her previous smile banished by quivering lips.

"What's happened?" said Shaeli.

"It's Ishaan. They…" She stopped, breathless. "You must come. I'll tell you on the way." She turned and started back out. She stopped at the top of the stairs. "Hurry," she said.

"But I'm still wearing a dress," Tarkoda mumbled as he stood up.

"Don't worry, Koda. You look very pretty," said Kirrit, taking his arm. "Come on."

They followed Cheval down and left the house, crossing the same garden where they had emerged the night before. They passed the building housing the stairs and went on until they reached a street.

The street was little more than a lane and everyone on it was walking. There were no horses, carriages or carts, only grassy, flower-lined laneways and white-stone houses set on verdant grounds. The houses, like Ishaan's, were all rounded, like piles of rocks or sand-castles built by some giant's child. Some had tiny balconies jutting out and all had at least one fountain, complete with a statuette or three, in the garden. They smiled at the people of Qorientae, yet nobody smiled back. Everyone they passed gave them strange looks in place of greetings. Ebony, riding high on Shaeli's shoulder sniffing the wind, was the only recipient of anything resembling a kind look.

They reached the edge of the island before Shaeli remembered that they were *on* an island. A very tall island. A thin bridge lay before her and it was a long way down to the calm waters of the lake. Ahead, another island waited, and she took a deep breath and a firm hold of Kirrit's arm as she stepped onto the bridge. It hung slightly, bowing down in the middle, yet it was steady, did not sway, and was wide enough to walk two or three abreast. Shaeli tried to concentrate on what Cheval was saying as they crossed it.

"Ishaan has been before the Elders since sunrise," she said. "I was worried when he did not return, so I left you some breakfast and went to look for him." She swallowed. "The gods I need a swim," she said, wiping her brow.

Shaeli wiped her own as the bridge ended and they reached the next island.

"They were not pleased he had brought us to Qorientae, I take it?" said Flin.

"No," said Cheval. "We are rarely permitted to intervene in… in such things. The people of your lands believe us myth. *Most* of the Ammerr prefer it that way." She said the last words harshly.

"But *you* do not think this way?" asked Blenny.

"No, Ishaan and I, a few others, we wish to travel openly as Ammerr, to not pretend to be your kind when we go into the World."

"Ammerr go into the World?" said Tarkoda.

"Oh, yes," said Cheval. "Much more often than you would think. But we are not permitted to… to interfere in your lives."

"You mean save people?" said Flin. "As you saved us last night?"

Cheval looked uncomfortable. "'Tis one of the subjects we debate often," she said. "And why Ishaan is still before the Elders. They do not believe, if you'll forgive me for saying, they do not think you *deserved* saving."

"And how are *we* to change that?" asked Blenny.

"Seeing you and Wendll, will be a start," she said. "Forgive me again, but a few of the Elders do not believe drell exist."

Blenny laughed. "We take no offence," he said. "*Many* drell do not believe in Ammerr."

They had reached another bridge, and Shaeli took this one a little easier than the first. The island ahead was smaller than the others, and only one building rose from its centre, a round white tower, like boulders of decreasing size piled on top of each other.

Cheval grew increasingly nervous as they crossed the bridge and the grounds surrounding the tower. They met few people on this tiny island, but these also gave them the frowning stares they had encountered on the other islands.

"Well, if the Elders think we're as interesting as everyone else seems to, Ishaan should be alright," Tarkoda said, smiling at a pretty, dark-haired girl.

"Remember you're wearing that dress when you're smiling at girls," said Kirrit, sweetly.

"So funny," said Tarkoda, with no trace of humour.

"Here we are," said Cheval.

At the base of the tower, two white-suited women stood on either side of the only door. Shaeli noticed they were barefoot, too, with decidedly large feet – in fact, everyone they had seen had been barefoot.

"We wish to see the Elders," said Cheval. "We come in defence of Ishaan."

The two women said nothing, merely nodded and stood back from the door, staring as sullenly at the strangers as the people in the street had.

The tower was not large, and inside there was nothing but a set of stairs winding up the wall. There was no railing and Shaeli hugged the wall as they ascended, Ebony clutched to her chest.

They heard voices as they neared the top, muffled angry voices. The stairs ended in a small room, and in its centre was another short staircase, two more Ammerr standing on either side. They recognised the man on the left as being one of Ishaan's friends from the night before, the one who had gone first through the doorway. It was obvious now he had been making sure they would not be seen. Cheval went straight across to him.

"They still seek answers, Olando?" she asked quietly. The voices from above were audible, but muffled. Olando glanced up before answering.

"They seem to be going in circles," he said. His hair was dark, his features finely chiselled, and his eyes were brown, the colour of sea-grass, dark and shining. "I can hear little but Ishaan seems to be holding his ground." He glanced at the others. "I'm glad you've come."

"May we go up?" asked Williver.

"I'll announce you," Olando nodded. "Luck be with you," he added, as he turned and went up the stairs, his silent companion at his side.

They followed a few steps behind.

"Forgive me," they heard Olando say. "There are those who wish to bear witness in Ishaan's defence."

"We have not asked for witnesses," a harsh voice replied.

The stairs ended in a room that encompassed the entire top of the tower. The walls were rounded, curved outwards, as if they were inside a bubble; the last boulder atop the larger ones. The walls were filled with large windows, these, too, of rounded glass, and every part of Qorientae could be seen through them; the ring of treeless mountains; each towering island rising high above the water; the rounded lumps of the houses looking like piles of stones across the distance; the rock-studded river inland that spread out along the ridge and fell in long lines from the cliff to the lake below, and far across the lake, the place where the tunnel led through the cliff to the sea, the mountains towering around all.

Ishaan stood in the centre of the room. Around him on a raised dais sat a half-circle of men and women, the faces all lined, the hair grey, but the eyes turned on Shaeli and the others were as bright as the sun on a calm sea. Each sat in an enormous carved chair, thirteen of them, and the woman in the centre stood as they entered.

She was not tall, yet gave the impression of it by her posture and long neck. Her hair was almost perfectly white, only a few dark strands showing the colour of its youth, and it fell past her waist. Shaeli instinctively bowed her head, knowing this was the leader of the Ammerr.

"What Brok says is so, Olando," said the woman, her voice as soft as the other's, Brok, had been harsh. "We have asked for no witnesses."

"I beg the Elders' pardon, Aneris," said Olando, bowing. "But I believe the outsiders may help." He moved to stand beside Ishaan. "And I wish to state before you that I, too, have gone against our laws. I aided Ishaan last night, and will face the fate the Elders decide for him."

"*No*, Olando," said Ishaan, looking at his friend in dismay. He turned to the Elders. "It is I who should face you and I alone. Olando was only acting out of loyalty."

"I also wish to stand with them," said Cheval, moving forward and bowing her head. "I also helped save the outsiders."

Ishaan looked at her, also in dismay, but dismay tinged with gratitude.

There were footsteps on the stairs and the seven others who had been with Ishaan burst from the stairwell. They stopped, breathing heavily and bowing to the Elders. A short stocky man stepped forward. His feet were enormous. Dark hair fell to his shoulders and he pushed it out of his eyes before he spoke.

"We wish to stand with Ishaan also," he said. "Despite Ishaan's wishes that we remain silent, we must support him."

"Thank you, Motin, Cheval, Olando," said Aneris, smiling briefly at them and the other young Ammerr clustered at the top of the stairs. "Your loyalty to Ishaan is admirable, even if your actions were not. You may wait outside for our decision."

They took the admonishment and the dismissal with bowed heads, and descended back down the stairs. Cheval walked slowly, looking back at Ishaan. He smiled encouragingly at her, but his smile faded when they had gone. He turned back to the Elders.

"I beg they not be treated harshly," said Ishaan. "'Twas at my request they saved the outsiders. I am responsible."

"I do not doubt it," spoke the harsh voice of the Elder, Brok. He sat at Aneris' left hand, a gaunt man with what remained of his hair plastered in a thin sheath over his bald pate, his lips as thin as a lizard's. "I doubt not that they were misled by your words, *and* that you are responsible. You had no right to endanger our people by bringing outsiders into our midst."

"With respect, Brok," said Ishaan, through clenched teeth. "These outsiders pose no threat to our people. And I resent the implication that I would bring danger. My loyalty should not be in question."

"I believe that is exactly what *is* in question," spat Brok. "For if you were *not* disloyal, you would never have brought these outsiders here." He threw an arm in the direction of the "outsiders", but his eyes did not touch them.

Ishaan looked imploringly at Aneris.

"You are wrong, Brok," Aneris said, quietly. She left the words hanging in the air as she sat back down and made a show of arranging her gown. "Ishaan's loyalty has never been in question," she said, when the gown was arranged to her satisfaction. "'Tis the wisdom of his *actions* that is in question, *not* his character. As I have said more than once." She looked up from her robe and fixed Brok with a cold stare. "I would appreciate it if you did not refer to it again."

Brok nodded abruptly and pursed his almost non-existent lips. Shaeli was liking Aneris more and more every moment.

Ishaan looked at Aneris gratefully, but the look was erased when Brok spoke again.

"My apologies, Aneris," Brok said, not sounding sorry at all. "And if the wisdom of Ishaan's *actions* is the question, then we have only to look at his history." He held up a hand and began ticking off fingers. "Numerous, *pointless* travels into the World. A long – also pointless – association with elves." Here he shot Williver a contemptuous look. "Constantly rousing our people to reappear into a World that has not seen us for centuries. Ridiculous claims of the finding of the elf Shahlita's wand, and now *this* betrayal ..."

He would have gone on but Shaeli stopped him.

"But the wand *is* real," she said, the words coming before she knew it. "And there's nothing wrong with elves. You couldn't find a better friend than Williver." She stopped herself then, realising they were all staring at her.

Aneris' lips held a slight smile when she spoke. The faces of a few of the other Elders also held smiles, but many mirrored Brok's frown.

"I'm sure you're right, my dear," Aneris said. "Personally I have always been very fond of elves. But, if I may ask, what would *you* know about an elfin wand?" She spoke as if amusing a small child.

Shaeli *felt* like a small child. "Well, it's mine," she said awkwardly. "The wand. At least I found it. I don't know if it's Shahlita's, but there *is* a wand. And it *is* elfin, according to our High Warlock."

"Nevertheless..." began Brok.

"No, Brok," interrupted Aneris. "We shall hear them. I grow weary. We were roused from our beds and have been here since the sunrise hours. The matter must be resolved. Besides," she said, the small smile playing about her lips again. "You may be wrong about the wisdom of saving these outsiders from the sea. It seems you were wrong when you said the drell had long since died out. These two look suspiciously like drell to me." She waved a hand at Wendll and Blenny.

"To me, also," chuckled a bearded man to her right.

Blenny stepped forward, pulling on his regal air as he came. "Your eyes do not deceive you," he said, bowing. "My companion and I are indeed of that ancient race. Allow me to introduce myself and my friends." He did so, leaving Shaeli until last. "And this outspoken young lady with the little jevvi is Shaeli, of Purple Leaf Trader, sister to young Tarkoda there, and a brave and loyal lass." He turned one eye to her, keeping the other on Aneris. Shaeli smiled gratefully at him, but the smile faded with his next words. "She, and rightly so, is the reason Ishaan has gone against your laws. If Ishaan had left the rest of us to drown, 'tis right that he saved Shaeli."

Again all eyes turned to her, and she quickly tried to downplay Blenny's words, not believing them for a moment. She blushed at the ridiculousness of the idea. "Oh, Blenny, that's not true," she said. "I'm no more important than anyone else."

"I'm afraid you're wrong, Shaeli," said Ishaan, quietly. "Blenny has guessed rightly. If I had not been able to save everyone, I would have made sure that *you* at least were safe."

"But... but, why?" she asked, almost forgetting they had an audience in her astonishment.

Ishaan did not speak for a moment. He gazed out the windows to the line of cliffs that hid the sea, and then he turned back to face her. "Because of your gift. Because of the wand. Because they seek you with such vigilance." Ishaan looked at her, his face weary, but his eyes as piercing as ever. "Because I owe you a debt. For what you did for me, and for the hurt I caused you." He smiled then. "And because I have already stolen you back from the sea once. I wasn't going to let Her have you now."

"Stolen me back...?" Shaeli asked, her brow furrowing. "What are you talking about?"

"Yes, Ishaan. What *are* you talking about?"

The voice of Brok brought Shaeli back into the room. Ishaan turned to him.

"Some Moons ago, my young friend was lost in a small boat, alone, and in dire need," Ishaan spoke shortly. "I was able to find her and return her to her own people."

Shaeli looked at him, incredulous. Ishaan had been there, in the Starisles, when she and Ebony had been in the storm? It did not seem possible.

"I'm sorry, but I'm a bit confused."

Shaeli turned to see Kirrit standing hands on hips, the stubborn look Shaeli knew so well upon her face.

"Excuse me," she said to the Elders with a small curtsey. "But I'm lost, and I'm sure I'm not the only one." She turned back to Shaeli and Ishaan. "Just when did he 'hurt you'? What 'debt'?" She looked at Ishaan. "And how did you know Shaeli was in that little boat?"

"They are several of many good questions, young lady," said Aneris. "And I agree with you, I am also confused. But I see there is more here than the mere saving of outsiders. There are tales to be told and the sun rises ever higher. We shall speak no more now. We are all weary and in need of immersion." She looked along the line of her fellow Elders. Each nodded as her eyes passed over them. "Agreed, then. We shall reconvene at sunset to discuss this further. And Ishaan," she said, fixing him with a stern eye. "I expect you to give us the *entire* story, not merely those truths you think we need to know."

Ishaan looked abashed, and bowed. "Yes, Aneris," he said.

The eyes of the Elders followed them as they went down the stairs, and they were met with the eyes of Ishaan's friends as they stepped into the sunshine outside.

"Nothing, yet," said Ishaan shaking his head at them. "We are to return at sunset."

"We shall be here," said the dark-haired man who had spoken to the Elders earlier.

"Thank you, Motin," said Ishaan, clasping his forearm. "My thanks to all of you."

"And ours also," said Williver. "We are all indebted to you for your aid last night."

The others added their thanks to Williver's, and the young Ammerr smiled and waved away their praise.

"Come, then," said Cheval. "Let's go for a swim." She looked at Ishaan. "You must be exhausted. A swim and then we'll eat."

He nodded. "Yes," he said. "But our friends may like to swim, too. Perhaps we could find them more suitable attire?"

The young Ammerr nodded, and they left the island. As Shaeli crossed the first bridge, she looked back to see Aneris and the other Elders leaving the tower.

* * *

Aneris watched the group go, the outsiders surrounded by her own young people. She was unsure what these strangers would bring to the Ammerr. She knew that they brought change, but for good or ill, only the gods knew.

* * *

Soon after they had returned to Ishaan's house, Motin, Olando and a few of the others arrived. They had clothes in which the others could swim; short light shifts for the girls and a pair of long shorts for the men, though the pants floated around the ankles of Blenny and Wendll. Tarkoda, for one, was pleased to divest himself of the "dress".

They went down the stairs to the little beach where they had arrived the night before, and Ishaan led them around the base of the island. On the far side the beach widened, and tucked beneath the rocks a few small trees and a patch of fine grass had taken root. Ebony leapt from Shaeli arms and scampered over to explore.

The water was azure in the shallows, turquoise in the depths. Across the lake a thin sheath of water fell slowly down, a silver ribbon in the midday sun, one of a dozen slim waterfalls that fell from the cliff face inland. At the bases of the other islands many of the Ammerr swam in the patterned water, but this small beach was empty.

Though autumn was beginning, the day was warm. Blenny and Wendll did not swim, but they were more than content to wade in the cool water and sit beneath the trees while the others swam across the lake to the waterfall.

As Shaeli and the others swam across, Ishaan and the other Ammerr disappeared for long periods beneath the surface. They climbed up on the rocks beside the falls, sunning themselves or diving back into the water while the Ammerr ducked and swam around them. One of the young men climbed up beside the waterfall and dove into a darkly blue patch, and he did not come up for a very long time. A few dolphins swam by, close enough to see their night-black eyes and smiling mouths. Ishaan splashed at the water, and one of the dolphins swam back and let Shaeli stroke its silken grey hide, then it dove beneath the water and came up on its tail, its body floating high above the surface. It skimmed backwards across the water and then leapt out in a long arcing dive. Shaeli clapped her appreciation, Tarkoda whistled loudly, and the dolphins all leapt from the water in a graceful synchronised dive before streaking off across the lake.

When they grew chilled, they swam back to the beach to warm themselves, and still Ishaan and his friends ducked beneath the water. When they finally returned to the beach, Shaeli was surprised to see Ishaan's eyes were bright and his shoulders lighter.

"You look better," she smiled.

"'Tis the water," he smiled back. "We need to immerse ourselves regularly. It is as food or drink is: vital to survival. Even sleep does not hold as much replenishment."

"But how do you stay under so long?" asked Koda. "How do you breathe?"

"We do not breathe underwater, like fish. We can retain air for long periods, in the same way a dolphin does, but like our dolphin friends we must surface regularly," Ishaan explained. "And like them we can also swim to depths that would kill your kind."

"And you swim so quickly," said Kirrit. "Cheval was over at the waterfall before I'd swum a few strokes."

Ishaan stuck out a foot. It was huge, the toes long and thick, the big toe as big as a thumb. He wriggled them, and pulled them apart. Between each toe was a thin web of skin. "These help," he smiled.

"I noticed you all had big feet," said Kirrit. "I was just too polite to say so." She giggled. "No wonder you can go so fast."

"Swimming for us is like running for you," Cheval said. "Ammerr find long walks without an immersion exhausting. Running is almost beyond us." She grinned. "'Tis like wading through mud."

"Oh, good," Kirrit said, throwing the grin back to her. "At least I'm better at something."

"Better?" spluttered Shaeli, looking at Cheval. "Kirrit is the best runner at Cave."

"Speaking of Cave," said Kirrit. "What's all this about Ishaan being in your debt? And what did you do for him that was so important? And Ishaan," she said, turning to him. "What did you do to Shaeli? To hurt her? I want to know whether I should be angry at you."

"And *I* want to know just when all this happened," said Cheval. "You never told me anything about going to the Cave of the Traders, Ishaan."

Ishaan held up his hands. He looked rather embarrassed. "I shall tell you all I can," he said. "After we eat."

* * *

They left the table laden with empty plates and sat on the terrace overlooking Ishaan's garden. The edge of the garden was also the edge of the island, much like Flin's house in Palveron, with a wide grassed area between the terrace and the edge. The tiny circuit of fish-filled stream that ran around the lower floor of Ishaan's house ringed the terrace, in one corner running into a lily pond where a fat-baby statue blew a fountain of water from a curved shell.

Olando, Cheval and Motin had stayed to eat, but the other Ammerr had gone to their homes. Kirrit, Tarkoda, and Shaeli knew of Ishaan's journey to Cave, but he told the story for his friends, the drell, Spotjaw and Flin. Williver sat with the

327

others, listening carefully as Ishaan spoke. When he recited the part about entering the Zoi cave, Kirrit drew a breath of horror.

"You *didn't*, Ishaan?" she said.

"Yes, Kirrit. I did, and I apologise to you and Tarkoda, as I did to Shaeli when she caught me."

"You *knew*?" Kirrit said to Shaeli. "And you didn't *tell*?"

Shaeli shook her head. Ebony was curled on her lap, drowsing under her fingers. "Not until after Ishaan had gone," she said.

"I'll bet Almarnoch was angry," said Tarkoda.

Shaeli nodded, remembering the sparks of fury that had flown from the Warlock. She shuddered at the memory and Ebony shuddered with her knees.

"No wonder you owe Shaeli a debt," said Kirrit. "You would never have been allowed to leave if the old ones had known."

"This is forbidden among the traders?" asked Olando. "To enter the cave of the Zoi?"

"Worse than forbidden," said Tarkoda. "It is the worst kind of betrayal." He looked at Ishaan when he said the words.

"Why didn't you say anything, Shaeli?" asked Kirrit. "Why didn't Almarnoch? I'm with Koda. I'll bet he was furious."

"Well, Williver intervened," said Shaeli, looking at the elf. "Almarnoch was *so* angry with me for not telling him about Ishaan straight away, for the first time I was almost frightened of him, but Williver visited him in the dreamworld and told him I was not to blame. Almarnoch decided afterwards that we would tell no one. Only Wyshka and Olver knew, because I was so upset. And Llevvis, too."

Kirrit looked at Williver in admiration. "You told Almarnoch what to do?" she asked, shaking her head. "Brave elf." She had always been more than a little frightened of the High Warlock. "Why did you, though? Because of Ishaan?"

"Because it was not right that he take his anger out on Shaeli," said Williver. "She was only being the loyal friend she has always been." He grinned slightly. "Though I did embellish the truth a little. Referred to the gods and such things."

Shaeli smiled at him. "When the Zoi returned happily to their cave, I knew it was alright," she said. "Ishaan told me he had done no harm, and despite being horribly angry and knowing I should tell someone, I believed him. I did as he asked and told no one until after he'd gone." She looked at him, remembering the spark of anger that had burned his cheek, ashamed still at wounding him. "It is only now that he is truly forgiven."

"And I thank you for that," Ishaan said, smiling at her.

"There *was* another thing that made me wonder about you, though," Shaeli said, the smile fading. "You went through my things. You looked at the wand. *And* you lied to me about it."

Ishaan looked surprised. "I didn't know you knew about that," he said.

"I did say something about it when I yelled at you in Cave, but I was ranting and you mustn't have understood, but you're not a very good liar," she said. "I knew something was wrong that day on the Lea." She looked at Kirrit. "I caught him coming out of Wyshka's hut. He said it was for his pipe." She looked back at Ishaan. "But you put the bag away backwards and I knew. Almarnoch and I thought you were just curious. That you'd heard about the wand and wanted to see it."

"I *had* heard about it," said Ishaan. "But it was Williver who told me."

"Williver told you?" said Shaeli.

Ishaan nodded. "'Tis the reason I went to the Cave of the Traders." He looked embarrassed again. "What I said about losing my way was also untrue."

"You went to the Lea to look at Shaeli's old wand?" asked Kirrit.

Williver answered her. "Since Shaeli first found the wand, Ishaan and I have discussed the possibility of it being Shahlita's. Long had Ishaan wanted to see it for himself."

"You're not talking about the wand made for the elf Shahlita centuries ago?" asked Motin. "The wand your grandfather made, that was lost the day the dragons disappeared?"

"Yes," said Ishaan.

"Your *grandfather* made this wand, Ishaan?" asked Flin.

Ishaan nodded. "'Tis the reason I wanted to see it for myself. It was his final masterpiece. He had seen a hundred and forty-seven Winters and he died three Moons after he'd presented it to Shahlita."

Motin whistled. "I thought it had been destroyed a hundred Winters ago."

"So did we," said Williver.

"Have you told *your* people about this, Williver?" asked Wendll. "Surely they would be keen to reclaim it."

"No," he said. "I thought it wise to keep it secret until Ishaan had identified it."

"The more I hear of the wand, the more eager I am to see it," said Flin.

"And you're sure, Ishaan?" said Cheval. "You're sure this is the one our grandfather made?"

"*Our* grandfather?" said Shaeli.

"Well, yes," said Cheval, frowning slightly. "Ishaan is my brother. I thought you knew."

"No," said Shaeli, and then she shook her head. "But there are a lot of things I don't know." She looked at Ishaan. "How did you and Williver first meet?"

"It was long ago, at the cave where the dragons once lived," Ishaan said. "We were both intrigued by the story, and wondered what had happened to Shahlita and the dragons. I had travelled to his lands and had managed to convince the elves to let me see the dragon's cave. Williver was my guide."

"Your guide?" asked Flin.

"Yes," said Williver. "Since the dragons left, my people have guarded the cave. Protected it from being ransacked or interfered with in any way."

"And when I found the wand, Williver told you about it?" asked Shaeli.

"Yes," said Ishaan. "But it wasn't until I found some old sketches my grandfather had made of the wand that we grew really suspicious, and then I had to see it for myself."

"So that's where you went the year you said you were going to Wokk?" said Cheval. "When you wouldn't let me come?"

Ishaan nodded again. He had been doing a lot of nodding. "Yes, Cheval," he said.

"And you lied to these people who thought you friend. Entered a forbidden place." Cheval shook her head. "I am almost ashamed to call you brother." She looked at Shaeli. "I apologise for him. Truly, he has been raised to behave with more honour."

"Cheval, please," said Ishaan, the embarrassed look returning to his face.

"Oh, don't look so pained, Ishaan," she said. "You have redeemed yourself a little by saving them from the sea. But only a little."

"You said that you saved Shaeli from the sea in the Starisles," said Flin. "I am curious about that, too." From the relaxed look on his face, no one could have known the anguish those days had caused him. He explained quickly to the others about Shaeli's mind being invaded, and how she and Ebony had been swept out to sea in a storm. "We thought her lost," he said. "'Twas little short of miraculous that she was returned to us."

"Williver contacted me, and at once I set out to find her," said Ishaan.

"But how did you know I was *in* the boat, Williver?" Shaeli asked. "My mind was almost gone."

"I found you in the dreamworld little one. Only for a moment, but it was enough. I don't think you recognised me," he said. "I knew that Ishaan was needed, and found him in the dreamworld too."

"I remember your voice," she said, softly, her eyes gazing at a place the others could not see. "Little snatches of it. Other voices, a child's, a man's, and... and Ishaan's." She looked at him, eyes widening. "I do remember. I *did* hear your voice."

"When we found the boat, I spoke to you," he said. "You were alive, but barely, and we took you to the closest island." He looked gravely at her. "You were east of the last island when we found you, still caught in the tail of a storm, Ebony clinging to your hair."

"East of the..." breathed Shaeli. That meant that when Ishaan had found her, there had been nothing between her and the Endless Sea. Nothing. She trembled at the thought.

"Who's 'we'?" asked Kirrit. "Who helped you? Cheval? Olando?"

They looked blank, and Ishaan shook his head instead of nodding for a change.

"No," he said. "I had need of faster aid. Aid with a much wider reach."

"The dolphins," said Cheval. "You used the pods."

Ishaan was back to nodding. "I did. There was no other way."

"We are grateful that you did," said Flin. "Otherwise Shaeli would have been lost to us."

"These dolphins are pets?" asked Spotjaw.

"No, not pets," said Ishaan. "Friends."

"It was dolphins who followed us from the Drell Mountains, wasn't it?" guessed Shaeli. "Remember, we saw them just as we sailed out, and again after the battle with the queen's ships."

"I remember," said Kirrit. "Can you talk to them, Ishaan?"

"After a fashion," he said. "I admit, I asked them to watch for you. Dolphins are clever creatures, and they found your little craft for me many times after you'd left drell waters."

"I saw them a lot," said Wendll. "I wondered why they followed us. I thought they must have thought we had fish."

"They saw you battle the ships in the northern waters, and they told me you were sailing past. I convinced the others to come with me, just watch you until you reached Meoro, but then we also saw you attacked by the flying ship," said Ishaan. "I had little trouble convincing them to intervene, but 'twas only by the grace of the gods that it happened so close to Qorientae, otherwise you may have been in the water much longer."

"Thanks be to the grace of the gods, then," said Blenny, shifting their memories from the black ship by changing the subject. "Your city is a beautiful place, Ishaan. Do all the Ammerr live here?"

"Oh, no," he smiled. "There is a colony or two on every Land, in places accessible only to the sea. Another city lies inland, in the mountains beside the river that falls into this lake. We have pastureland there. Our parents live there," he said, looking at Cheval. "'Tis many Moons since we saw them."

"Too many Moons," said Cheval, rising. "And any more questions can wait. The afternoon is almost over. It is time we went back to the tower."

* * *

CHAPTER TWENTY

The thirteen Elders sat stern-faced as Ishaan recited the story of the wand. They asked Williver to confirm aspects of the story, and as the sunset changed the World from pink to grey, the Elders began to look at Shaeli more and more curiously. When Ishaan spoke of her gift for throwing, they looked almost impressed, and when Flin added his praise, Shaeli felt enormously uncomfortable. Williver then told them of the journey from Trilby, how they had been hunted throughout the Land and on the sea.

"And now they seek to destroy her and her gift," spat Brok in his crow-like voice. "Some force follows this girl, intent upon her demise, and our *loyal* subject brings her into our haven," he said, the words coated in sarcasm. "How clever."

"They *did* seek her, Brok," said Ishaan. "Now they think her dead, smashed upon the rocks. That strange craft watched as we carried them towards the shore. Their safety now is assured with the assumption they are dead."

"How did those who seek her know of the wand's existence?" Brok shot back. "If it truly is what you say it is, there are many who would covet it." He slid a look at Williver. "The elves not least."

"That would be true," said Williver. "If I had told any of them. There is but one elf who knows of this and his allegiance is beyond question. It is more than likely the wand was seen when Shaeli's mind was invaded."

"But if there was not knowledge of Shaeli's possession of the wand, *why* would her mind have been searched in the first place?" said Aneris, quietly. "This invader of minds sought the wand specifically. They *must* have known it was in the hands of the traders."

There was silence as they pondered the question. It was one Shaeli had asked herself many times: how did they – whoever *they* were – how did they know about the wand? She looked up at Aneris.

"I don't know how they found out about the wand, or that I had it," she said. "But it seems to me that it doesn't really matter now."

Aneris looked back at her, empathy plainly upon her face. She smiled. "You are right, my dear," she said. "How we are led to a road barely matters, once our feet are walking upon it."

"But who has this power to invade minds?" asked the bearded man beside Aneris. "I have heard of dream-walkers, but never of this power to invade and strip minds."

"We know not, Rizar, but it is almost certain it is the same force that flies the black ship," said Williver. "I was saying to my companions earlier that there must be some connection. Of this I am sure. Some of those who have seen this ship have been driven to madness, and only one with great power could go into another mind in order to break it."

"Why have you not come to us with any of this, Ishaan?" asked a tiny round woman at the end of the line of chairs.

"I could not, until I was sure," replied Ishaan. "And when I was," he shrugged. "I wasn't sure it meant anything."

"Surely you're not thinking this *child* worthy or capable of wielding such a weapon?" said Brok.

"And even if she could," said a sharp-faced woman near him. "To what end would it be wielded?"

"An apt question, Una," nodded Brok. "There is no need for such a thing in the World."

"There is not *now*," said Ishaan. "But that does not mean there'll not be, in the future."

"The World outside is troubled," said Flin. "This black ship is only part of the shadow that hangs over Zirrus. If the wand *does* need to be used, there is no one living, of any race, who is more worthy than Shaeli. Her gift is unsurpassed. With her abilities with the stones, she also has the gift of levitation."

"What rubbish," cried Brok.

"Ridiculous," spat the sharp-faced Una.

"If what you say is true, it should be easy to prove," said Aneris calmly. She looked at Shaeli. "If you would be so kind, my dear."

Shaeli looked at the faces, all turned her way yet again. Her friends gave her nods of encouragement, while the faces of the Elders held varying degrees of speculation. She had listened to the conversation with amazement. *Using* the wand had never occurred to her. It was old and battered, useless without stones, but she pushed the thought aside, shrugged and stepped forward. She looked about.

"What do you want me to lift?" she asked.

"Oh, please, let me help," said Brok, standing and smirking. "Take my chair."

Tarkoda and Spotjaw moved Brok's chair into the centre of the room. Tarkoda grinned at her when she gave him Ebony to hold.

"Show them, Shaeli," he said, quietly.

Williver winked at her and she turned to the chair. She drew the vistrella from her amulet and aimed. She heard Brok mutter something which she knew was unpleasant.

She set her lips and threw the beam. It caught the chair around the seat. There were gasps from the Elders as the purple light filled the room. One or two cried out in amazement as Shaeli lifted the chair and floated it across the room, setting it back in place beside Aneris, then she dropped the stone into her amulet and looked out at the night. Darkness had wrapped itself tightly around the tower and stars had begun poking holes in its blanket. She looked back at Brok as he took his seat, unable to help a little smugness from creeping into her face.

"Her gift with the other stones is just as great," said Flin, the smugness more than obvious upon *his* face.

"Do you see now why I had to save her? Save them all?" said Ishaan.

"I see the gift lies in her as strongly as you say," said Aneris. "But you have no proof this wand is the one lost. The wand and the bangles have been lost for more than a century, and ..."

"No they're not," Shaeli interrupted. She glanced at Williver and he nodded imperceptibly. She turned back to Aneris. "The bangles aren't lost," she said, slowly. "I have them, too."

There was silence in the room.

"I beg your pardon?" said Aneris at last. She no longer spoke to Shaeli as if she was speaking to a small child.

"Well, at least, I *did* have both," said Shaeli. "Williver helped me find one many Winters ago." She looked at Ishaan. "Did you not see it when you looked at the wand? It was there in the bag."

Ishaan shook his head. "I knew nothing of this. I looked at the wand only." He looked at Williver. "You have not told me this, my friend."

"I thought it best to keep it secret," Williver replied, with a shrug of his shoulders. "I did not wish you to see the wand knowing Shaeli also had one of the bangles. I thought it may bias your opinion."

"How did this elf help you find the bangle?" said Brok. "It *had* been found on Romynn, a score of years ago, but they lost it again in the Sea of Aa'liu when the ship on which they travelled sank in a storm. They chose to save *people* instead of the bangle." The words were said in disgust.

"I'll not see women and children drown needlessly," said the bearded man on the other side of Aneris, Rizar. "And it seems the bangle was not lost after all." He smiled at Shaeli. "Tell us about it."

So Shaeli told them about Nol and his family, how she had found them by the sea near Orrellis and reunited them, and how Nol had given her the bangle as reward.

"He and his family were on the ship that sank, and the box was beside him on the beach when he woke. For many years he had thought his family drowned," said Shaeli.

"Then it is fortuitous indeed that you did save those people, Rizar," Aneris said to the bearded man beside her.

"Yes, I always felt it was right, somehow," said Rizar, nodding. "I have told that story many times, about the woman and her children, the old locket I found later, when I was looking for the bangle." He squinted over at Williver. "In fact," he said, after a moment, "in fact, I told *you* that story, you and Ishaan, a few, well, it must be ten Winterings ago, over a bottle. *And* I showed you that rusty locket. By the gods, now that I think upon it, I have not seen the locket since then."

Williver looked sheepish. "I thought it should go back to its owner," he said. "So I took it to Orrellis, near where the family live, and hid it somewhere Shaeli could find it when next she was there. My apologies, Rizar."

"But tell me, *how* did you tell her of this? Was it coincidence that this man was in Orrellis at the same time as the child's Trader?" Aneris said to Williver. "Were *you* in Orrellis?"

"No," said Williver. "I was not there." He looked at Ishaan, then back at Aneris. "I have the gift of travelling within the dreamworld. What Rizar called a dreamwalker."

"A dreamwalker?" The word rippled along the line of tall carved chairs.

"Yes. I have been able to travel the dreamworld at will since I was young. Some dreamers make unusual patterns in the sky of the dreamworld," said Williver. "It was in this way I saw the man, Nol, for his dreams were dark with grief. The bangle featured strongly in these dreams, and after I heard Rizar's story, I knew these people were one and the same.

When I knew that Shaeli would be in Orrellis, I... I persuaded Nol to travel there also. A small nudge from the dreamworld."

"Williver has been in my dreams since I was a small child," said Shaeli, wondering if it would be helpful or not.

"Then *he* may invade minds also," said Brok, as eager as ever to find fault. "*He* is no different than the one who seeks the wand."

"He is *very* different," said Shaeli. "Williver sends dreams of peace. The other is a black wind that sweeps through your mind. They are *not* the same."

"You'll forgive me if I reserve judgement," said Brok, dismissing her words with a wave of his hand. "I see no difference."

"And you said you had *both* these bangles, miss," said Una, beside him. "If one is at your Cave, where is the other?"

"In the Straits of Nebillonia," Shaeli said, her voice blunt with annoyance. "It was on the boat with us. It was sunk by the black ship. The one Ishaan and the others saved us from."

None of the Elders spoke. They looked at Shaeli with varying expressions of surprise and disbelief. Finally Aneris did speak.

"If this is true, then we must search for it," she said. "At first light every Ammerr will search the straits for signs of this boat. Anything that is found is to be brought to me."

* * *

The sun had not risen above the line of cliffs when the first remnants from their little boat began to arrive at the beach. They stood with Aneris as bits of clothing, crockery, and baggage were brought from the sea.

The Ammerr had waded into the lake in the first grey light. All except for the very old and the very young had swum out the tunnel to search the floor of the straits. Now the pile before Aneris grew and grew as broken and singed things were added to it, and after Aneris had looked at each object, it was reclaimed by its owner, and those things useless or broken were laid in a pile. As the sun rose higher, so did the pile.

Williver was pleased to see his bow and quiver appear; Tarkoda regained his knife; Blenny his pipe. Other weapons, clothes and sundry were found undamaged; many more things were ruined.

Shaeli had described her bag and the pouch containing the bangle, but when Cheval brought the bag to shore mid-morning, it was empty, the side burnt away. She began to think that the bangle was truly lost, just as she had begun to hope again. She had been elated when she thought there'd been a chance the Ammerr would find it, but as the sun reached its zenith, more and more Ammerr returned with empty hands. Ishaan was the last to return, and when Shaeli saw his face, hope burned again.

He had a bag tied to his waist as he waded from the water, and he fumbled in it as he walked up the beach to stand before Aneris. He laid several pieces of clothing on the sand, and then pulled a small pouch from the bag.

"When I found this it was empty," he said, laying it on the sand beside the clothes. "I kept going, following the path of the tide, and just as I had begun to despair, I found it, wedged between rocks." He pulled the bangle from the bag and held it out in the bright sunshine.

It gleamed green and violet and aqua, and the gathered Ammerr murmured as Ishaan passed the bangle to Aneris. She studied it a long time, her face without expression. Finally she looked up, walked over and handed the bangle to Shaeli.

Brok exploded. He had not taken part in the search, had merely sat with Una making more and more disparaging remarks as the morning wore on. "You're not *returning* it to her," he cried. "It should be kept *here*, in Qorientae, not given to an inept child."

"Again, Brok, you are wrong," said Aneris calmly. "You have no forethought. This child has been given a gift by the gods. They have also given her the wand and one of the dragon-scale bangles. Who am I to ignore their wishes?" She looked at the Ammerr crowded around silently. "Do any disagree with my decision?"

Brok turned and strode away, the sharp-faced Una following, but everyone else stood calmly, saying nothing.

"Good," Aneris smiled. "Then it is so." She looked at Shaeli. "Tonight you shall all dine with me and we shall discuss the best way to get you home, to the Cave of the Traders."

* * *

"We *were* going to try and find somewhere to land above Meoro, and travel overland until we reached the Pass," Flin explained to Aneris and Rizar later that night.

They sat by a broad pool, fountains spurting water from the mouths of squat, ugly gargoyles perched in each corner. Aneris' house was a rambling structure with domed rooms set in a circle around the central pool.

"We could still do that if we had another boat," said Tarkoda.

"The Ammerr have no boats, young man," said Rizar. "We have no need of them."

"Where... how do you go?" asked Wendll. "When you travel in the World?"

"We swim," answered Rizar. "To Xenel or Argon usually, if we want to travel by ship, but 'tis just as easy to go to Meoro Village or over to Ashkanna."

"It is not possible for you to travel to the Pass along the coast," said Aneris. "Perhaps you may have to go back northward. The way is not without dangers, but it is possible. From there you could travel inland."

"There is not time," said Williver. "Autumn will pass quickly and the Wintering must dictate our course." He glanced at Ishaan, and took a breath. "Ishaan and I feel we can go inland."

341

"We can go upriver, and then to Williver's people at Lythnori," said Ishaan.

"And then where, Ishaan?" said Rizar. "There is no pass between the mountain of the dragon and Zerrinius. No one has ever found a way over those mountains. North and west, yes, but not south."

"But we shall not go *over* the mountains, Rizar," said Ishaan. "We shall go under."

"*Under*?" said Kirrit. "I don't like the sound of that."

"You're not serious?" said Rizar. "What makes you think there is a way beneath the mountains?"

"Williver and I have travelled extensively through the old dragon cave," said Ishaan. "In its furthest reaches there is a tunnel, broad and darker than a night without moon. At its entrance lies a symbol. I found the same symbol inside the Trader's Cave, and another in the cave of the Zoi beneath Mount Zerrinius."

Kirrit and Shaeli gasped, Tarkoda's mouth dropped open.

"*That's* why you went into the Zoi cave, Ishaan, to see if this symbol was there?" said Shaeli.

"It was something else we had long speculated on," Ishaan nodded. "That the tunnels reach that far, and the presence of these symbols seems to confirm this. 'Twas another reason for going to the Cave of the Traders."

"You really think they are connected?" asked Aneris. "You think they are two ends of the same tunnel?"

"I do," said Ishaan.

"I also believe this," said Williver. "It is not a route we would choose to take but now it seems there is little choice."

"You *really* think so, Williver?" said Shaeli. "You really think this tunnel leads all the way to Cave?"

"Yes, little one," he said. "I do. There are legends among my people of a trade route between us and the southern lands. That Traders used to fly in from the south, in the times before

342

the races moved apart from each other. I am sure this is the only way."

"Then we shall see you have everything you need for your journey," said Aneris. "And we pray the gods go with you."

"I also wish to go with them," said Ishaan, bowing his head.

"I don't think so, Ishaan," Aneris said. "You may lead them to our inland settlement, surely, but beyond that…"

"Please, Aneris," he said. "They may need my help."

She looked at him for a long time, then she studied the other faces awaiting her reply.

"Very well," Aneris said. "You may go."

* * *

Three days later they stood beside the waterfall looking down at the towering islands of Qorientae. The city lay far below them, the wide river that fed the falls shattered by rocks piled at the lip, splitting the slow-moving river into dozens of smaller tributaries that pooled along the cliff top before falling in long slow lines to the lake below. Unlike the churning river and falls in the Drell Mountains, this river meandered towards the lip, the falls tumbled slowly, as if they had all the time in the world to mix with the salty waters of the lake. The islands rose green-topped above the patterned water, the houses looking like nothing more than lumped boulders, only the tower where they'd spoken to the Elders held any hint of a meaningful structure.

Far across the other side of the lake, the line of cliffs cut darkly across the sunrise. Here, they were high enough to see over the thick cliff hiding Qorientae from the Straits, and on the sea a ship could be seen sailing north, so far away it was a mere spot.

"Kirrit," said Shaeli, gazing at the tiny ship. "Remember when we were on Captain Mahi's ship in that storm? When we went up on deck?"

Kirrit nodded. "Do I?" she said. "Of course. That was one of the best storms I've ever seen."

Flin looked at her. "You are a strange girl, Kirrit," he said, dryly, shaking his head at her. "I remember that storm as one of the most miserable experiences of my life."

"That's because you were down in that stuffy old cabin," Kirrit grinned. "If we'd been friends then, I would have come down and made you go and look at it."

"If you'd done that," said Flin, even more dryly. "We would never have *become* friends."

Kirrit grinned, and Shaeli continued.

"Remember that light I saw? It could have come from here."

"That may be so, Shaeli," said Ishaan. "When we expect travellers from inland and the weather is bad, we light a beacon to guide their way. Here by the path."

"That *must* have been it," said Shaeli. "The entire ship thought I was seeing things."

"I'm sure that Brok would think that was for the best," said Cheval, with a smile.

Shaeli grinned back at her.

Cheval, Olando and Motin had all been given permission by the Elders to accompany them. They had lobbied the Elders constantly during the past days, citing more and more outrageous reasons for the trip, and in the end they had won and the four Ammerr were now part of the company.

At sunrise they had watched as the four took a final swim in the lake. They had swum several times with the Ammerr, once they were again joined by the pod of dolphins that had followed them from the Drell Mountains. The dolphins had pulled them through the water, playing games and squealing, Shaeli sure it was with the same delight she felt, and this morning the dolphins had again swum with them. Afterwards, many of the Ammerr had farewelled them at the last island, waving as they crossed the bridge to the mainland.

Now, with a collective sigh, they took one last look at the city and then turned inland, shouldering their burdens, the packs and cloaks gifts from Aneris, looking at the mountains ahead. The tops were already white and they would soon be glad of the warm cloaks.

Many of their clothes were found on the floor of the straits, and most had suffered damage, so they all wore trousers and vests supplied by the Ammerr, light clothes patterned with faint markings. They were made from fish skin, Cheval told them, and would adapt whatever the weather, and they all wore new boots, soft and light, made of sharkskin, and they knew they would be glad of these also.

Beside them, the river continued to meander as the day passed, taking up half the valley through which they walked. All day they followed the river valley west, stopping only once to eat as the river sauntered past on its lazy way to Qorientae.

As the sun dropped towards the mountains ahead, the valley narrowed, and late in the afternoon they reached the end. Before them stood a bare cliff face, and falling from it a wide waterfall, slow and graceful. Ishaan smiled at his sister.

"Almost home," he said.

"I hope Mam won't get too much of a shock, us turning up with ten spare mouths to feed," said Cheval.

"She'll be fine," said Ishaan. "You know she will. She'll be so pleased to see us, she won't care how many beds she has to find."

"She won't be so pleased when she finds out where we're going," said Cheval. "I vote *you* tell her."

"Fine," he said. "Just pull the rope so they know we're here."

They stood before the rocky cliff, the long waterfall to their left mirroring the one back at Qorientae. Hanging down the cliff was a long slim rope. Cheval went over and tugged on it. Somewhere high above a bell echoed.

"As if they haven't seen us, Ishaan," she said. "They'll be readying it."

"Readying what?" asked Shaeli, looking up the cliff-face.

"That," said Cheval, as something fell off the cliff above.

They started, jumped back, and the four Ammerr laughed.

"I'm sorry," said Ishaan. "I should have warned you. The basket must seem odd."

"The cliff is too steep to climb," explained Cheval. "The basket is the only way up to the village."

"Why is it up there?" asked Shaeli. "Why not have the village here in the valley?"

"This valley often floods with the spring run-off," said Cheval. "Besides…"

"Besides, you'll see," interrupted Ishaan. "Stand back now."

The thing descending down the cliff was just above their heads, and Olando grabbed a rope dangling from it, and guided it to the ground.

It was indeed like a basket, a very big basket with a hinged door in one side. Motin opened the door and inside there was room for them and more to stand. When they were in, Motin closed the door, and then they were rising up, the cliff-face sliding by, the valley floor shrinking beneath them. Shaeli kept her eyes on the horizon as the basket rose higher and higher, Ebony on her shoulder chittering in excitement. When the cliff top came into sight, they saw they were hooked up to a giant pulley. The arm swung in and deposited the basket on the top of a cliff.

Tarkoda looked admiringly at the enormous cogs and pulleys. "Just like we have on Purple Leaf," he said. "Only much, much bigger."

When they left the basket, Shaeli could see why, beside the occasional flood, they did not build in the valley below. They were on an enormous plateau, ringed by high, green-skinned hills. Vast fields carpeted the enormous plateau, studded with woodlands and sprinkled with streams. Houses, again all smooth, rounded shapes, like bunches of mushrooms stuck together, sat plumply beneath umbrella-shaped trees. To the left stretched a lake almost as big as the plateau, a mirror in the late sun, a huge bowl of water, so blue it was nearly black. The water seeped over the edge of the bowl, falling into the valley below, and they knew now why the waters flowed so slowly, so reluctantly from this place. Shaeli had never seen anywhere more beautiful.

They thanked the men who had operated the basket and left the cliff-side, following a grassy path running beside the lake. They walked slowly, admiring the unusual houses, the pretty orchards, some with unpicked fruit still hiding between leaves. Here, there were wider roads than the grassy lanes of Qorientae, and they passed several carts laden with produce. In one field, a group of ponies munched thick grass. People here looked at them curiously, but smiled and happily greeted the four Ammerr as they walked through the community.

As the sun sank behind the mountains, they entered a low-walled garden. The mushroom house was large, and as they neared it they heard a cry from inside. A woman flew through the door and hugged first Cheval and then Ishaan. Behind her came a young girl who threw herself into Ishaan's arms, squealing with delight.

The woman was tall, her hair dark and short, her eyes like Cheval's. The young girl was obviously their sister, her face very like Cheval's, but softer and sweeter, and she had Ishaan's eyes, but in palest blue. After she had kissed her siblings, she smiled shyly from behind Cheval's shoulder at the others clustered in the path.

"'Tis a fine sight you are, my children," said the woman, and she too looked at the others, but not at all shyly. "Olando and Motin I know, but these others are unmet." She smiled. "And unusual, if I may say."

"You may, Mother," said Ishaan, smiling. "Allow me to introduce my friends." He went through the group, and then holding his mother's hand said, "And this is my mother, Yahnna, and my very pretty sister, Fynz'l. Fyn is almost ten."

"Eleven," hissed Fynz'l, clearly insulted.

347

"My pardon," smiled Ishaan. "You grow far too quickly."

Fynz'l was mollified, and Yahnna took her hand.

"Come inside," she said. "Your father will be home soon and I'd say he'll be surprised to find so many for dinner. I see we shall have to find something more than the fish and salad I was planning."

"Forgive us, Mam," said Cheval. "There was not time to warn you."

"Our apologies also, madam," said Flin. "We are a large company and come uninvited."

"If my children invited you, you are welcome," Yahnna replied. "And to have them here I would feed thrice your number. Come inside."

The house was all earth tones and ocean blues, the windows with patterned glass depicting seahorses and shells and fish. The rooms were filled with unusually-shaped furniture, couches like sea sponges and tables with two or three tops, lamps like strings of sea-weed. Yahnna showed them where they could put their packs and sleep, then she ushered them into a large kitchen. It filled one of the mushroom-shaped rooms, an enormous range on one side and a big table on the other.

Fynz'l sat beside her sister, staring at Shaeli, and after a moment Shaeli knew why. The child was staring at Ebony, who was perched on Shaeli's shoulder.

"Would you like to meet Ebony?" she asked, smiling at the pretty child.

Fynz'l nodded and came over. Shaeli placed the jevvi in the girl's lap and she stroked the soft fur. Ebony chittered and nuzzled the child's hand.

"Look, Mam," Fynz'l said, a smile lighting her face. "It likes me."

"So I see, my girl," smiled Yahnna. "But then, everyone likes you."

Fyn beamed.

"Where's Da?" asked Cheval.

"Helping someone with a table," said Yahnna. "He'll be home shortly."

"He's home now," said a voice, and a blue-eyed man walked into the room, carrying a net filled with fish.

Ishaan and Cheval went and kissed him, and Yahnna came over and took the net from his hand.

"How did you know?" she asked, looking at the fish.

"I heard my children had come up the basket with a band of outsiders," he said. "It's all over the plateau. I thought you'd not have enough of that trout."

"A good thought it was," Yahnna smiled, kissing his cheek.

Ishaan introduced his father, Pykkal, to the others. Pykkal took out a pipe and began stuffing it. He looked at Ishaan.

"Quite a stir you've caused, lad," he said, a dimple creasing his cheek. "The talk of the village."

"I expected as much," Ishaan said. "But we'll not be here long."

"And where are you going, son?" said Pykkal.

"Into the mountains, Da, but it's a long story," said Ishaan.

"It can wait until after dinner, then," said Yahnna. "I shall need some help."

She directed them all to various tasks and soon they sat before a well-filled table. After the soft pink trout had been eaten, Ishaan told his family about the wand, about travelling to the Long Lea and confirming the wand's origins, about Shaeli's gift and the journey they now planned to make to Cave. Then he told them of the black ship, and how it had destroyed the boat, and Fynz'l's eyes grew rounder and rounder.

"I saw this black ship you speak of," said Pykkal mildly, when Ishaan had finished.

"What?" his wife gasped.

Pykkal took his time stuffing his pipe as they all waited for him to tell them. It was obvious he rather enjoyed the waiting.

"Once," he said, lighting the pipe, and making a show of drawing heavily on it. "Once as I travelled from here to Qorientae beneath a full moon, I saw something pass through the night sky. It seemed unnatural to me then, not Trader, not falling star. I thought my eyes played tricks."

"Your eyes saw true," said Flin. "How many Winterings ago was it?"

"Oh, near ten, I'd say," said Pykkal. "The year after Fyn was born. What do you think it is?" he asked. "How does it fly?"

"We know not," said Flin. "We don't know what it is, or how it flies. Nor who flies inside it."

As they talked more of the black ship, no one noticed that neither Wendll nor Blenny had anything to say on the subject.

* * *

The next day they pored over the old drawings of the wand Ishaan had found, Shaeli comparing them to the picture of the real wand in her memory. Yahnna and Pykkal voiced their amazement over and again at the wand's reappearance, not for a moment doubting Ishaan's word that it was so. Over and again they also remonstrated with him for not telling them of the discovery sooner. Williver took much of the blame for this, saying he did not want a dispute to arise between elves and the Ammerr.

"Why did our Warlocks think it elven, if it was made by the Ammerr?" asked Shaeli, to shift the subject, and because she wanted to know.

"The wand appears elfin because of the writing, the symbolism, and the style," said Yahnna. "But my father was a master craftsman, renowned even amongst the elves, and Shahlita would have no one but him craft her wand. There are clues it is Ammerr made, if one knows where to look, but your Warlocks would not see them. Pykkal would see them, Ishaan also, but there are few in the World who know our art." She smiled. "Though many wear it without knowing."

"Wear it?" said Shaeli.

"Yes, our jewellery is worn throughout the World, unknown to most," said Pykkal.

"Ishaan said his family made jewellery when he first came to Cave," said Kirrit. "But then he also told us he lived on Argon, or was it Xenel?"

"Everything I told you of my family is true, except for where they live," said Ishaan. "Our jewellery is sold through merchants on Argon. Mother makes jewellery, and my father makes the finest furniture in any land."

"I've admired many of the pieces in the house," said Flin. "It is a pity we do not stay longer. I would love to see more of the plateau."

"When are you leaving?" asked Yahnna.

"We thought to go at first light," said Ishaan.

"Tomorrow?" she said. She looked at the four young Ammerr. "I suppose you're all going?" They nodded, and she sighed. "We'd best go and ready supplies then," she said.

"You have weapons?" Pykkal asked, and at their blank looks, added. "You'd best come and look at the armoury."

"Perhaps I forgot to mention that my father also makes weapons," smiled Ishaan.

They followed him down into a room below the ground. The walls were filled with swords, knives, bows. Hatchets and clubs dangled from the ceiling. Pykkal gave them all new weapons. He gave out bows and tightly packed rolls of arrows, and insisted on giving each of the girls a small dagger to carry on their belts. Kirrit stroked a small cross-bow, a tiny thing no bigger than a dinner plate, her fingers caressing it as if it were fur.

"You have good taste," said Pykkal, watching her.

"Oh, I love it," said Kirrit. "It's just so cute."

Tarkoda looked at her and shook his head. "Cute," he said. "You're a strange girl, Kirrit."

"'Tis yours, lass," said Pykkal. "Take it, with my compliments."

* * *

There was a chill in the air when they left the next morning. Fynz'l cried as they left and Shaeli sent up a little skylight for her. She let it blossom just above their heads, and the light bloomed into a braid of flowers that floated down to dissolve at the child's feet. Fyn's blue eyes grew round with delight and she waved until the dusky morning had swallowed them.

It took them all day to cross the plateau, past open fields and through pretty forests where bright birds sang, through communities of lumpy houses where they were hailed and offered meals. It took them all the next day to climb the hills behind the vast plain. The hills sloped down to the plateau like the sides of a bowl, treeless, covered in thick, spongy moss and dark rocks. As the sun began to set, they made camp at the top, beneath a rocky overhang.

Below, the bowl of lake and valley was thick with shadow. Lights twinkled and smoke pooled around houses. Ahead lay the mountains, dark shapes edged against the dying light.

* * *

"How long will it take to reach your home?" Flin asked Williver as they shouldered their packs next morning.

"Five, perhaps six days," the elf replied. He pointed to the closest hulk. "Beyond that first mountain lies the valley of my home, and further to the south, the mountain of the dragons."

"And how long will it take to reach that?" asked Blenny.

"Another two or three to reach the dragon's lair," said Williver.

Kirrit shivered. "It sounds scary when you call it that," she said. "A lair."

"That it was, when the dragons were there," Williver said. "And still it is an eerie place."

They walked down a long slope dotted with trees whose needles covered the ground.

352

"I wonder how long it will take to get through to Cave," said Shaeli. "Once we're in the lair."

"We have no way of knowing," said Ishaan. "What lies beneath is a mystery."

"Do you suppose there's water down there?" asked Motin. "We'll need to swim sometime. I'm already starting to feel the need for immersion." He looked at Ebony bounding down the slope. "Even the jevvi has more energy than I."

"I don't know what lies beneath the mountain of the dragon, my friend," said Ishaan. "But I know there is a stream at the bottom of *this* slope."

"Excellent," said Motin.

They reached it mid-morning, and after the Ammerr had swum, they ate something, re-filled their water bottles, and went on, following the stream down a thin valley. By evening the mountain they were headed for loomed above, and next morning they began the trek over it.

They took a route low over the hip of the mountain, following an invisible trail known only to Ishaan and Williver. Olando had travelled to the dragon mountain several times with Ishaan, but he only vaguely knew the way.

For three days they travelled over the edge of the mountain, the bulk of it rising to their right, the slopes growing treeless high above. The air grew colder, hawks and eagles trawled the skies, and nearby tiny blue-cheeked birds flitted from bush to bush. Huge rocks pushed from the mountainside, their sides covered in spidery lichens, bright orange fungi growing around their bases like deformed feet. Twice they saw jenka, the mottled wildcats stalking through the slopes above, and once they saw a drebell, a nuggety ball of fluff and muscle. Williver pointed it out, wedged high in a tree, eyes closed as it slept through the sunlight hours, thick black claws hooked into the bark, and they took a wide berth around it, for the drebell was an angry little creature, inclined to drop down and attack if it took fright. At night they heard the creatures calling to each other, a strange cry like croaking laughter which mocked them through the midnight hours.

The next day they went steeply downhill, and by nightfall they were camped at the bottom of the mountain's slope. They had stopped in the upper reaches of a valley, and the next morning Williver led them down to where a small creek ambled from the hills. It was not deep enough to swim, but they filled their bottles and the Ammerr put their faces in the water. Further on the creek widened, and they followed its course as it was joined by other tiny creeks, and became a wide stream.

The valley spread out, and down on its floor the sun beamed. They left the drab, rocky slopes behind and went down into a land still clinging to the last of the summer. Above, the mountains were beginning to show patches of white, but here there were still patches of late flowers. They stopped to eat and to let the Ammerr swim, but Williver urged them on; they would reach his home by nightfall, he said, if they hurried.

The valley grew broader still, and mid-afternoon it opened out entirely. Before them lay a great stretch of land, a place where two mighty valleys met. In the centre two broad creeks flowing from each valley met also, forming a river that ran out to the north between high-sided canyons. Studding the great expanse of valley were small forests and copses, and far down to the right, beside where the two creeks formed a river, rose a hill.

It was an enormous mound, a hill almost worthy of being called a mountain. Its base was bare, battered piles of trees flung into mounds like driftwood were testament to spring floods, but above the flood line, the entire hill was covered in tall forest. Several towers rose above the trees at its peak, between the trunks there were puddles of smoke, and they knew this was Williver's home. They left the stream and headed straight for the tree-studded hill across the valley floor.

The afternoon was waning, but the sun still warmed them as they reached the base of the enormous hill. Williver's step quickened as they neared the first trees, and somewhere, high above, came the sound of a horn.

"They herald our arrival," said Williver. "'Tis probably best if I speak for us all. I have kept many secrets and now the time comes to tell them." He did not seem to relish the prospect.

They entered the trees, dark-trunked giants with pale, lacy leaves. It was dim and cool beneath the boughs, silent and breezeless. After the brightness of the afternoon sunshine in the valley, the trees here seemed almost too quiet, too enclosed; the afternoon disappeared as soon as they were within the trees, and it seemed the World went with it. They were somewhere else now, moving upwards through green twilight, and although they could not see anyone, Shaeli was sure she felt eyes upon her back and she moved to walk closer to her brother. Tarkoda smiled at her, but the smile looked odd and she knew he also felt uncomfortable. Kirrit came up on her other side, slipping her arm through Shaeli's and squeezing it. She felt it, too. The too-quiet. The green, other-worldliness.

There was no sound but their footfalls as they walked up the slope between the dark, thick-trunked trees. No birds called from the branches, nothing moved on the leaf-patterned ground. The top of the hill was in sight before they saw anyone.

Two figures moved from between the trees ahead. One was a tall man, broad-shouldered, with dark hair reaching to his shoulders and showing streaks of grey at the temples, his beard also thick with grey. The other was a woman, her hair holding silver lines among the pale strands also, yet she stood with a straight back, her face unlined, with high cheekbones and full lips. The two faces were lit by the last rays of the sun slanting between the trees; pale, beautiful faces, ears high-set and pointed, the man's face grim, the woman's unreadable. Neither spoke.

The group stopped. Williver went forward and bowed before the two elves.

"Why do you bring these strangers to our Lands, Williver?" said the man. His voice was deep, the words clipped and terse.

There was no greeting. No welcome. Shaeli felt a chill run down her spine. She looked at Williver, saw his hands were pressed into balls at his sides. Something was terribly wrong.

"Forgive me, my lord Xyllo," said Williver, bowing again. "But I would not have done so if the need were not very strong. I had no choice. The gods have guided us here."

"But *why* are they here?" Xyllo asked again. "We do not bring outsiders to Lythnori, this you know. Ammerr are one thing, but *this* is unheard of."

"I would not have brought them without the need being very great," Williver repeated. He hesitated just a moment before continuing. "And Lythnori is not our destination."

"What *is* your destination then?" said Xyllo. "You could have escorted them inland without bringing them here."

"We do not travel inland, my lord, we travel to the Mountain of the Dragon," said Williver. He said the words quickly, as if distancing himself from their content. He licked his lips. "And from there to the Cave of the Traders."

"What?" said Xyllo. "That is ridiculous. You can't be serious."

The woman spoke before Williver could answer. "*Why* do you do this, Williver?" she said. Her voice was as cool as the shadows between the trees.

Williver took a breath before he answered. Shaeli knew then that he was nervous, very nervous, and her heart began to thump against her breast for him. She had never seen Williver nervous before.

"Because the wand of Shahlita has been found, my lady Mithrina," Williver said. "It has been found and we go to protect it."

* * *

The Lady Mithrina looked at him for a long time. Williver's news appeared to make little impression upon her face. Xyllo's face, however, had covered a dozen emotions before she spoke.

"You may lower your weapons," she said at last, speaking to the trees.

There was nothing for a moment, and then dozens, scores of elves moved from behind trunks and down from the branches over their heads, bows and small swords in all their hands. No wonder Williver was nervous. No wonder they had felt so uncomfortable.

The elves stared at them, all curious, most unsmiling, but here and there Shaeli saw Williver catch a wink or a nod from a friendly face.

"You may bring your company into Lythnori, Williver," said the Lady Mithrina. "But each must lay aside their weapons. Armed strangers do not walk these lands."

"You have nothing to fear from anyone here, Mithrina," said Williver.

"This I know," the lady replied. "Yet it shall be so or you shall not enter." The words were said simply, but with absolute assurance.

"But..." began Williver.

"Do not trouble yourself, my friend," said Blenny. "'Tis easily done."

He untied a short knife from his waist, walked forward and dropped it in the grass before Mithrina and Xyllo. He smiled, bowed, and backed away. Wendll followed his lead. One by one, the others came forward and dropped what weapons they held. The Ammerr each held a thin sword, Cheval and Olando also had a bow each. Tarkoda laid his sword and his sling beside them. Spotjaw added a stubby knife, his only weapon, to the pile. Kirrit had been given the tiny crossbow and a quiver by Pykkal, and she walked forward and lay these and her knife beside the others. Flin and Shaeli had not moved.

Mithrina looked at them. "Yours also," she said.

For a moment Shaeli thought she meant the small knife given her by Ishaan's father, but then Flin walked forward, taking his throwing stone from his pocket. He handed it to Mithrina and laid a long knife on the ground, then walked back, his lips pursed, clearly unhappy. Shaeli had unbuckled the knife, but now she looked down at her amulet, and then back at the tall elfin lady.

Mithrina looked at Shaeli, and for the first time her face softened. "I will take care of it. Do not fear," she said, holding out her hand.

Shaeli had never thought of her amulet as a weapon, but as she walked forward, slowly undoing her belt, she knew fully for the first time that it was.

Mithrina looked at her as she handed over the amulet and knife, her eyes green fire, and she smiled. "Thank you, little one," she said, and Shaeli smiled back. She couldn't help it. That was what Williver called her.

She went back and stood beside Kirrit, pulling Ebony down from her shoulder and holding her in her arms while Mithrina looked first at them, and then at the elves gathered in silent knots among the trees.

"Take their weapons and prepare the guest house," she said. "They will dine with us after the sunset hour."

She took Xyllo's hand, and they turned and went up the slope. The silent elves followed, the pile of weapons disappearing from the ground as they went. Most ignored the group, a few offered smiles, but the elves followed Mithrina and Xyllo up the hill, until all but four remained.

A small elfin woman came forward. She embraced Williver, kissed him fondly, but looked at him sternly. "What adventure have you found yourself in this time, my son?" she said.

Williver smiled, but the smile was worn, like the threads of an old carpet. "My apologies, Mother," he said. "I have embarrassed you again. But this time…"

"Yes, yes, 'this time'," she said, with a flap of her hand. "I will hear it later. Kiss your father, and introduce your friends."

He did so, embracing a tall elf standing quietly watching. Beside Williver's father stood another elf, older still, and similarly featured. Williver embraced him also, and then he turned to the last figure.

It was an elfin girl, only a little taller than Shaeli, her brown eyes uptilted, her mouth the same, her hair a dark rope down her back. Williver hugged her until her feet left the ground and she laughed aloud, but she did not speak.

"These are my parents," he said to the others, leading the girl over to stand beside them. "Wattle and Charel. My uncle, Tylerrin, and my friend, Llianas." They smiled at the four elves as Williver introduced them, one by one.

"Come then," said Wattle, a tiny woman for an elf, her eyes the same bright blue as Williver's. "We shall take you to the guest house as Mithrina said."

She took her son's arm and led him up the hill, and the others followed. Shaeli found herself walking near Williver's uncle, Tylerrin, and she smiled at him.

"Are you Qiren's father?" she asked.

He looked at her, eyebrows raised. "You know my son?" he said, clearly astounded.

"Oh, yes," she said. "He helped Flin train me. Flin," she called. "This is Qiren's father."

"Pleased to meet you," said Flin, joining them. "Your son is a fine thrower and a good friend."

"Ah, you're that lad from Palveron," said Tylerrin. "The one he's been staying with."

"That's right," said Flin.

"But if you are here, where is my son?" asked Tylerrin. "Where are Qiren and his wife?"

"At the Cave of the Traders," answered Flin, looking at Shaeli.

"*What?*" said Tylerrin. "Why?"

"Illen is my aunt's sister," said Shaeli. "They travel with my family, on Purple Leaf Trader."

"I know of Illen's sister," said Tylerrin, obviously puzzled. "But why are they on her Trader?"

"It's a long story," said Shaeli.

"It shall wait then," said Tylerrin. "Welcome to Lythnori."

The hill had levelled out and the trees thinned, and between their trunks grew the houses of Lythnori. The houses lay between the trees, within them, around them, spreading up into the branches above. Each house was uniquely shaped, each seemed a part of the forest; living, like the trees. Peaked ceilings jutted between forked branches, latticed verandas ran along others, coloured windows glittered in the late sun. Here and there, the thin towers they had seen from the valley rose into the canopy, reaching into the sky above the treetops.

The top of the hill was flat, a vast expanse, and they walked through the trees and between the amazing houses until they emerged into the last sunshine of the day. The centre of the hill was bare of trees and houses, the size of a small field, rounded, and in the middle was a wide pool, a low wall built around the perimeter, the water brim-full. It reminded Shaeli of the spring pool at Cave, but instead of one stream flowing from it, this pool had six arms, flung out like the spokes of a wheel. The arms flowed across the round grassed expanse and down through the forest.

Williver led them across the centre of the expanse, over little half-circle bridges spanning the arms of the pool. Across the field lay a rambling structure, its front door open between the trunks of two enormous trees. As they neared, several elves left the house and two others appeared in the doorway.

"Greetings, my friend," said one, bowing.

The other echoed him, bowing also, and Williver laughed.

"I thought you were going to ignore me," he said.

"Never," cried the first. "We thought only to ready your rooms."

"And to find a few bottles to toast your return," said the second.

"Typical," said Wattle, lips pursed. "Ky and Jocovar are always the first to find reason for a toast. Lead on, then," she said to them. "Don't keep us waiting outside the door."

Ky, the first elf, was very tall, the tallest person Shaeli had ever seen, his thick, sun-streaked hair falling across dark-lashed, green eyes. Jocovar, the second, was much shorter, his eyes uptilted and merry, his cheeks round and ruddy.

They led the way through a tiny entry hall into a large room nestled between the trunks of five trees. Between the trunks, thin staircases led up to oddly-shaped bedrooms. Shaeli, Kirrit and Cheval found one with a tiny balcony that looked over the field and the pool. There were branches growing across the ceiling; another that was a seat below the crooked window. None of the windows in Lythnori were square, every one was uniquely shaped to fit the tree-house into which it was built, and many had no glass, only tiny shutters of woven branches, but wherever there *was* glass it was delicately coloured and patterned with pictures.

There was little time to talk with Williver's family and friends. They washed the grime from their hands and faces as the sun sank. Tylerrin lit lamps with a small gem, and the flame glowed more brightly than Warlock fire. They drank Ky and Jocovar's wine, and soon after a solemn elf called them to meet with Mithrina and Xyllo. The older elves were told to accompany them, and the three younger elves, Ky, Jocovar and the silent Llianas watched as they walked away, obviously disappointed at being left out.

They passed by the pool again, walked over the tiny arched bridges and across the clearing to a structure that encompassed dozens of trees. Above soared a tower, its turret high above the canopy, the top open to the sky.

Inside, there was a large entry hall with several trees growing up through the floor and into the ceiling, and before them was a wide staircase. Dozens of miniature lights lit the space and the stairs, and as they ascended, Shaeli saw the stairs were made of living branches, a few sprouting new leaves, and some of the lights seemed to be embedded in the treads of the branch-stairs. There were even more of the tiny lights glittering from the walls and ceiling on the next floor, and the trees from the entryway continued their path up through this room. Here and there, a branch unfurled soft leaves, and in one corner flowers grew from the floor, their pastel scent matching their subtle colours. One side of the room was open to the night, leaf-covered branches framing the view of the clearing. In the centre of the room a large round table was set, covered with garlands of flowers, and Mithrina and Xyllo stood beside tall chairs. Both greeted them formally as they entered the room.

Shaeli felt grimy and plain as she sat in the beautiful leafy room, but she greeted the two elves in formal elf, surprising them both. The two had changed for the meal and sat in regal splendour as the meal was served and eaten, and inevitably, when the plates had been cleared, Williver had to tell the story.

He told it much the same way Ishaan had recited it to his parents, adding his own part of travelling the dreamworld, of meeting Shaeli there many times. Xyllo asked many questions, berating Williver as expected for his secrecy, but Mithrina rarely spoke, her eyes turning more and more often to Shaeli's face.

Shaeli sat looking at her hands, or at Ebony, who wandered around the room delighting at trees inside a house. Shaeli did not really want to listen as the tale was being told again. She hardly believed it herself, and every time she heard it out loud it seemed even more absurd. She rubbed at her eyes, wishing she could sleep for a Moon, wishing it would all just go away. Her eyebrows began to pull together, as if straining to shake hands.

She realised Mithrina's eyes were on her again, even before she raised her own to meet that calm gaze. The elfin lady's green eyes seemed to ask questions Shaeli did not want to hear, let alone answer, yet when Mithrina did ask her a question, it was so simple that Shaeli could barely answer.

"Would you like to sleep, child, before we talk more of this?" she asked. "I see you are all tired, and when one is tired thoughts are hard to find, and emotions too easy. Take them to their beds, Wattle. Let them sleep, take the Ammerr to swim if they wish in the morning, and then bring them here again."

"We shall sleep on this matter also," said Xyllo. "But know this. Dark things can only come from this, and we will not let the wand fall from our hands again."

* * *

Shaeli slept, her dreams thankfully absent, and when she woke it was to green-dappled sunshine playing on the walls and the soft sounds of Kirrit and Cheval still breathing deeply in their beds. She rolled her face to the wall and closed her eyes against the morning, luxuriating in sleeping in a bed for the first time since they had left the plateau. Yet her mind would not let her find that gentle place between waking and sleeping, the place where it was easy to let thoughts drift off into nothingness and dreams. Her mind began to ask questions, to replay events, to search the future for answers. In the end she gave up trying to find the drifting spot and just got out of bed. At least if she found someone to talk to, she wouldn't have to listen to her own thoughts.

Ebony woke as she dressed, and she stretched and leapt off her cushion. Shaeli picked her up and nuzzled her.

"You need a bath," she said. Ebony looked at her and flared her little nostrils, and Shaeli laughed. "I know. I smell, too. We'll both have one after breakfast."

She found her brother downstairs, pouring tezz from a large pot. He poured a second cup as she entered, added a generous serve of sugar and handed it to her. She put Ebony down and the jevvi bounded out the door.

"Don't you go far," she called after her. "Thanks," she said to Tarkoda, sipping at the brew. "Where is everybody?"

Tarkoda looked at her over the rim of his cup. "Everybody?" he said, raising an eyebrow. "*All* of them?"

She nodded, and Koda sighed.

"The Ammerr have gone to swim with Ky and Jocovar," he said. "There's eggs in that silver thing there." He pointed to a table. "And rolls, if you want something. Spot's still snoring. I know that because we shared a room." He rolled his eyes. "Never again." Shaeli giggled and her brother continued. "The drell are outside, enjoying the looks they're getting from the elves. I presume the girls are still sleeping?"

She nodded. "What about Williver?"

"He went somewhere with that other elf," said Tarkoda. "That girl, Llianas."

"And Flin?"

Tarkoda shrugged. "Guess," he said. He took an orange from a bowl and began to peel it.

"He found the bathroom?" smiled Shaeli.

"Of course," said Koda. "And I'm next, so don't get any ideas. Is that everyone?"

"I think so," she said. "Let's see, four Ammerr, two drell, you, me, Kirrit, Williver, Spotjaw, Flin. That's it. Twelve. Thirteen, if you count Ebony."

Tarkoda shook his head. "Imagine their faces when we turn up at Cave with two drell, four Ammerr, and an elf," he said.

"Coming out of the Zoi cave," she added.

Koda laughed. Shaeli laughed, too, but she also felt a little like crying.

Flin came in, rubbing his damp hair with a small towel. "All yours, Koda," he said. "Pour me some of that tezz, please, Shaeli."

"Thanks, Flin," said Tarkoda. "Is it up to standard?" he added cheekily.

"It's fine, Koda," said Flin, dryly. "On your way." He flicked the towel at Tarkoda, who laughed and left the room.

Shaeli handed Flin a cup, trying not to smile. Flin ignored the fact that she was trying not to smile.

"Williver not back yet?" he said.

She shook her head, swallowing a giggle. "There's eggs, if you want them," she said, after she'd swallowed.

"I've had some," he said. "Though the elves don't like us being here, they are certainly hospitable."

"I know. I suppose we'll have to go and talk with them again soon."

"Yes," he said. "It bothers you, doesn't it? Talking about it all the time?"

She looked at him, and nodded. "It doesn't matter though," she said. "It can't be helped. Besides, there's hardly anyone left to tell."

"No," he agreed. "I suppose not."

"And when we reach Cave... well, Almarnoch will know what to do. Him, and the old ones, and my parents. And we'll be safe with the Fleet, at least while the Wintering lasts." She sighed. "Once we reach Cave, everything will be alright."

"Let's hope so," said Flin.

"Let's hope what?" said Kirrit, coming down the stairs, all tousled red hair and yawns.

"Nothing, Kirrit," said Shaeli. "Do you want tezz?"

"Yes, please. And do I smell eggs?"

* * *

They were not summoned until the morning had passed.

Mithrina and Xyrrol did not wait for them in the round-tabled room as they had the night before, but in a room open to the sky, a room that was almost a courtyard. Its floor was grassed, the walls filled with vines and ribbons of minute lacy flowers. On one side of the room burbled a small fountain, and Xyrrol stood unsmilingly beside it.

Mithrina stood feeding tiny grey-brown birds. The birds flittered around her feet, their fire-red beaks darting at the grains she threw down. There were scores of them scattered about the grass and in the trees and vines, their voices piping across the lawn.

The garden room was surrounded by the rest of the house – was part of it – but the open sky and the birds made them feel they were outside. It reminded Shaeli of Arinola's conservatory, and she looked around, much more relaxed than she had been the night before. She felt less plain, less travel-worn than she had, and she set her shoulders and waited to hear what Xyrrol and Mithrina would say.

Xyrrol watched their arrival, his brows lowered, and when he spoke his voice held a sharp edge. "What do you intend to do with the wand once you reach the Cave of the Traders, Williver?" he said.

"We had not thought beyond reaching the Cave, my lord," said Williver. "We thought only to protect it, and Shaeli, from whatever seeks them."

"And you, young woman," Xyrrol said to Shaeli. "What are your intentions towards the wand?"

Shaeli was surprised. She kept being surprised by people thinking she wanted to *do* something with the wand. She frowned. "I never had any *intentions* towards it," she said, annoyance edging her voice. "I just *found* it, that's all. I didn't *know* it was special. It's just an old broken thing. I'm sure it won't work, and if it did, I wouldn't *use* it. How could I?"

"There are ways," said Xyrrol. "But if that is the truth, then our decision is this." He stopped, looked at Mithrina and she met his gaze unblinkingly. He pursed his lips, and then continued. "You shall be allowed to complete your journey. If, and I have my doubts, but *if* you are correct and the Cave of the Traders can be reached from this side of Zerrinius, then you are to return to Lythnori, *with* the wand. If it is as you say, the Lady Shahlita's, we shall consider further."

"But Xyrrol," said Williver, "the Wintering will be upon the Land soon. It will not be long until first snow."

"I *know* when first snow is, young elf," said Xyrrol, his brows and his voice lowering further. "But beneath the *mountain* there are no blizzards."

"But three days journey lie between Lythnori and the Dragon Mountain," said Williver. "And that is in good weather. It would not be possible to return until after the Wintering, at the earliest, and…"

"Then you shall travel when it *is* possible," Xyrrol cut in, raising his voice.

Flin tried to help Williver. "But why should we travel back to Lythnori, my lord?" he asked. "Forgive me, but there will be no need to come back."

"You may find a need, young thrower," said Mithrina. They were the first words she had spoken since they'd arrived.

"Forgive me again, my lady," said Flin. "But we are obviously not welcome here, and…"

"That has nothing to do with it," she answered. "'Tis not so much that you are unwelcome as unexpected. This tale is entirely unexpected, but must be dealt with, as *you* have been, swiftly and with forethought. There is no proof the wand is what you say it is, but if it *is* so, then you *will* have need to return to Lythnori. Whether you wish to or not."

"Forgive me also," said Ishaan. "But there is no doubt about the wand being Shahlita's. I have seen it and it was made by my grandfather. It is hers."

Xyrrol raised his eyes to the sky, obviously unconvinced, but Mithrina looked at Williver. "You say the wand of Shahlita is badly damaged?"

"If it *is* Shahlita's," muttered Xyrrol.

Williver glanced at him, then nodded at Mithrina and she continued.

"*If* it is what you suspect, and it is damaged, it cannot be returned to power," she said, with a glance at Ishaan. "Even with someone to repair the metal and reset the stones, if you *had* stones, the power is elven power, and we alone have the magic it needs."

"There is no talk of restoring it, Mithrina," said Williver. "We seek merely to protect it."

"This I know," she said. "But there will come a time when it will be coveted, not just sought, and if the World outside sits on the brink of disaster as you say, then that time will come all too soon." She sighed. "Mankind are so *hasty*." She looked at the group, encompassing them all in her gaze. "There are many things left unsaid. Many secrets clutched tightly." Each of them squirmed under her gaze; those without the secrets she spoke of, as well as those with them. "Yet we will not push you to reveal them. They will reveal themselves when their time is right. You have one more day to stay in Lythnori, and then you shall travel to the mountain where dragons once lay." She looked at Flin, and the shadow of a smile passed across her lips. "And you *are* welcome here. All of you."

* * *

CHAPTER TWENTY ONE

That night the elves of Lythnori gave them so grand a feast that their welcome was no longer in question. Mithrina and Xyrrol oversaw all, and were of the last to seek their pillows.

Throughout the evening, Williver's friends, Ky and Jocovar, pleaded with Xyrrol to be given permission to accompany them beneath the mountain. Again and again they were denied, until Xyrrol grew so sick of them that he forbade any elf from even mentioning joining the company in his presence. The two elves were sorely disappointed, but heeded him and did not mention it again; at least not when Xyrrol was nearby.

They slept late, and when they did wake it took them most of the morning to pack their belongings, the supplies given them, and to talk with the elves who came to wish them well. Williver's mother, Wattle, scuttled about giving orders to everyone she saw. His father, Charel, patiently bore with her, and Qiren's father, Tylerrin, stood smiling and watching the parade which trouped through the house. Shaeli had spoken with Tylerrin the night before of his son and Illen, and of the time he had ridden with her grandfather, Povann, to rescue the girls taken prisoner by the half-elf, Periqol. She could sense some of the horror of that time in his face as he spoke, but he talked so highly of her grandfather she could tell they had liked each other, and wished anew she had met Povann.

Apart from the first tense beginnings, the elves had enjoyed the rare visit and many came to farewell them. Ky and Jocovar gave them all a wine skin to add to their bundles, and bemoaned the fact they were to be left behind. Of the little elf, Llianas, there was no sign, and Shaeli guessed she was so saddened with their going that she did not want to watch it.

The sun was nearing its zenith when they finally left the cool shade of Lythnori. Xyrrol and Mithrina stood beneath the last trees waiting for them. The weapons which had been taken upon their arrival lay on the grass at their feet, and each claimed their own as Mithrina handed Flin and Shaeli their throwing stones.

"May the gods keep watch over you," she said, and they all bowed before her and Xyrrol, and then stepped from beneath Lythnori's trees.

The bright sunshine seemed almost unnatural after the cool green of Lythnori, and they squinted in the brightness of it as they said their final farewells. Many of the elves had come down the wooded hill, and they stood beneath the trees as the company went down the final slope to the valley floor, yet when they reached it and turned to wave, there was no one there. Not one elf remained in sight, but when Williver raised an arm, they all did the same, knowing that not seeing elves was no indication they weren't there.

Across the valley, the hills hazy in the distance, lay the crooked peak that sat like a carrion bird over the valley for which they were headed. There were few trees across the expanse, and those that were there sat in clumps around the edges, but the ground was green, full of mossed boulders and thick grass. They had two rivers and several watercourses to cross before they reached the valley that would take them to the dragon's lair, and they edged the valley, crossing at wide fords, and with the Ammerr to help, traversing the first river and the other streams was no problem. They camped the first night between the two rivers, crossing the second just after sunrise the next morning, and then they entered the last valley.

The valley leading to the Dragon Mountain was a wide, shallow stretch of land, empty of trees, the crooked peak hanging above, but it was still grassy, with a shallow creek meandering from it. As they followed the valley to higher climes, the grasses began to die out, replaced by thick, spongy vegetation that grew close to the ground and which looked and felt like giant moss. The creek ran at their right, the water freezing cold after its journey from high in the peaks where there were already great drifts of snow. Soon even the thick moss which covered the hills died out and the ground grew uneven; gritty rubble replaced soil underfoot and small stones became ugly rocks. The way grew steeper, the shallow creek now tumbling down at a rapid pace, flowing back the way they had come. It seemed to Shaeli that the creek went eagerly from this place and she did not blame it. As the afternoon wore on she dreaded the thought of spending the night in this grey ugly place, yet just before sunset they rounded a bend and there, on a steep bluff above the rocky valley, was a square fortress, its one turret a squat unroofed lump. It lay on the other side of the creek, and Williver led them to a place where they could cross, and they climbed higher, the fortress growing ever larger. It was as grey as the valley, drab and alone, but there was a kind of beauty in its stark lines.

Williver told them this was a final outpost. It was used to protect the approach to the dragon's cave, for many had tried over the years to reach the lair and the treasure within.

They spent the night beneath the garrison's grey roof. The elves there shook their heads when they heard Williver's plan, looking at the rest of them as if they'd gone mad.

They were still shaking their heads when the travellers left the next morning, and while the garrison was in sight, the elves stood atop the tower watching them go on and up into the valley.

Higher they went that long, cool day, ever higher. The valley they followed shrunk into a series of clefts that became the side of the mountain, the shallow creek that they followed still ran beside them, now on their left, and as night fell they came to a place where the water pooled beneath a rocky overhang. At the back of the overhang the rocks had been cleared away, and a blackened ring of stones showed the remains of past fires.

"Well I guess this is home for the night," said Tarkoda, sliding the pack off his shoulders.

"Looks cosy," said Kirrit. "What do we use for wood?"

"There's a flood-pile upstream," said Williver. "We'll have to carry it down. Tarkoda, will you help?"

"Sure," he shrugged. "Nothing else to do."

"I'll help," said Spotjaw, laying his pack beside Tarkoda's.

"I'll come, too," said Flin.

"I like the look of that pool," said Motin. "I could do with a swim if you have enough for the wood?"

"Yes, Motin," said Williver. "Immerse yourself while you can. There is only one more pool that we know of, the dragon pool itself, and then we must hope to find something beneath the mountain."

Motin almost shuddered at the thought.

"Where is this dragon pool?" asked Cheval.

"Near the entrance to the cave," said Ishaan. "We camp beside it tomorrow night."

"And then we go in," said Wendll. He did not look any more delighted with the prospect than Motin.

"Then we go in," agreed Williver, smiling grimly at Wendll's less-than-enthusiastic face. "You can see the entrance of the cave from the flood-pile," he added.

"I'm going to come and have a look then," said Kirrit. "Shaeli?"

"Alright," Shaeli groaned. "I'll come."

"Good," said Kirrit. "Anyone else?"

"No," said Cheval. "I might try the pool, too. Olando?"

"The pool," he nodded.

"I'll stay also," said Ishaan.

"And Wendll and I might start finding something to eat, so we might," said Blenny. "Eh, Wendll?"

Wendll nodded, his usual grin returned to his face. "Aye, Blenny," he said. "Drell legs are not made for all this walking any more than Ammerr legs."

Motin was already easing himself into the water and the other three were unlacing their boots. Kirrit shivered.

"I'd rather go and fetch wood than get in there," she said. "It must be freezing in that pool."

"It is," said Motin. "Freezing, shallow, and delicious." He grinned, and his dark head disappeared beneath the water.

The Ammerr had coped with the journey from Qorientae well so far. Each day they had been able to find somewhere to immerse themselves, if not swim. While in Lythnori, they had swum many times, but beneath the mountain was another matter, and Shaeli was worried for them. She knew Williver was, too. She had also noticed the Ammerr drank enormous quantities of water, but they did not sweat. Even when they had been much lower and closer to the sea, when it was as warm as summer coming over that first mountain behind the plateau, they had not perspired, though it was obvious they felt the heat of the day.

She called to Ebony and the jevvi picked her way across to Shaeli from where she had been watching Blenny pull packages from different packs. She scrambled up Shaeli's arm, sneezing at the dirt and brushing it from her little hands, and Shaeli laughed at her as she followed the others up the valley.

The flood-pile Williver spoke of was more of a flood-hill. Not far above the pool a wall of rock thrust out from the side of the mountain. Behind it were the piled remains of mighty trees, tangled bushes, and craggy boulders, all snarled together in a giant knot.

Above rose the mountain, and high up a dark gash where the mouth of the cave lay. They stared at it wordlessly for a long time, and then each gathered an armful of sticks and small logs and they went back down to the pool.

* * *

At noon the next day, the pool was far beneath them. The dusty overhang with its bright fire seemed a much more cheerful and preferable place to where they were now.

They had left the little creek behind and headed up a steep ridge, in itself exhausting enough, but now the slope they were trying to climb seemed intent on keeping them at its base. It was all grey pebbles and sliding rocks, the surface alive with sharp-edged stones and grit. For every two steps they staggered up, they slid one, or five, back again. Williver eventually managed to make it to a solid rock jutting out three-quarters of the way up the slope, and he tied a rope to it and threw it down so the others could reach his perch.

They sat panting against the rock for a while, the top of the slope tantalisingly close. Williver assured them the going was easier after this.

"'Tis a wonder you need anyone to guard the cave, young elf, so it is," panted Blenny. "This slope would deter most, I would imagine."

"It does," said Williver. "But there will always be those for whom greed supplies its own strength."

"Aye, lad," Blenny answered. "You're right there, so you are. Sadly."

"Koda," said Ishaan. "Do you think you could throw the rope around that outcrop?" He pointed to a mound above.

"I can try," said Tarkoda.

His first try went wide, the second pulled down the rock when they tested its weight, creating a landslide that turned the hill into a live thing that slid crashing and clattering into a cloud of dust below, but the third toss held, and one by one they hauled themselves up. The ground levelled a little after that and they clambered higher, almost crawling the last section of slope until they lay panting at the top, on solid ground once more.

"Oh, no," said Tarkoda, after a moment. "I left the rope tied around that rock."

"Leave it," said Williver. "We have plenty and it would be difficult to retrieve. Come, the afternoon wanes and we still have to make the dragon pool by nightfall."

Make it they did. The last slope was steep, the way covered with rock-piles and patches of slippery gravel, but it was an easy climb compared to the hillside of sliding stones. The sun had dipped behind the mountain when they came upon the place where dragons once drank, but there was still plenty of light to see around them.

The pool was not large, nor deep. It was a spring, for no water flowed into it, at least not this late in the year, and only a trickle flowed from it to tumble into the rocky valley below. Tall outcrops surrounded the pool; misshapen towers of dark-streaked boulders keeping silent sentinel over the water. The ground itself was littered with bones. Most of them were small, their origins lost in obscurity, with still-recognisable skulls scattered amongst them, cows or sheep, but in three places the bones were huge. They were the bones of dragons. Great curved rib-bones cut sharp white lines against the rock; three skulls with teeth like spear tips in lipless grins leered across the expanse; bones of tails curved like enormous snakes along the ground. Nothing moved.

The slight breeze had dropped with the sun and a chill shivered through the group, yet it was not the chill of nightfall they felt, it was the death, the remnants of a long-past battle that still lingered in this place. The echo of anguish. The stench of betrayal. This was a graveyard, not only for the creatures who had been meals, but for the dragons themselves.

They did not speak for a long time. Each knew what had happened here. It weighed heavily on the air in this place. They moved as far from the pool and the bones of the long-dead dragons as they could to make camp for the night.

* * *

Shaeli woke late in the night. The moon still shone, but it was low, giving only thin light. She shivered, felt Ebony turn and resettle beside her, and looked to where Olando sat watch on a nearby rock. Though there was nothing around them for many days walk, they'd all felt better having a lookout. She squirmed, trying to find a comfortable spot on the hard ground. She would be stiff in the morning, she knew. She closed her eyes and was trying to fall asleep again when she heard it. A soft rattle. A slide.

She opened her eyes and lifted her head. She looked at Olando. He still sat on his rock, but his posture was stiff, his head cocked slightly. He had heard it, too.

She sat up and he looked over at her. He raised his hand and put a finger to his lips, and she nodded. Ebony woke and looked up at her and she repeated Olando's movement. The jevvi scuttled up her arm and snickered in her ear.

Another soft fall of stones came from somewhere below their eyesight, from the steep rise they had climbed before sunset. Olando was on his feet, and he poked Ishaan with a boot as he passed on his way to where the path became flat ground. Ishaan was up and following him before Shaeli had reached her feet. Williver lay nearby and she touched his shoulder. His eyes opened instantly, and again she put a finger to her lips before whispering.

"Someone's on the path," she said, and he was up and following the others.

Ebony again snickered in her ear. She was not disturbed by whatever was on the path, Shaeli could tell, but merely curious. She followed Williver to where Olando and Ishaan stood behind an outcrop peering through the moonlight.

At first she could see nothing, and then she caught a glimpse of a thin hunched figure clambering over a pile of rocks. The figure scrambled from shadow to shadow, climbing ever closer. Every now and then another soft rattle from dislodged stones reached them.

Olando raised his bow and trained an arrow on the figure. They could hear it breathing now, harsh rasping breaths.

Shaeli's heart had begun to pound, but Ebony snickered softly again.

Olando had pulled his bow tighter when the figure stumbled and fell. They heard a soft curse and Williver drew a breath.

"Stop where you are," said Olando, loudly. "Or this arrow flies."

"Wait," said Williver, putting a hand on Olando's arm.

Olando eased his bow and lowered it, watching with a frown as Williver stepped out into the moonlight.

"Some light please, Shaeli, if you will," he said.

Shaeli pulled out her finger of quartz, hearing the others stirring with the sound of Olando's shout as she fired a ball which blossomed above the path into a glittering umbrella. Standing in the light, eyes shielded from the sudden glare, was the thin figure of an elfin girl, a small pack on her back, braid askew, breathing deeply. She had dirt on her face, her knuckles were grazed, and one knee of her trousers was torn, blood showing through the tear.

"*Llianas?*" said Williver. "I *thought* it was your voice, but I knew I must be dreaming." He shook his head. "What are you doing here?"

"I'm going with you," she said, squinting up at them.

"*What?* Why?" he said. "Xyrrol said no one was allowed to go with us."

"Xyrrol said no one was to *ask* to go," she replied. "So I didn't ask. He expressly forbade Ky and Jocovar, or anyone, to accompany you, but he never said anything about *following* you, did he?"

"So you just followed us?" said Williver. "Oh, Llianas, Xyrrol will be so angry."

She shrugged. "Well, I'm not there to hear it, am I? I'll worry about it when I see him next. And I left Mithrina a note."

"A note?" Williver shook his head and laughed. "Well, you'll have to come now, for there's no going back."

"That was my plan," she said. "Now, are you going to help me? I've been sliding down that stupid rocky hill half the night."

Williver laughed again and went down the slope. He hugged Llianas, took the pack from her back, and helped her to where the others, all of them now awake, stood at the top of the slope.

"I thought I'd never make it," she was saying as they reached the top. "Only you'd left a rope dangling and that saved me."

"Lucky for you, then, that Tarkoda forgot it," said Williver. "When did you leave Lythnori?"

"The middle of the night after you'd gone," she said. "I thought you shouldn't be the only elf on this journey, and Ky and Jocovar were being watched." She shrugged again. "So I came."

"But why wait until now to reach us?" asked Ishaan. "It must have been very hard on you, travelling alone."

"Well, first I had to catch up," Llianas said. "And then I thought I should wait until you were well past the garrison. I almost came last night, the fire looked so good, but I was afraid Williver would have taken me back." She smiled at him, a smug little smile. "You can't now. We're much too far away from the garrison." She shared that smug little smile with the whole group. "So here I am. Is there any tezz?"

Cheval warmed her some and they were amazed that the formally silent elf suddenly had so much to say. She sipped on her tezz as she told them of her journey – crossing the rivers, her encounter with a group of jenka, sneaking past the fortress – and then she put down her cup, mumbled something, lay down, and was promptly asleep.

The others talked a little longer, until one by one they began yawning. Williver took watch for the rest of the night. He was not tired, he said, and would wake them at first light.

* * *

In the morning they were all stiff and the Ammerr were in need of a swim. Williver assured them the water in the pool was fine and they picked their way between the piles of bones, keeping as far from the dragon skulls as possible. They filled their water bottles, drank and washed as the Ammerr swam. Shaeli bathed and treated Llianas' wounds, and they patched her trousers while she pulled the knots from her hair with a tiny comb and re-braided it. As they ate, Kirrit asked Williver where the entrance to the dragon's cave lay. He pointed across the pool.

"On the far side," he said. "See where the ground goes around that ridge?"

On the other side of the pool the ground curved around a long ridge, but across the ground before it lay the bones of one of the dragons.

"We have to go through the dragon bones?" Kirrit said. "Great."

"And 'tis no use to put it off," said Williver. "Are we all ready to go?" They picked up their packs, and looked at him. "Very well then," he said.

They followed him around the pool, the bones of the dragon growing larger until the great skull was before them, the teeth bigger than their heads, the great dark holes where there were once bright eyes, each knowing the dragon was long-dead but fearing it anyway. Between the ribs they walked, picking their way beneath an ivory archway, the huge backbone on the ground at the centre. They climbed between the bones, feeling themselves within the heart, the very stomach of the creature, and when at last they reached the other side, each breathed a sigh. They looked back to the bones starkly white in the morning sun.

It was quiet still. They had seen no creature in the time spent there, not a bird, a lizard, nor even an insect. They had heard nothing either, only the sound of their own voices and the far-off splash of water falling to the valley from the pool.

They turned their backs on the graveyard and walked around
the ridge to face the lair itself. The ground was as wide and
smooth as a road, the way between the lair and the pool worn
with centuries of passing dragons. Only one rock-slide marred
the path, and beyond lay the entrance to the cave.

From below in the valley it had looked a dark gash on the
side of the mountain, but here it was a yawning hole, wide at
the bottom and narrowing into a slit high above. A great black
triangle impossible to see into.

To their left the valley fell away, and Shaeli realised just
how high they had climbed. Down the valley floor they could
see the grey garrison on its high ridge, and far beyond that the
green of the valley where Lythnori lay, yet as high in the
mountains as they were, they were still merely at their knees.
Above, the cloak of snow was lengthening, the top of the
mountain hidden in thick cloud; the Dragon Mountain filled
the sky.

They drank in the sight of the World, and turned their
faces to the morning sun. They did not speak of never seeing it
again, though it was in all their minds.

Finally they turned, and together, the two drell, four
Ammerr, five people, two elves, and one tiny jevvi walked into
the blackness of the dragon's lair.

* * *

CHAPTER TWENTY TWO

Far to the south-west, a large band of rebels rode away from the still-burning remains of a guard's outpost. The fort had been built on the northern edge of the Royal Parklands, initially to keep poachers from the forest. Or so it was said. Of late the only thing the soldiers had indulged in was pillaging the countryside, not only of food, but anything else they might take a liking to; horses, jewellery, paintings, furniture, a farmer's daughter. Any that stood up to them were promptly flogged, locked in cupboard-like cells, or just killed outright. Those found hiding produce were also punished, yet everyone hid something; it was the only way they ensured their families would eat.

As the mood of the guard had shifted, as they had moved from watchful soldiers to overbearing thugs, a few in their own ranks had protested. One, a young man brought up in a village not far north, had objected stubbornly to their tactics. He spoke loudly about taking all of a farmer's livestock, about taking every bushel of grain from a couple with six children, of expecting the publican to supply endless ale. He also spoke loudly about petitioning Great Court, of reporting to superiors, of leaving the guard. He must have spoken loudly one time too many, for one dawn he was found hanging from a Landing, his face almost unrecognisable, a sign saying "traitor" hanging from the noose around his neck.

Another soldier, a woman, friend to the young man, spoke out also, yet not for long. They found her in a ditch beside a road, outside a home where she'd shielded a girl from the unwanted attentions of one of her fellow soldiers. The girl had been safe, that day at least, but the woman had not. When they found her a few days after the incident, what had been done to her was whispered about with horror; men told each other what they'd heard in mumbled conversations in taverns, but never spoke of these things to their wives. They kept them close to home, kept their daughters locked away or sent them somewhere deemed safer. People began to forget what it felt like to laugh, to feel safe. They met seldom, at least openly, watching the guard to see where next they'd turn; there were no more dissenting voices within the ranks of the royal guard – though it was said that a few had disappeared into the night after the ugly death of the woman who was left in the ditch. The people could do nothing but wait for the next monstrosity.

One of those soldiers who had disappeared into the night had made his way north. He had found someone who would take him to the rebels. He had told them what was happening in the towns and villages to the south.

Less than a Moon later, Fezzik led the attack on the fort. Supplied again with a map of the place and the lax routine of the guard, he had struck when they were snoring after a drunken feast. The guard were easily overcome, dying as they struggled sleepily from their rooms. The prisoners were freed, and stolen items removed before they fired the place. He had watched the blaze turning the night sky crimson, and when the thin light of dawn streaked the east he had turned his back upon the conflagration and ridden into the morning.

His fellow rebels drifted off in ones and twos to their homes and Fezzik rode on with just a few men, these fugitives like himself. The female Warlock, Bekerra, was his constant companion, travelling with him on each raid on her enormous horse, her indignation growing with each of the guard's atrocities, her strength and humour sometimes the only things that kept Fezzik from despair. Her magic had saved his life on more than one occasion.

With him also was the former guard, Bithani, who had given him the information about the fort above Boccra which had led to the release of Verlie and Pemba. She had sought him out after leaving the guard, and she had brought her parents and sisters with her. She'd said that there were some who wished to leave the queen's service; that there were those besides her who could not condone what the guard were doing to the Land. Yet one who had left before her had had the guard turn up at his home in a small village and his parents had been put to the sword for his "betrayal". Many were the rumours of such happenings, and while she had been told of that one occurrence by the soldier in question after he had returned to his duties, she was sure the tales were more than rumour. Fezzik had sent her family to safety in the north and now she rode with him against her former comrades. He advised others who left the queen's service to protect their families, to remove them from their homes to ensure their safety. Those fugitives were like his own, bereft of their homes and their former lives.

His life was transient now; no long, quiet days in the forge in Boccra listening to his father gossip with the villagers, no quiet meals with his family. Verlie, Pemba and the children lived at an isolated farm to the north and he saw them often. Verlie and Pemba both continued to make weapons, and there were few he trusted enough to fetch them, so he usually went with Bekerra to add the weapons to their arsenal. The two women had recovered from the deaths of their loved ones by growing more determined, much as Fezzik had, their thoughts always on the people who suffered and the guard who caused the suffering. Every day brought tales of destruction and terror, starvation and death; his own brother, Fozar, had been thrown from his house, and their brother-by-law killed by the guard. Fozar was now a fugitive like Fezzik, leading a band of rebels further south. They met regularly and it had been Fozar who'd given him the paper that had fluttered from the tower of the Glade. There had been a small brown spot in one corner; blood from the woman who had followed the papers from the tower.

With the paper that had come from Great Court they had doubled their efforts; the knowledge there was another who deserved the throne gave them something tangible to hope for, to work towards. No further rumour of Tenelon's heir was heard, but Fezzik was not bothered. The Wintering was not far away now, and he would be able to spend it with his wife and children. Arral had regained much of himself, though he smiled less and thought more, but little Florry was still far too quiet, inclined to dissolve into tears with very little provocation, and he had not heard her speak Zeffy's name since they'd left Boccra. He hoped that he could wheedle her back to herself a little during the long days of blizzards.

He also had plans to finalise. An idea had come to him that he had at first dismissed as ridiculous, but the idea had festered in him, and each objection brought up by one part of his mind was resolved by another. The plan grew. He had discussed it with Fozar and Bekerra, who added a few details. They agreed Great Court and Palveron should feel the same pain as the people in the rest of the Land, and though they knew they would never wholly succeed – the Traders and ships would see to that – still, they would try. When spring came they would start.

Fezzik, riding into the morning with the smell of the burning fort still clinging to him, could hardly wait.

* * *

Dari was there when the queen was given the news that the rebels had burnt the outpost on the northern edge of the Parklands, and for a long time afterwards he wished he hadn't been.

They were dining with the queen and fifty of her closest courtiers. The meal had been sumptuous, as ever, the wine excellent, and he and Garrit had partaken generously of each. He was enjoying his new position, though how they had come to be there he was unsure, for it was highly unusual. When Garrit had found him on the Warlock Island one morning in late summer and told him he wanted him to come again to court, he was surprised. That he had been given permission to go was itself odd – he had final training to do, the Lift spell was still unlearnt – but when Garrit told him they were not going to the Warlock House, they were to live in the castle itself, Dari had been astounded. He had not quite finished his training, and to be taken into the court was an honour, yet he knew he'd done little to deserve such a thing.

Garrit had waved a hand at him, and told him such a gift was not to be questioned. His eyes had been overbright, Dari had thought, his manner unusually agitated. Dari did not know that Garrit had come from the queen's quarters where he been interviewed at length by she and her master-at-arms; he did not know Garrit had been horrified to learn the queen knew about the wand Dari thought so useless; that Garrit had grovelled before her and promised to do anything she asked of him, anything. Dari knew only that he grew quickly to love his new status, Garrit even more so, and, though he had been plagued by strange dreams since he had arrived at the castle, he was enjoying himself immensely by the time the herald came with the news on that autumn day. He had drunk much wine and seemed to be impressing the two young Wokkii seated on his left, so he did not even see the herald enter the room.

The first he knew was when the yelling started. It took him a moment to realise that it was the queen. As he turned, a thick cup flew past his head and crashed into the wall behind him. Everyone stopped speaking, their eyes on their monarch as she ordered them from the room, and then they scuttled away like beetles before fire. Only Sir Azeron sat unmoved by the tirade, his wine still in his hand as the others hurried away. Dari scuttled with the rest, Garrit was already out the doors, and the last words he heard as he ran gave him nightmares for days.

"*Enough*, do you hear," she was screeching. "It's time they were put in their places. I am ready now, and they will pay for their treason, every last one, traitors, rebels *and* those miserable traders. They will die, every last one of them."

Dari had looked back and met the dark eyes of Sir Azeron. Azeron did not blink. Dari turned and ran on. He had to find Garrit.

* * *

On the Long Lea, Eenis was also plagued with strange dreams. Like the others of Purple Leaf, she had made herself useful, helping in the kitchen bottling fruit and preserves and cleaning the old ones' huts up at Cave in preparation for the return of the Traders. She was as worried about Shaeli and Tarkoda and the others, but she was pleased she had Illen with her and the two spent much time together.

When she began to be plagued with dreams, she put it down to the worry, to how unsettled things were, to missing Dari. The dreams always had Dari in them, and although they were innocent enough – merely talking together as she told him of their journey to Cave, of Shaeli's quest, of what little she knew of the time the old Queen Irinesta had left the heir on Purple Leaf – there was some dark feeling about them, as if they were speaking secrets that were listened to by a malevolent ear.

In the dreams they were in the grounds at Great Court, sometimes sitting beside the well in the inner courtyard, the towers overlooking them; other times they walked in the gardens, but the flowers and trees were all dead and thick cloud covered the sky. It was always night, and always the wind blew about them, tugging at their hair and clothes. Yet she was with Dari and his hands were warm, his eyes the same, and she was so pleased to see him that the setting was irrelevant. She would ignore the oppressive feeling of the dream, the feeling of eyes watching, the incessant wind pulling at her hair, and she would smile at her youngest son and hold his hand and tell him what news she could; he was always so interested in her life. It was so gratifying to be close to him when he was so far away.

And yet, when she woke from the dreams her skin crawled and she felt as if she had escaped from some horror. As if the happy dream of being with Dari was really a nightmare.

***

CHAPTER TWENTY THREE

As the World faded behind them, Shaeli and Flin pulled their stones out. They waited until the entrance was a small triangle far behind them before they threw light into the tunnel, yet not before everyone had turned and said a silent farewell to the sun.

They threw their lights up and in front, creating round light balls that hovered overhead, and as they walked beneath them, Flin or Shaeli would throw another one or two ahead, the light balls blossoming like round lamps, the orbs hanging in the air and fading behind them so there were always three or four above their heads. It would be almost the only light they would see while they travelled beneath the mountain. Almost.

The floor of the tunnel was not sandy, as it was at Cave, but hard and smooth like the path back to the dragon pool. It narrowed a little as they went on, losing the little triangle of sun when they rounded a bend, and they began to see the ceiling of the tunnel above the light balls. Their footfalls echoed in the dark, and here and there, water dripped from above or slid down the walls.

They rounded another bend and Shaeli felt her nostrils prickle. She walked near the front with Flin, Williver and Ishaan. Behind came Kirrit, Cheval and Llianas, the others just behind them.

"What's that smell?" said Kirrit. "It smells like... like the Marshes." She did not sound at all happy.

"'Tis the scent of dragons," said Ishaan. "You may want to tie something around your faces. It is not the most pleasant of smells."

"Why didn't someone *mention* that dragons smell?" said Kirrit.

"My apologies, Kirrit," laughed Williver. "I did not think to warn you. Just be thankful there are no bats, for their stench is much worse than dragon. And very old dragon, at that. The smell has faded much with the years."

"Well, I hope I never go into a bat cave," said Kirrit, tying a kerchief around her nose. "Poisoned Marshes and old dragon lairs are quite enough for me."

The smell had grown stronger and they all pulled out something to tie around their faces. Even after a century, the smell was overpowering.

"We're almost there," said Ishaan. His voice was low, as if there were a need to whisper in this dark, empty place.

The tunnel curved again and they all felt the walls disappear from either side of them. The sense of space was vast, and only those of the Fleet knew what it felt like, for they had felt it during their Cave year, before Almarnoch and the Warlocks had sent their tiny lights spinning through Cave. Only they knew the enormity of the cave they were in. Thinking of Almarnoch's lights gave Shaeli an idea and she whispered to Flin.

When they stood beneath the last light ball, they both fired up, high into the air, bursting the skylight into a hundred pieces, sending them spinning out to the walls and the ceiling. Each tiny light clung to the rock of the dragon's lair, illuminating it instantly. The space opened around them, the heavy shadows gathered in corners, but in the few hundred lights sent out by Flin and Shaeli, a thousand flames flickered.

The floor was dark, the same smoothly polished rock as the tunnel, and there was little upon it, no small bones, no piled rocks. There was only one pile of bones, identical to the one they had passed through beside the dragon pool, its head angled crookedly, as if its neck had broken, its huge tail stretched across the floor.

The lair of the dragons was a vast space, empty of anything but them and the bones of the dragon, but the walls were filled with holes. Dozens, scores of pockets were hollowed into the dark rock on every side, layer upon layer of them, almost to the roof. The cave walls were peppered with the dark holes, the shadowed pockets, each hole huge, and each glittering with reflected light; light from the faces of a million gemstones. Each hole glittered with gems, the facets glowing with soft colour, as if there were the beginnings of rainbows nestled within them. In a few of the dark pockets, the white bones of dragons lay in lumpy piles.

"This is the lair of the dragons," said Williver, pulling down his mask, his arm sweeping across the sight. "This is where they once slept. This is why we protect the cave from the World."

His voice was hushed with reverence and they could see why. The gemstones in each nook glittered brilliantly, the backdrop of shadow making them shine even more brightly.

"Each dragon had its own niche," said Ishaan. "Younger dragons at the bottom, the older ones higher up."

"A dragon spends its life in search of shiny things for its bed," said Williver. "They are great miners, as well as great hunters. No one knows how they polish the gems, but they do, and they line their nests with them."

"There must be thousands of stones in this cave," said Spotjaw. The lair had finally broken Spotjaw's calm veneer. He had been mostly unimpressed by the things they had seen on their journey, but this cave had his mouth hanging open like a boy at his first fair.

"Millions, I'd wager," said Tarkoda.

"You'd win that wager, lad," smiled Ishaan. "Even the young dragons have a healthy hoard. Come and see."

They walked across to the nearest hole. Its base was at Blenny's eye level, and he had to stand on his toes to see in.

Gems lay scattered in a depression in the rock. Most were tiny, but here and there lay a fist-sized gem, the largest in the centre of the nest. The stones lay in a rough circle, sparkling in the lights thrown by Flin and Shaeli.

"How do you know these were the young dragons?" asked Shaeli.

"Because the higher up you go, the larger the nest," said Williver. "The more gems and the larger the nest, the older the dragon. The nests at the top are thick with stones."

"I can see why this place needs your protection," said Blenny. "Many are the people of the World who would covet what lies in here."

"That is true, though not many try," said Williver. "At least, not any more." He smiled wryly. "There was a time, a decade or so after the dragons disappeared, that many tried, but they were... discouraged. Legend now keeps most away, but every now and then, some still try."

"The skylights are fading," said Flin. "Shall we throw some more?"

"No need," said Williver, donning his mask again. "You have seen it, and our path lies across the cave."

"And away from this smell," said Kirrit.

"Yes," said Williver, and they could see him smiling beneath his mask. "Away from the smell."

They walked across the smooth floor, their footfalls echoing, their voices seeming far too loud even though they spoke in low tones. On the other side of the lair another tunnel led further into the mountain, but they stopped at its entrance to watch the skylights fade from the dragon's home. One by one the lights went out, and with each light, some of the glittering reflections from the dragons' nests also went out. The nests became first black holes, then part of the great creeping shadow that reclaimed the cave.

Before the last lights went out, Flin and Shaeli threw their light balls into the tunnel. They turned away from the lair and went deeper into the mountain. This tunnel was the same as the first, wide and smooth, and as it went on, Tarkoda tested the air.

"It's not so bad, now," he said at last. "Musty, but not so dragony."

They took off their masks, and followed the tunnel until they reached a fork. To the right, the wide, smooth tunnel went on. To the left, the tunnel was smaller. A dank smell came from it.

Williver stopped. "Our way lies down there," he said, pointing to the left, as Shaeli had known he would.

"Where does the other way lead?" she asked, looking wistfully at the wide smooth tunnel that continued to their right.

"To the dragon's mine," he said.

"Is it far?" asked Tarkoda. "I'd like to see it."

"There are no gems left," smiled Ishaan. "Whatever was mined there is long gone. Only a cavern and mostly dead-end tunnels remain. One tunnel leads back out to the mountainside, high up in the peaks, but there is not much else there."

"Still," said Tarkoda. "I'd like to see it, if it's not far."

"There is something else there," said Williver. "In the old mine. We may look, it is not far, but you should know, the bones of another dragon lie there."

He led them down the tunnel, and soon they came to another cavern. Shaeli and Flin threw lights as they had in the lair, and they were in a cave much smaller than the first. A dozen tunnels led from it and there were a few rock piles scattered around. In the centre was a skeleton like those by the pool outside and back in the lair. Its teeth were bared at them as they came from the tunnel, the bones of its tail curved around to point at them also, the ribs standing between like sentinels.

Shaeli shivered. "Why is it here?" she whispered.

"We don't know," said Williver. "It died at the same time as the others, this we know. We thought perhaps it was protecting something, but we have searched these tunnels many times and found nothing."

"It may have been wounded and come here to die," said Flin.

"We think that is most likely," agreed Ishaan. "For nothing has ever been found here, not even a forgotten gemstone."

They began to roam about, Spotjaw and Tarkoda exclaiming over broken rocks covered in claw-marks. Blenny and Wendll talked knowledgably about the tunnels and the veins the dragons had followed. Olando asked Flin to fire a skylight down a few of the tunnels and they all went over to look, but there was nothing to see, an empty tunnel much like the one they had left.

Shaeli was wandering back to the main tunnel with Kirrit and Williver, Ebony on her shoulder, when it happened. She felt suddenly light-headed, and stopped, putting a hand to her eyes.

"Are you alright, Shaeli?" she heard Kirrit say, but her voice seemed to come from far away, as if she was down one of the tunnels.

When she took her hand from her eyes, the World had changed, and if it had not happened to her before, she would have been very afraid.

The walls of the cave had faded, the skylights too. Ishaan, Koda and the others were looking at her, but they were soft imitations of their former selves, their clothes colourless, their hair, eyes, skin, all non-descript and vague. The rocks seemed insubstantial, as if they were merely pictures floating on air and, if she tried, she would be able to put her hand right through one. Almost everything in the cave had taken on a pale, washed-out, *watercolour* look. Only one thing seemed solid. Only one thing was painted in bright strokes, in *oils*. The skeleton of the dragon.

Every bone was etched in fine detail, each tooth blinding in its whiteness. She could see each tail bone precisely, each indentation, each whorl. And there was something else. Beneath the great white arch of the rib cage lay a mound of bones, and though, when she'd looked before, she hadn't been able to make them out, it was now clear to her that it was the clutching remains of the dragon's arm and the bones of its massive wing which had been curved protectively across its chest. And beneath the mound of bones lay something that cast white-hot rays of light into the pale cave, the way the sun casts light-shafts between thick cloud. She could not see the source, as one cannot see the sun behind the cloud, but she knew the source of this white fire was there, blindingly bright, buried beneath the blanket of bones.

She looked at Williver. He was a soft, watery image, and she sensed, more than heard what he said.

What is it? What's the matter?

She shook her head, tried to raise an arm, to point at the blinding light tearing through gaps between the bones; to say, *there's something there, can't you* see?, but she could not speak, could only turn back to gaze at the bones of the dragon. She sensed the others gather nearby, felt their questions, but her eyes did not leave the long-dead dragon.

The light-rays streaming from the mound of bones began to pulse. She could feel them lighting her face as they throbbed and she squinted against that white-hot light. The moment seemed to stretch, everything around her moved slowly; everything but the pulsing of the light. Faster and faster the light beneath the bones throbbed, and then with one final, blinding flash, it stopped.

After a moment, everything shimmered before her eyes and the World shifted back to its usual colours. The rock walls and piled boulders lost their see-through look, the faces of her companions returned to their solid selves.

Her knees wobbled, threatened to buckle, but she wouldn't let them, and they began to steady themselves. Suddenly she could hear the others talking around her, asking what was happening, what was going on, what was the matter with Shaeli? But she took no notice of them. She looked at Williver.

"There's something there," she said, her voice a croak, her pointing finger wobbling. "In the bones."

She could say no more, but Williver followed her as she walked clumsily over to the dragon. Her legs felt stiff, knotted at the knees, but her eyes were fixed on the spot where she had seen the pulsing light.

She took Ebony from her shoulder and handed her to Kirrit. She walked between the enormous skull and the curved tail until the mound of bones lay at her feet and the arch of ribcage towered overhead. She felt none of the fear of the skeleton that she had before. She felt as she did when walking with Williver in the dreamworld, as if nothing could hurt her.

She knelt and pushed an arm in through a gap. She felt about, pushed in further, unmindful of the bones now pressed against her cheek. She stretched her fingers out and they brushed against bone, cold and smooth, and then against something colder, smoother, and she pushed in more until her fingers wrapped around it, something hard and cold and bigger than her fist, but when she tried to pull it out, to bring her arm back through the gap, she couldn't do it, not without letting go.

"I'm stuck, Williver," she said, her voice still a croak. "Help me. Move the bones."

"What is it, Shaeli?" he said. "I'll pull you." He grabbed her arm.

"*No*," she said. "I'll have to drop it. Move the bones."

"Drop what?" he said. "What happened to you?"

"Later," she said. "I'll tell you later. Just move the bones so I can pull it out."

He asked no more questions, and he and the others shifted bones over Shaeli's head.

"Why don't you just let it go?" said Tarkoda. "Whatever it is."

"No," she cried again. "Just get me free."

So they lifted bones away, passing them over to Ishaan and Spotjaw who stacked them in another pile.

"That's it," she said. "I'm almost... there." She pulled, and her arm and the thing in her hand came free, and she fell backwards. Her hand and the thing thunked into her chest, and she sat up and looked at what she held.

She heard Cheval gasp behind her, Kirrit and Llianas both made strange gulping noises. Some of the others called to the gods. She looked up at Williver, her eyes round and huge. Williver looked from her eyes to her hand and back again.

"How did you *know*?" he said. "How *could* you know it was there?"

He leant over, took her arm, and helped her to her feet. His eyes never left her face. Shaeli had never seen them so blue.

They both looked at the thing in her hand. Ishaan came closer. The others gathered around. There were more gasps and naming of the gods as they looked at it. Shaeli's hand seemed very small beneath it.

The huge gem shimmered in the fading skylights, its facets mirroring their faces, rainbows dancing in its depths. It was double-ended, each thick end coming to a sharp point. It was clear, criss-crossed inside with lines of fairy-hair, yet one could see every colour glimmering in the heart of the stone. The white shadows of Shaeli's fingers beneath the stone had rainbows shimmering at their edges. It was weighty in her hand, and she knew with unwavering certainty what it was. She had seen the place where it had once rested many, many times.

She looked back up at Williver.

"How did you know?" he said, again. "How did you *know*?"

* * *

Above them, in almost every one of the dragon's nests, a gemstone began to glow, softly at first, and then more brightly.

* * *

Later, Shaeli told them about the time she had seen the colours of the World shift; of the strange fugue state which had come upon her at the Autumn's Eve Hunt.

They had left the cave of the dragon bones and returned to the place where the smaller tunnel forked away. The others sat clustered around her as she told them of the watchers, and how she had realised the queen was destroying Zirrus, piece by piece.

"I thought it was some leftover from your dream," she said, looking at Williver. "Some strange window into the dreamworld." She swallowed and looked down at the stone she held in trembling hands. "I guess that's not right."

"No," said Williver. "I don't think so, either." He shook his head. "I have no explanation."

"I think I may have one," said Blenny, and they all looked at him, surprised. He had sat quietly, stuffing his pipe as Shaeli spoke. He lit it and drew deeply before he went on. "What Shaeli describes, the fading of the world around her, the brightness of certain people or objects, this is what happens when one looks into the smoke, when futures are told and messages given. It seems Shaeli has a touch of drell magic in her, so she does, and the gods have sent her a great prize."

"Drell magic?" said Shaeli. "But how could I do that? I can't do what you do, Blenny. I can't see the future."

"Maybe ye can lass, and ye just didn't know it," he said. "It starts like that, so it does, random, and there is a lot of training to be done before one can see into the smoke at will, to see past reality to those things which have not yet happened."

"Like training for your skylights," said Wendll. "I'd wager you didn't learn to throw overnight. It takes many Winterings to master the visions in the smoke, and then to interpret what is seen."

"What *did* it mean when I saw all those men watching for each other at the Hunt, then?" she asked.

"I'd say those men will see each other face to face in Winterings to come," Blenny answered. "The atmosphere must have been highly-charged by them, and you must have tapped in on that energy. Realising what was happening in the Land was just another facet of the vision. There are often several messages. When I saw you in the smoke in Trilby, the visions I had were for other people, but involved you."

"I heard a man yell, too, in that vision. He stood near us at the Hunt," she said, remembering the big, bearded man. "It was a terrible yell, but like something still inside him, a yell he hadn't used yet."

"So a little bit of his future was mixed up in it, too," nodded Blenny. "Visions are like that."

Shaeli frowned. "When I went looking for Nol's family, at Orellis after the twins' barrel ride, it happened then too. Just a little bit. The locket showed me the way. I remember the colours were bright then too."

"Aye," said Blenny. "That was another thing you needed knowledge of, and it was given."

"But this time it wasn't a vision of the future," she said.

"Aye, lass," said Blenny. "But it was still something you needed to know, so it was, and mayhap there's something ahead we don't yet know."

"So *why* do I have them?" she asked. "Why do they come?"

Blenny shrugged. "Without training they are as random as summer storms," he said. "And they come as do your other gifts, from the gods. But do not deny or fear them, they do not come without reason." He pointed with his pipe at what she held in her hand. "As you see."

She looked down at the stone, still unable to believe she held it. In the hovering light of the orbs the stone shivered. It was impossibly clear, its depths crossed with fine lines, the "fairy hair" like those in Shaeli's smoky quartz, each patterned with minute rainbows as she moved it in the light. It covered her palm, its points almost reaching her fingertips on one end and tapering over her wrist on the other. Its pointed ends and the edges of its facets were unmarked, not even the smallest chip damaged their perfect lines. The stone lay heavy in her hand and she could feel the power running within it as strongly as she felt the weight of responsibility *for* it laying heavily upon her heart. She wondered if they knew.

She looked up at the faces around her, all of them eager and concerned at once.

"You know what it is, don't you?" she said, her voice cracking. "It's hers. It's... it's Shahlita's."

Williver and Ishaan were the only ones who did not register an element of surprise, and she clung to that. At least they already understood the magnitude of her find.

"It... I mean, the dragon," she said, the words coming in broken pieces. "It must have been trying to protect the stone. Keep it from whoever wanted it. It must have... must have had it clutched under it, so they couldn't reach it."

No one spoke. The silence in the cave was broken only by the sound of their breathing, until the dry voice of Spotjaw snapped the silence as sharply as if he had snapped a twig.

"Swallowed it, I'd say," said Spotjaw. "From the look of where she pulled it out, right under those ribs. Stands to reason," he said, looking back up the dark tunnel. "It ate it."

They were quiet again as they thought of the dragon, cornered and fighting for its life, putting the stone where it could not be retrieved – at least not for a very long time.

Kirrit shuddered. "I thought you said that cave had been searched," she said.

"It had been," said Williver. "How this was missed, I know not. Perhaps the searchers were somewhat wary about disturbing the bones. But it was waiting for Shaeli, that much is certain."

Shaeli smiled at him, a weak, trembling smile.

"'Tis also certain the day passes outside," he continued. "We should move on, if you're able."

"I'm fine," she said. "I'm just wobbly at the knees with amazement, that's all. Thunderstruck, my Da would say."

"We should probably eat something while we're stopped," said Cheval.

"My stomach agrees," said Olando.

As they pulled supplies from bags, Shaeli found a cloth to wrap the stone in. She took a long look at it before she rolled it up and pushed it far down into a corner of her pack beside the dragon scale bangle. It would not have fit into her amulet even if she'd wanted it to, and she didn't want it to. It wasn't hers.

Ebony was watching with interest as a scant meal was pulled from packs. They had been well supplied by the elves of Lythnori with dried fruits and meats, tezz, smoked cheeses and fish, and hard, thin cakes of bread, but they ate sparingly; there would be no more supplies. They each carried two or three water bottles and a small wine-skin courtesy of Ky and Jocovar, and all but the Ammerr drank sparingly. Ebony chewed on some fruit, and then she dashed over to Tarkoda, who had a supply of nuts to tempt her with, given him by the guards at the grey fortress in the valley below. When they had eaten, they shouldered their packs and gathered at the entrance of the other tunnel.

Though smaller, this tunnel was still broad, broad enough, as Spotjaw said, to run their wagon through and then some, and the floor was softer, a thin sandy layer covering the dark rock. Its smell was dank and musty, but not enormously unpleasant, and they soon became used to it.

Despite its size, the tunnel would have been a tight fit for a dragon, and after a short distance it was clear the dragons had not used it. Ancient rock falls were piled here and there, reducing the path to a size impossible for a dragon to have passed through. Several times they had to go single file around a pile of dark rocks, and once they had to step over a wide crack that appeared running diagonally across the passage. For a long time the tunnel was level, and then it began to fall away, slowly at first, until it was obvious they were going downhill. The rock falls were less on this downhill stretch, but the walls began to drip more consistently, and it grew colder. They walked on and on, past black, lesser tunnels, round sweeping bends and long straights, ever downwards, and when the tunnel floor levelled out again, they felt they had been beneath the mountain for days. When the tunnel forked, they gladly stopped.

To their left the tunnel ran straight and level, directly ahead was a thinner tunnel, wide enough only to walk two abreast, and to the right a third tunnel fell steeply away. Again Shaeli instinctively knew this was their route.

Beside the third tunnel flowered a great symbol, and Shaeli knew she had been right. She had seen this symbol before. It was on the wall, far at the back of Cave beside the entrance to the cave of the Zoi.

* * *

Williver surprised her when he led them down the higher, left-hand tunnel, yet the surprise was short-lived, killed by the appearance of a small room. It lay at the tunnel's end, a thick door rusted open at its entrance. Inside, a dozen benches studded the walls. A table was hewn out of the rock in the centre, and a fire-pit had been gouged out of the floor on one side, a small stack of rocks beside it. Opposite, a bowl had been cut into the wall beneath a steady drip, and it was brimful with fresh water.

"All the comforts of home," said Ishaan.

"Almost," smiled Williver. "We'll spend the night here, and go on tomorrow."

"What's 'the night' anyway?" asked Kirrit. "How would we know down here?"

"We'll just have to guess at it, lass," said Blenny.

"And at least we can have a fire," said Cheval. "That's something."

"Lucky there's some fire-stones here," said Tarkoda.

"Luck has nothing to do with it," said Williver. "Ishaan and I carried them up here, a few at a time. Several times we have spent the night here, exploring the tunnels."

"'Tis a fair-sized tunnel," said Wendll.

"Aye," said Spotjaw, pulling a slab of bacon from his pack. "Room enough to turn a wagon, right outside this door." He tested a knife on his thumb. "What's below? Down that steep tunnel we'll be tackling in the morning?"

Shaeli grinned at him as he began to cut the bacon into strips. He knew where they were going as well as she did.

"We have not ventured far," said Ishaan. "Another room, similar to this lies below, what I guess would be just over half a day's journey. We will rest there again. Beyond that..." He shrugged. "We know not, only that the symbol you saw out there is repeated below, and repeated again in the Cave of the Traders."

"'Tis our hope that further symbols mark the path," said Williver. "So we may easily find our way."

"I think we all hope that, lad, so we do," said Blenny. He had been busy laying some of the fire-stones in the pit. "But we shall take it one step at a time. The first step is lighting this fire and cooking some of that bacon, isn't it, Spot?"

"You speak a true word," said Spotjaw.

"I'll light those fire-rocks," said Flin.

"My thanks," said Spotjaw, pulling a flat frying pan from his pack. "If someone will just toast that hard bread, we'll be eating quicker than you can say 'sleeping underground'."

"I'll do it," volunteered Llianas. "If you brush it with a bit of water first it softens it."

"Couldn't make it much harder, lass," said Spotjaw. "Like a slab of rock, that bread."

"Elven bread like this will last for several Winterings," laughed Llianas. Her voice was low, her laugh a soft chuckle. "Wait until I show you the sweetbread pudding it makes, you won't think it like rock."

"I'll look forward to it, lass," said Spotjaw.

"I'll fill the water bottles," said Motin. "I need a drink. A long one." He looked as if he did. His dark hair was hanging limply on his forehead and neck, and he was panting as if he'd just run a long distance.

He went to the bowl that had been gouged out of the rock wall. It was a shallow basin, full of cold water, fed by a thin rivulet which seeped from the wall. After Motin had filled a few of the bottles, he upended one on himself, pouring the whole icy bottle over his head, wetting his cloak and shirt beneath it. The others looked at him, eyebrows raised, and he looked back sheepishly.

"I could not help myself," he said. "The need to be wet was too strong."

"Before we leave tomorrow, we shall be able to douse ourselves," said Ishaan. "*After* the water bottles have been filled, we may drain the pool and leave it to the long task of refilling."

"Yes, Ishaan," said Motin, still looking a little embarrassed, but definitely the better for his dousing.

They ate the bacon, and the bread, which, after also being given its own dousing, became softer, as Llianas had said it would, and toasted nicely. Then they found somewhere to lie down and rolled themselves in their cloaks. As the last light ball was fading away, Shaeli spoke.

"Williver," she said, her voice as soft as the fading light. "Do you... do you think it was Wipp? Do you think it was Shahlita's dragon who swallowed the stone?"

"I don't know, little one," he said. "But it seems to me that Wipp would have done such a thing, to protect her and the wand."

Shaeli nodded at the fading light and rolled over. It was as she thought.

* * *

Williver woke them. They had no idea how long they had slept, but both Williver and Llianas vowed it was somewhere near sunrise, and they ate a hasty meal and went back to where the tunnel went further down into the mountain.

They had decided to take the rest of the fire-rocks with them. There were not many, enough for only a few fires, but Olando and Motin both had fine, strong nets with them, and it was no trouble to load one with the rocks. They were light enough and the few hot meals they would provide would more than outweigh the trouble it took to transport them, and there were many hands to help with the carrying. They left enough for one fire in the little room beneath the dragon's lair, in case they had need of it, should they have to return this way.

They stopped to look at the symbol carved into the wall beside the tunnel mouth. To Kirrit, Tarkoda, and Shaeli, it was familiar, like a star-burst surrounded by strange writings, but even with every race there to see it, none could decipher the writing, yet they did not linger and followed the tunnel down further into the belly of the mountain. Water dripped from the roof and walls, and here and there they encountered strange insects, beetles and centipedes of unusual size that skittered away from the light.

Later, they came to the other room Ishaan had spoken of. They stopped there only long enough to eat, and then they went on. Soon they came to another branch. Two tunnels led off to the left, and the main tunnel went on. Beside it was the symbol.

"This is as far as Ishaan and I have been down this tunnel," said Williver. "The tunnels to the left lead back to the surface, these we have followed, but the symbol leads down."

"That is our way, then," said Blenny.

"It would appear so," said Flin. "No point waiting. Let's go."

He threw four lights in quick succession, and the dark tunnel lit up. He held out an arm to Shaeli.

"Shall we?" he smiled, and she laughed and took his arm.

They went down for a long time and then the floor levelled out. Shaeli and Flin took turns throwing orbs to light their way. The rock-falls they had passed above had petered out and finally stopped altogether, and Blenny seemed to think the falls higher up had been due to the tunnelling of the dragons nearby, but down this deep, the tunnel was as perfect as when it had been created. Much of the tunnel was probably made, he said, by some underground watercourse that had dried out, or been diverted elsewhere eons before. It was obvious some race had used it as a pathway, in a past too distant for memory.

On they walked, and when they were all weary and the Ammerr were dragging their feet, they came to another room carved in the tunnel wall. There was no door, only the same table of rock in the centre, and a fire-pit carved into the floor, but the Ammerr were overjoyed to find a long trough of water. The seepage had filled it to overflowing, and the floor around it was damp where the overflow drained further into the mountain's roots.

They did not bother to light fire-rocks, they were too tired. They ate something, warmed their bellies with the richness held within the wine-skins, the Ammerr doused themselves, and they slept until Williver woke them again.

They passed another day in this way, walking beneath the mountain, finding a room carved in the rock when they were on the brink of exhaustion. The Ammerr in particular, despite regular dousing, were feeling the need for proper immersion, for even the long trough had not been big enough for them to cover themselves completely. They lit another fire the third night, and Llianas cooked a meal of the hard bread flavoured with berry preserves in Spotjaw's pan, surprising them all with the soft, sweet delicacy.

The next day they went on. The tunnel went uphill on a gentle slope, and then levelled, and they walked on even ground. Kirrit noticed it first, not long after they'd stopped to eat.

"Oh, the gods," she said. "What is that smell?"

"It smells like, I'm sorry to say this, Kirrit," said Williver. "But it smells suspiciously like bat."

Kirrit groaned. "Typical," she said, pulling a kerchief out of her pack. "It's been one stench after another on this journey."

As they went on, the smell became worse, and they all tied something around their noses. The beetles that ran away from the lights became more numerous, the centipedes longer and fatter. The path took a steep, uphill slant, and when the smell had become almost unbearable, Llianas spoke.

"Does that look like daylight up ahead?" she said. "Up past that last orb."

At first they could see nothing, but gradually it did seem as if there was daylight ahead, weak, but there. Flin and Shaeli stopped throwing lights, and they found they were in a dull gloom, a deep, thick dusk, but they could see. They hurried towards the source of the light, the beetles and centipedes growing more numerous and impossible to miss, squashed beneath their eager feet as they came closer to the source. Suddenly the tunnel opened up either side of them and they were in a cave, not nearly as large as the dragon cave but still big, and it was very high, the upper reaches soaring above, and the light source came from somewhere over their heads. Their faces turned as one to the light, and there, far above, a thin beam of sunlight shone into the highest point of the cave. They could not see the sky, but that thin shaft of far-off light lifted their spirits, but the smell here was revolting, and though the glimpse of the world outside had pleased their hearts, their nostrils were not nearly so grateful.

"Which way do we go from here?" asked Cheval.

"I'm not sure," said Ishaan.

"I think the tunnel continues on over there," said Williver, pointing to the right.

"Let's have a bit more light then, shall we," said Flin, and he threw a few beams.

"*No*, Flin," said Williver, but it was too late.

As Flin fired, the walls of the cave began to move. Pieces of wall, tiny pieces, hundreds of them, started to fall, yet they did not hit the ground. They darted, screeching around the cave.

"Run," yelled Tarkoda.

They ran across a floor that was uneven and slippery all at the same time. Thousands of beetles and centipedes and roaches scurried under their boots, their bodies making ugly crunching noises as they were splattered beneath thudding feet. The smell their feet kicked up was almost unbearable, gaggingly gross, but they kept running towards the light Flin had thrown, seeing the dark mouth of the tunnel beyond the hanging orb. All the time the cave walls darted at them, screeching and clawing.

The tiny bats had been woken by Flin's sudden light. This was their home, the distant shaft of sunlight their door, and there were intruders in their midst. Hundreds of the creatures flew at them, tiny teeth and claws bared. Shaeli pulled Ebony from her shoulder and tucked her inside her shirt just as a bat flew at her head. It tangled in her hair and she swiped at it as she ran, throwing it off but not before it had scratched her head. She heard the others yelling as they pelted across the disgusting floor, then she heard a cry for help behind her and she looked back.

The four Ammerr stumbled behind the others, Ishaan and Olando helping Cheval, Motin staggering after them. Bats circled their heads, darting at them, and she ran back, firing at the cloud of black bats swirling around the heads of the Ammerr and dozens of the creatures fell into the guano, but scores more replaced them. Tarkoda and Williver were there before her, Spotjaw and Flin on her heels. A bat flew in her face

and when she could see again she saw Koda had scooped up
Cheval and was carrying her. He darted past Shaeli, Cheval
bumping in his arms, her face pressed against his shoulder.
She reached Olando, taking one arm as Flin took the other.
Williver had his arm under Ishaan's shoulders, Spotjaw was
dragging at Motin; all four Ammerr were gasping for breath
and waving free arms at the swarming bats.

They staggered towards the darkness of the tunnel, the
bats swooping and scratching at them, tearing at their hair,
their faces, their hands, the light of the skylights pushing the
darting creatures to madness. Shaeli dragged at Olando,
willing him towards the tunnel, seeing its darkness as safety,
its shadow as sanctuary.

But the bats loved darkness and it seemed Flin understood
this, for he threw the brightest of lights into the tunnel.
Llianas, Kirrit, and the drell flew before them into the tunnel
beneath the lights Flin threw as he ran, one arm around
Olando, the other outstretched. Shaeli threw lights behind her
until the tunnel around them was ablaze. The bats scattered
and Flin and Shaeli kept throwing as they ran, tossing ball
after ball into the wide tunnel that opened before them.
Llianas, Kirrit, Wendll and Blenny tumbled through the tunnel
in front, carrying the last of the fire-rocks between them.
Williver, Flin, Shaeli, Spotjaw and Tarkoda ran behind,
dragging the Ammerr. Gradually, the assault of the bats
receded, and they stumbled their way on, away from the
grasping, scratching, darting flight of the bats. On they
stumbled, and on, down the tunnel, uphill, level, and then
down again, and they kept going, pulling the Ammerr along
with them long after the bats had stopped flying at their heads.
Their pace slowed, they jogged into the lights Flin kept
throwing into the tunnel, and then Llianas ran into a carved
room, the door miraculously whole except for a dark square at
the top. They followed Llianas inside and pushed the door shut
behind them.

One by one their breathing slowed, their hearts returned to normal pace, and they began to laugh with relief. The bats had given them all scratches, scared them silly, but they had done little real damage. Compared to the queen's fleet, the black ship, or the Poisoned Marshes, the bats were less than nothing, a minor hiccup, at worst the most horrible stench they had encountered, and even that had been left behind, the guano dropping away from their running feet. They began to giggle as the door closed behind them, the silence and weariness pushing them all to hysteria. The laughing passed and the weariness took over. They rolled themselves in their cloaks where they fell, away from the running, the tunnel, and the bats.

* * *

Later, as Shaeli slept, her dreams were plagued by things that swooped and nibbled and sucked. She woke with Kirrit's cries in her ears.

"Help, someone," Kirrit was crying, her voice as small as a child's. "It's drinking me."

Shaeli felt groggy. Her ankle hurt and she was very tired. She was almost asleep again when she heard Llianas calling Tarkoda, Williver, Ishaan, somebody, *anybody*. Her voice was indistinct, but high and insistent. After a moment she heard her brother reply, but she could not make out what he said; his voice was muffled, distant.

Ebony cowered beneath her armpit, and she thought it strange, because Ebony liked to sleep beside her, not tucked tight beneath her armpit, shivering. Shaeli opened her eyes but struggled to find awareness, hearing first Koda, and then Blenny and Williver calling, their voices like echoes. Llianas' voice still called insistently. Shaeli's eyes almost focussed on Flin's last skylight, a pale indistinct yellow ball hovering against the rocky ceiling. She felt strange, and her ankle hurt. She looked down and saw a tiny, fuzzy shape. Her eyes stumbled their way to Kirrit and Cheval.

Kirrit had a fuzzy shape at her wrist, Cheval one at her throat. Both fuzzy shapes were suckling madly. Both Kirrit and Cheval were far from awake.

"Get it off," cried Kirrit, her voice weak, sleepy.

"Bats," she heard her brother say. "It's the bats."

Shaeli found her hand in her amulet. Ebony jittered beneath her arm as she pulled out a stone, she didn't know which one, and fired at the ceiling. Bright white light blossomed in the darkness and she heard a screeching, felt a flutter beside her face as the door grew bright in her vision. Black shapes fluttered at it and through it, dozens of them. She watched in groggy fascination as the black shapes bumped through the hole in the door, and at the edge of the grogginess she heard the others were muttering, then calling to her. Williver rose in front of her, and she sat up, sleep still clawing at her.

She shook her head, her sight cleared, and the hurt in her ankle was real, the blood seeping down onto her boot, bright red in the light she had thrown. Her head hurt too, and when she touched the place her fingers came away bloody. Blenny stumbled over to her, blood seeping from a wound on his temple. Spotjaw swayed over his shoulder and Koda was staggering across the room. Behind them Llianas stood shaking against the wall, her dark eyes horrified pools.

"More light, Shaeli," Williver panted. "More light."

She threw again as Tarkoda pushed his pack into the open space in the top of the door. In the brightening light, she saw three shapes still fluttered in the room, crimson patches marking their faces. Williver hit one with an arrow clenched in his fist and Koda killed the others with a stone from his sling. When they were dead, their bodies still twitching on the floor, they found that Kirrit, Wendll, Cheval, Flin, Motin and Olando had slept through the assault. Ishaan swayed where he stood, his eyes blinking slowly as if the lids were very heavy. Shaeli pulled the jevvi from where she huddled beneath her shirt, crooning to her and checking for wounds, but Ebony was the only one unmarked by the bloodthirsty bats. Each of them, those standing and those still asleep, had at least two wounds, damp places where the bats had suckled, and they all felt groggy.

Williver guessed the bats secreted some kind of poison, a drug to keep their victim quiet while they feasted, and they shuddered at the thought. Shaeli had never heard of bats that drank blood, but Blenny had. There was a colony of them, high in the eastern Drell Mountains, he said.

Tarkoda picked up the bodies, took them out and threw them back up the tunnel, and they all felt better after the red-faced bodies were gone, the door shut again, Tarkoda's pack stuffed in the hole. Koda went over to where Llianas still stood shivering against the wall.

"I thank the gods you were here," he said, putting his arm around her and drawing her away from the wall. He looked at the others. "It was Llianas who woke me," he said. "I don't know what would have happened if she hadn't."

"The noise they made, it was in my dreams," Llianas whispered, shuddering. "And when I opened my eyes I could *feel* them on me." She shivered again, and clutched her cape more tightly about her. There was a bright wound on one of her wrists, another on her collarbone.

Williver thought it near the time they should be waking, and they decided to light some fire-rocks and brew some tezz. Ishaan fell asleep as it brewed, but they did not wake him, nor any of the others, thinking it best to let them sleep off the bats' drug, but they wiped their wounds and were pleased to see the bleeding stopped almost instantly. They drowsed in front of the thin flame, soaking up the warmth, and every now and then Shaeli threw another orb to hang above them, casting comfort with its light. It was a long time before the others woke. Each was told the tale, and each shivered with revulsion. Motin was the last to wake, his face pale behind his dark hair, and while he drank deeply, he ate little and spoke less. They cleaned their wounds again, and found they were small and easily dressed, though they itched terribly, and when they finally regained strength enough to pull on their packs and venture back to the tunnel, they saw the bodies of the three bats Tarkoda had thrown up the tunnel were now tiny skeletons, every bit of flesh removed from the bones. They shuddered, thinking of the oversized beetles that inhabited the tunnels, then they turned their backs on the bones and went on.

Down they went, round great bends and then uphill. They went slower, partly because the Ammerr were not capable, and partly because they were all tired, weary from the bats' poison and of being beneath the mountain. Finally the uphill battle stopped, ahead the tunnel went down, steeply down, but at the peak lay one of the small rooms. They fell into it, the Ammerr making straight for the water-trough in the corner. They lit the last of the fire-rocks, ate meagrely of their dwindling supplies, and slept.

* * *

When they woke, they felt better, the effects of the bats' poison almost gone, and they started down the steep incline. The tunnel forked again, and though the wide main tunnel continued on, they found the starburst symbol beside a smaller tunnel. They followed it down and round sharp corners, and it began to thin, to shrink around them, and still they were going down. At last, the floor levelled, but the tunnel remained small, barely room to go two abreast, and the skylights were so close above their heads that at times they could have reached out and touched them. Ahead the tunnel grew narrower still.

They stopped in a tiny triangle of space where three thin tunnels met. They had to hunt for the symbol on the walls, and at last they found it, small and faded, beside a tunnel that was no longer a tunnel, but a set of stairs, carved through the rock, leading upwards almost as steeply as a ladder. They ate something standing up, for there was not room to sit, and drank a little of the remaining wine as Shaeli and Flin discussed the best way to light the tunnel ahead, for the light orbs would not work in such a low space. Shaeli pulled out her finger of smoky quartz and threw up into the darkness, pulling at the beam so it shattered into hundreds of tiny pieces that clung to the walls, the low ceiling and the steps. It was the same way they'd lit the dragon's lair, but on a much smaller scale. They went in single-file, Williver and Flin first, Ishaan and Spotjaw bringing up the rear.

They were silent as they went up, feeling the weight of the mountain more than ever on these steep steps, the rock crowding them on every side. Up they went until the steps grew more level and then stopped altogether, but the tunnel grew no bigger and it began to wind this way and that, and then there were more steps, these going down as steeply as the others had gone up. In the light of the skylights they followed them down, and when they reached the bottom, the space around them opened, though the path beneath their feet did not grow wider.

Flin and Shaeli threw beams ahead, but instead of clinging to tunnel walls, the lights spun off around them, clinging to rocks far away. The path lay before them still, but on either side of it there was nothing; the path hung in emptiness, a bridge of rock over a dark canyon. On either side, across the emptiness, in pockets and crevices in the far-off edges of the canyon, were hundreds of stalactites and stalagmites of all sizes, minute to giant, all glittering in the light. Some of the skylights clung to them, the surfaces shining with milky rainbows. Far to one side there were minute caves, filled with the tiny points of crystals clustered tightly together, sparkling pockets of shimmering light, and nearby Blenny pointed out a thin vein of gold. Everywhere drops of water hung like tears, dripping into the unseen bottom of the canyon. Through the centre of this beautiful cavern ran their tunnel, now reduced to a thin bridge with nothing but darkness beneath.

They did not admire the spectacle for long. Flin threw orbs that hovered above the bridge like great lamps, until they could see the place where the bridge became tunnel once more. It was a long way ahead and Shaeli fixed her eyes to the spot, willing herself to stay calm. There were poles set into the rock bridge at irregular intervals, the remains of a thick chain hanging from them here and there, but most of the links were long since rusted to dust. She took a deep breath and followed Williver and Flin onto the bridge.

As the path fell away either side of her feet, she fixed her eyes ahead. She let her gaze flow over the wonders around her but she did not allow it downwards. She kept Ebony clutched in one hand and a firm grip on Flin's pack with the other. When they reached the other side, the tunnel pooled before continuing, and there was room for them all to sit and rest.

Llianas sat near where the bridge became tunnel again, and she called Williver over. They talked for a moment, and then Williver walked back out across the bridge a few paces. He stopped, stood motionless for a while, and came back.

"Did you hear it?" Llianas asked.

Williver nodded.

"Hear what?" asked Ishaan.

"Water," answered Llianas. "A small stream, I think."

"Where is it?" asked Motin, looking at the emptiness beneath the bridge. "Can we reach it?"

"No," said Williver, shaking his head. "I'm sorry, it is far beneath us. Llianas and I can barely hear it."

Motin sighed.

"It does not mean we will not encounter it further on, my friend," said Ishaan, pointing ahead. "See? The tunnel goes downhill again."

"Let us follow it, then," said Motin. "My head grows fuzzy with the lack of immersion."

The tunnel here was wider than the thin shaft they had left on the other side of the bridge, enough to walk two or three abreast, and the way was not steep but it wound about, and after a while they all heard the rustle of distant water. Eagerly they went ahead, the others almost as anxious as the Ammerr to find water, rushing around bend after bend as the sound grew louder and louder. Around the last bend they went, the sound loud enough to touch, sure there was a tumbling stream in their path, but when they reached the bend there was nothing but more tunnel beyond it; no water, no rushing stream. Only the sound of it was there, removed from them by a wall of rock, and although the wall was wet and the sound of it echoed in the tunnel, they could not reach through rock. Motin leant his face against the wall, but after a moment he turned stoically back to the tunnel, and they went wordlessly on.

Later, they slept in the tunnel and then they went on; how long they did not know, up and around and down. Twice they came to a fork, found the symbol and went on. A few times more they heard the rushing of the stream; the last time it seemed to be coming from somewhere above their heads. There were no more rooms to shelter in, and when they thought they would have to sleep in the tunnel again, the ground turned soft beneath their feet, and the tunnel ended abruptly.

They stepped out onto dark sand. Dark sand and vast, darker space. Flin and Shaeli threw light up and out.

They were on a crescent-shaped beach, the sand beneath their feet black and gritty. To their left huge rocks dotted the small beach, their shapes as crooked as huddled figures. To their right was a stream, the one they had heard through the rock, falling from high above into a lake of epic proportions, its surface a black mirror broken only by the thin stream. The lake stretched before them, studded here and there with black rock islands, and Flin threw more light out across the lake until the shoreline opposite became visible. They looked for the way round, for the path that would lead them around this enormous underground lake, but they could see nothing, no pathway, no symbol etched into rock.

No one noticed Motin slip the pack from his back. They only noticed when he was running at the water, running as if his legs were made of wood, but running, dropping his cloak as he went.

"Wait, Motin," yelled Ishaan.

But Motin did not stop. He ran at the water, and when he reached it, strange sparks flew from each splash of his foot, but he either did not notice or he disregarded it. When the blackness of the water reached his knees, he pushed himself off into a long shallow dive.

When his feet first hit the water, Shaeli saw the water flicker off to her right, as if a lamp had gone on and off beneath the black mirror. As Motin pushed off into his dive, a shriek shattered the silence in the cavern. Llianas screamed.

"What was that?" cried Kirrit.

The water closed around Motin. Lines of light flashed beneath the surface, light that moved and shuddered. More lines of light began to appear across the dark water until the whole lake was flickering with scores of the pulsing, streaking lights. Each line of flickering light was headed towards them. Another shriek rang across the water. They could not tell from which direction it came.

Motin's head broke the surface with a scream. Around him the water flickered and boiled, long shapes moving through it. Motin screamed again, his body jerking strangely, his face bleeding from a line of puncture wounds, his arms flailing.

"*Motin*," screamed Cheval. She threw off her pack and ran to the water's edge.

Olando caught her with her toes in the water, dragging her back as Motin was dragged beneath the surface. A dark shape slid from the water and lunged at Olando, a line of light flickering along its body. He leapt back, dragging Cheval, and the creature merely brushed against his boot, yet he screamed in pain.

"They sting," he cried. "The lights sting."

The shriek echoed again, closer, but they did not have time to wonder at it. They drew weapons, raining arrows and rocks and lights around the spot where Motin had gone down. They could see him in the flicker of the lights beneath the water, a writhing, jerking shape surrounded by other long thin shapes. That he was still alive was barely possible.

Across the water the shriek came again and the lake's surface was broken by a huge shape, a shape that was bearing down on them with amazing speed, a massive stream of light flowing along its length as it came. They backed away from the water, Olando dragging a screaming Cheval as the shape ploughed through the water towards the still-struggling body of Motin. When it reached him it swept him up in a great, gaping mouth until his body was lifted from the water. Down the great head went, dragging Motin with it.

They had a brief moment to see his face and the terror in his eyes before he and the creature disappeared beneath the surface, their passing marked by a huge splash. Around the splash the smaller forms flickered, small weak screeches of protest coming from them, the water a frenzy as they fought over scraps. Yet the screeching and the flickering lines of light did not disappear with the body of Motin.

Along the shoreline the water kept flickering. Here and there a long shape pushed itself up the beach towards them, some as thick as a branch, some like tree trunks. Other bodies seemed to unravel endlessly from the black water; all had lines of white light skimming through their bodies, their heads ugly lumps, the mouths pushed forward with sharp, pointed teeth. The creatures seemed maddened by the light in their cavern and the smell of blood, pushing their way up through the black sand, sliding back into the water and surging forward once more.

They moved closer to the tunnel. The water foamed as the light-filled bodies pushed their way up the sand, pushing higher and higher in a frenzied effort to reach them, and then the huge shape that had taken Motin rose out of the water and turned towards them.

"Off the beach," yelled Williver, and they turned towards the tunnel.

Shaeli saw the long shape pick up speed before she began to run, saw the bright white light streak down its body. As the tunnel loomed, she saw a line of steps run off to the right.

"Steps, Koda," she yelled. "Up the steps."

Tarkoda was in front, helping Olando with a weeping Cheval. He looked at where she pointed and changed direction. He left Olando to help Cheval and bounded up the steps. At the top there was a flat rock and a black hole.

"Up here," he yelled. "Hurry." He pulled out his sling, scrabbled at his feet for stones, and began firing them down at the beach.

Olando dragged Cheval up and into the dark hole, Kirrit, Llianas and the drell behind them. Ishaan ran over to Tarkoda and began firing arrows down at the beach. Kirrit pulled her little cross-bow from her pack and joined them as the others leapt up the stairs. Williver threw with his wand. Spotjaw threw rocks.

Flin and Shaeli were last. Flin had Shaeli by the arm and was pushing her ahead of him when the creature hit the beach.

Shaeli heard the screams from above and the shriek from the creature blend together. She turned her head in time to see the body of the thing leap from the water and thrust itself towards them. Across the beach it came, pushing itself out of the water, its huge head rearing, mouth agape and reaching for them across the black sand. She thought it would never reach them, never cross the beach, would never touch them, but on it came, unravelling from the water like a fishing line, a huge, fat fishing line with a mouth gaping sharp points like hooks eager to catch her. Bright light was pulsing down its body as it came, so white it was almost purple in its intensity.

Flin pushed at her as the thing stretched out for them, reaching across the beach until the head was lunging at them on the stairs. The wide mouth full of pointed teeth opened a body-length from her face and the creature screeched at her, the heat and the stench of its breath washing over her. She could see a scrap of Motin's clothing caught between its teeth. She held up the stone in her hand but she did not have need of it. Flin threw a beam into its face and it shrieked and drew itself back, yet the beam seemed not to have harmed it. Again it leapt across the beach at them, but this time they had gained the safety of the rock platform, and when the creature screamed again, this time it was in anger at being robbed of a further meal.

Along the shore, the smaller creatures still threw themselves futilely up the black sand, but the giant slithered back into the water, flickered a line of light down its length and was gone. As the skylights faded, the other creatures stopped trying, dragging themselves back into the water, pulling their dead companions with them, feasting on the dead in a frenzy that lasted only moments. The lake stopped moving and flickering, the surface stilled, the lights ceased. No sign of the creatures remained. It was over.

They stood on the rock, breathing hard, looking down at the black water.

"What were they?" Kirrit whispered.

"Eels, I think," said Ishaan. "But like no eel I have seen before. Once I encountered a group of eels with sparks in their bodies like these, but I have never seen them grow to this size. Never." He sighed and passed a hand over his eyes. "I must see to my sister," he said, and he went to the black hole behind the platform. "May we have some light in here, please?" he asked, as he reached its entrance.

"Of course," said Shaeli. "I'll come with you, Ishaan, she must be very upset."

She threw a light into the darkness, and she and Ishaan followed it and the sound of Cheval weeping. They found a room similar to those they had used throughout their journey, but this was much larger. There was a pool in one corner, fed by a smaller bowl sitting brimful above it. The pool was easily big enough for the Ammerr to immerse themselves in. When Shaeli saw it she wanted to cry too.

* * *

CHAPTER TWENTY FOUR

None of them were very hungry. Cheval would not eat at all, taking only a sip of the elven wine, and there were no more fire-rocks to warm them in this dark place. They rolled themselves in their cloaks, and slept.

When Shaeli woke, Flin had thrown a few dim skylights around the roof. He, Tarkoda, Williver and Ishaan stood out on the platform, looking into the blackness over the lake and talking in low voices. The others still slept. Only Ebony woke when she sat up, and she picked up the jevvi, stepped over Kirrit, and went out.

"Well, we're going to have to light it up so we can see where we're going," Tarkoda was saying. "That thing can't reach us up here, so it doesn't matter."

"I think they see us better in the darkness, anyway," said Ishaan. "They live their lives surrounded by nothing but black water. Did you see how big its eyes were? It probably watches us now."

They all looked out over the unseen lake, but there was nothing, not the smallest flicker of light, only the white splash of the stream breaking the darkness, the sound of it falling the only thing to be heard.

"So, like the bats, you think the darkness will give them advantage?" asked Williver.

Ishaan nodded. "I have seen creatures from deep in the oceans, creatures that live in darkness like these," he said. "They develop other ways to survive. Some are blind, with others, the eyes grow huge, they generate their own light, as these do. If they were merely eels, even those with lights that sting like these, we may be able to deal with them." He shook his head. "But *these*. That giant. 'Tis impossible. We *must* find a way around the lake."

"And to do that, we must be able to see," said Flin.

"Just as I was saying," said Koda, throwing an affectionate arm around Shaeli's shoulders. "What do you think, little sister?"

"I think as long as we don't have to go near that water, I'll be happy," she said. "We must be nearly to the other side of the mountains, surely, so..."

She was stopped by a distant thud. The ground trembled beneath their feet, and the lake began to flicker with lines of light. There was a second thudding boom, and then a series of irregular smaller pops. The rock beneath their feet shuddered, but the trembling of the ground lasted only a moment and then all was still. The lines of light in the lake slowed, and stopped.

"What was that?" said Shaeli.

"I know not," said Ishaan. "Some earth tremor, perhaps."

"Not like any earth tremor I've ever felt," said Flin.

"Nor I," said Blenny, from the entrance to the cave room. "And we have many tremors in our mountains, so we do."

The others stood behind him, pale and dishevelled.

"Whatever it was must remain a mystery. We have to find a way around this lake," said Ishaan. "We must find the next part of the tunnel."

"And to do that, we must have some light," said Flin, pulling his stone from his pocket. "Shaeli, if you will?"

Shaeli found her quartz, and together she and Flin began to throw skylights across the cavern. First the black crescent of beach became visible, then the surface of the lake and finally the distant shore. Beneath the still black waters, lines of light began to flicker, and from the distance came the shriek of the giant, but they kept throwing light after light out across the water and around the edges, all of them looking for a sign of a path or steps that would lead them away from this place. But look as they might, no matter how many lights they threw, none of them could see a way around the lake. The beach ended in sheer cliff, no other tunnel or stair led from it, and there was no way to go past the ends of the beach without going in the water. Flin and Shaeli threw more light across the lake, until the cliff on the opposite shore was clearly visible. Williver could see the entrance to a large tunnel, far across on the right-hand edge of the distant shore. Llianas saw it, too, but neither could see any way to reach it.

Shaeli looked longingly at the far-off shore, knowing that Cave must lie somewhere beyond. She followed the black islands from where they stood, wishing they could leap from one tumbled island to the next. The stumpy islands lay in an almost direct line between them and the far-distant tunnel, almost as if they had once been connected. As if they had once been...

"A bridge," she said. "It must have been a bridge."

"What?" said Tarkoda, frowning at her. "*What* was a bridge?"

"Those islands," she said, pointing. "Look. They're almost in a straight line between us and that tunnel. This platform, the islands, they must have once been connected. The islands must have been a bridge. That's how they crossed."

"And that's why we can't find a way forward," said Ishaan. "I think Shaeli's right, for I can see no other way to go around."

"What are we going to *do*, then?" said Kirrit. "How do we reach that tunnel without going in that water with those *things*."

"I don't know," said Williver. "But find a way we must, or we shall have to go back."

"We *can't* go back," said Shaeli. "Cave must be so close now. First snow will fall soon. We can't go back."

"No, Shaeli," said Cheval quietly, her eyes filling. "We cannot go back. That would mean Motin has died for nothing. We *must* find a way to pass."

A long time they stood upon the rock as Flin and Shaeli threw light after light into the lake cave, searching for a way across or around. They ate something, the three Ammerr immersed themselves in the deep trough inside the room, and the others washed some of the grime of their journey from their bodies.

Tarkoda sprinted down to the beach to retrieve what arrows he could salvage, as well as Motin's pack and cloak. Cheval's eyes filled with tears when she looked at them and then she raised her head and scanned the cavern for a way to cross. They had been there a long time and were beginning to despair when Wendll pointed down at the lake.

"Look," he said. "Look at the eels."

While the skylights had blazed above the lake, the eels had shivered with light, a small cry escaping from one every now and then, and they had grown used to the noise. Nothing had been heard or seen of the giant beast, but now its shriek cut the air. The lights of the eels in the black lake had begun darting about, the lights running up and down them shooting faster and faster, more squeals and shrieks began to drift into the air, and across the lake came the long light of the giant.

The smaller eels flocked towards it as it drew its huge head from the water. The bright light in the dark cavern seemed to bite at its eyes, for it shrieked again and threw its head about, but it did not submerge. From across the lake hundreds of lines of light sped towards the giant, like offspring hurrying to their mother.

The companions standing high above heard a dull whirr in the distance, a throbbing sound that grew louder and louder. The sound came from across the lake, from the tunnel above the far-off cliff. The giant beast turned to face it.

To Shaeli, the sound was familiar. She looked up at her brother as he cried out.

"I don't believe it," he said. "It sounds like... it sounds like... Zoi!"

And then she understood, and she looked back across the lake just as they burst from the tunnel.

They flew in, a thin stream at first, and then more and more. They seemed puzzled by the lights filling the cavern, but not afraid, merely flying around the hanging orbs, the whiteness of their bodies shining like stars in the cavern of the black lake. As the giant birds flew from the far-off tunnel, the eels began to shriek.

The air in the cavern was soon full of the flock, their wings flapping slowly as they soared above the lake's surface. The giant in the lake shrieked and snapped at the air, but the Zoi circled it leisurely, unperturbed by the display, some landing on the islands looking down at the dark water, but most wheeled about. Then they began diving.

The giant eel, head rearing from the water, snapped at the Zoi flapping around its head. They darted at it, the huge birds almost dwarfed by the beast, yet it could not come close to capturing one. Down and around the huge head the birds darted, distracting the giant, while first one, then another swept down to the water, grabbed a smaller eel and flew off with it, back across to the tunnel on the far shore. The smaller eels screeched as they were carried off, light flickering down their bodies as they were carried back into the tunnel, the giant shrieking in fury and the Zoi fluttering around its head. Dozens of the white birds took turns worrying the eel while dozens more darted around it, plucking its brethren from the churning water.

They stood mesmerised on the rock watching the Zoi fishing for the eels. It seemed that the stinging light generated by the eels did not affect the great birds, for they flew unperturbed back across the water with the flickering eels clutched in thick talons. They saw one Zoi lurch out of the water with a particularly long fat eel struggling and flickering in its claws, and another bird flew over to grab a piece of the eel and together they carried it back across the water.

One of the birds landed on the closest island and stood surveying the scene. It looked curiously up at the hovering

425

skylights and then around the cave. It saw the group on the flat rock staring back at it, and it let out a loud call. The cry of the Zoi is a wondrous sound, a chiming of rich bells, but they all heard the warning cry in this call.

"Best go back into the room," said Tarkoda.

"But they won't hurt us," said Kirrit. "*Will* they?"

She looked across at the bird. It had been joined on the island by two more, and a few others were starting to fly over from where the giant eel battled the darting flock.

"I don't know," Tarkoda said. "Outside, no. But down here, I'm not so sure. Not unless..." He stopped and sent out a piercing whistle across the water. The three Zoi on the island took off at that moment and headed towards them. "Inside. Quickly," he said, herding them back towards the entrance of the room.

"Do as Koda says," said Ishaan. "I don't like the look of them."

"Look out," yelled Flin, as the first of the three birds swooped towards them.

The drell, Ammerr and Spotjaw darted into the room as the first bird landed. Williver and Flin followed with Kirrit and Llianas.

"Come on, Koda," yelled Shaeli from the door.

Her brother had stopped and turned to face the birds. All three had now landed on the rock where they'd just been standing. "No, wait," he said. "They're still the Zoi of our Fleet."

He bowed in the traditional greeting, and for a moment the Zoi stood looking down at him. Tarkoda did not raise his eyes, but stayed down. The Zoi looked at him and at each other. Several more birds circled in the air above the rock, the rainbow feathers beneath their wings glittering. The Zoi crooned to each other, and then they turned back to the kneeling figure of Tarkoda. The bird in the centre raised a talon, the others stepped forward, beaks outstretched.

"No," cried Shaeli, and she ran forward and assumed the same position as Koda, willing the birds to understand they were of the Fleet and meant no harm.

Kirrit ran forward too and knelt beside Shaeli. Shaeli took her hand and grabbed Tarkoda's as they kneeled, heads bowed, before the birds, then Shaeli heard the fluttering of wings and looked up, expecting to see a sharp beak poised before her, but instead she saw another bird flying towards them, low across the lake. It flew swiftly, landing in the space between the three birds and the crouching figures of Shaeli, Kirrit and Tarkoda.

Tarkoda looked up at it. "Thank the gods," he breathed, and he lowered his head again. This time when he raised it he stood and walked towards this new bird. He lowered his head again as he stopped beneath the great head.

The Zoi looked down at him, its head cocked, great dark eyes taking in his every move. Then it opened its wings and Tarkoda walked beneath them. He reached up and began to scratch at its armpits.

"Good girl," he crooned. "Good girl."

Shaeli looked back over her shoulder at the others clustered in the doorway. Pointed at them were three arrows and Flin's stone.

"It's alright," she said. "It's the lead female from Purple Leaf. She loves Koda."

"As I see," said Flin, lowering his stone. "But will she love the rest of us?"

Shaeli looked back as one of the other birds called over to the female, whose eyes were closed with the enjoyment of Koda's attentions. The female opened her eyes and looked back at her kindred. She chimed a few notes, ruffled her feathers, and shook her head at them. The three looked calmly back at her and then they turned and flew back to where the battle with the eels still raged.

Tarkoda came out from beneath the female's wings and bowed again to her. She lowered her head in return and then she just stood staring at him. Other Zoi flew over and wheeled past, looking down, and two of the new birds landed. Koda greeted them in a similar matter as he had the female. These two were also birds of Purple Leaf and they all looked down at Koda.

"They look as if they're wondering what you're doing here," said Kirrit.

Tarkoda looked up at the birds. "I think you're right, Kirrit," he said. "I wonder if..." He raised an arm and pointed down at the tunnel where they'd come out onto the black beach. "We came from there," he said, and then moved his arm in a wide sweep so it pointed across the water. "We need to go there."

The birds followed the arc of his arm, the female cocked her head to one side, but no sign of comprehension sparked in their eyes.

"Good thought, Koda," said Shaeli. "But I don't think they understand."

"We came from *there*," said Tarkoda, again, repeating the movement from tunnel mouth to distant shore. "We need to go *there*."

The female just stared at him and then it ruffled its feathers, turned, and flew back across the lake. The others watched them for a little longer, and then they too flew back over the water.

"Oh, well," said Kirrit. "It was worth a try."

"If only they would carry us over," said Llianas. "We'd be there in moments."

Tarkoda smiled at her. "We would," he said. "Yet they do not love even me enough to let me ride on their backs."

The birds of Purple Leaf flew back to the screeching eels and the flock taunting them. The battle was winding down now, the giant was obviously tired, thrusting its head less and less from the water, the Zoi toying with it, fishing almost at will. It was not long before the birds began to head back towards the tunnel on the distant shore, a few final eels flickering and writhing in claws. Soon the cavern grew quiet, the giant disappeared beneath the surface, and the lines of light grew less frantic as the eels headed back to corners of the lake. There was quiet in the cavern again, and one by one the skylights faded. They did not bother to throw any more.

* * *

They went back into the room, ate a morsel of the remaining supplies, and sat despondently. After a while, they slept.

Shaeli woke to a soft fluttering. She lay close to the door, Kirrit on one side, Ebony curled into the crook of her arm. She wondered what the fluttering was, but she could not hear it anymore, and she tried to find a more comfortable spot on her pack for her head. She'd almost forgotten what it felt like to sleep in a bed with a pillow, to wake to see the sun. She was lying there, wondering when she would next see the sky, when she heard it. A far-off splash. More flutterings. She sat up, and saw by the dim remains of a skylight that Llianas was also awake and rising from the floor.

"What was that?" she whispered, and Llianas shrugged her shoulders and they went to the door to peer out into the darkness.

Again there came the sound of a distant splash, then another. Shaeli and Llianas looked at each other as the fluttering sound echoed in the cavern outside. One final splash echoed across the lake and there was silence for a while. The fluttering began again. This time it began to come closer, accompanied by a soft slapping sound. Llianas went and shook the shoulder of Williver. He sat up instantly and looked at her.

"Listen," she said.

He did, a frown creasing his forehead, and then he stood up, went over, and shook Tarkoda. He sat up as quickly as Williver had, sling in hand.

"Does that sound like Zoi to you?" Williver whispered.

Tarkoda listened, nodded his head slowly. "Sounds like them flying, yes, but that other sound, that slapping sound, I don't know what that is."

The others woke at the sound of their voices and they all listened as the flapping, slapping sound came closer. Then it was right beneath them, and they heard a crunch, a grind, as if something was being dragged up the beach.

The fluttering came again, and then the bell-chime of a Zoi sounded right outside the doorway.

Tarkoda walked over to the door. "I'll need some light, please, Shaeli," he said.

She pulled out a stone and followed him out onto the rock platform, the others close behind. She could see the pearlescent feathers of the birds shining in the darkness before she threw a couple of beams into the air.

There were four of them, all birds of Purple Leaf. They blinked in the sudden light, but did not flinch at it. The female lowered her head as Koda stepped forward, and he lowered his in return. She chimed a great note and one of the others flew down onto the black sand below. The great female looked down at it, back at Tarkoda, and then down into the darkness once more. There were flickers of light across the lake, but they were few.

"Throw some light, Shaeli," Tarkoda said, excitement plain in his voice. "Throw some light onto the beach."

As she did, a shriek echoed in the distance, yet they ignored it with the sight that blossomed below.

Pulled half up on the gravelly black sand was a long punt, little more than a raft, really, but they could see it floated, and that there were several paddles on its deck.

Tarkoda looked back up at the Zoi and she lowered her head once more. He grinned at her, leapt into the air with a whoop, and threw himself at the bird.

If she was startled, she did not show it. It seemed she was almost smiling as he scratched his way down her breast. She waited as he scratched her and praised her and the other birds, and then with a final cry the four birds rose into the air and flew back across the lake.

* * *

They sat eating on the rock, looking down at the long punt. It sat on the black water, barely moving, the front pulled up on the beach, the remains of several ropes dangling forward and rear.

"They must have pulled it over with those old bits of rope," said Tarkoda. "They knew what I was saying after all."

"'Tis a wonder it still floats," said Spotjaw. "It must have been here an age."

"That it must," said Blenny. "And a sight for these tired eyes, so it is."

"Do you think it will carry us all?" said Kirrit. "What if it starts to sink while we're out there?"

"You'll be bailing to make sure that doesn't happen," said Tarkoda, grinning at her, promptly ignoring the tongue she stuck out at him. "I count six paddles."

"That should do," said Ishaan. "When should we leave?"

"I've been thinking about that," said Williver. "We don't want to have to battle the giant when we're out there. We should wait until the eels are distracted."

"Next time the Zoi come, you mean?" said Wendll.

"Yes," Williver said. "We know when they're coming by the sound, and if we're ready, we should be able to reach the far side before the eels know we're out there."

"Or at least before they can do much about it," said Olando, standing. "Let's ready everything and stack it out here."

"Good idea," said Ishaan. "And we'll plan exactly where we'll sit in the punt, so there's no hesitation when it's time."

These things were quickly done and they settled eagerly on the rock shelf to await the next arrival of the birds. A long wait it proved to be. They ate, talked over their plan again and again, and dozed on the rock shelf. Flin and Shaeli threw orbs to hang over them and the punt on the beach below, for the sight of it made their spirits soar, but elation was eventually overtaken first by boredom, and then exhaustion. They talked and ate and dozed again. Ishaan was the only one awake when the first eels began to stir. They had seen little of them as they waited; here and there the flicker of light or the occasional screech from a lesser eel, but they had seen no sign of the beast that had taken Motin.

They heard the distant whirr of the birds as Ishaan woke them, and by the time the Zoi flew from the tunnel on the far shore, they were lined up on the steps ready to dash to the punt. Flin and Shaeli threw lines of orbs across the lake in all directions to guide them, and to distract the beast from their passage.

The birds flew from the tunnel in flurries of white, wheeling out across the lake like great drifts of wind-blown leaves. The giant eel shrieked its chilling call across the water as its brethren gathered around it.

Down the steps they went, crunching their way across the black sand, trying to make no noise, yet their footfalls seemed to grow louder with each step. Into the punt they scrambled, Shaeli, Williver and Llianas in front, Tarkoda and Spotjaw next with Kirrit between them. Then Wendll, Cheval and Blenny took the next low seat, and with a shove Flin, Ishaan and Olando pushed them off the beach and leapt aboard, trying to touch the water as little as possible. A few bright splashes leapt from their feet and Shaeli scanned the eels for a sign they'd been spotted, but the eels were now in full battle, screeching as the silent Zoi began to pick them out of the water.

The great beast thrashed about, snapping at the darting birds, as they began to row, iridescent splashes marking each stroke. Shaeli kept watch on the eels while Williver and Llianas scanned the way ahead with their keen elven eyes, searching for the landing on the far side. Kirrit and Cheval bailed the water that seeped between cracks in the bottom of the boat and Flin manned the ancient tiller. Though they sat low in the water, the black surface almost lapping over the sides, the punt's leaks were surprisingly few – at first.

They headed to the right, towards the thin waterfall and away from the flashing, shrieking eels. The Zoi were in full flight now, darting at the great eel's head, teasing it away from the ones fishing, swooping down at it and sheering off at the last moment as the beast wailed its fury, its lights flashing and pulsing along its body as the other eels churned up the water around it.

Past the thin waterfall they paddled, keeping the line of islands that had once been a bridge between them and the battle. Here and there, Williver would silently point and steer them round some jagged rock near a huddled island, and in the light of the hanging orbs they all began to see the cliff of the shore across the water and the dark mouth of the tunnel. On they went, paddling and watching the battle between beast and birds until they were more than halfway across the water.

Shaeli was scanning the lake, Ebony on her shoulder sniffing at the air, when she felt her feet grow damp. She looked down to see Kirrit bailing black water over the side, her face grim and slightly panicked. Beneath her, the punt was awash with water, and she could see the place where it seeped in, a long welling line like a wound seeping blood. Shaeli pulled a cloth from her pack, and handed it to Kirrit, hoping she could stuff the seam closed, and then she turned back to watch the beast.

Kirrit and Cheval were both bailing frantically when the Zoi began to fly back up the tunnel. The battle was winding down and they were still only three-quarters of the way across the lake. Shaeli saw one line of light leave the frenzy around the giant and head towards them. She pulled a stone from her amulet, the amber, for she intended to fight light with molten light, if it came to that.

433

Williver tapped her on the shoulder, and he pointed out across the water, his face alight. To the right of the cliff where the Zoi were starting to disappear into the darkness of the tunnel, a small bay was coming into view, shielded by a rocky outcrop. He signalled back to Flin and the rowers, who saw the bay and paddled harder towards the black beach and the path that led up to the tunnel, the promised sanctuary of dry land.

The Zoi flying around the giant's head were less eager now, the game over. Many eels had been plucked from the black water and the birds were thinning. The line of light beneath the surface had come closer, but a Zoi flew down and picked it out of the water and Shaeli smiled thankfully as the bird flew past them, the eel in its talons writhing. The tunnel was now clearly visible, and the little beach below it was much like the one they'd left, a stark patch of black sand, but it still seemed so far away. She snapped her head around as the giant eel shrieked.

It was tired, she could see that, its head thrusting less and less from the water, but it was also furious. The great birds were toying with it now and it knew it. Most had flown back up the tunnel, but a dozen or so still flew around the giant. Four more soared through the air between the eels and the punt, and Shaeli knew that they were the birds of Purple Leaf, watching the water, protecting them.

The beach lay tantalisingly close when the last of the Zoi stopped gliding lazily around the giant's head. Taking a few last squirming eels from the water, they flew across the water, over the punt and up the tunnel. The only birds that remained above the black water were those of Purple Leaf.

Now the giant beast turned its head towards them, as they had known it would. Its smaller brethren, some as long as carts, longer than their punt, began to stream towards them. They paddled harder as the lines of flickering light sped towards them beneath the surface, the giant in their midst. It stopped long enough to shriek at them as it passed the islands, and the four birds flew at its head, but now it seemed unmindful of them, intent on making a meal of its own. Through the water it came, cutting a path through the lesser eels, the fury at being taunted by the Zoi now directed at them.

Shaeli felt the crunch and shudder go through the punt as they reached the beach. Williver was already leaping out, helping Llianas, throwing sodden baggage up the beach where a path led up to the cliff and the tunnel.

"Up the path, Llianas," he said. "Hurry."

She grabbed a few bundles and sprinted up the beach and Williver turned and helped Shaeli out, and as soon as her feet touched the ground, she spun around and threw a huge ball of molten honey light at the beast.

The giant eel had reached the long rocky outcrop that had sheltered the beach from their sight when Shaeli's light-ball connected with it. It swerved at the last moment, and the bolt hit it on the side of the head. It shrieked and dropped beneath the surface, but it did not slow its pace.

Kirrit, Spotjaw, Cheval and the drell were out of the punt, grabbing bundles and weapons as they ran for the path. Shaeli told Ebony to go with Kirrit and the jevvi leapt from her shoulder, landed halfway up the beach and scurried after Kirrit. Tarkoda leapt out, throwing the last of their packs up the black sand. Llianas had almost reached the top of the path as the others scrambled up the beach.

Shaeli adjusted the pack on her back and threw two more beams at the eel as Flin's feet hit the sand. The beams flew across the surface and then dropped beneath it to collide with the eel below the water. Again, it did not stop, but raised its head and threw itself through the diminishing stretch of water. They grabbed the last of the packs and ran, pushing Olando and Ishaan before them. From above, arrows began to fall from those who had already reached the cliff. Williver stood at the base of the path, his hands a blur as arrow after arrow flew from his bow. Shaeli looked back in time to see the beast hit the beach.

Many of the smaller eels came with it, flickering their stinging lights and wailing as the giant hit the beach in the same place they had landed, ploughing through the punt as if it were not there. The ancient wood splintered with a crash, pieces flying through the air, but the huge head smashed heedlessly through it.

Tarkoda, Olando, Ishaan, Flin and Shaeli were still on the beach when it hit, Williver ahead of them at the bottom of the path. A chunk of wood flew at them, knocking Tarkoda off his feet, and as Shaeli stopped to help him, the eel stretched out its mouth for them.

Flin threw a bolt that hit the beast in the throat but it ignored it, its teeth dripping black foam as it ploughed up the beach. From out of the air flew the female Zoi, talons outstretched, poisonous barb revealed. She hit the eel directly in its great eye and the eel screamed and shook its head. The bird was shaken off, her body thudding into the black sand, but she had done enormous damage. Before the eel slid back into the water, they saw the gash in its eye, the wound seeping an ugly grey fluid, yet the eel did not stay in the water for long. It was in pain now and even more furious. Around it, the beach was coming alive as the fat bodies of the other eels heaved themselves out of the water.

Tarkoda had regained his feet, but he did not run up the beach. He ran back to the female Zoi, for she was struggling to rise. She was dazed by the blow, floundering on the sand, and as Tarkoda reached her, the giant reared from the water again and swept back towards them. The other three Zoi swooped the giant but it did not stop. Through the splintered remains of the punt, shrieking as it came, ploughing its way up the sand towards them, its wounded eye seeping grey mucous, the giant eel headed straight towards Tarkoda and the Zoi. Tarkoda heaved at the bird, and she shook her head and looked down at him groggily.

Shaeli ran to stand between them and the eel. She planted her legs wide in the black sand, raised her arm, and threw a bolt at the beast, throwing her most intense beam at the eel's weeping eye. The bolt hit the already damaged eye dead-centre, and it exploded in a gush of milky grey liquid. Behind her, Flin threw a dozen huge balls into its face. The eel screamed, thrashed its head, and began sliding back into the water.

The Zoi regained her feet, then her wings, and she soared off to rejoin the others, chiming a cry as she rose in the air. Tarkoda grabbed Shaeli's arm and they ran to Flin, who was picking off the smaller eels that still surged towards them. The three of them raced to the path, the agonised shriek of the giant filling their ears.

Olando, Ishaan and Williver stood at the bottom of the path, firing arrows at the lesser eels pushing their way up the sand. One huge brute leapt from the water and grabbed Tarkoda on the heel as he ran, and he cried out as the flickering light in the thing leapt up his leg. His leg shuddered with the sting as the eel sought for better purchase with its teeth, and then three arrows smacked into its body. Its light flickered and went out.

The four birds from Purple Leaf circled above as they staggered up the path, dragging the last of their packs and helping Tarkoda, whose leg was numb from the stinging light. At the top of the path was a broad open platform, three times the size of the one they had left, the tunnel a dark space beyond. They looked back across the line of huddled islands to the crescent of beach they had left far across the water. The door to the room was lost in shadows, the platform indistinct.

Below, in the black water along the shore of the beach, pieces of their punt floated amongst the writhing bodies of the eels. At the far end of the sand they could see the sunken remains of several other punts in the shallows. There were drag marks leading back into the shadows, where more punts lay pulled up on the black sand. The punts must have been stored here, pulled far up on the sand for centuries, and the Zoi must have tried several before they'd found one that floated. Here was the explanation for the strange splashes they'd heard before the birds had brought the punt across the water. Now the remains of their punt lay splintered, some pieces on the sand, some drifting off across the water.

The lesser eels still pushed flickering lines of light from the water. They shrieked and writhed along the empty beach, snapping at the bodies of the dead, too dull to realise it was all over.

When the birds chimed overhead, Tarkoda led the bow they all gave the Zoi. Every head lowered to the birds, for without them they would have been truly lost. The birds circled one last time, and then they flew over their heads and followed their kin up the tunnel. As the white bodies disappeared into the thick shadows, one last chime from the female echoed back at them.

They heard one final shriek from the giant before the last light orbs faded. The beast had disappeared beneath the water when Shaeli had shattered its eye, and they did not see it again. There was only that final agonised screech from across the water, its echo trembling in the air for long moments, and then nothing. They watched as the lights from the lesser eels moved back across the water and went out.

The lights Flin and Shaeli had thrown finally faded. One by one the hanging orbs went out, and the black lake slowly disappeared from sight. They were not sorry that it was so.

Shaeli threw a soft light a short way up the tunnel and they followed it in, wanting to leave the black lake behind them. The tunnel was high, broad enough to easily accommodate the wing-span of even the largest Zoi, but they did not go far. They ate the last of their rations, pulled their cloaks about them, and slept. Again.

In her rooms at Great Court, Queen Virrisian watched the patterns swirl and shimmer in the half stone. The cracked voice that came from it was triumphant.

"I have what we seek," it said.

"That is news I have waited long to hear," she replied. "Bring them here."

"Is that wise?" said the voice. "It may be better if I keep them."

"No, I want them here," said Virrisian. "I wish to show them to her. It will be a pleasure to watch her face and tell her what I intend."

There was a bark of laughter. "You are a cruel woman, my dear."

"Yes," she said. "Just as you like me."

***

CHAPTER TWENTY FIVE

Shaeli woke with a scream in her throat.

The dream had been filled with cries of pain and grating crashes and plumes of bright fire, but the darkness to which she opened her eyes trapped the scream in her throat before it was given voice. She closed her eyes again and waited until her breathing slowed, yet the feeling of the dream was still wrapped tightly around her chest.

She could tell by the sounds around her that the others still slept, but she could not return to it. Cave was so close – it must be, the Zoi were here – and she wanted to be there so badly it hurt. Beside her, Ebony stirred as she put her hand into her amulet and felt for a stone. She pulled out the rose quartz and threw a soft pink light up into the darkness, and around her the walls of the tunnel and the sleeping bodies of her companions blossomed, their forms patterned in rose and shadows. Llianas stirred as the light blossomed. She sat up and looked at Shaeli, her hair a scruffy rope, her eyes dark pools.

"You are anxious for your home," she said.

Though it was hardly a question, Shaeli nodded, sudden tears rushing her throat. "Yes," she said, willing the tears to stay where they were.

Llianas stood and silently walked over. She knelt and gave Shaeli a gentle hug. It was too much. The tears fell and Llianas held her until they were spent.

"We shall wake them, then," she said, smoothing the hair from Shaeli's face. She hoisted Shaeli to her feet and went over and shook Williver's shoulder.

It was not long before they were all awake and readying their packs. Ebony danced around their feet and Shaeli felt like dancing with her. She grinned at Kirrit. Tarkoda grinned at her. They grinned a secret smile at each other. Home. They were nearly home. The tears that had fallen when she woke had been banished by the knowledge that they would soon be at Cave, yet the elation was overshadowed by the remnants of the dream. She thrust the memory away from her mood – it was just a dream – and looked at Williver.

"Ready, little one?" he said, and she nodded.

She threw a few light balls into the tunnel and took Kirrit's arm. Kirrit squeezed it, and together they went into the tunnel.

At first they strode ahead. Tarkoda's leg was still stiff from the eel sting, but he pressed on, as eager as Shaeli for Cave. Ebony sat expectantly on Shaeli's shoulder, chittering with the mood of her companions, every now and then doing one of her long, gliding leaps to the floor and scampering ahead.

The tunnel was wide, the floor soft with fine sand, and to begin with it was level. Then for a long time it went uphill, not a steep slope, but enough to tire them and make the three Ammerr struggle, then it began to wind about in long curved sections, right and left and right again, and always uphill. They stopped to rest at the top of one long slope, foraging in their packs to produce a final meal. When the scant offering had been consumed and the last drops of wine wrung from the skins, they shouldered their now light packs and went on into the tunnel, on and up. When they thought they would have to sleep again beneath the mountain, they began to hear a noise ahead, a soft cooing, a distant flutter. They went faster, the noise grew louder, and a strange glow began to light the tunnel ahead. Flin and Shaeli found they could stop throwing light orbs as the glow lit the tunnel with a strange white light.

The last slope was the steepest, and when they reached the top they were breathless and the light dazed them. They stopped in the last shadow of the tunnel, chests heaving as their eyes adjusted and they took in the spectacle before them.

The cave of the Zoi was enormous, not half the size of Cave, nor even as big as the lair of the dragons, but it was still a cavern of great proportions, yet the spectacle did not come from its size. Around the floor of the cave, growing in epic numbers, were thousands of fungi. Mushroom-like they grew, from thumb-size to misshapen lumps like small bushes. Tiny clumps started at their feet, just inside the mouth of the tunnel, spreading across the floor of the cave, and amazingly, from each lumpy growth, light glowed. Each shone with a deeply white light, a white rich with purple undertones, as if a lamp was turned on inside each one, as if their skins were light itself. They were all oddly-shaped, some flattened as thin as a fan, others lumped together like mounds of pudding, or doubled over as if reacquainting themselves with the floor, but from the smallest to the largest, each one glowed with the faintly iridescent light, the sum of them all bathing the cave in a soft, violet-white hue. Amongst the shining fungi were the bones of the eels, pale ivory in the light of the glowing growths; great heads with pointed teeth grinned silently at the roof, necklaces of backbones curled in piles, lesser bones lay scattered and crumbling at the bases of the iridescent lumps. Among the glowing mounds, tiny impossibly green frogs plopped from fungi to fungi, their soft skin luminously bright in the strange purple-white light.

Far to the right, a thin stream of water fell from the roof. It pooled in a wide pond, and then the water ran out from the pool, tinkled along the wall, and disappeared through a hole in the floor. They could barely hear the sound of its falling. It was overpowered by the sounds of the Zoi.

The cave was filled with the chiming calls, the coos, the flutterings of the great birds. Their whiteness glowed with fluorescent ferociousness in the light of the fungi, making them brighter, even more majestic, even more beautiful. Some flew around the cavern roof, some stalked amongst the fungi, feeding on them, some bathed in the water of the pool. Others perched in nests around the walls or upon towering outcrops.

Like the dragon's lair, the cave was pocked with scores of holes, and in these the Zoi had built huge nests. In the soft glow of the fungi, the nests looked to be made of feathers, the feathers of the birds themselves, new white feathers on top, old grey feathers like long sticks beneath. There were more nests built on the high rock formations scattered throughout the cave, hundreds of Zoi sitting, standing, or gliding around them. From a score of nests the heads of baby Zoi were peeping at their brethren.

A distant sparkling drew their eyes across the cave. Across the vast expanse, in the place where the cave narrowed again into a tunnel, the walls were studded with crystals. The walls and roof around the distant mouth were covered in points of quartz, millions of the stones clouding the mouth of the tunnel, so thickly that the rock was unseen, covered by the archway of glittering stones.

"It was from there I saw this place," said Ishaan in a low voice, pointing across to the crystal archway at the opening of the tunnel. "This cavern was empty then, but it still was amazing to me, yet now, with the birds here, it is even more incredible."

The whites of his eyes and his teeth glowed strangely. Everybody's eyes and teeth were glowing strangely, their skins four shades darker. Llianas looked like one of the Irikai from across the Endless Sea. Shaeli stifled a giggle and looked at her hands. Her fingernails glowed white-green against her brown skin.

"You did not come to this side of the cave?" said Williver. "You did not venture down this tunnel?"

"There was no need," said Ishaan. "Above this tunnel lies the symbol, big enough for me to see from the far side. We will not see it until we venture out, but it was large enough for me to be sure it was the same as the one on the far side, and I did not wish to disturb the cave in any way."

"Well, we're going to disturb it now," said Tarkoda quietly. "They've seen us."

They had stayed inside the tunnel mouth, but now several birds were flying towards them and others were turning their way.

Tarkoda took a breath, walked boldly out into the cave where he was easily seen, and assumed the bow of greeting. The others followed his lead, kneeling around him on the soft, glowing fungi carpet, the spores collapsing beneath their knees, giving off a damp, mushroomy smell, the juices seeping through their clothes. Tiny glowing frogs plopped away in fright. Shaeli glanced behind her before she lowered her head and saw the symbol Ishaan had spoken of above the tunnel mouth, as big as the front of a Trader. No wonder he had no need to go further.

Across the cave, the voices of the birds grew louder, the tone climbing as more and more birds saw the intruders. Cries of distress and indignation echoed through the cave, black eyes turned towards them. Dozens of the birds flew across to the bowing group, but there was no cry of greeting from them, no sign of recognition in their eyes. They did not see people of the Fleet, they saw intruders in their private cave. A threat.

In moments they were surrounded, cowering on their knees in a circle as the birds towered over them and around them, cutting off the tunnel behind. There was nowhere for them to go. Hands went slowly to weapons. Hearts thumped against chests. Again the birds of Purple Leaf came to their aid.

Talons had been raised and beaks lowered when the lead female flew into the circle. She squawked and ran around the kneeling group, her wings outstretched, pushing the ring of threatening Zoi back. Another bird joined her, and then two more, and another three, and then they were surrounded by the Zoi of Purple Leaf, the female chiming loudly at the rest of the flock.

They remained on their knees, watching from beneath lowered brows, hands still firmly on weapons, as some kind of exchange took place.

As their female kept calling, the noise in the cave gradually diminished. She kept calling, the chiming of her voice becoming softer, more soothing. Several of the other birds cried back at her, their voices shrill, but the more she crooned at them, the fewer their cries of discontent.

Finally the birds stepped back and a pathway opened between them. The female looked down at Tarkoda and Shaeli, nuzzled them both, and then she raised her wings. Shaeli and Tarkoda stood beneath them, the shining wings a protective shield above them, and as the others rose to their feet, the other birds of Purple Leaf raised wings above their heads also.

They walked across the cave with the wings of the birds spread like rainbow umbrellas over their heads, the other Zoi watching them, standing either side of the path they created with their huge bodies. Others watched from where they perched in their nests or peered down from rock formations, each Zoi's eyes following their every footstep. There was no sound from the birds as they went, no chiming, no calls. In eerie silence the Zoi watched the intruders leave, each black eye upon them, the fluttering of wings and the fall of water the only sounds. The walk across the Zoi cave seemed very long, and when they reached the crystal archway the birds of Purple Leaf lowered their wings.

They bowed, unable to express their gratitude. Tarkoda gave each bird a final scratch, bowed again, and then he followed the others through the crystal archway. When the tunnel closed about them they loosened their hands from their weapons and the breath they held in their lungs, wiped sweat from brows and found their mouths bereft of moisture, yet they did not linger, they felt the eyes of the Zoi upon them still.

The crystal arch continued on through the tunnel for a long time. Behind them the glow from the Zoi cave began to fade, but the walls around them glittered still. They ran their hands across the cool, spiky surface, Shaeli and Flin marvelling at the energy unspent within these walls, wishing they could pry just

445

a few stones from the thousands around them. They scoured the floor looking for fallen stones, but there were none, the crystals remained tightly packed within the walls of the tunnel, and when at last the crystal arch around them stopped, fading away into the rock in long thick veins, the dark rocky walls of the tunnel ahead looked incredibly dull by comparison. The light from the Zoi cave had long since faded, and Flin threw orbs ahead as the tunnel again began to wind uphill. Though it had been a long time since they'd slept, and it seemed they had been walking longer than any of them could remember, none of them thought to stop and rest; they were far too close.

"How far is it now, Ishaan?" asked Shaeli.

"Not a great distance," he said.

"But how far is *that*?" she persisted.

"Not far," Ishaan smiled.

They went on, always upwards, round many bends, tired and sore, but talking of the feast they would be given, the spring stream and the pool on first terrace where the Ammerr could swim, the faces they would see, the sun.

Eagerly they went forward, and at last the air warmed, the tunnel levelled, the sand beneath their feet grew thicker. Tarkoda, Kirrit and Shaeli rushed ahead, throwing themselves beneath Flin's skylights, laughing and running, sure that the light of Cave would be just around the next bend.

When they finally saw it, they whooped with delight.

"It must be night," said Tarkoda. "It's so dark out there."

"It doesn't matter," crowed Kirrit. "We'll wake them up."

"We're *here*," cried Shaeli. "We're home."

They ran to the end of the tunnel.

They ran laughing into Cave.

They did not recognise it.

***

LOOK OUT FOR

THE TOWER OF THE GLADE

BOOK THREE OF *THE TRADERS*

ABOUT THE AUTHOR

R.L. Aiken lives on the eastern coast of Australia in a small town with the ocean out the front and kangaroos out the back. She has been writing this very big story in this very small town for a very long time, and is very happy to finally put it in your hands to be read. Thanks for holding it.